BATMAN and ROBIN and Howard

Batman and Robin and Howard

By Jeffrey Brown

with colors by Silvana Brys

BATMAN created by Bob Kane with Bill Finger

Jim Chadwick .... Editor
Courtney Jordan .... Assistant Editor
Steve Cook .... Design Director - Books
Louis Prandi .... Publication Design
Tiffany Huang .... Publication Production

Marie Javins .... Editor-in-Chief, DC Comics

Daniel Cherry III .... Senior VP - General Manager
Jim Lee .... Publisher & Chief Creative Officer
Joen Choe .... VP - Global Brand & Creative Services
Don Falletti .... VP - Manufacturing Operations & Workflow Management
Lawrence Ganem .... VP - Talent Services
Alison Gill .... Senior VP - Manufacturing & Operations
Nick J. Napolitano .... VP - Manufacturing Administration & Design
Nancy Spears .... VP - Revenue

BATMAN AND ROBIN AND HOWARD

Published by DC Comics. Copyright © 2021 DC Comics. All Rights Reserved. All characters,
their distinctive likenesses, and related elements featured in this publication are trade-
marks of DC Comics. The stories, characters, and incidents featured in this publication
are entirely fictional. DC Comics does not read or accept unsolicited submissions of ideas,
stories, or artwork. DC - a WarnerMedia Company.

DC Comics, 2900 West Alameda Ave., Burbank, CA 91505
Printed by Worzalla, Stevens Point, WI, USA. 10/1/21.
First Printing.
ISBN: 978-1-4012-9768-8

Library of Congress Cataloging-in-Publication Data

Names: Brown, Jeffrey, 1975- author. | Brys, Silvana, colourist.
Title: Batman and Robin and Howard / by Jeffrey Brown ; with colors by
    Silvana Brys.
Description: Burbank, CA : DC Comics, [2021] | "Batman created by Bob Kane
    with Bill Finger" | Audience: Ages 8-12 | Audience: Grades 4-6 |
    Summary: "Sidelined by Batman after a crimefighting excursion goes
    wrong, Damian Wayne must learn how to live as an average kid. But life
    in his new school becomes more challenging than Damian expected when he
    meets his match in a rival named Howard."-- Provided by publisher.
Identifiers: LCCN 2021025290 | ISBN 9781401297688 (trade paperback)
Subjects: CYAC: Superheroes--Fiction. | Schools--Fiction. |
    Friendship--Fiction. | LCGFT: Superhero comics. | Graphic novels.
Classification: LCC PZ7.7.B78 Bat 2021 | DDC 741.5/973--dc23
LC record available at https://lccn.loc.gov/2021025290

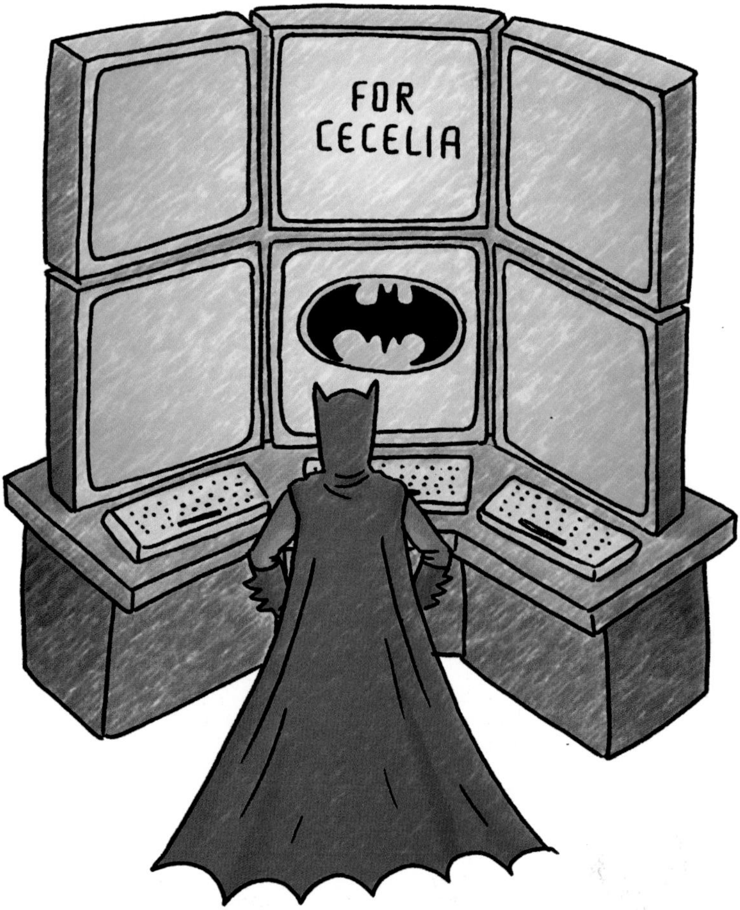
FOR
CECELIA

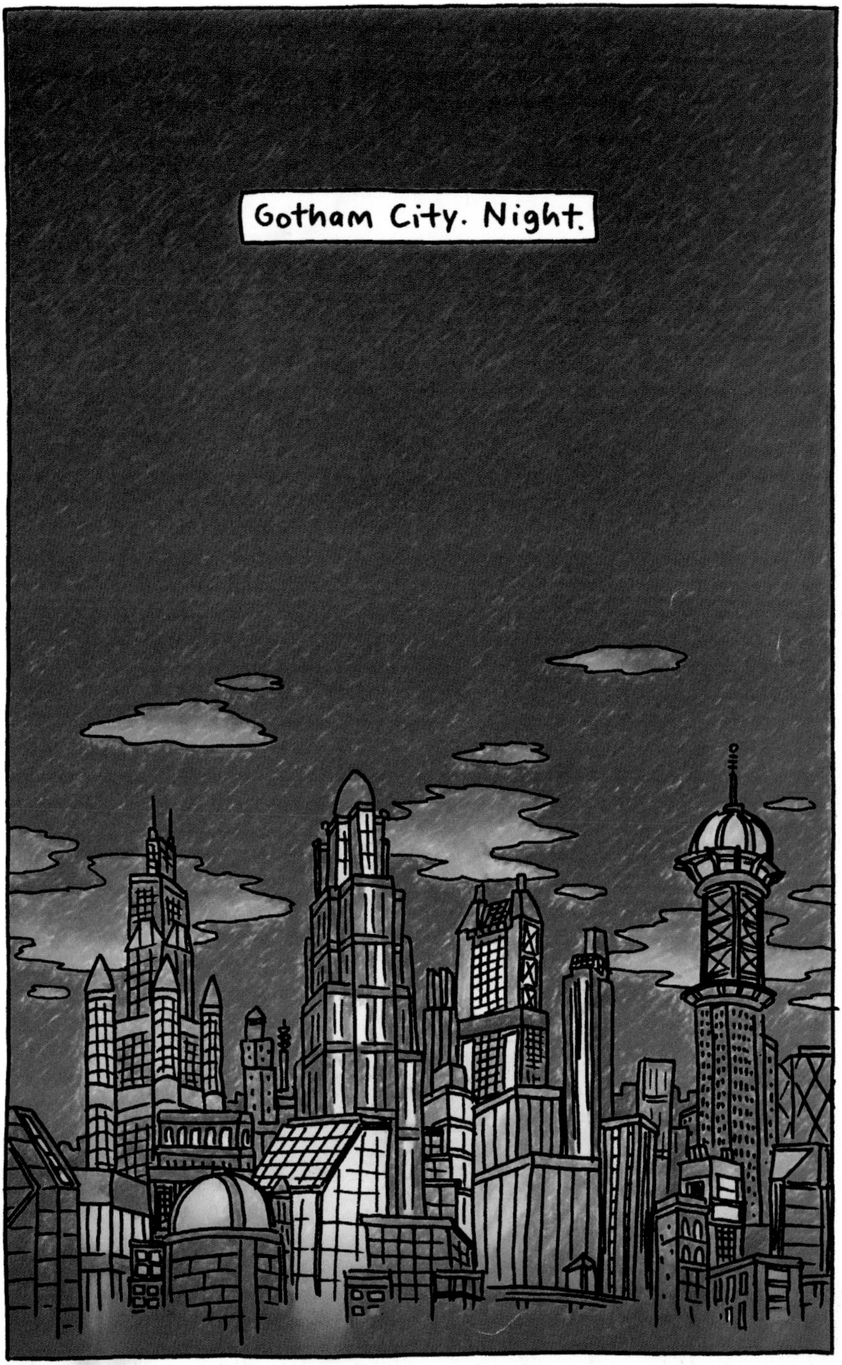
Gotham City. Night.

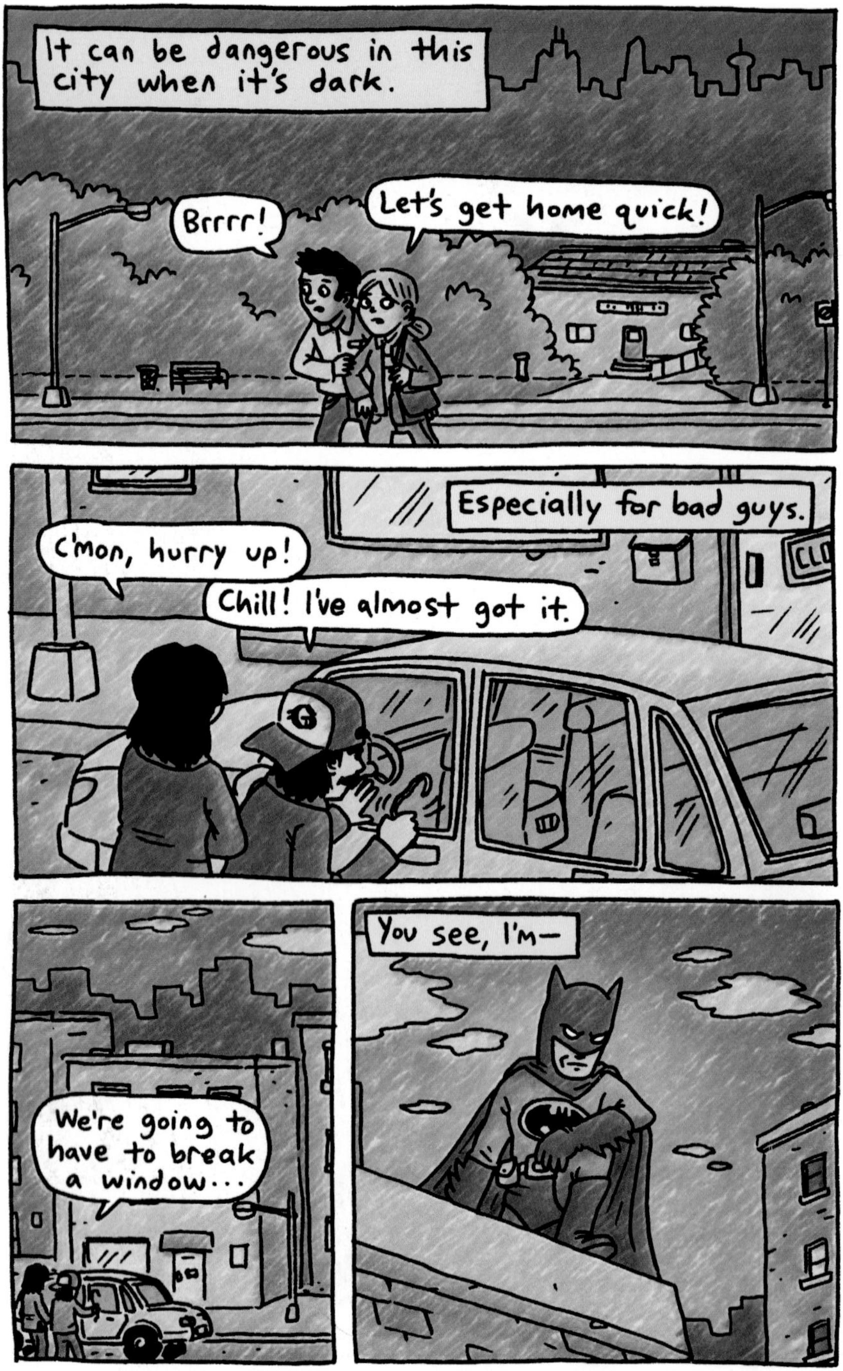
It can be dangerous in this city when it's dark.
Brrrr!
Let's get home quick!
Especially for bad guys.
C'mon, hurry up!
Chill! I've almost got it.
We're going to have to break a window...
You see, I'm—

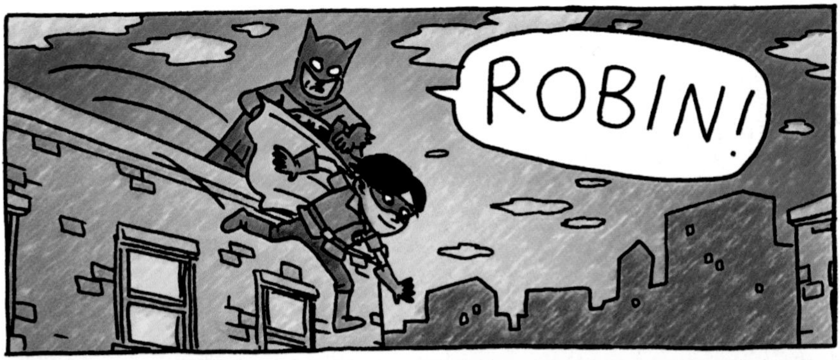
ROBIN!

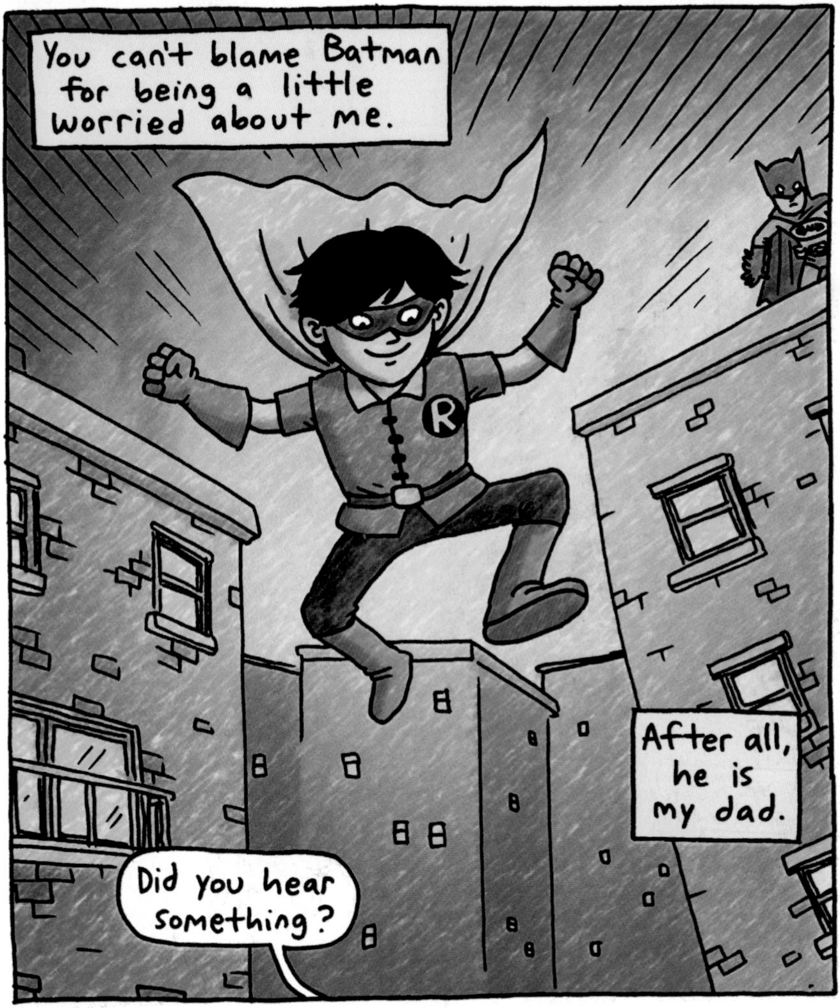
You can't blame Batman for being a little worried about me.
After all, he is my dad.
Did you hear something?

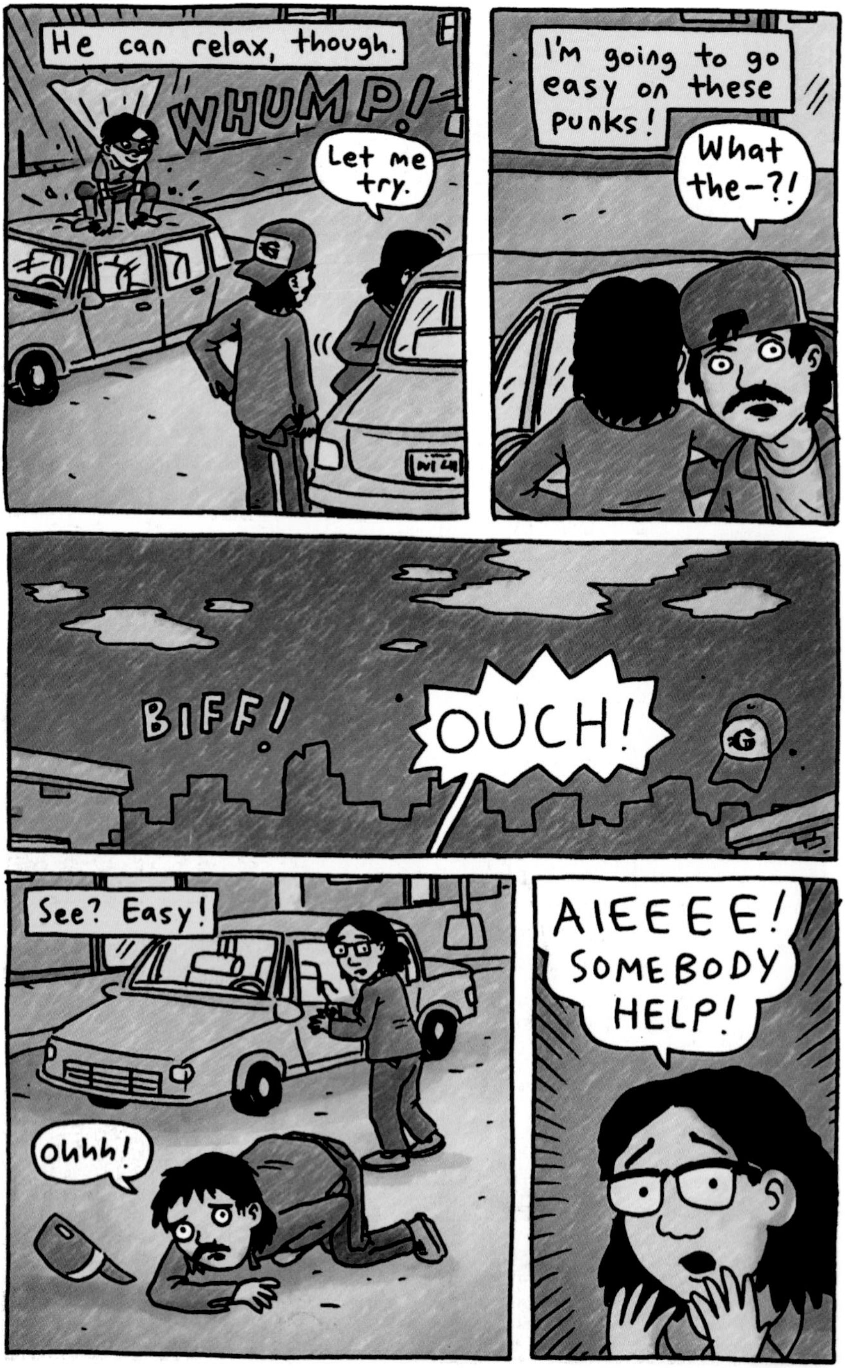
He can relax, though.
WHUMP!
Let me try.
I'm going to go easy on these punks!
What the-?!
BIFF!
OUCH!
See? Easy!
Ohhh!
AIEEEE! SOMEBODY HELP!

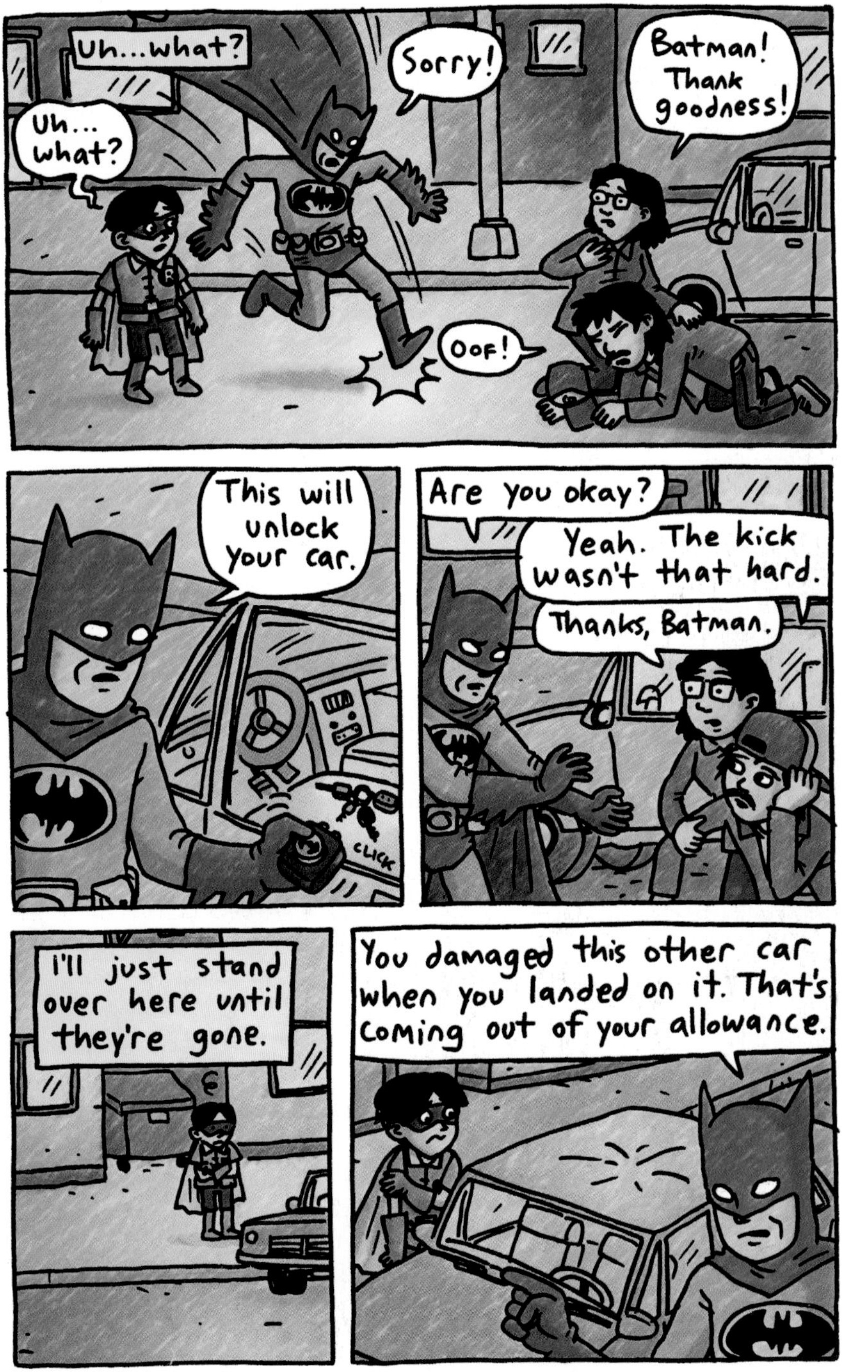
Uh...what?
Uh... what?
Sorry!
Batman! Thank goodness!
Oof!
This will unlock your car.
CLICK
Are you okay?
Yeah. The kick wasn't that hard.
Thanks, Batman.
I'll just stand over here until they're gone.
You damaged this other car when you landed on it. That's coming out of your allowance.

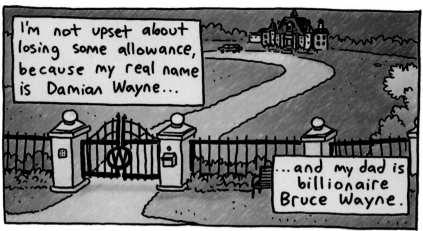

I'm not upset about losing some allowance, because my real name is Damian Wayne...

...and my dad is billionaire Bruce Wayne.

How was I supposed to know that was their own car and they just locked themselves out of it?!

Observation. Deduction. Patience!

We can't rush into situations based only on how they seem, Damian.

You still have a lot to learn.

Is that why you're making me go to a stupid new school?

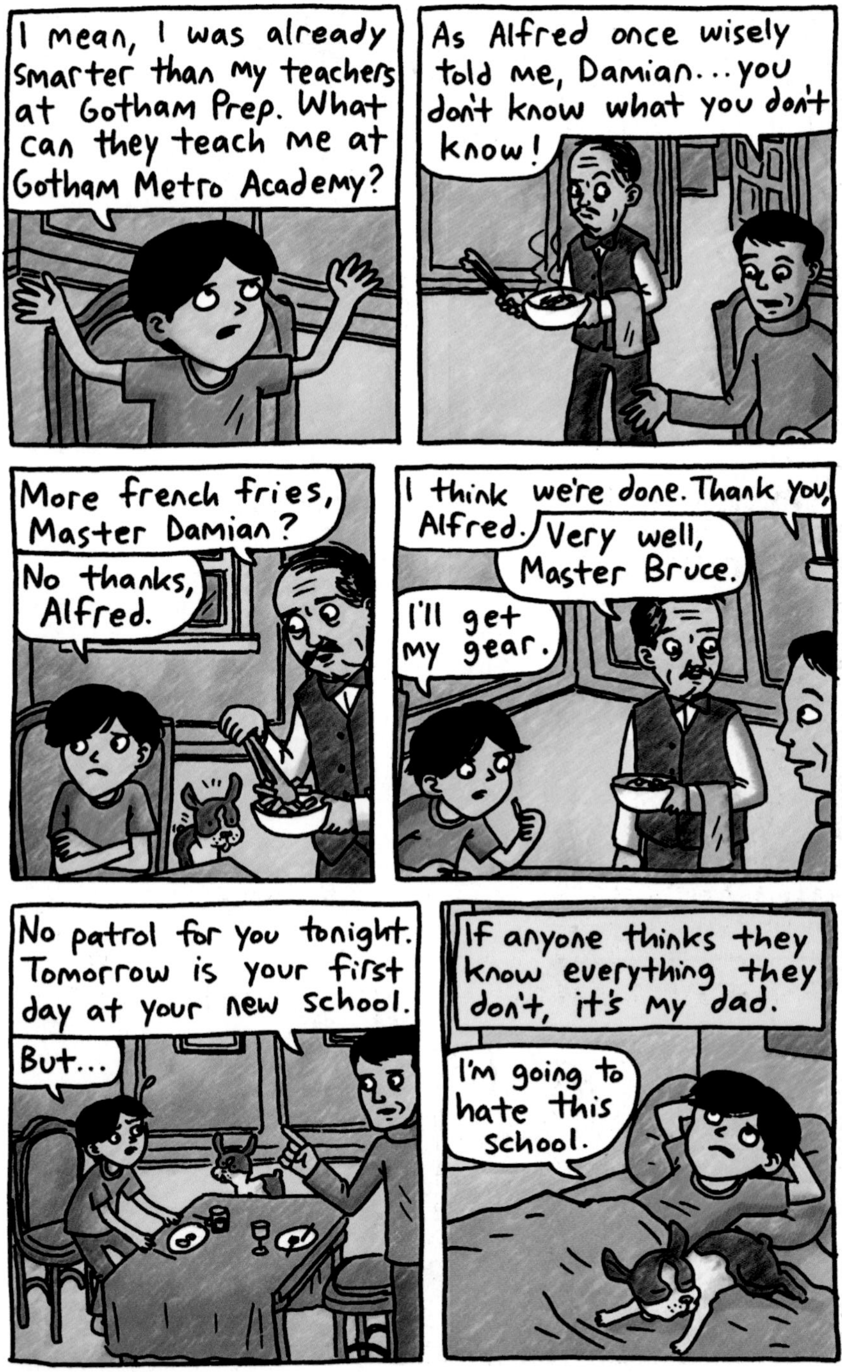
I mean, I was already smarter than my teachers at Gotham Prep. What can they teach me at Gotham Metro Academy?
As Alfred once wisely told me, Damian... you don't know what you don't know!
More french fries, Master Damian?
No thanks, Alfred.
I think we're done. Thank you, Alfred.
Very well, Master Bruce.
I'll get my gear.
No patrol for you tonight. Tomorrow is your first day at your new school.
But...
If anyone thinks they know everything they don't, it's my dad.
I'm going to hate this school.

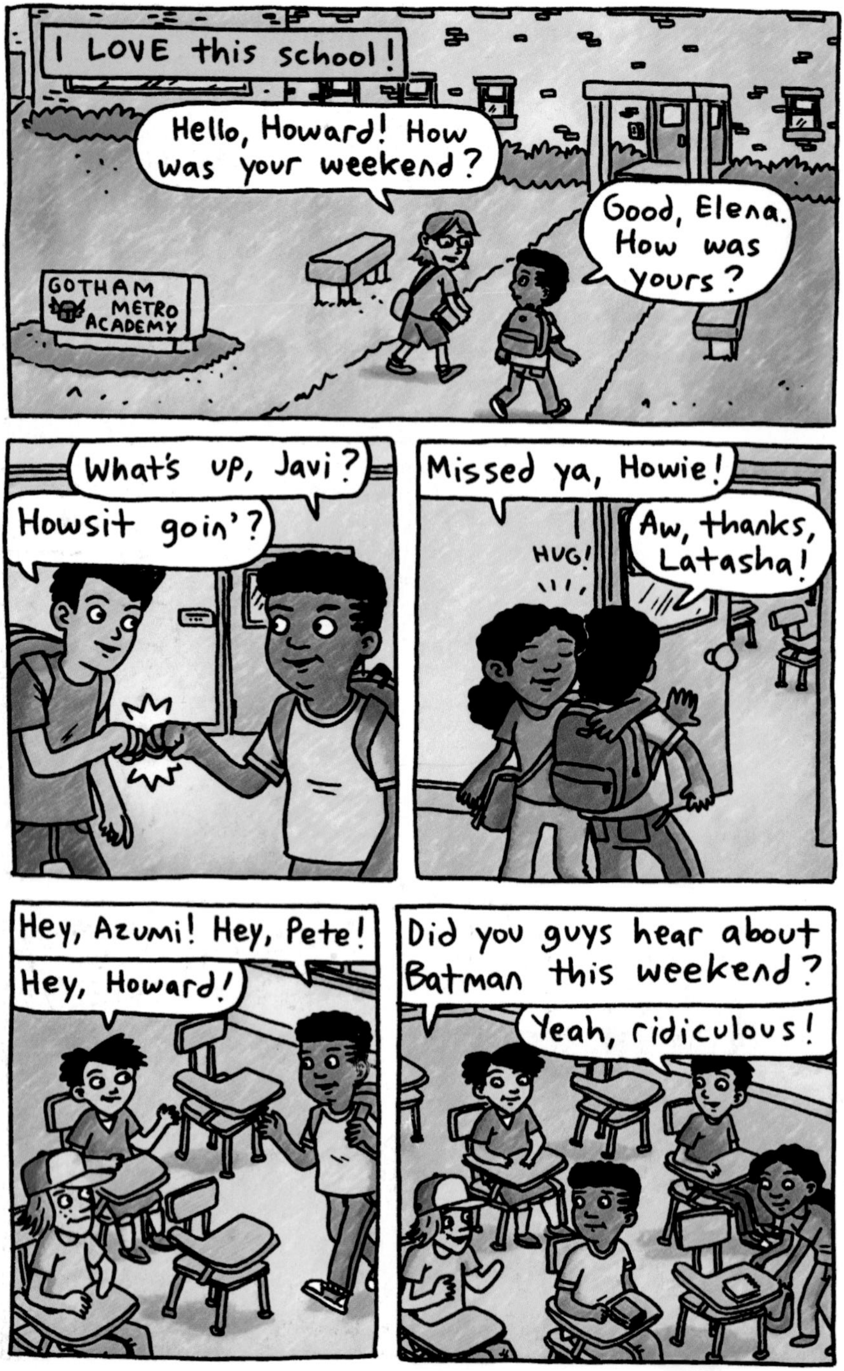
I LOVE this school!
Hello, Howard! How was your weekend?
Good, Elena. How was yours?
GOTHAM METRO ACADEMY
What's up, Javi?
Howsit goin'?
Missed ya, Howie!
HUG!
Aw, thanks, Latasha!
Hey, Azumi! Hey, Pete!
Hey, Howard!
Did you guys hear about Batman this weekend?
Yeah, ridiculous!

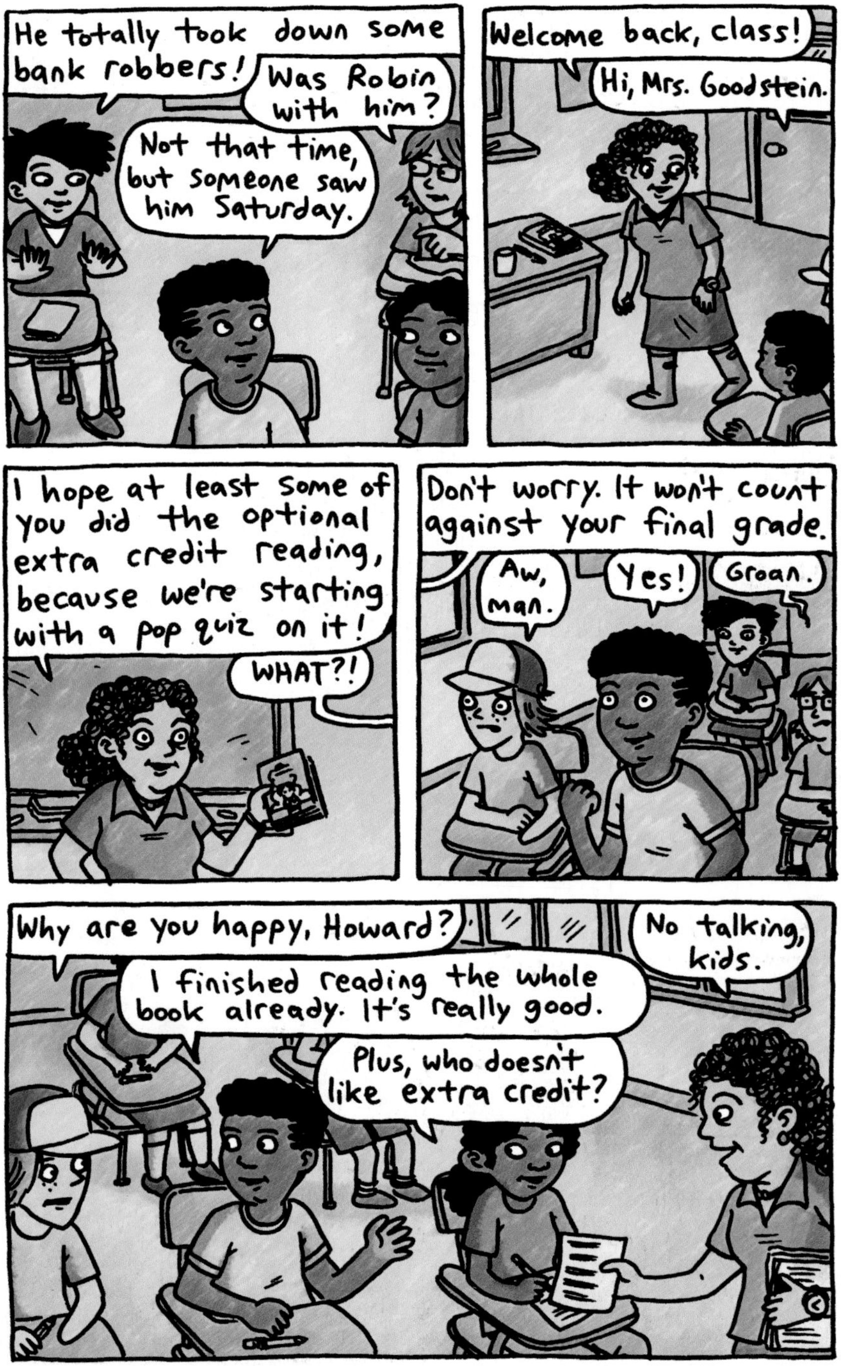

He totally took down some bank robbers!
Was Robin with him?
Not that time, but someone saw him Saturday.
Welcome back, class!
Hi, Mrs. Goodstein.
I hope at least some of you did the optional extra credit reading, because we're starting with a pop quiz on it!
WHAT?!
Don't worry. It won't count against your final grade.
Aw, man.
Yes!
Groan.
Why are you happy, Howard?
I finished reading the whole book already. It's really good.
Plus, who doesn't like extra credit?
No talking, kids.

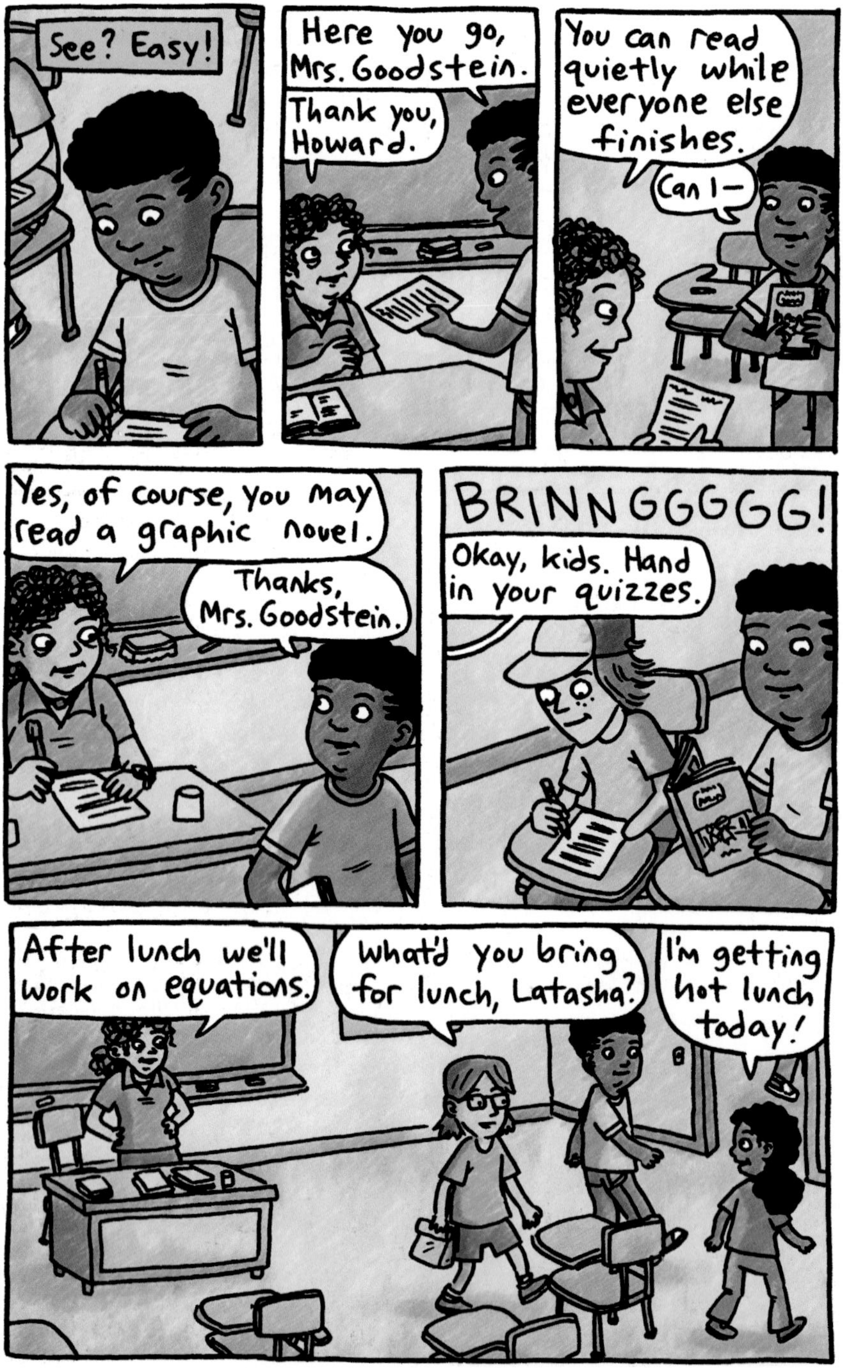
See? Easy!
Here you go, Mrs. Goodstein.
Thank you, Howard.
You can read quietly while everyone else finishes.
Can I—
Yes, of course, you may read a graphic novel.
Thanks, Mrs. Goodstein.
BRINNGGGGG!
Okay, kids. Hand in your quizzes.
After lunch we'll work on equations.
What'd you bring for lunch, Latasha?
I'm getting hot lunch today!

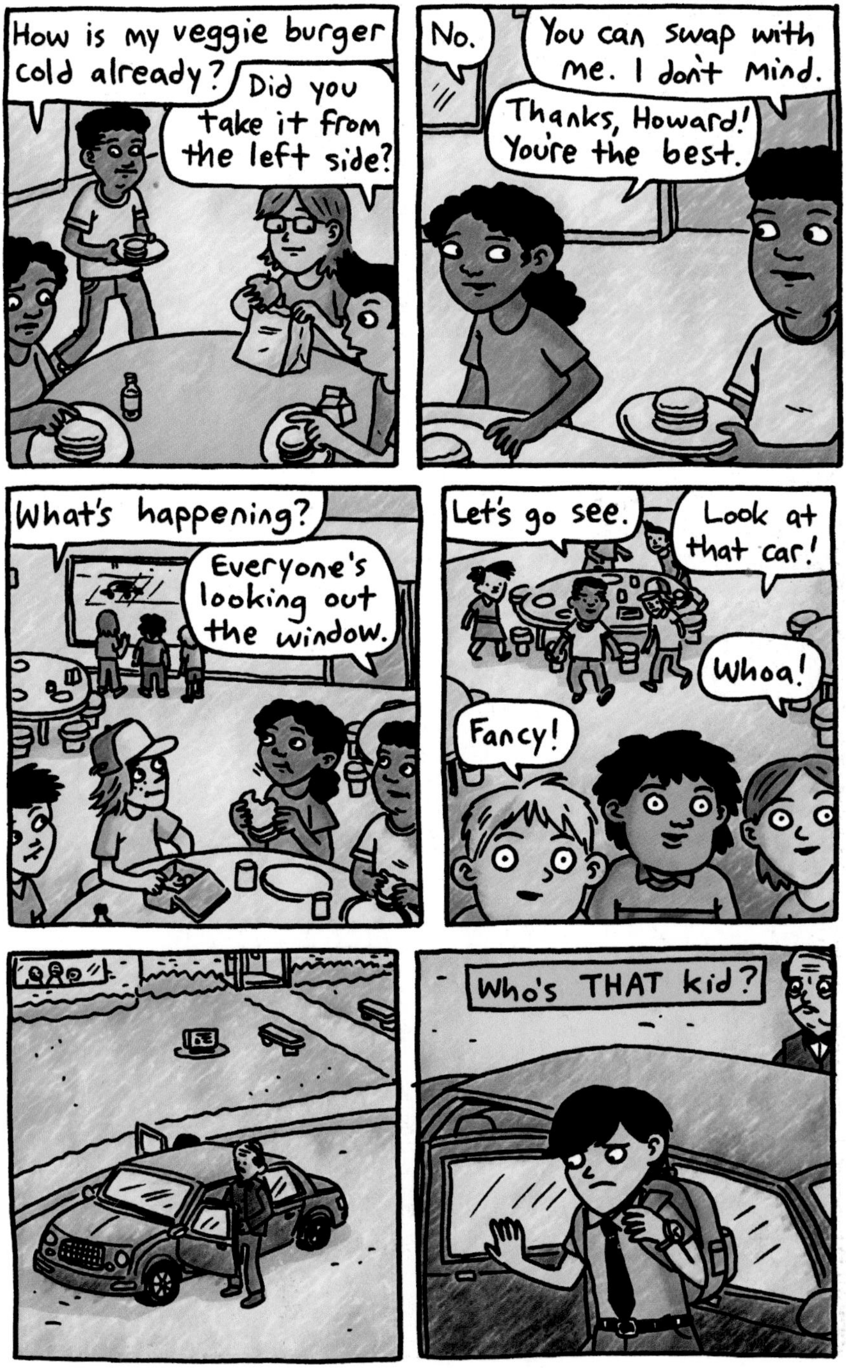
How is my veggie burger cold already?
Did you take it from the left side?
No.
You can swap with me. I don't mind.
Thanks, Howard! You're the best.
What's happening?
Everyone's looking out the window.
Let's go see.
Look at that car!
Whoa!
Fancy!
Who's THAT kid?

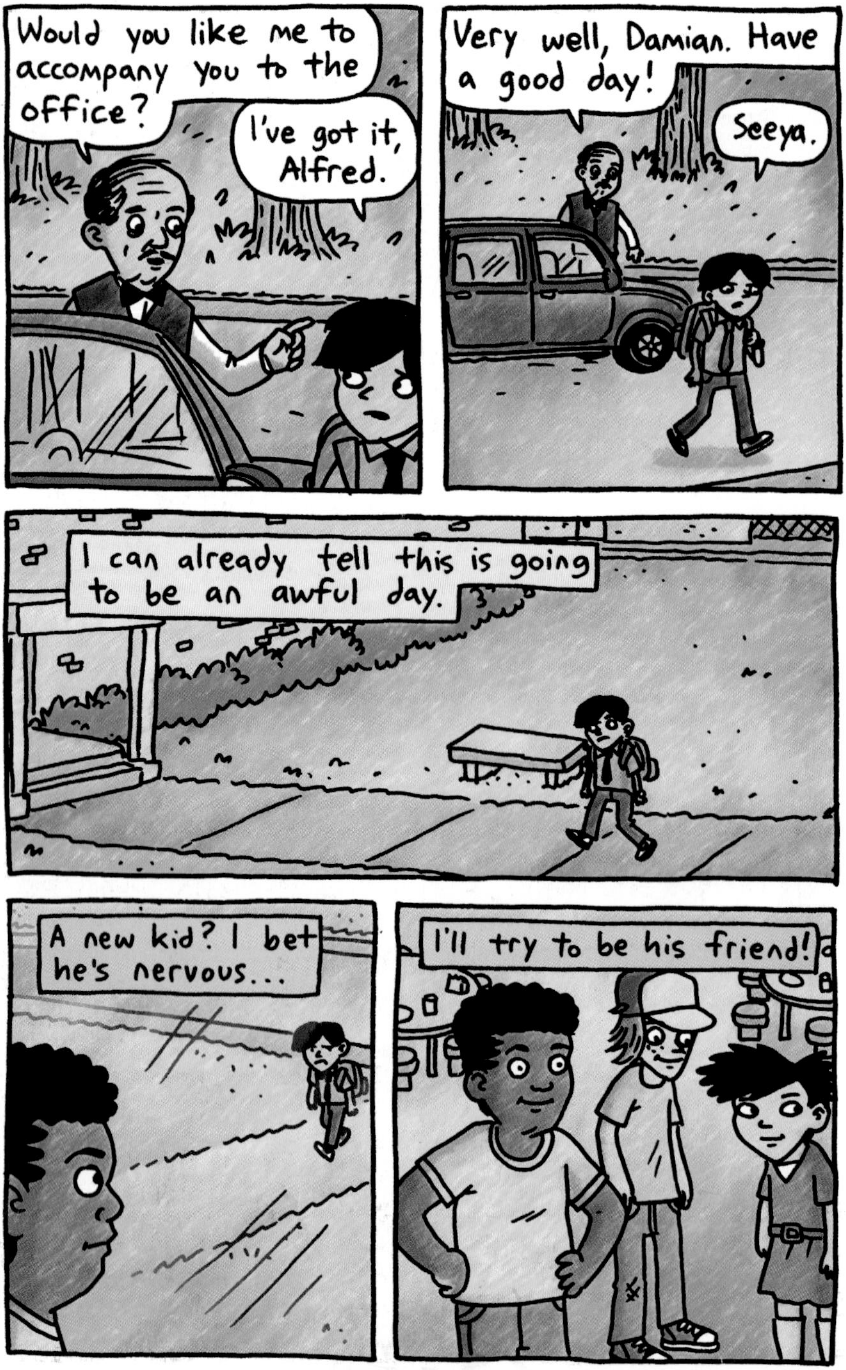
Would you like me to accompany you to the office?
I've got it, Alfred.
Very well, Damian. Have a good day!
Seeya.
I can already tell this is going to be an awful day.
A new kid? I bet he's nervous...
I'll try to be his friend!

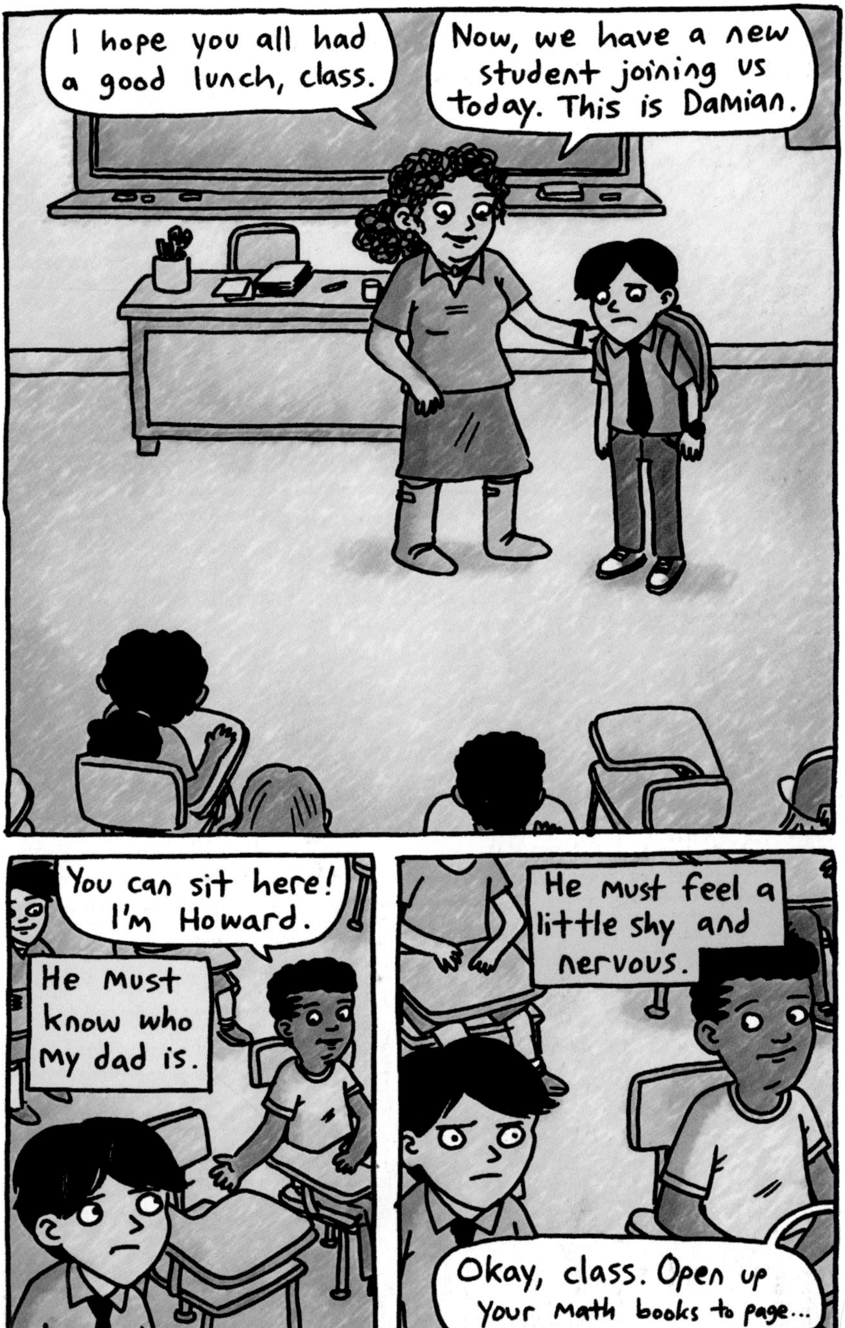
I hope you all had a good lunch, class.
Now, we have a new student joining us today. This is Damian.
You can sit here! I'm Howard.
He must know who my dad is.
He must feel a little shy and nervous.
Okay, class. Open up your math books to page...

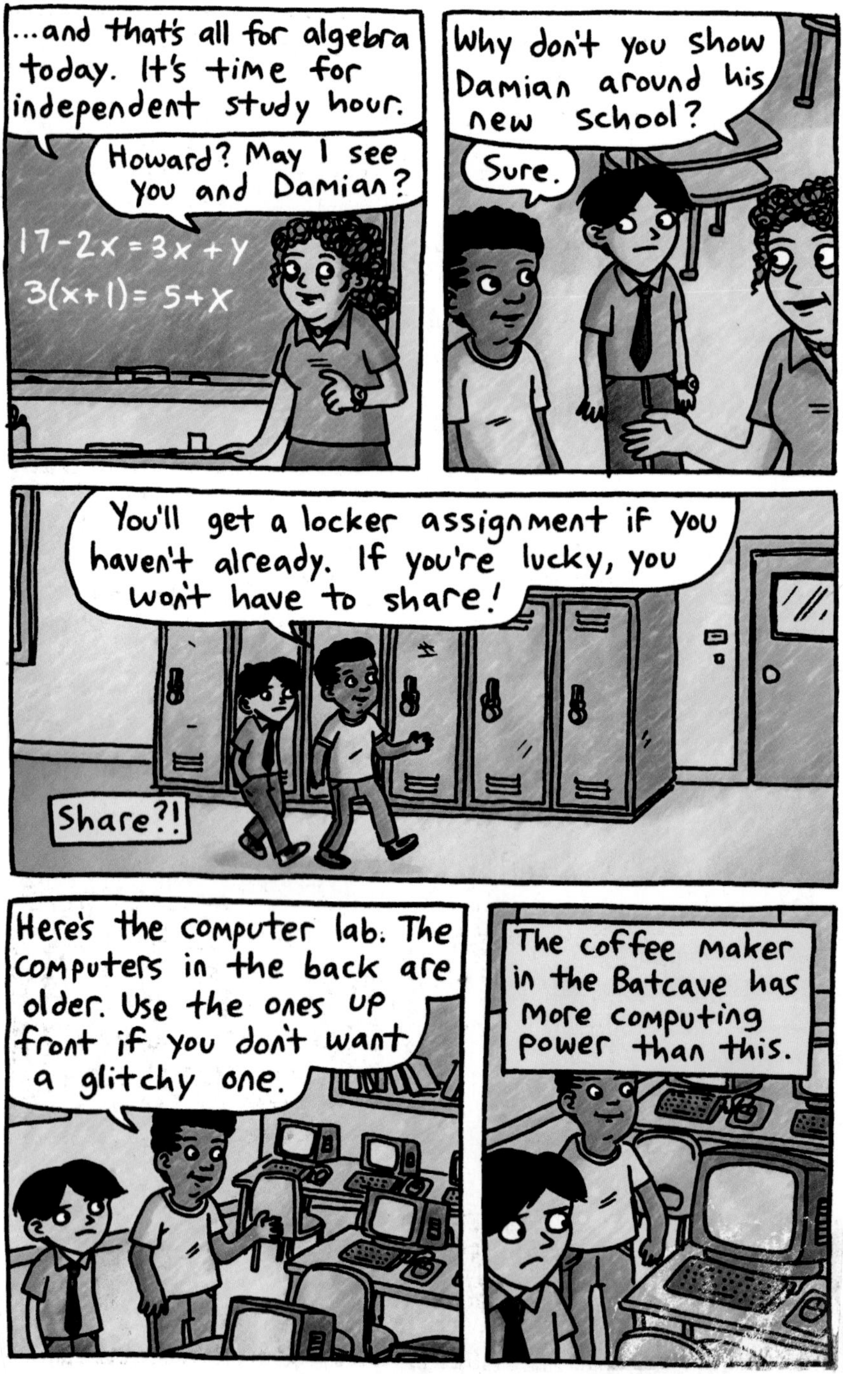
...and that's all for algebra today. It's time for independent study hour.
Howard? May I see you and Damian?
17-2x=3x+y
3(x+1)= 5+x
Why don't you show Damian around his new school?
Sure.
You'll get a locker assignment if you haven't already. If you're lucky, you won't have to share!
Share?!
Here's the computer lab. The computers in the back are older. Use the ones up front if you don't want a glitchy one.
The coffee maker in the Batcave has more computing power than this.

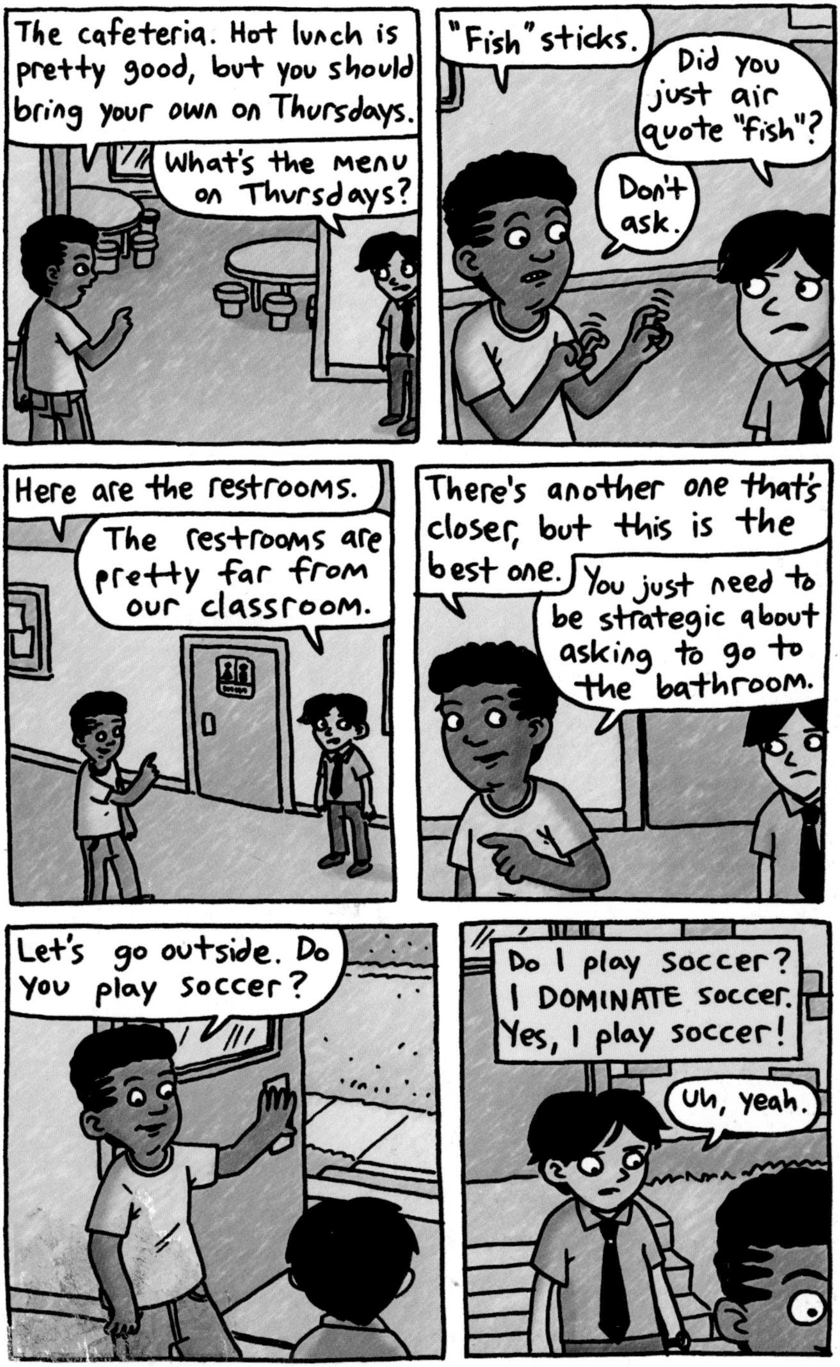
The cafeteria. Hot lunch is pretty good, but you should bring your own on Thursdays.
What's the menu on Thursdays?
"Fish" sticks.
Did you just air quote "fish"?
Don't ask.
Here are the restrooms.
The restrooms are pretty far from our classroom.
There's another one that's closer, but this is the best one.
You just need to be strategic about asking to go to the bathroom.
Let's go outside. Do you play soccer?
Do I play soccer? I DOMINATE soccer. Yes, I play soccer!
Uh, yeah.

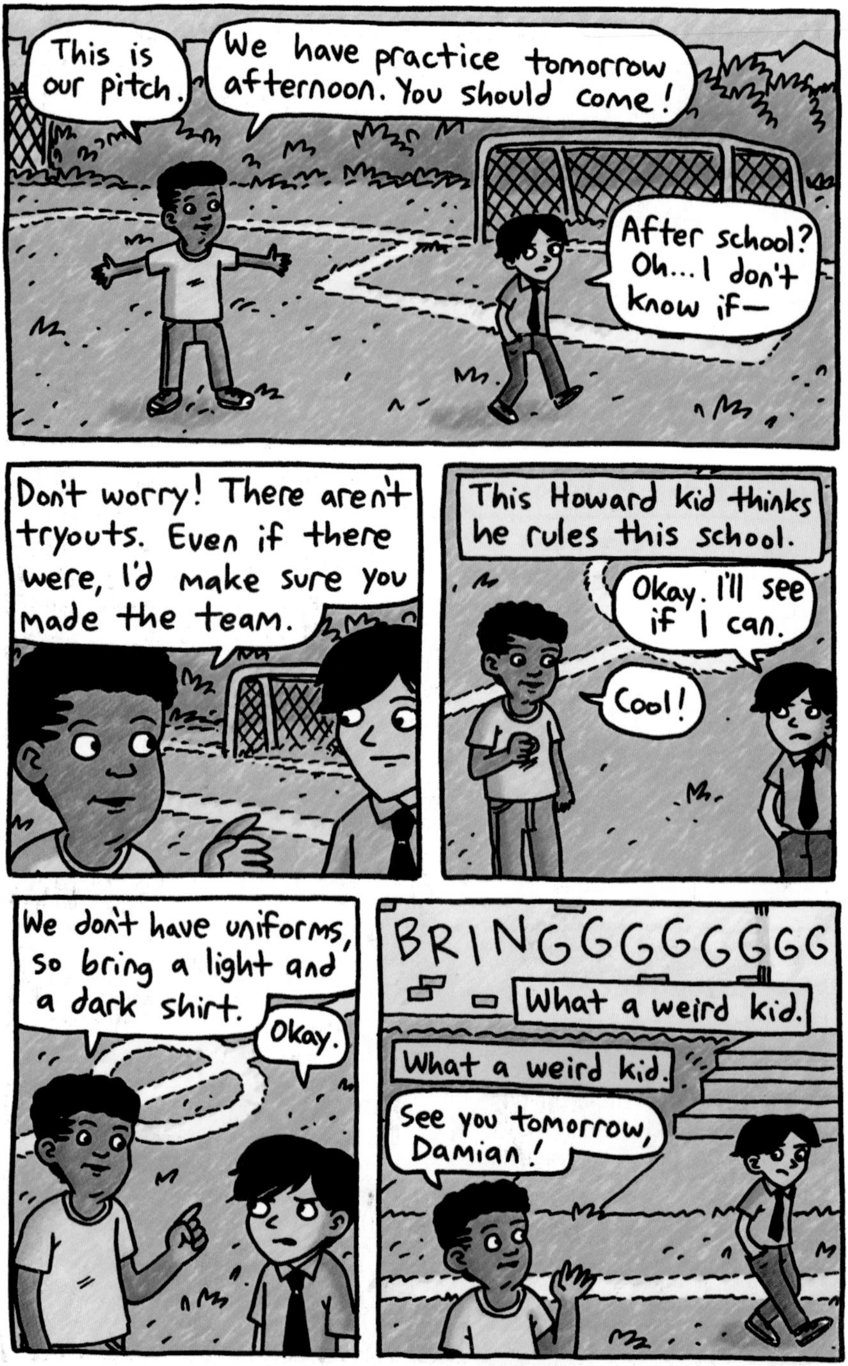
This is our pitch.
We have practice tomorrow afternoon. You should come!
After school? Oh... I don't know if—
Don't worry! There aren't tryouts. Even if there were, I'd make sure you made the team.
This Howard kid thinks he rules this school.
Okay. I'll see if I can.
Cool!
We don't have uniforms, so bring a light and a dark shirt.
Okay.
BRINGGGGGGGG
What a weird kid.
What a weird kid.
See you tomorrow, Damian!

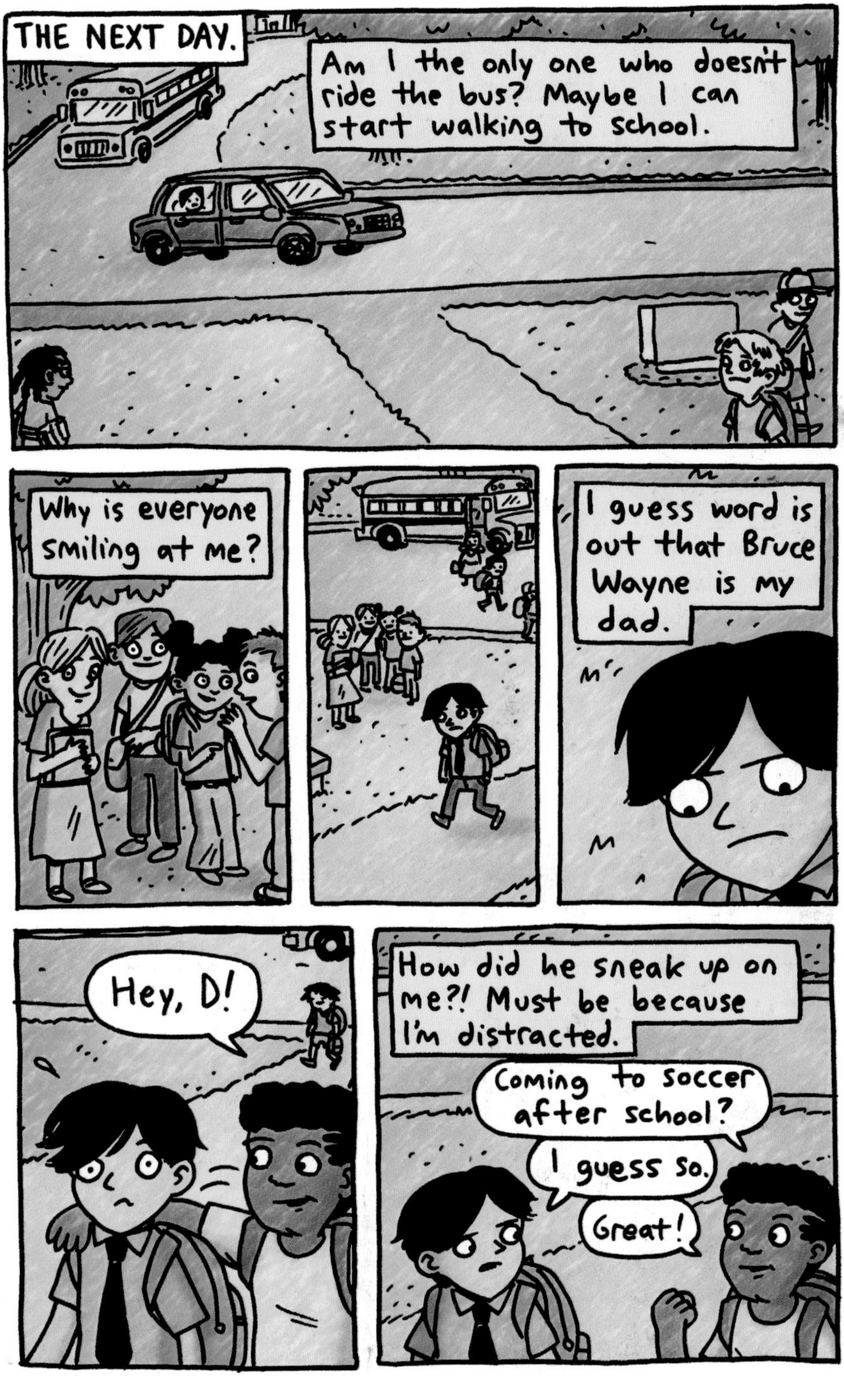
THE NEXT DAY.
Am I the only one who doesn't ride the bus? Maybe I can start walking to school.
Why is everyone smiling at me?
I guess word is out that Bruce Wayne is my dad.
Hey, D!
How did he sneak up on me?! Must be because I'm distracted.
Coming to soccer after school?
I guess so.
Great!

Today, class, we're going to study the cell.

Plant and animal cells have differences. Bacteria can be even more different.

Now, from our text, who can tell me the three parts that all cells have in common?

Yes...

Damian?

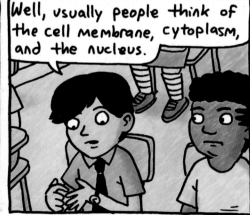

Well, usually people think of the cell membrane, cytoplasm, and the nucleus.

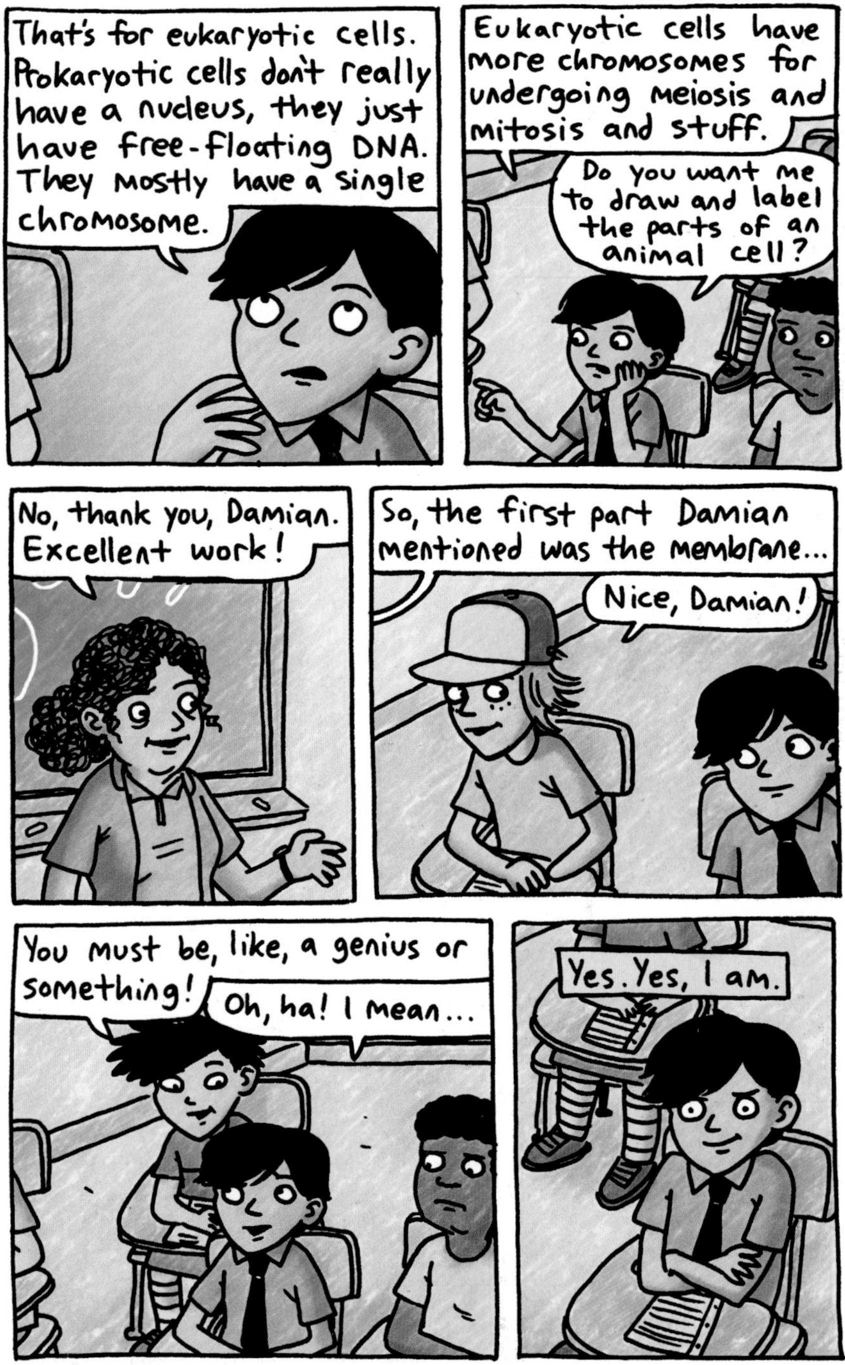
That's for eukaryotic cells. Prokaryotic cells don't really have a nucleus, they just have free-floating DNA. They mostly have a single chromosome.
Eukaryotic cells have more chromosomes for undergoing meiosis and mitosis and stuff.
Do you want me to draw and label the parts of an animal cell?
No, thank you, Damian. Excellent work!
So, the first part Damian mentioned was the membrane...
Nice, Damian!
You must be, like, a genius or something!
Oh, ha! I mean...
Yes. Yes, I am.

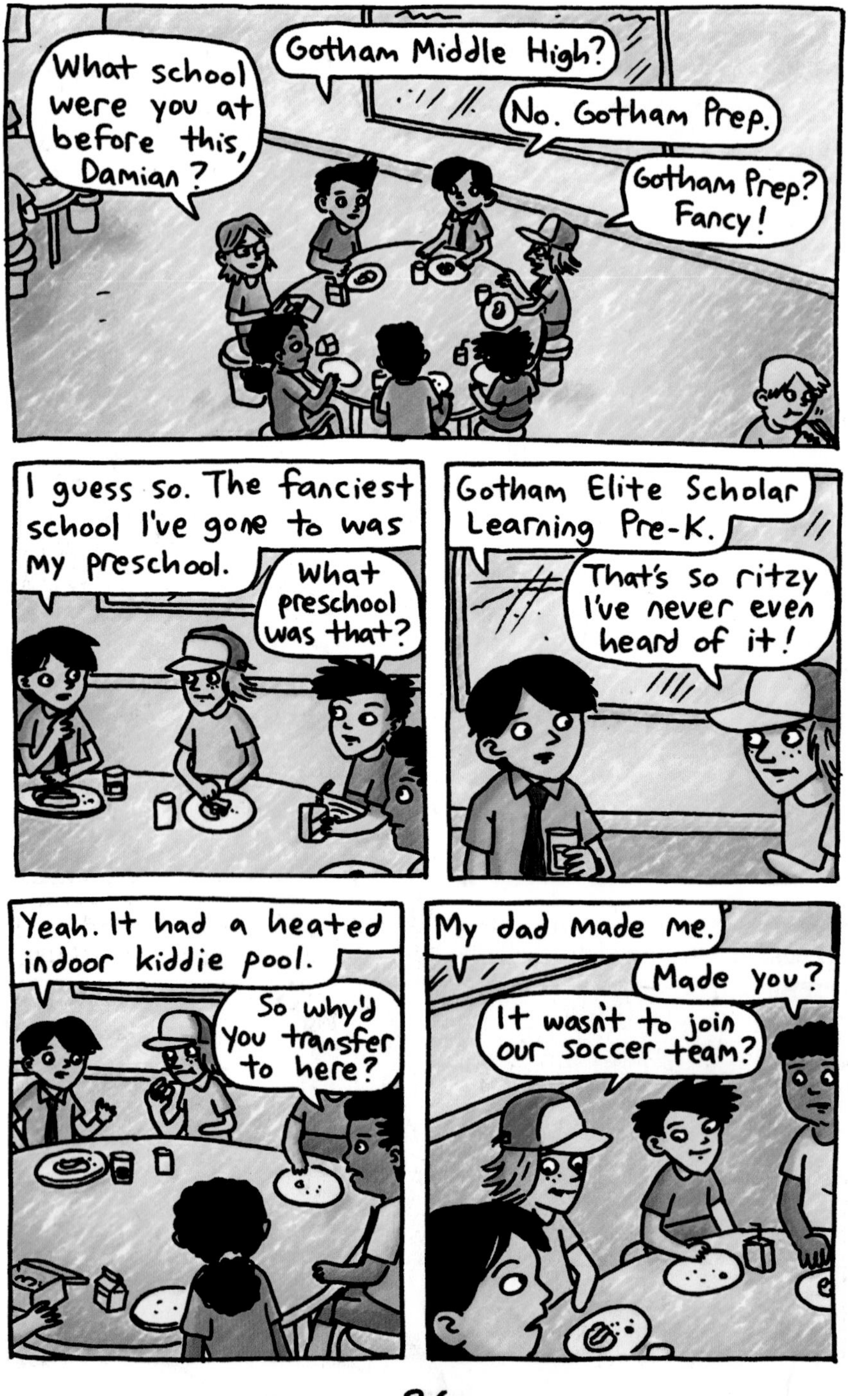

What school were you at before this, Damian?
Gotham Middle High?
No. Gotham Prep.
Gotham Prep? Fancy!
I guess so. The fanciest school I've gone to was my preschool.
What preschool was that?
Gotham Elite Scholar Learning Pre-K.
That's so ritzy I've never even heard of it!
Yeah. It had a heated indoor kiddie pool.
So why'd you transfer to here?
My dad made me.
Made you?
It wasn't to join our soccer team?

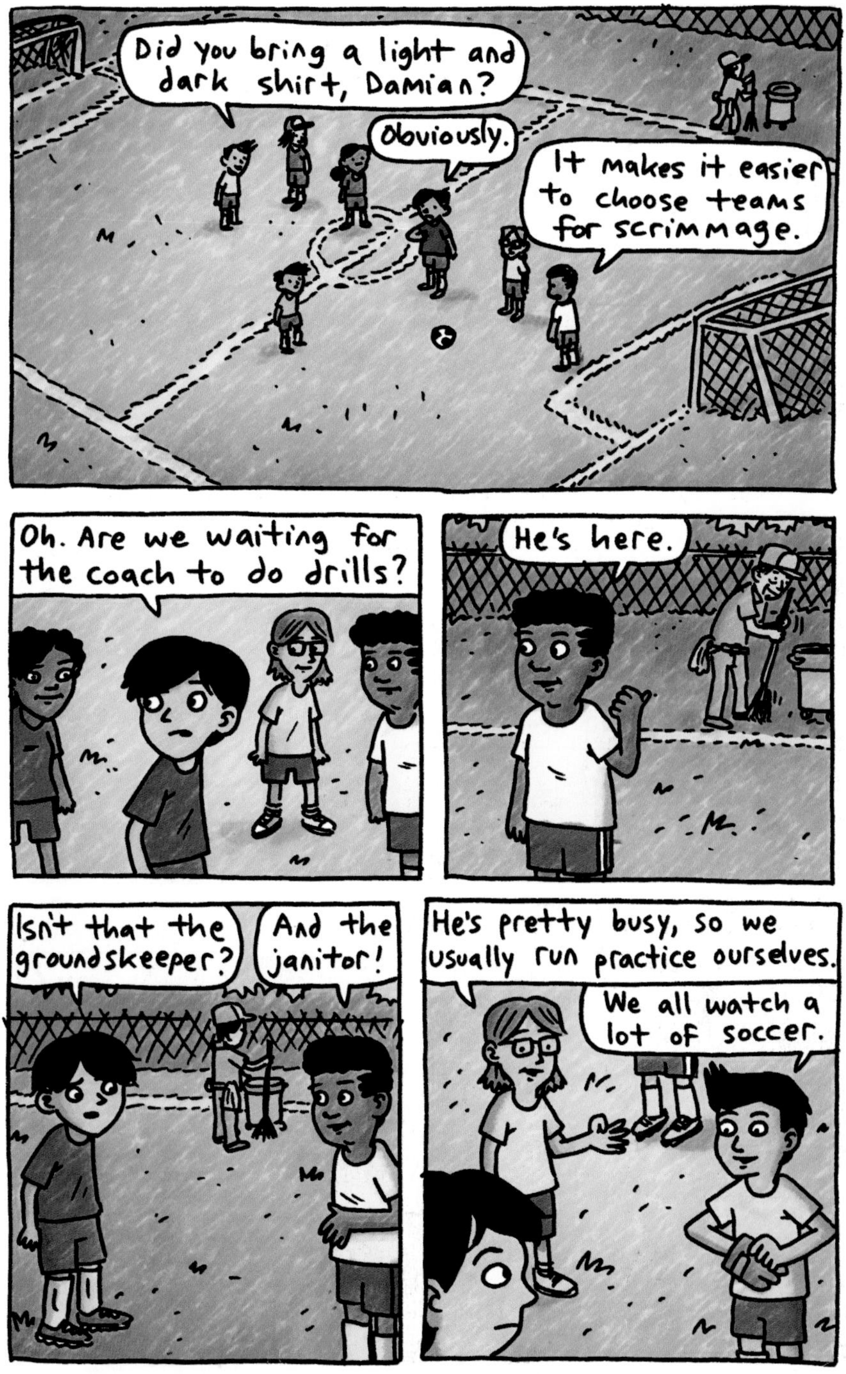
Did you bring a light and dark shirt, Damian?
Obviously.
It makes it easier to choose teams for scrimmage.
Oh. Are we waiting for the coach to do drills?
He's here.
Isn't that the groundskeeper?
And the janitor!
He's pretty busy, so we usually run practice ourselves.
We all watch a lot of soccer.

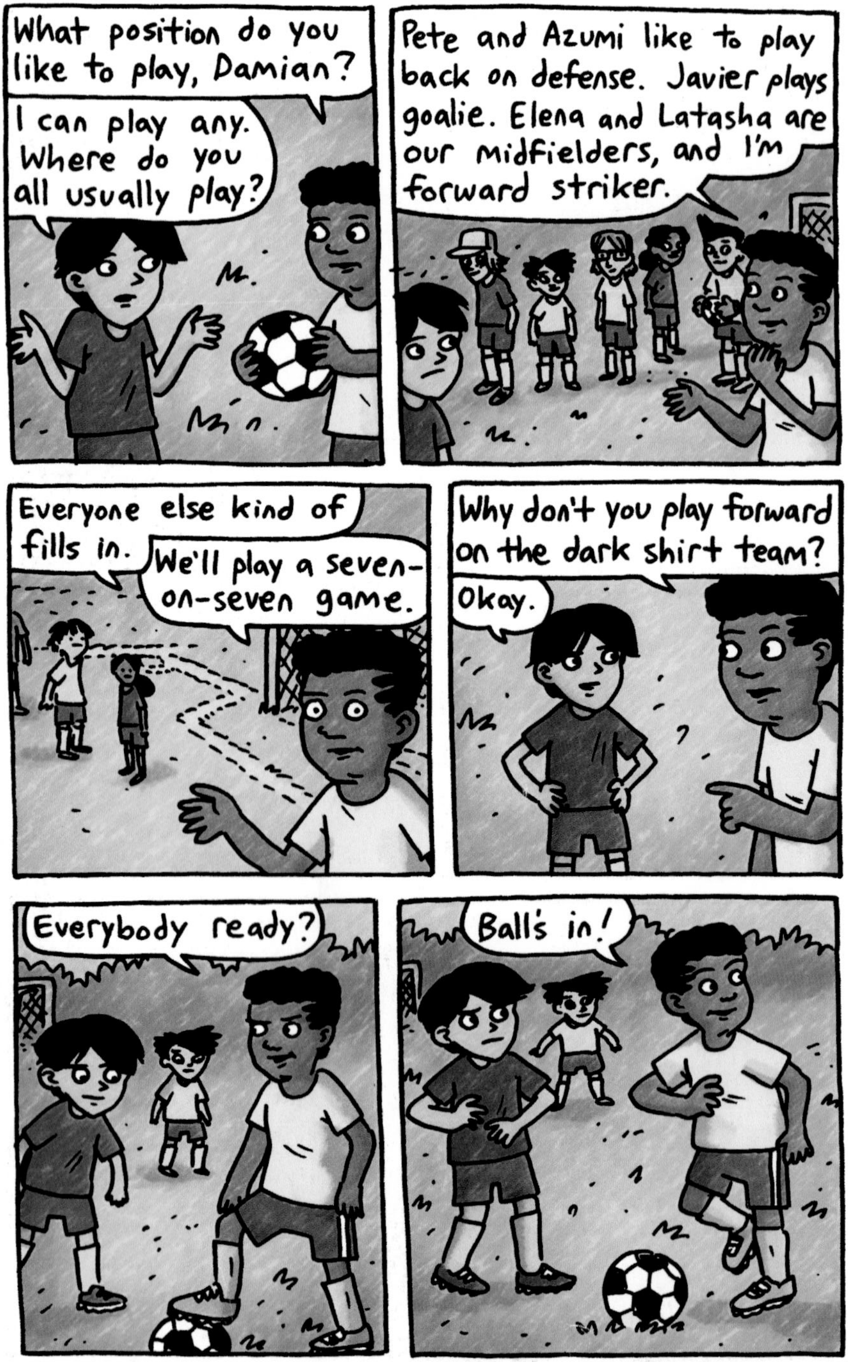
What position do you like to play, Damian?
I can play any. Where do you all usually play?
Pete and Azumi like to play back on defense. Javier plays goalie. Elena and Latasha are our midfielders, and I'm forward striker.
Everyone else kind of fills in.
We'll play a seven-on-seven game.
Why don't you play forward on the dark shirt team?
Okay.
Everybody ready?
Ball's in!

Huh?
STEAL!
Flick!
BLAST!
Whoa!
That was sooooo cool!
Ha! You got me. Nice work.
Let's see him do that again.

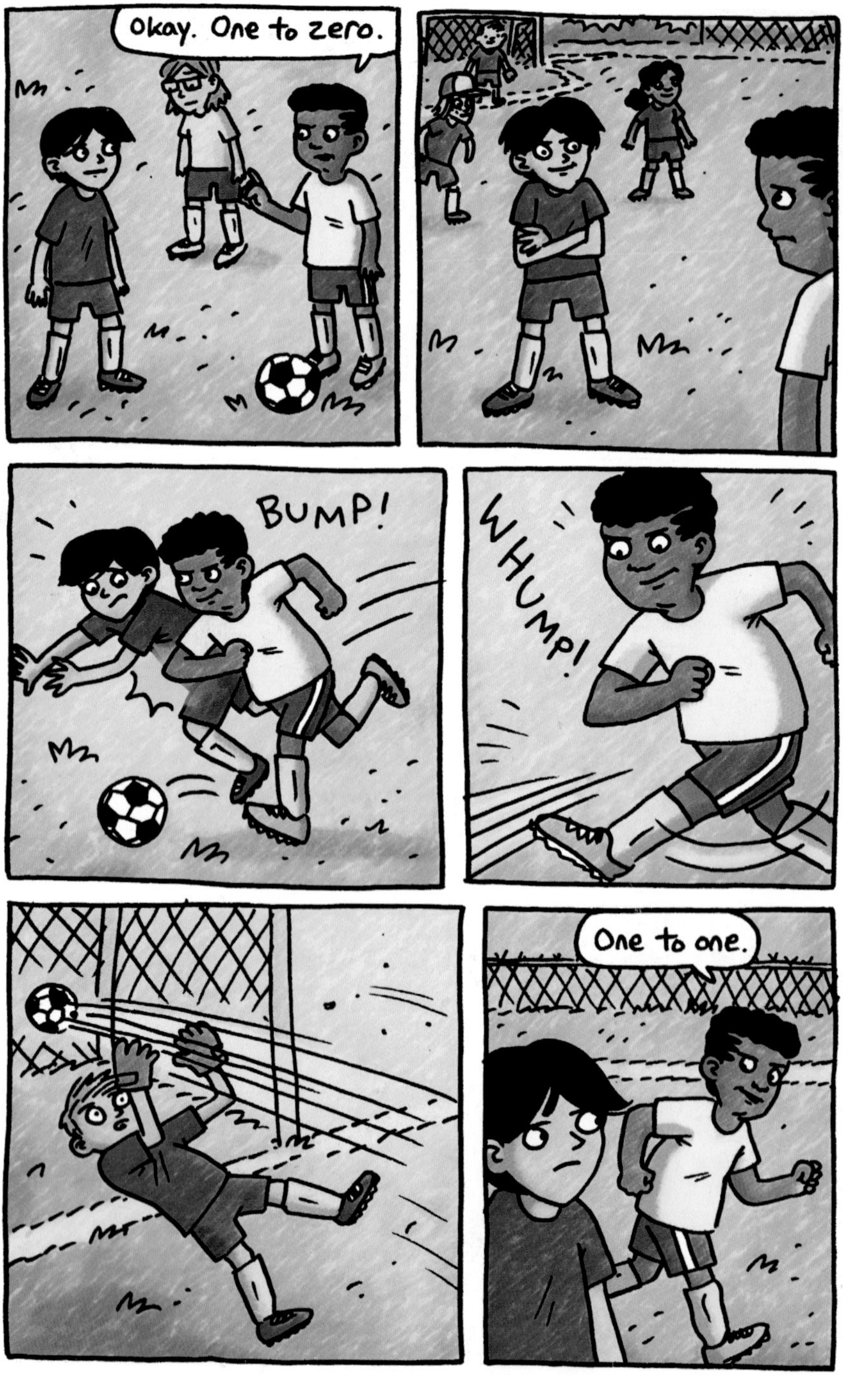
Okay. One to zero.
BUMP!
WHUMP!
One to one.

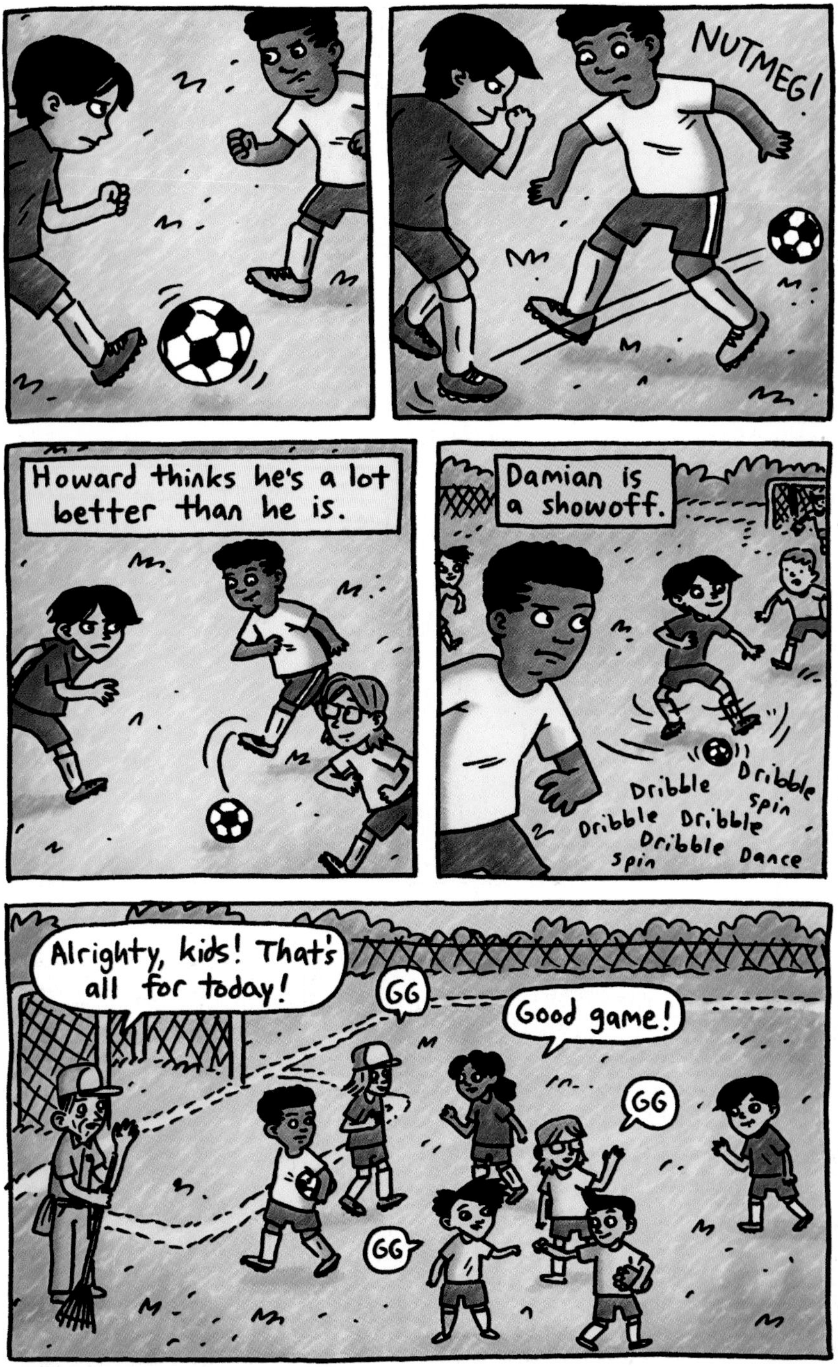
NUTMEG!
Howard thinks he's a lot better than he is.
Damian is a showoff.
Dribble
Dribble
spin
Dribble Dribble
Dribble
spin
Dance
Alrighty, kids! That's all for today!
GG
Good game!
GG
GG

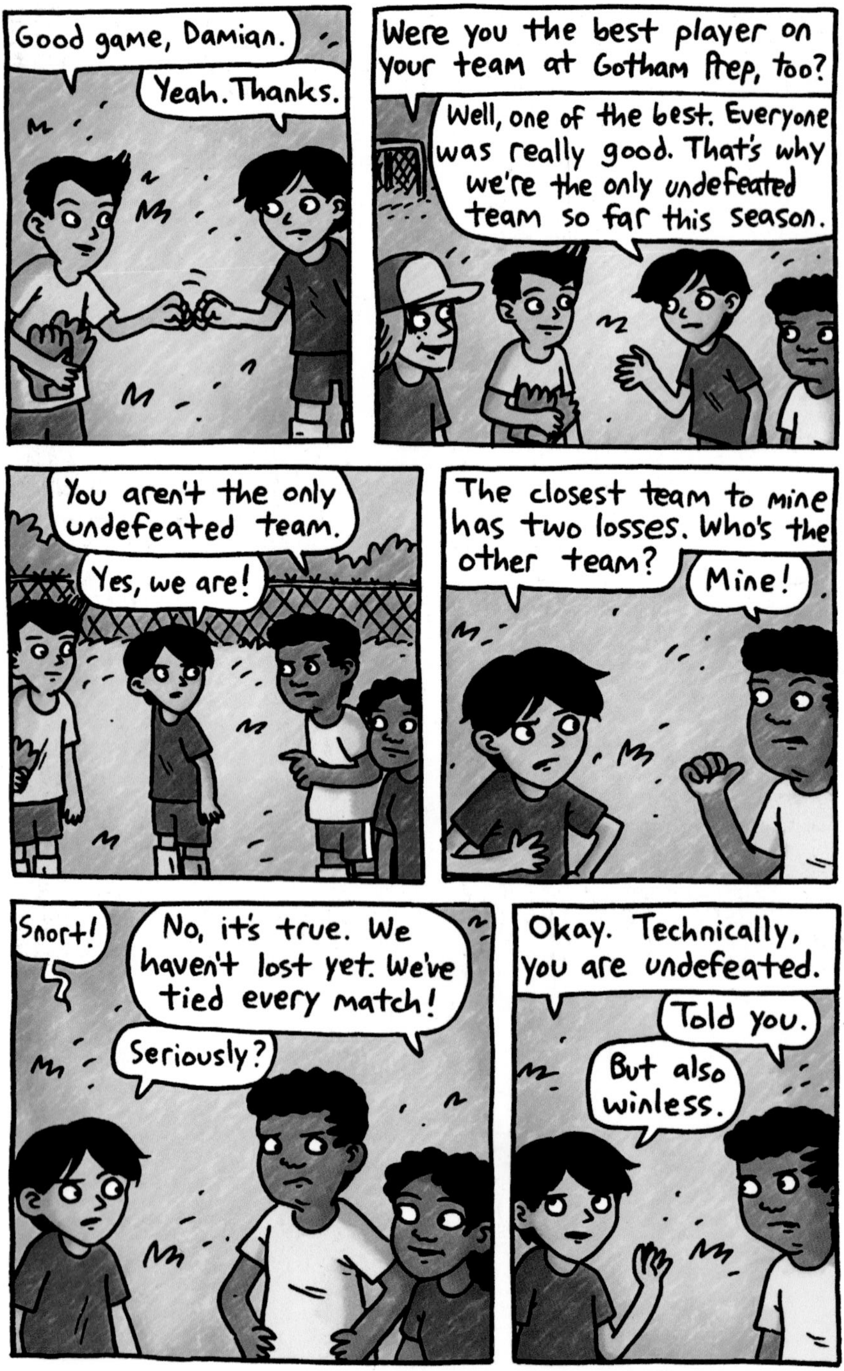
Good game, Damian.
Yeah. Thanks.
Were you the best player on your team at Gotham Prep, too?
Well, one of the best. Everyone was really good. That's why we're the only undefeated team so far this season.
You aren't the only undefeated team.
Yes, we are!
The closest team to mine has two losses. Who's the other team?
Mine!
Snort!
No, it's true. We haven't lost yet. We've tied every match!
Seriously?
Okay. Technically, you are undefeated.
Told you.
But also winless.

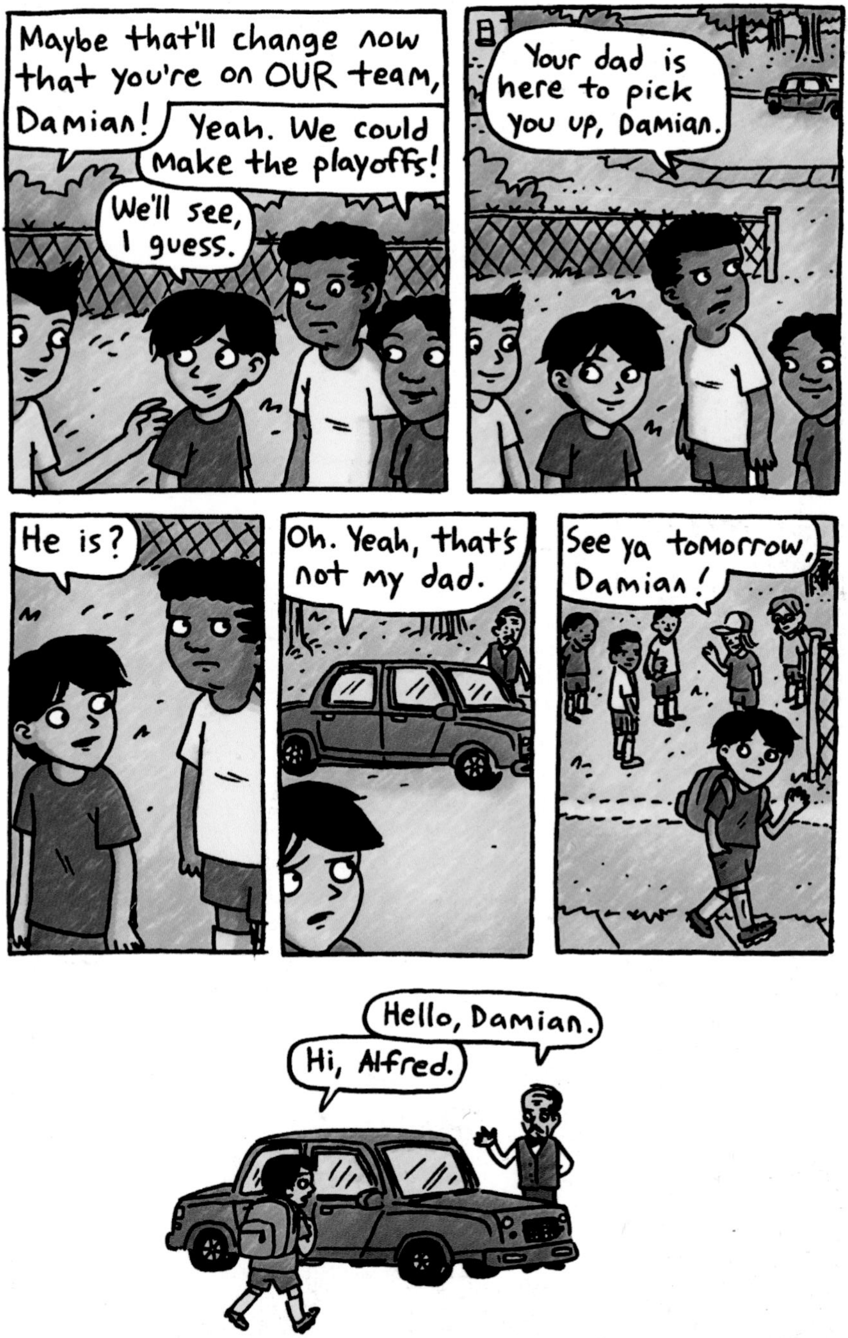

Maybe that'll change now that you're on OUR team, Damian!
Yeah. We could make the playoffs!
We'll see, I guess.
Your dad is here to pick you up, Damian.
He is?
Oh. Yeah, that's not my dad.
See ya tomorrow, Damian!
Hello, Damian.
Hi, Alfred.

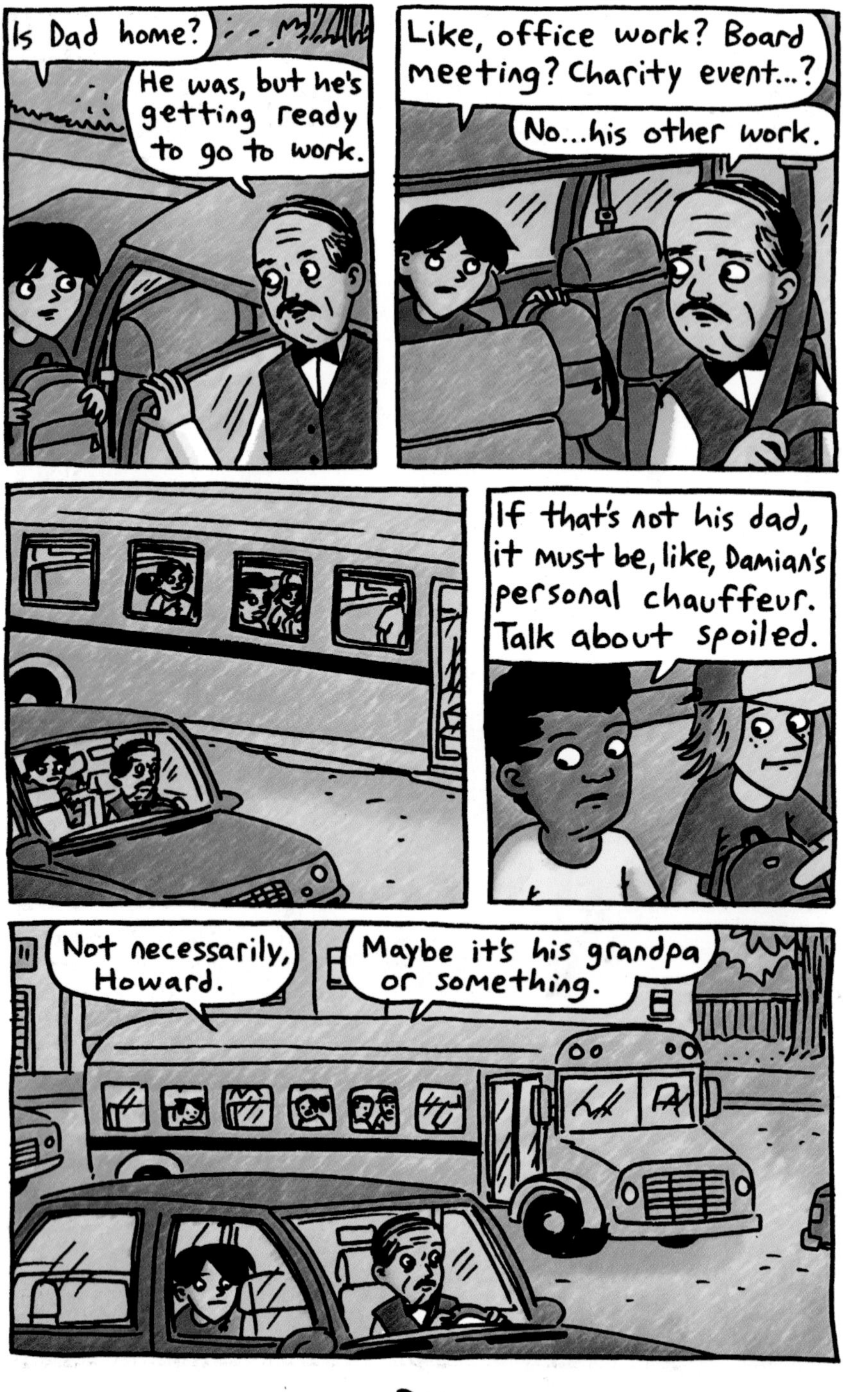
Is Dad home?
He was, but he's getting ready to go to work.
Like, office work? Board meeting? Charity event...?
No...his other work.
If that's not his dad, it must be, like, Damian's personal chauffeur. Talk about spoiled.
Not necessarily, Howard.
Maybe it's his grandpa or something.

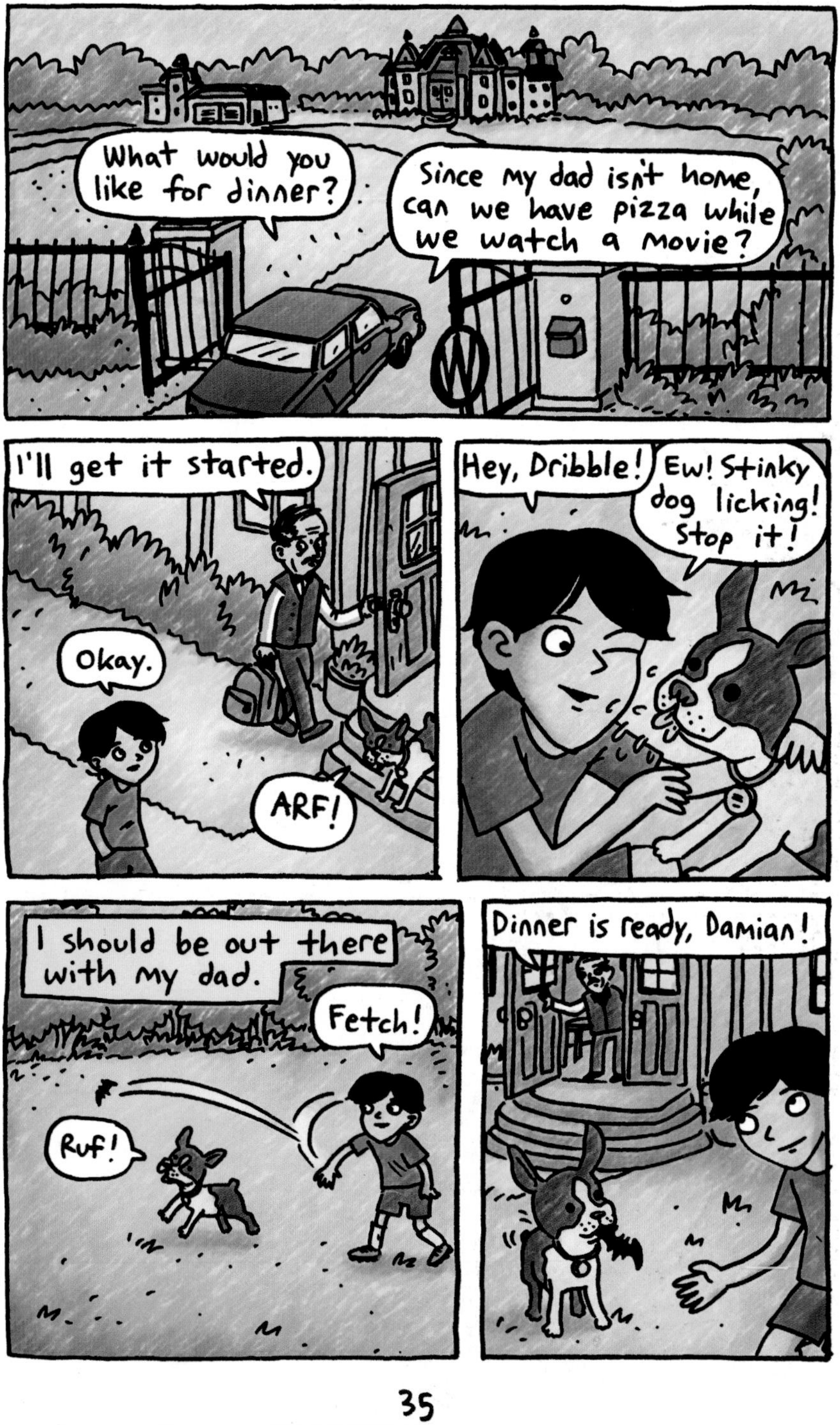
What would you like for dinner?
Since my dad isn't home, can we have pizza while we watch a movie?
I'll get it started.
Okay.
ARF!
Hey, Dribble!
Ew! Stinky dog licking! Stop it!
I should be out there with my dad.
Fetch!
Ruf!
Dinner is ready, Damian!

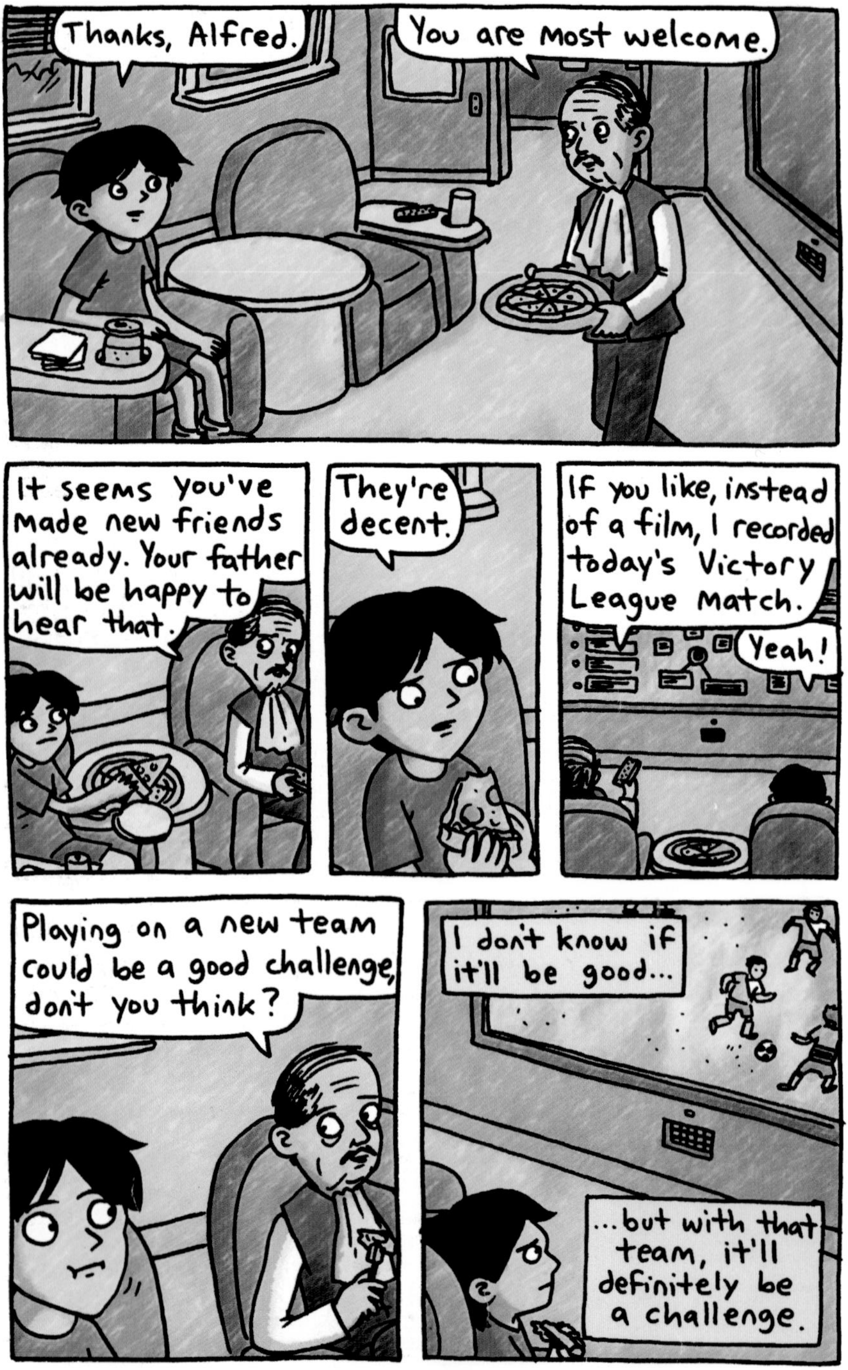
Thanks, Alfred.
You are most welcome.
It seems you've made new friends already. Your father will be happy to hear that.
They're decent.
If you like, instead of a film, I recorded today's Victory League Match.
Yeah!
Playing on a new team could be a good challenge, don't you think?
I don't know if it'll be good...
...but with that team, it'll definitely be a challenge.

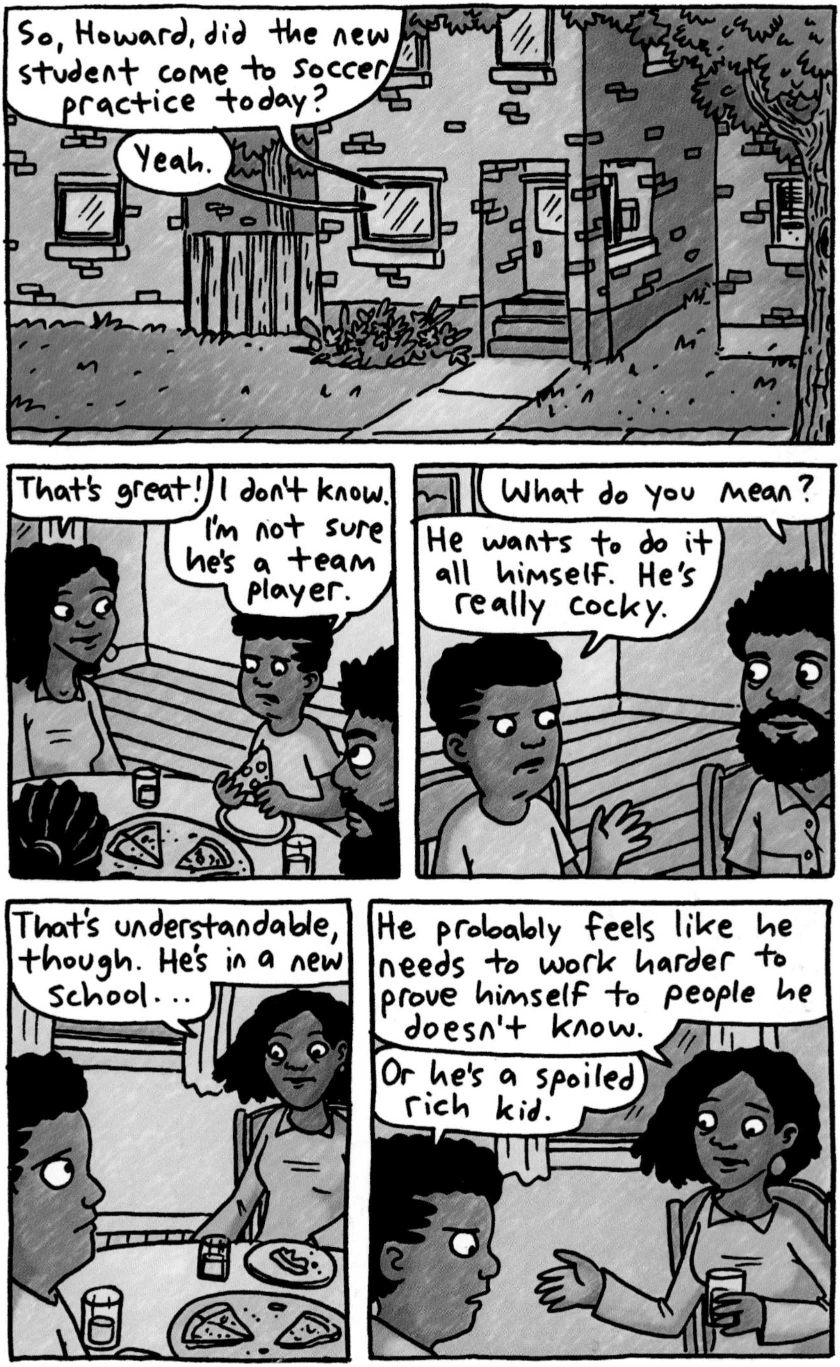
So, Howard, did the new student come to soccer practice today?
Yeah.
That's great!
I don't know. I'm not sure he's a team player.
What do you mean?
He wants to do it all himself. He's really cocky.
That's understandable, though. He's in a new school...
He probably feels like he needs to work harder to prove himself to people he doesn't know.
Or he's a spoiled rich kid.

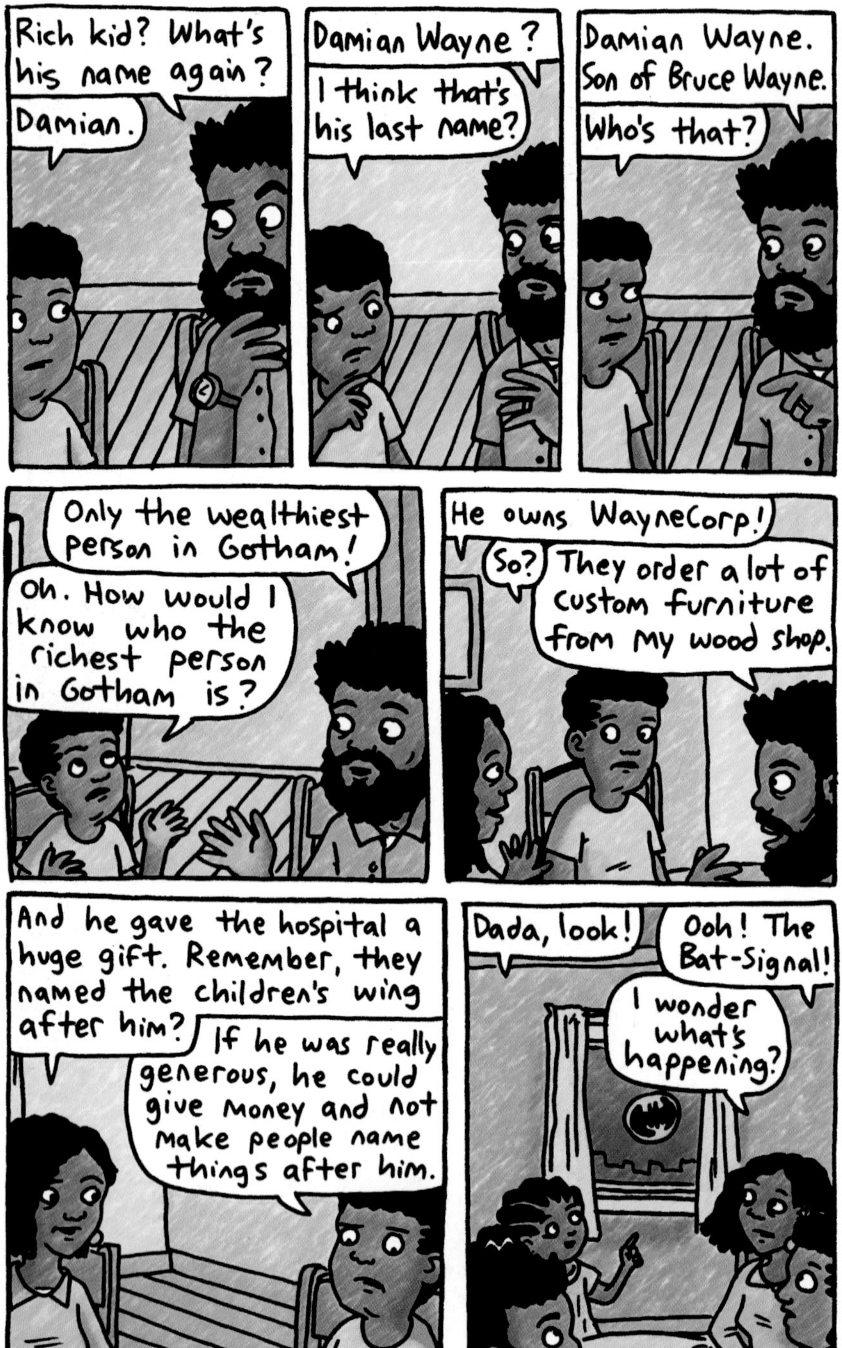
Rich kid? What's his name again?
Damian.
Damian Wayne?
I think that's his last name?
Damian Wayne. Son of Bruce Wayne.
Who's that?
Only the wealthiest person in Gotham!
Oh. How would I know who the richest person in Gotham is?
He owns WayneCorp!
So?
They order a lot of custom furniture from my wood shop.
And he gave the hospital a huge gift. Remember, they named the children's wing after him?
If he was really generous, he could give money and not make people name things after him.
Dada, look!
Ooh! The Bat-Signal!
I wonder what's happening?

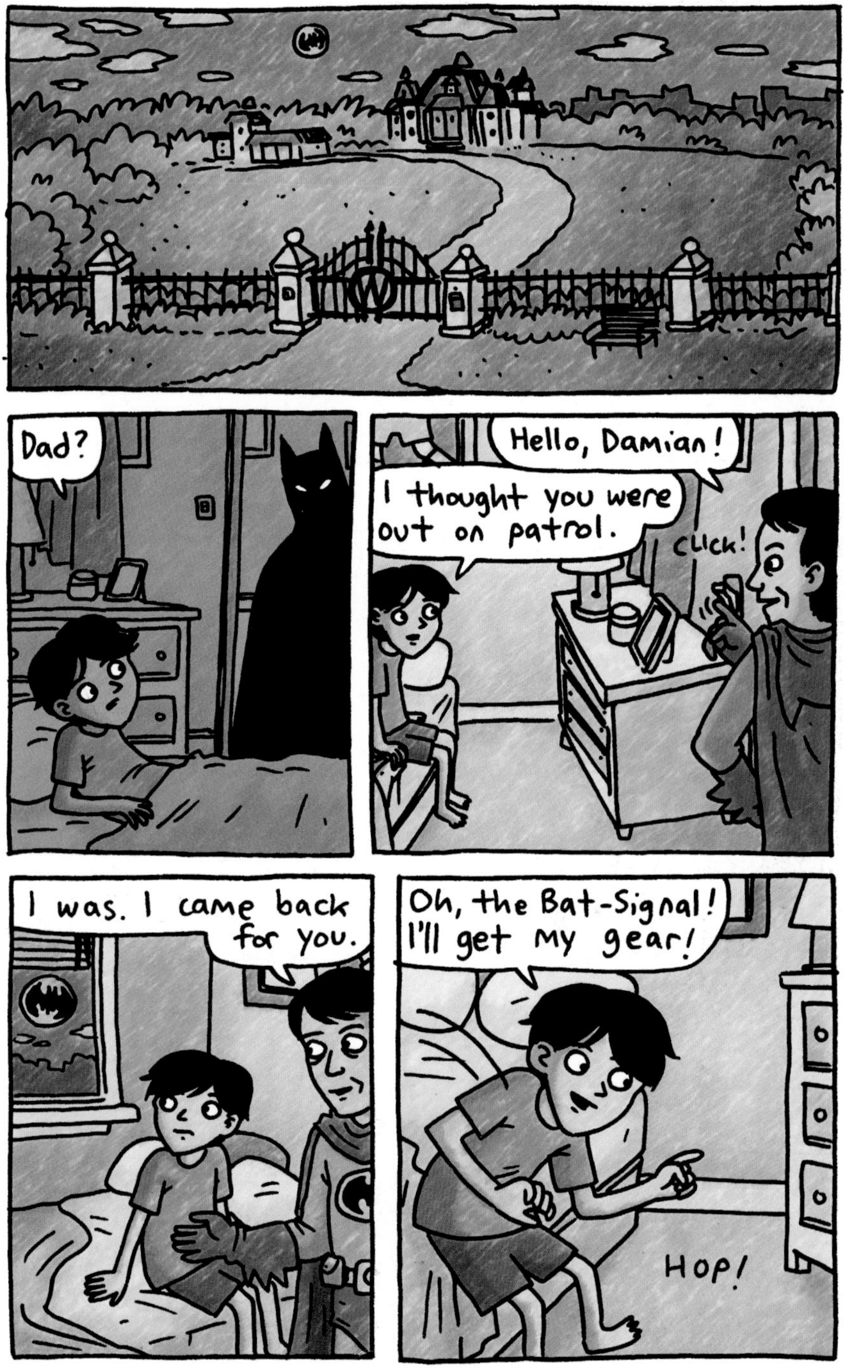
Dad?
Hello, Damian!
I thought you were out on patrol.
CLICK!
I was. I came back for you.
Oh, the Bat-Signal! I'll get my gear!
HOP!

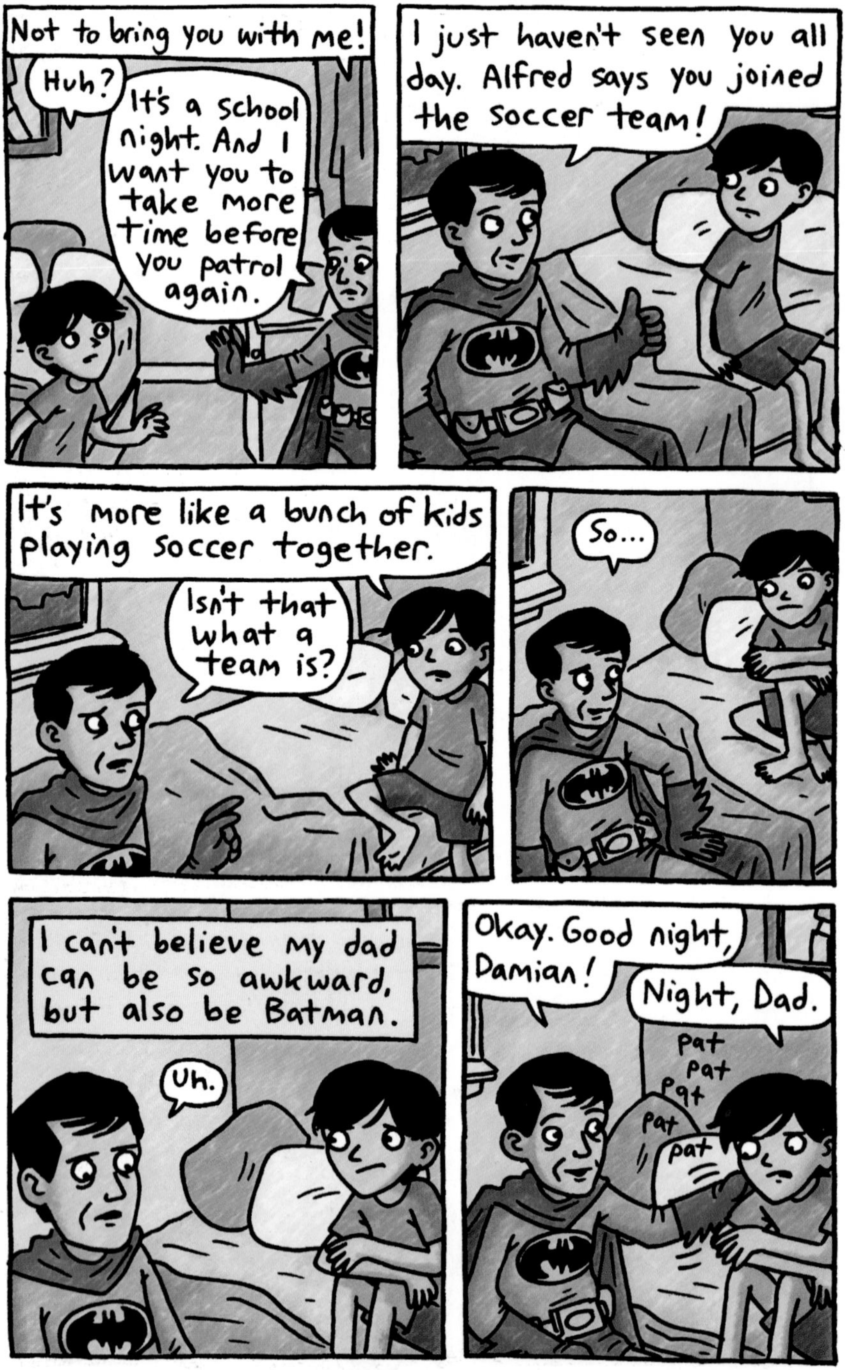
Not to bring you with me!
Huh?
It's a school night. And I want you to take more time before you patrol again.
I just haven't seen you all day. Alfred says you joined the soccer team!
It's more like a bunch of kids playing soccer together.
Isn't that what a team is?
So...
I can't believe my dad can be so awkward, but also be Batman.
Uh.
Okay. Good night, Damian!
Night, Dad.
pat
pat
pat
pat
pat

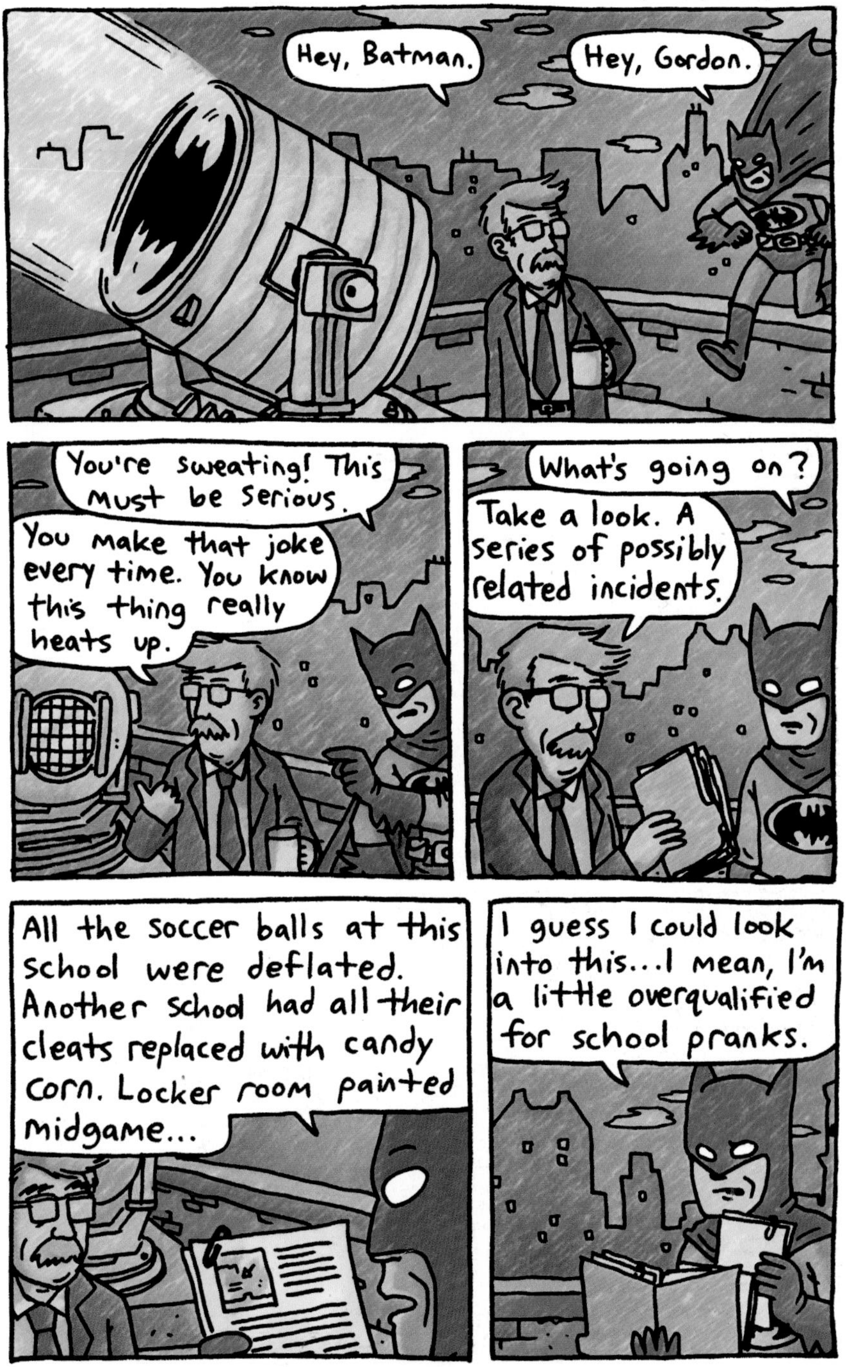
Hey, Batman.
Hey, Gordon.
You're sweating! This must be serious.
You make that joke every time. You know this thing really heats up.
What's going on?
Take a look. A series of possibly related incidents.
All the soccer balls at this school were deflated. Another school had all their cleats replaced with candy corn. Locker room painted midgame...
I guess I could look into this... I mean, I'm a little overqualified for school pranks.

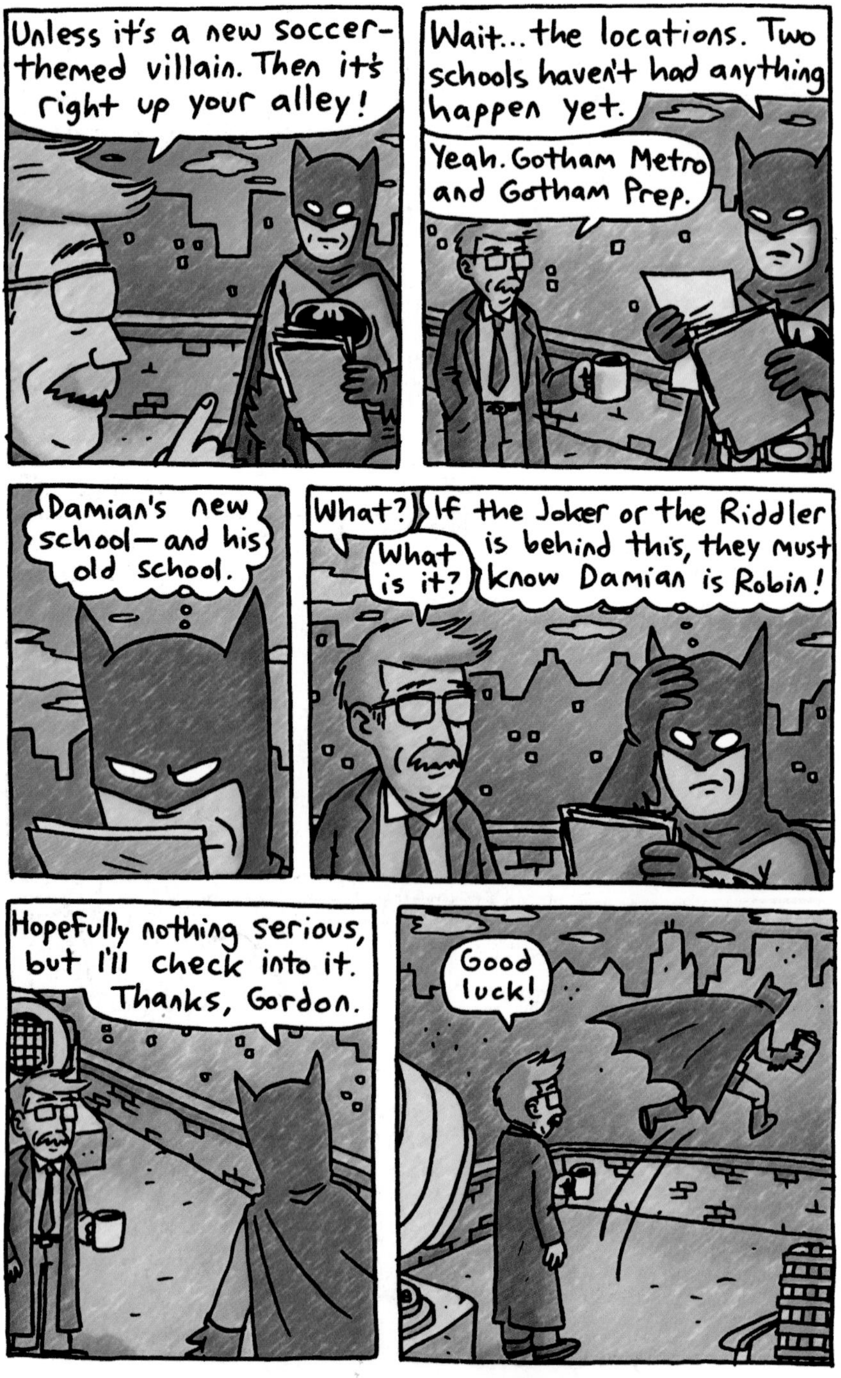
Unless it's a new soccer-themed villain. Then it's right up your alley!
Wait... the locations. Two schools haven't had anything happen yet.
Yeah. Gotham Metro and Gotham Prep.
Damian's new school—and his old school.
What?
If the Joker or the Riddler is behind this, they must know Damian is Robin!
What is it?
Hopefully nothing serious, but I'll check into it. Thanks, Gordon.
Good luck!

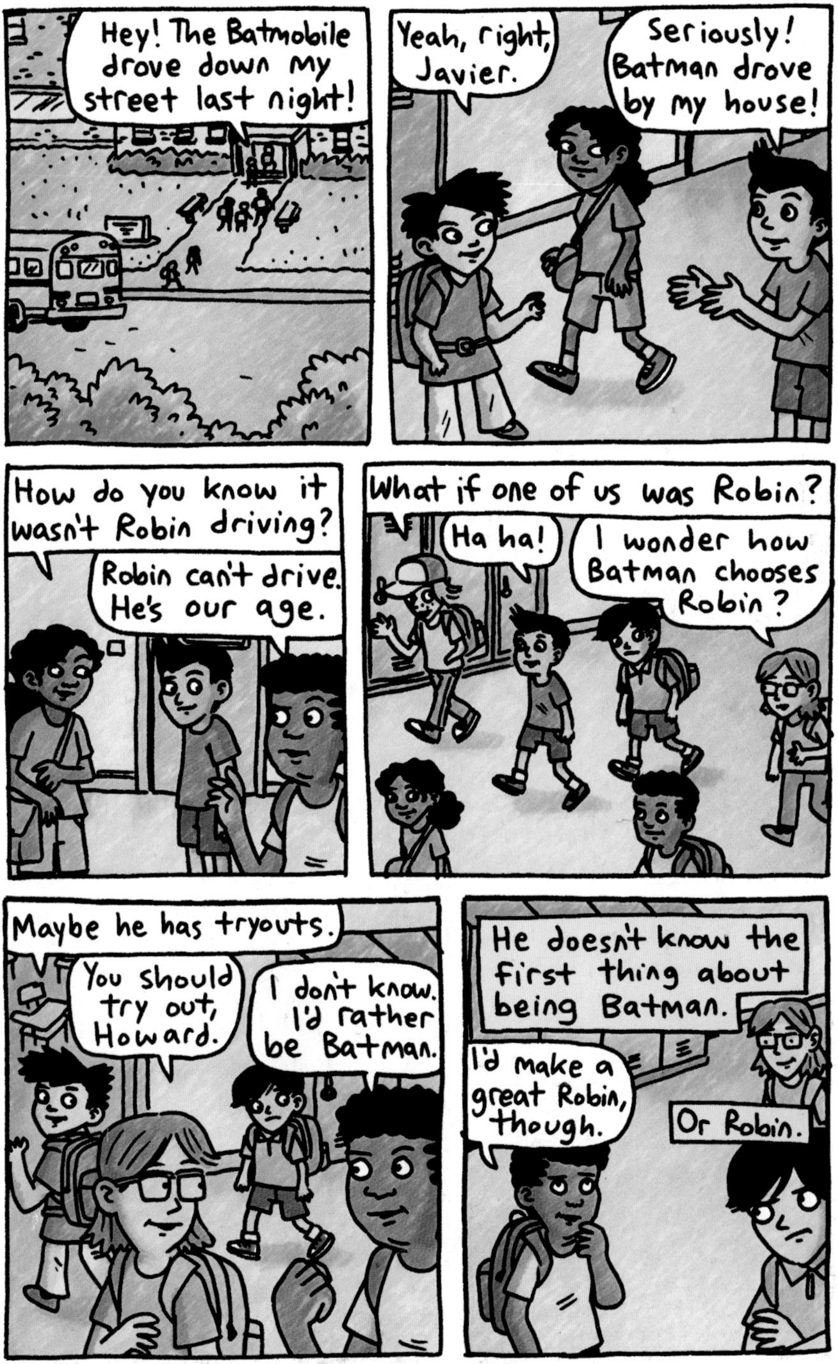
Hey! The Batmobile drove down my street last night!
Yeah, right, Javier.
Seriously! Batman drove by my house!
How do you know it wasn't Robin driving?
Robin can't drive. He's our age.
What if one of us was Robin?
Ha ha!
I wonder how Batman chooses Robin?
Maybe he has tryouts.
You should try out, Howard.
I don't know. I'd rather be Batman.
He doesn't know the first thing about being Batman.
I'd make a great Robin, though.
Or Robin.

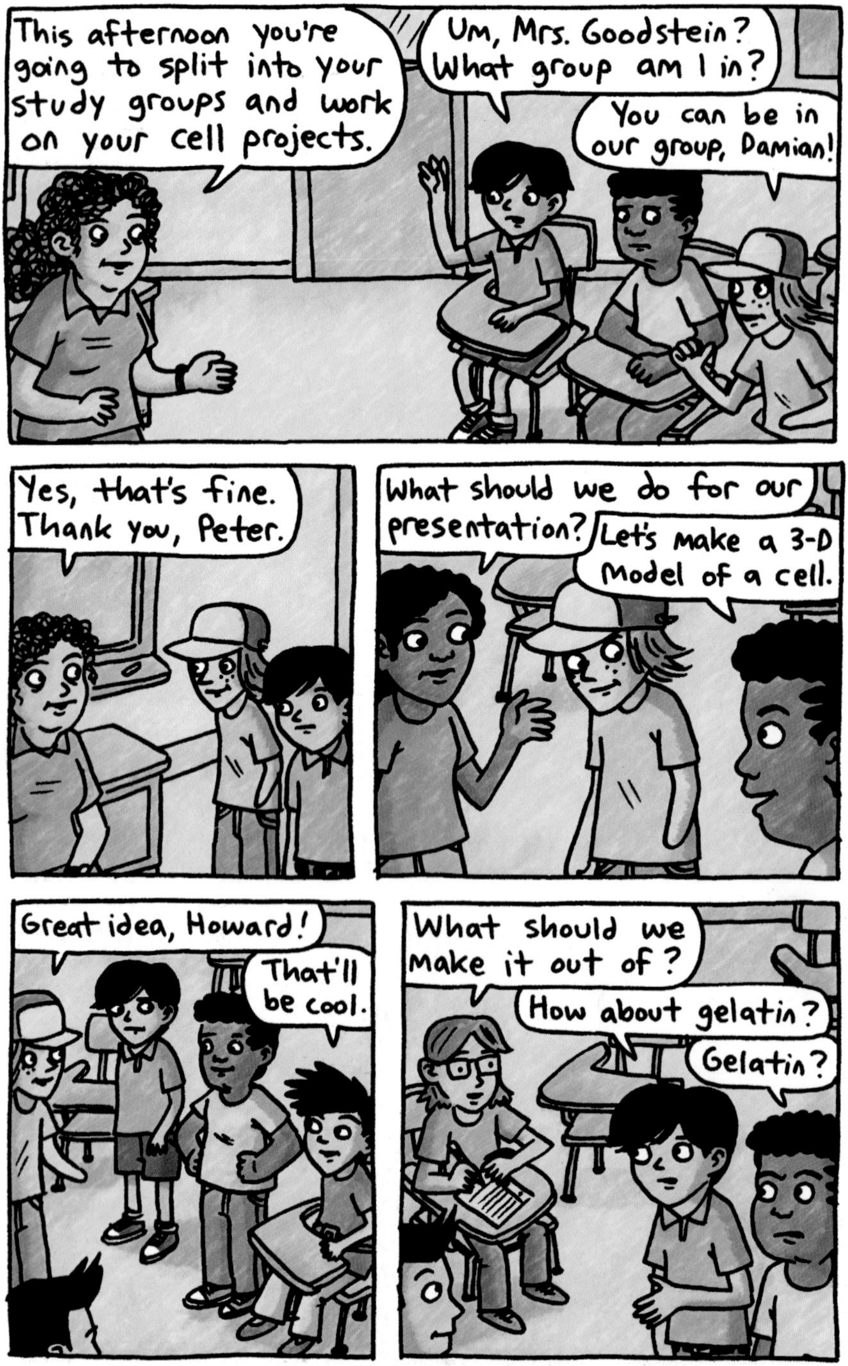
This afternoon you're going to split into your study groups and work on your cell projects.
Um, Mrs. Goodstein? What group am I in?
You can be in our group, Damian!
Yes, that's fine. Thank you, Peter.
What should we do for our presentation?
Let's make a 3-D Model of a cell.
Great idea, Howard!
That'll be cool.
What should we make it out of?
How about gelatin?
Gelatin?

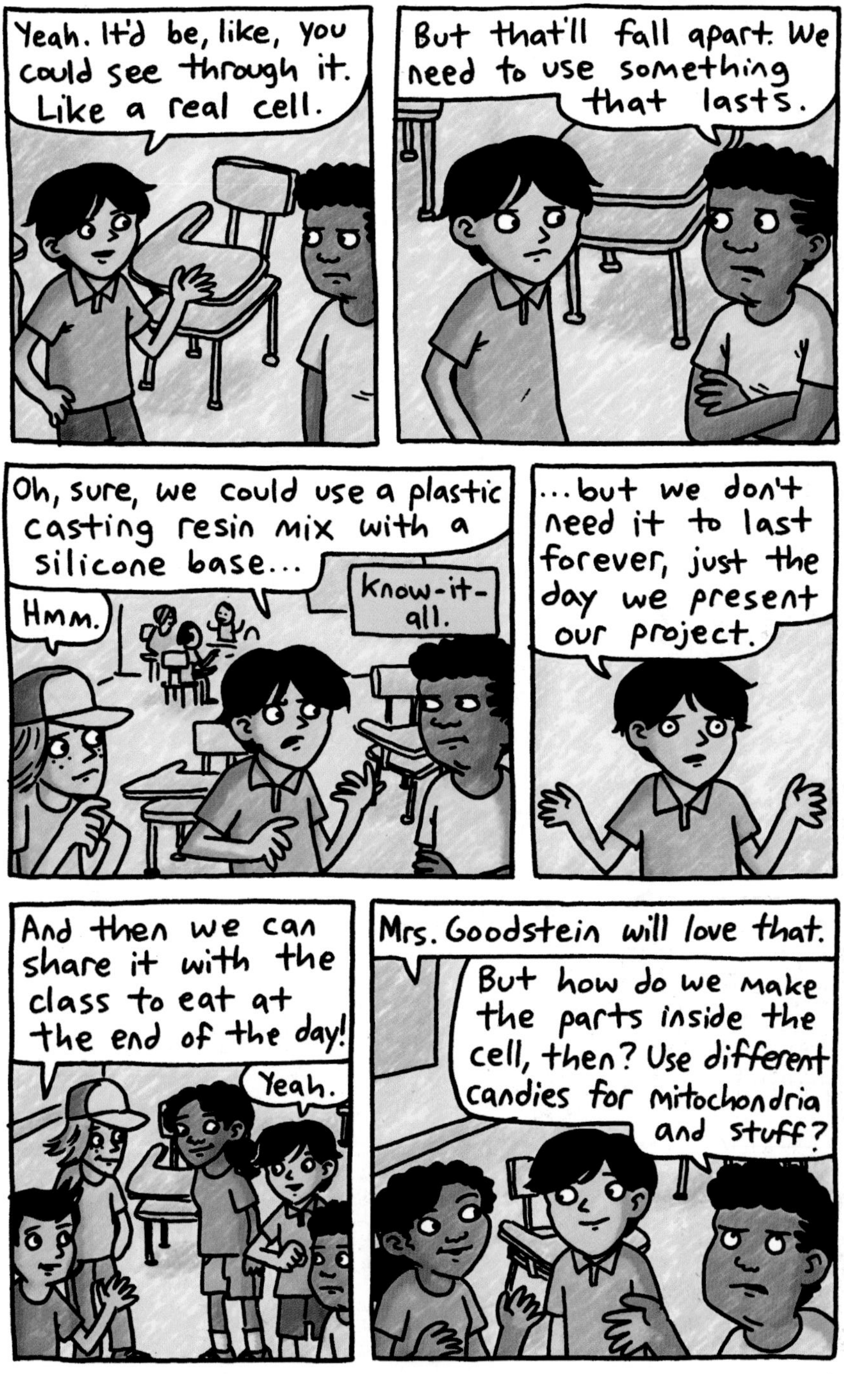
Yeah. It'd be, like, you could see through it. Like a real cell.
But that'll fall apart. We need to use something that lasts.
Oh, sure, we could use a plastic casting resin mix with a silicone base...
Hmm.
Know-it-all.
...but we don't need it to last forever, just the day we present our project.
And then we can share it with the class to eat at the end of the day!
Yeah.
Mrs. Goodstein will love that.
But how do we make the parts inside the cell, then? Use different candies for mitochondria and stuff?

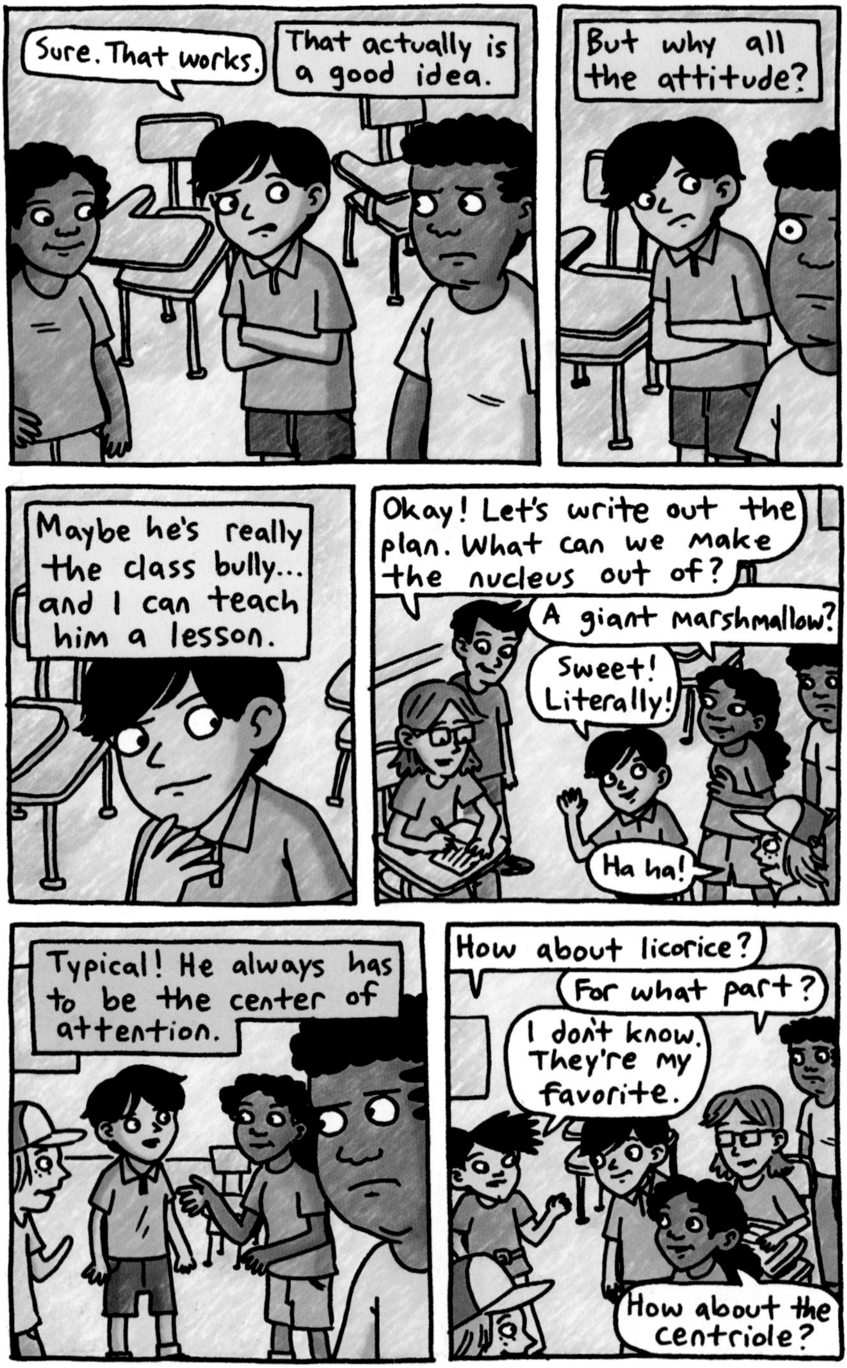
Sure. That works.
That actually is a good idea.
But why all the attitude?
Maybe he's really the class bully... and I can teach him a lesson.
Okay! Let's write out the plan. What can we make the nucleus out of?
A giant marshmallow?
Sweet! Literally!
Ha ha!
Typical! He always has to be the center of attention.
How about licorice?
For what part?
I don't know. They're my favorite.
How about the centriole?

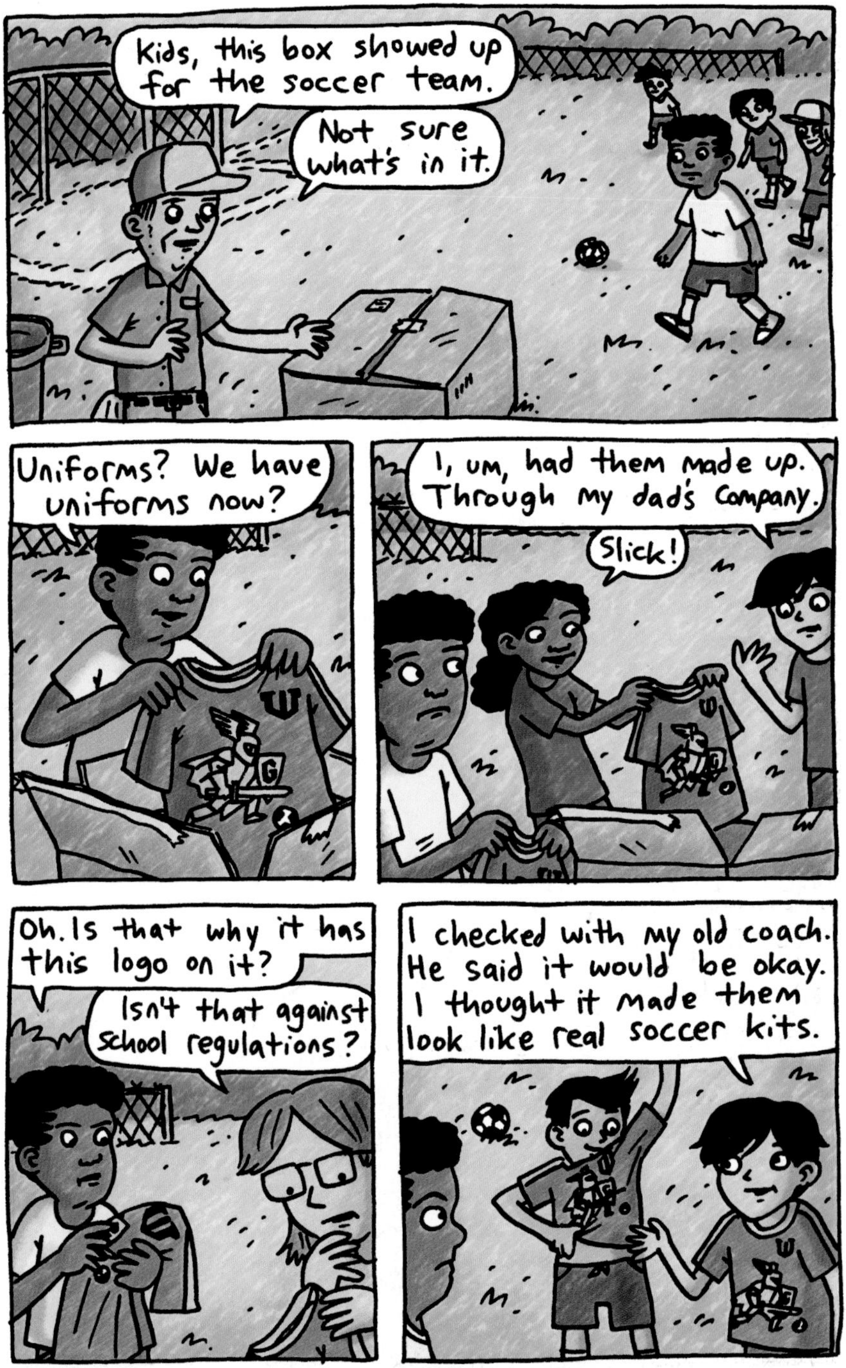
Kids, this box showed up for the soccer team.
Not sure what's in it.
Uniforms? We have uniforms now?
I, um, had them made up. Through my dad's Company.
Slick!
Oh. Is that why it has this logo on it?
Isn't that against school regulations?
I checked with my old coach. He said it would be okay. I thought it made them look like real soccer kits.

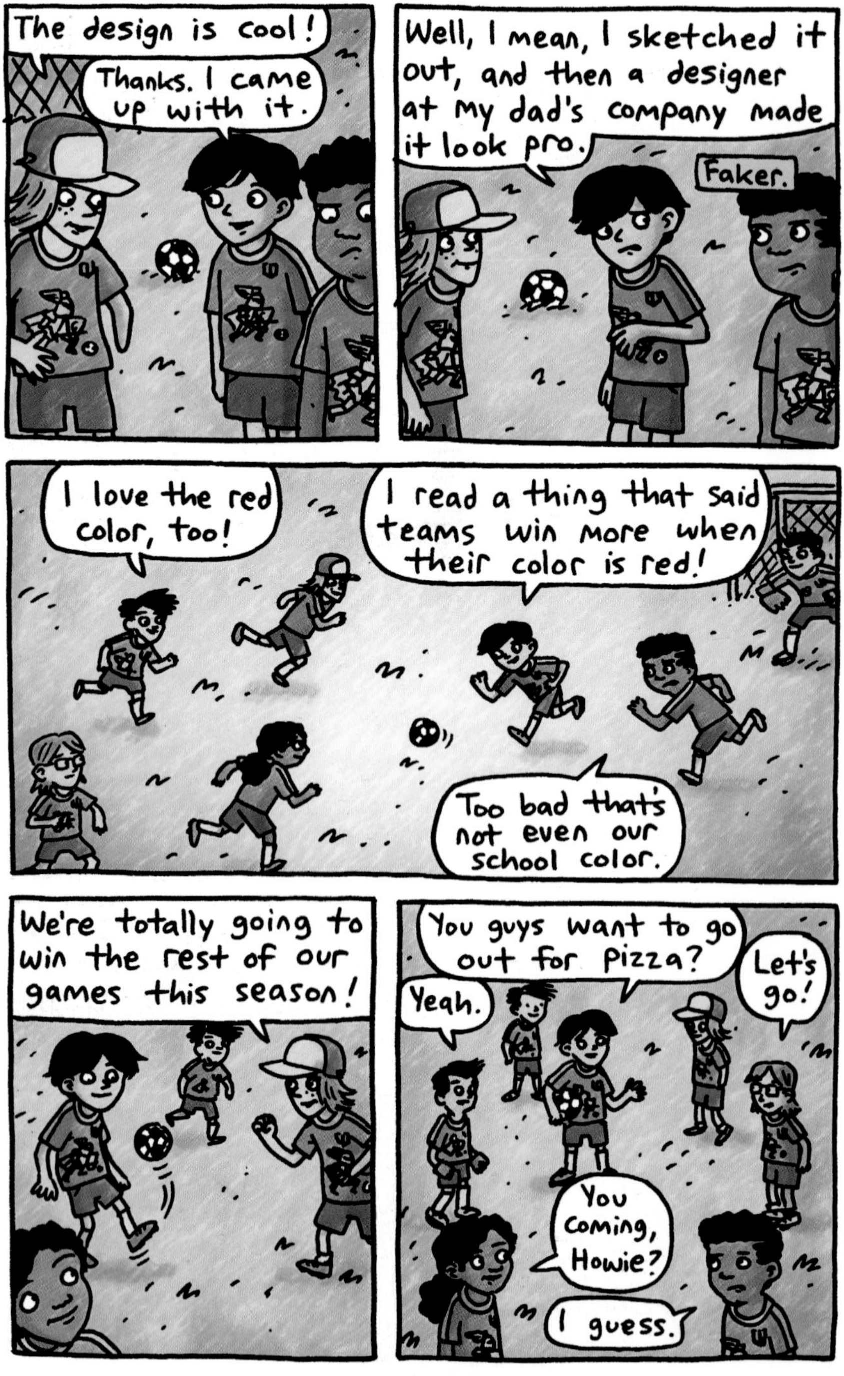
The design is cool!
Thanks. I came up with it.
Well, I mean, I sketched it out, and then a designer at my dad's company made it look pro.
Faker.
I love the red color, too!
I read a thing that said teams win more when their color is red!
Too bad that's not even our school color.
We're totally going to win the rest of our games this season!
You guys want to go out for pizza?
Yeah.
Let's go!
You coming, Howie?
I guess.

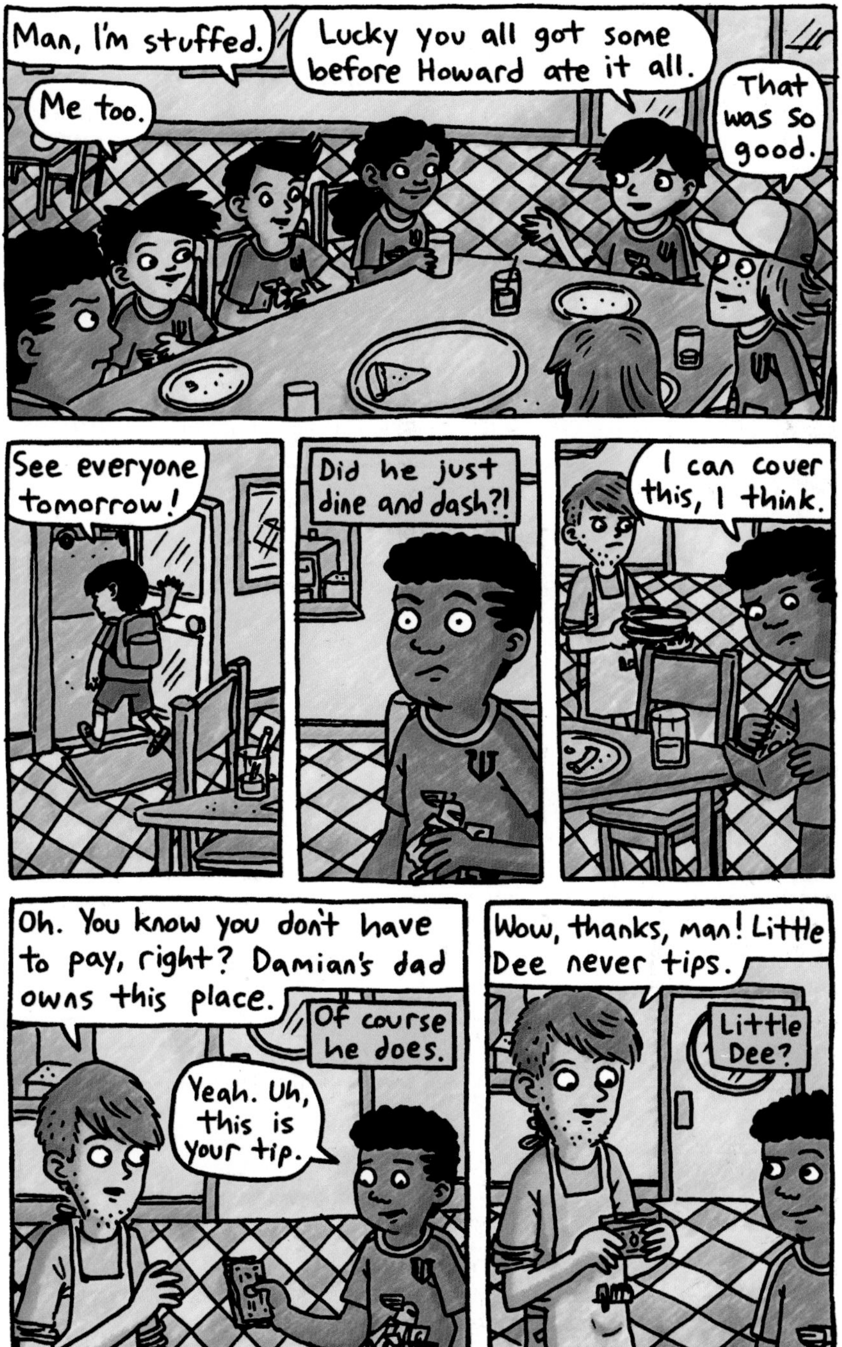
Man, I'm stuffed.
Me too.
Lucky you all got some before Howard ate it all.
That was so good.
See everyone tomorrow!
Did he just dine and dash?!
I can cover this, I think.
Oh. You know you don't have to pay, right? Damian's dad owns this place.
Of course he does.
Yeah. Uh, this is your tip.
Wow, thanks, man! Little Dee never tips.
Little Dee?

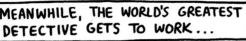

MEANWHILE, THE WORLD'S GREATEST DETECTIVE GETS TO WORK...

The first school with an incident: Gotham Central. Where I attended!

The equipment room is this way.

No unknown fingerprints.

Environmental detector unable to operate due to sweaty sock smell.

Coincidence? Or did whoever did this cover evidence with the smell of dirty gym clothes?

Very clever. That means it MUST be a super-villain. But why did they do this?

50

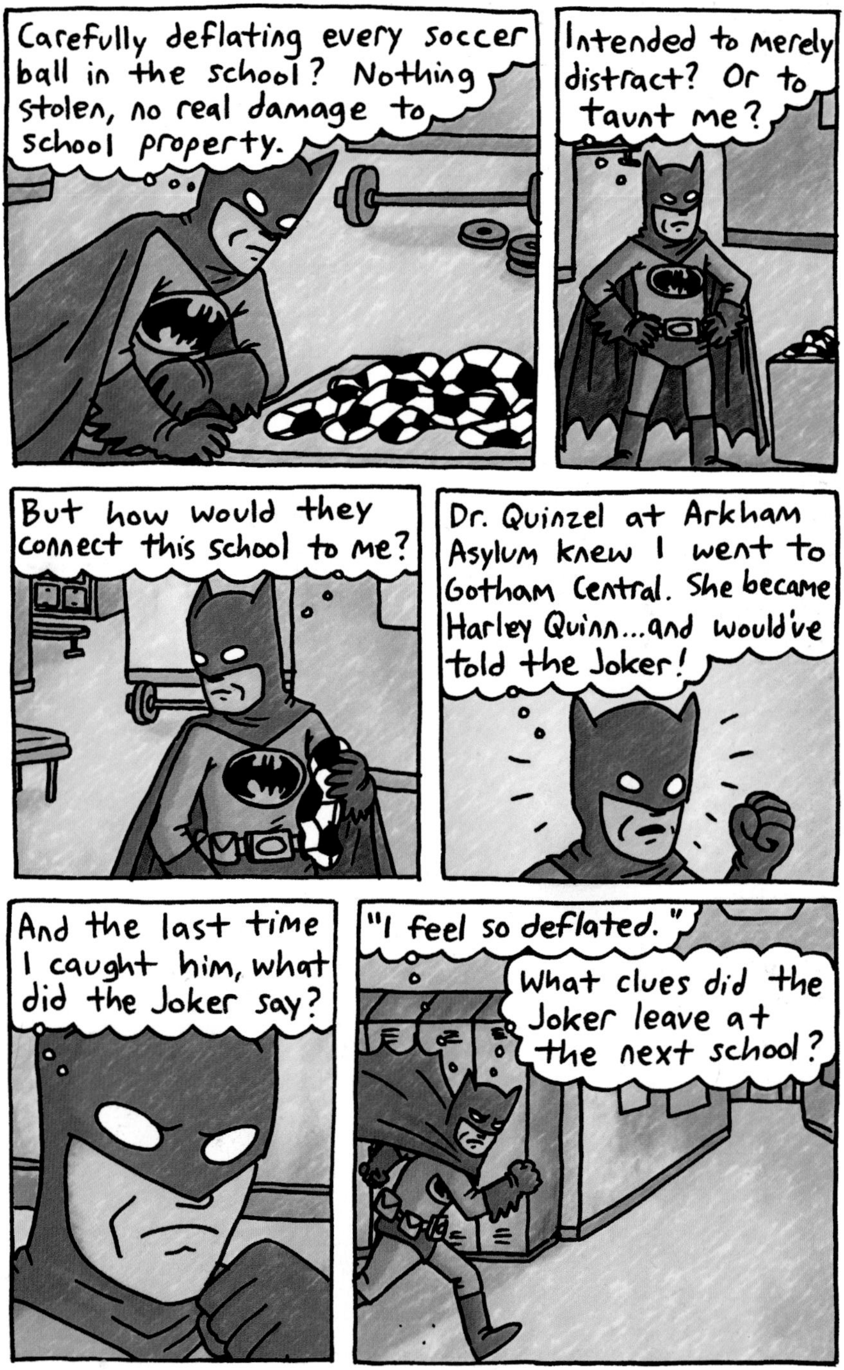
Carefully deflating every soccer ball in the school? Nothing stolen, no real damage to school property.
Intended to merely distract? Or to taunt me?
But how would they connect this school to me?
Dr. Quinzel at Arkham Asylum knew I went to Gotham Central. She became Harley Quinn...and would've told the Joker!
And the last time I caught him, what did the Joker say?
"I feel so deflated."
What clues did the Joker leave at the next school?

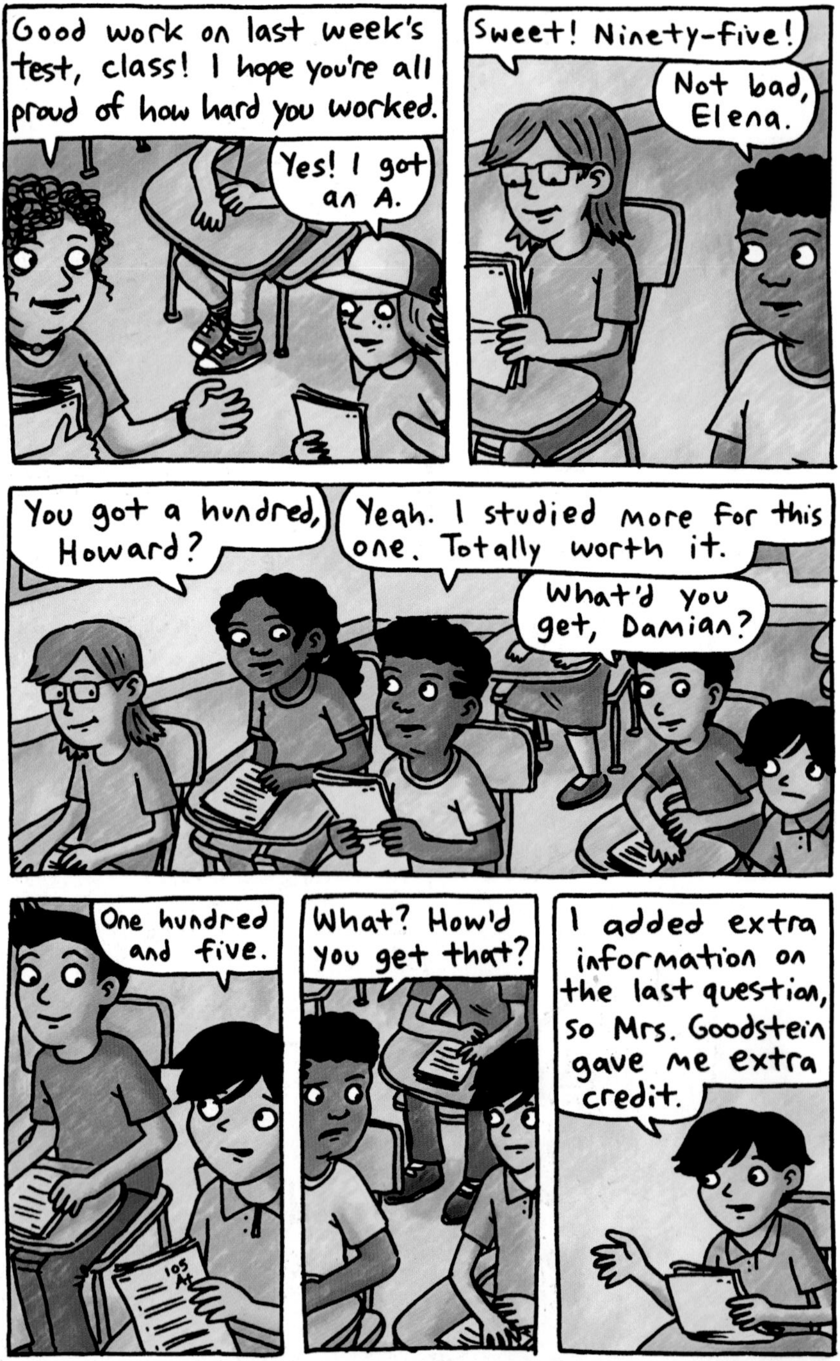
Good work on last week's test, class! I hope you're all proud of how hard you worked.
Yes! I got an A.
Sweet! Ninety-five!
Not bad, Elena.
You got a hundred, Howard?
Yeah. I studied more for this one. Totally worth it.
What'd you get, Damian?
One hundred and five.
105 A+
What? How'd you get that?
I added extra information on the last question, so Mrs. Goodstein gave me extra credit.

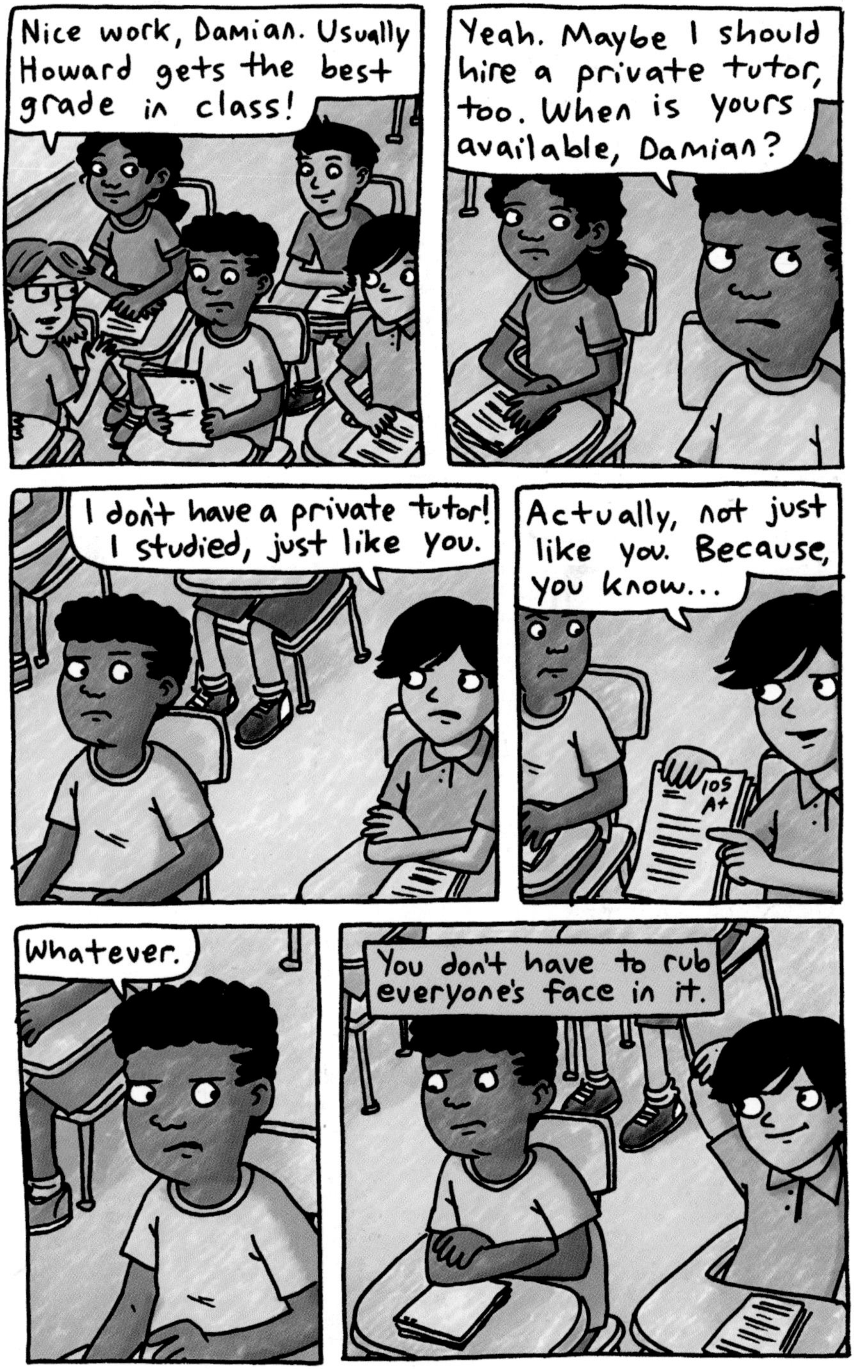
Nice work, Damian. Usually Howard gets the best grade in class!
Yeah. Maybe I should hire a private tutor, too. When is yours available, Damian?
I don't have a private tutor! I studied, just like you.
Actually, not just like you. Because, you know...
105
A+
Whatever.
You don't have to rub everyone's face in it.

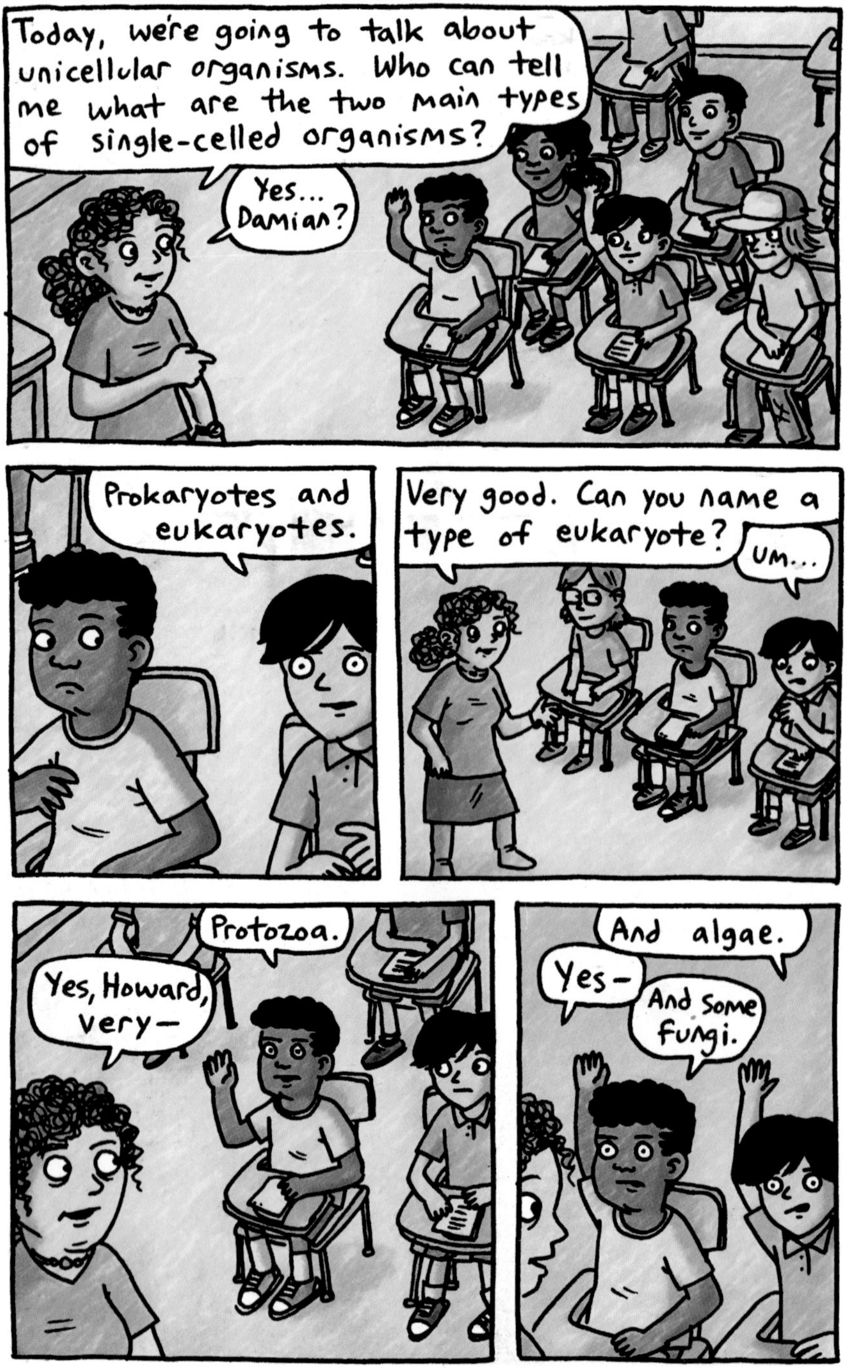
Today, we're going to talk about unicellular organisms. Who can tell me what are the two main types of single-celled organisms?
Yes... Damian?
Prokaryotes and eukaryotes.
Very good. Can you name a type of eukaryote?
Um...
Protozoa.
Yes, Howard, very—
And algae.
Yes—
And some fungi.

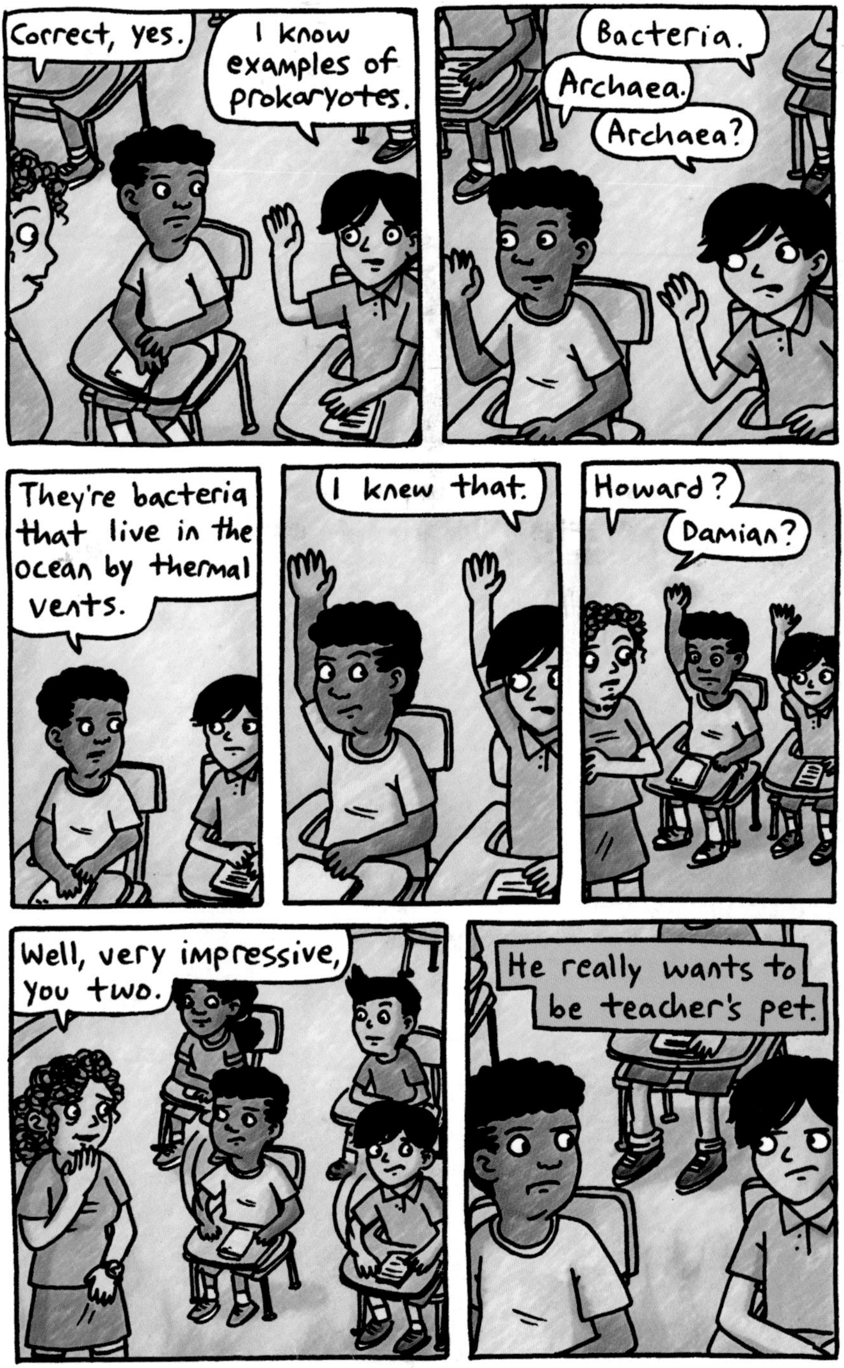
Correct, yes.
I know examples of prokaryotes.
Bacteria.
Archaea.
Archaea?
They're bacteria that live in the ocean by thermal vents.
I knew that.
Howard?
Damian?
Well, very impressive, you two.
He really wants to be teacher's pet.

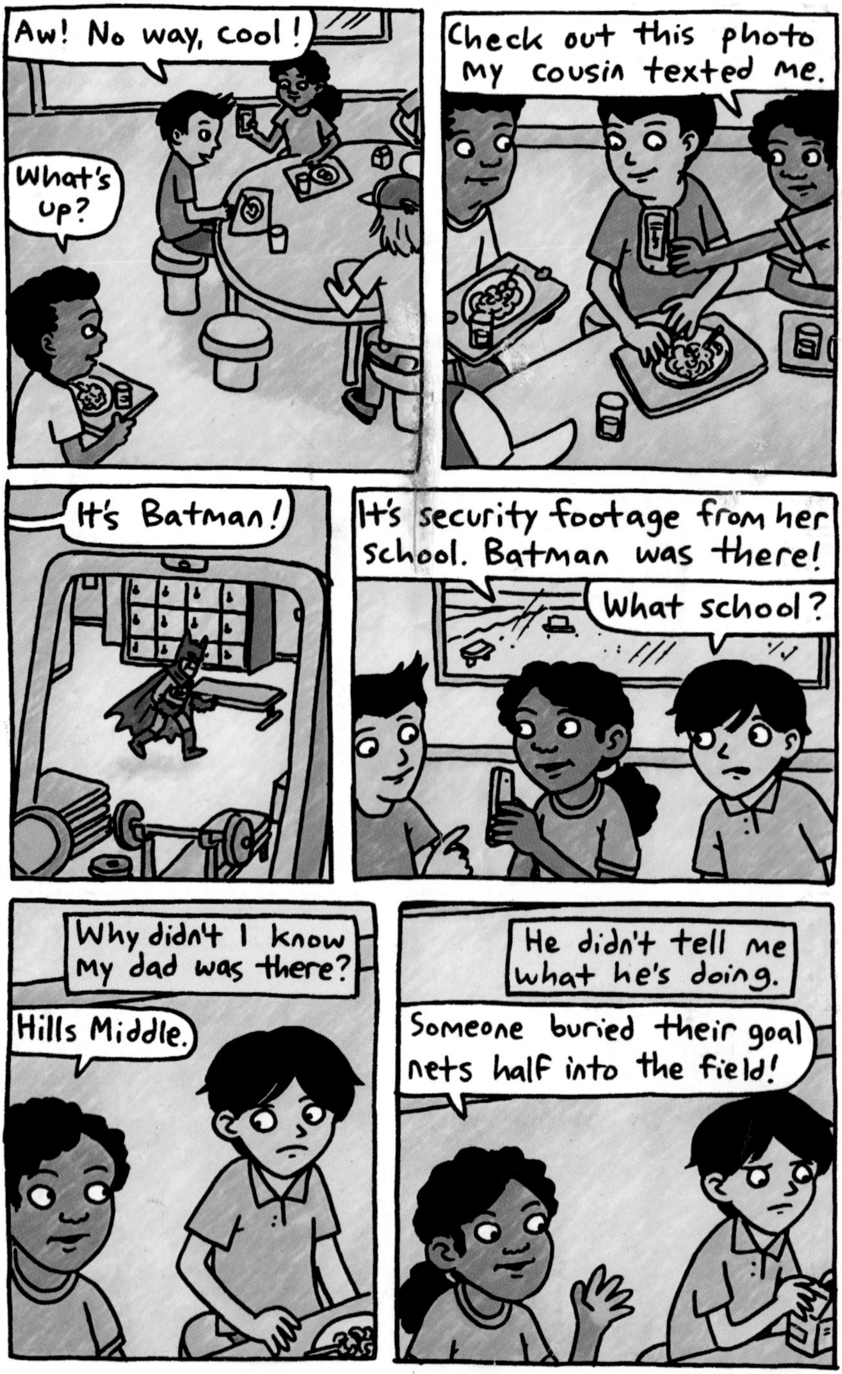
Aw! No way, cool!
What's up?
Check out this photo my cousin texted me.
It's Batman!
It's security footage from her school. Batman was there!
What school?
Why didn't I know my dad was there?
Hills Middle.
He didn't tell me what he's doing.
Someone buried their goal nets half into the field!

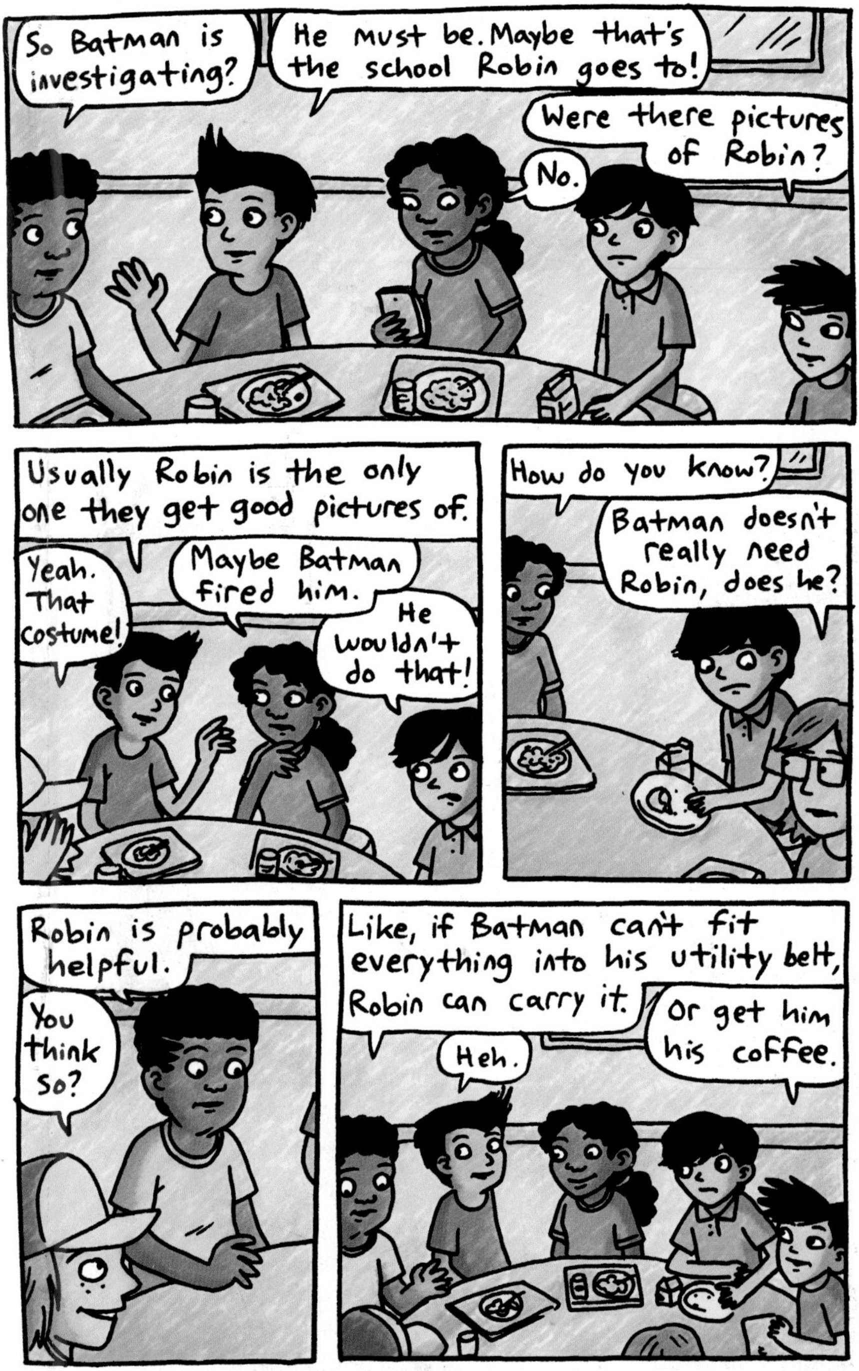
So Batman is investigating?
He must be. Maybe that's the school Robin goes to!
Were there pictures of Robin?
No.
Usually Robin is the only one they get good pictures of.
Yeah. That costume!
Maybe Batman fired him.
He wouldn't do that!
How do you know?
Batman doesn't really need Robin, does he?
Robin is probably helpful.
You think so?
Like, if Batman can't fit everything into his utility belt, Robin can carry it.
Heh.
Or get him his coffee.

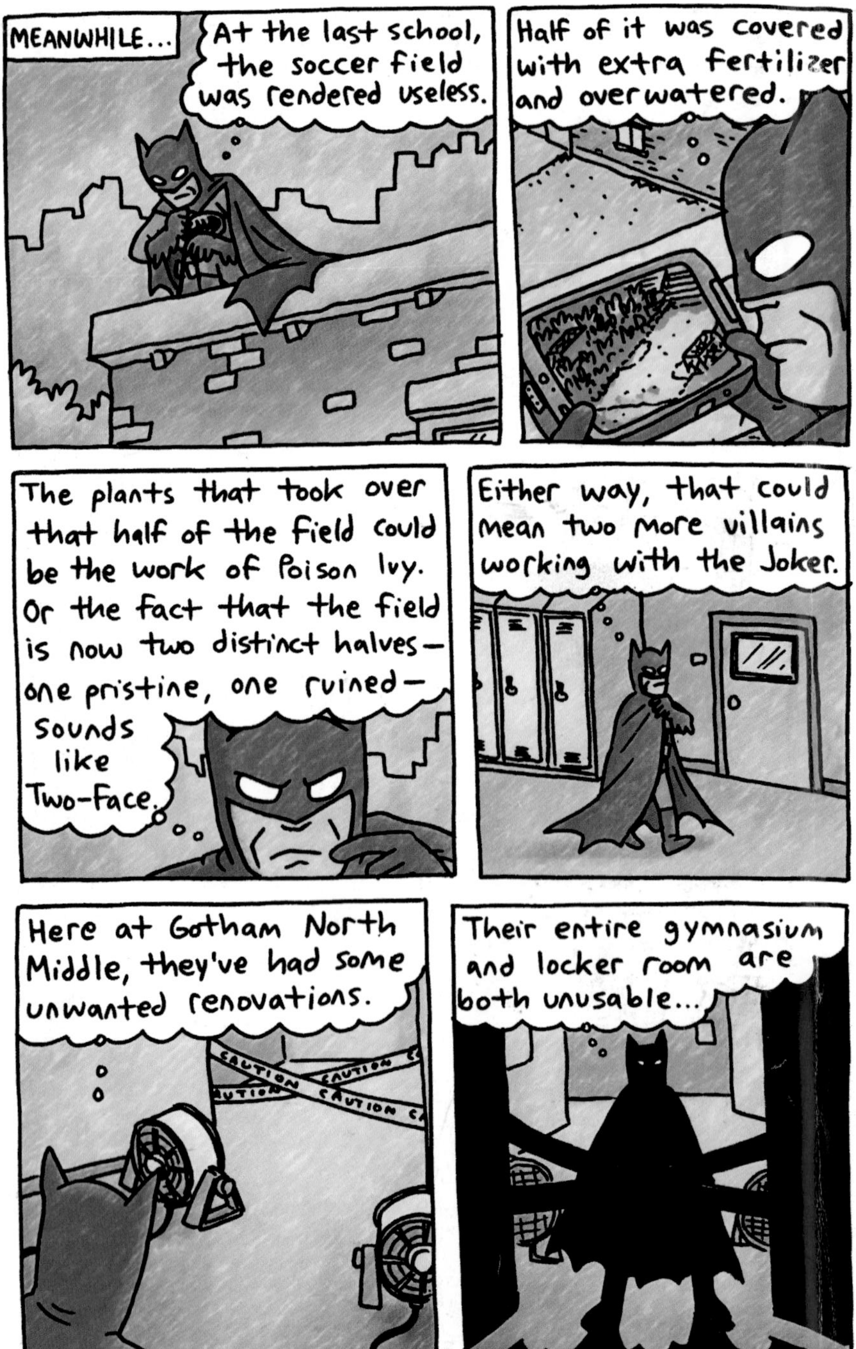

MEANWHILE...
At the last school, the soccer field was rendered useless.
Half of it was covered with extra fertilizer and overwatered.
The plants that took over that half of the field could be the work of Poison Ivy. Or the fact that the field is now two distinct halves—one pristine, one ruined—sounds like Two-Face.
Either way, that could mean two more villains working with the Joker.
Here at Gotham North Middle, they've had some unwanted renovations.
CAUTION
Their entire gymnasium and locker room are both unusable...

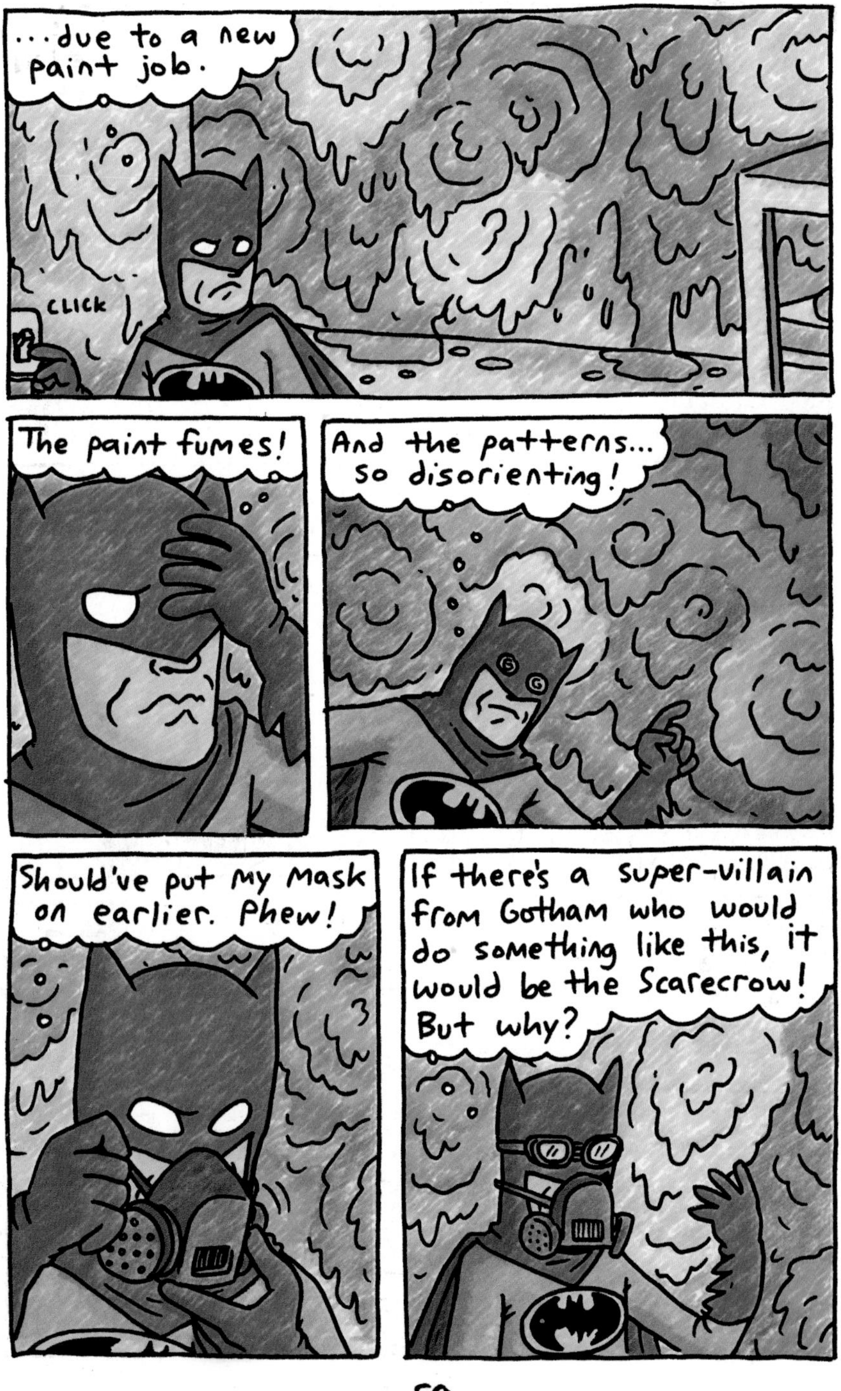
...due to a new paint job.
CLICK
The paint fumes!
And the patterns... so disorienting!
Should've put my mask on earlier. Phew!
If there's a super-villain from Gotham who would do something like this, it would be the Scarecrow! But why?

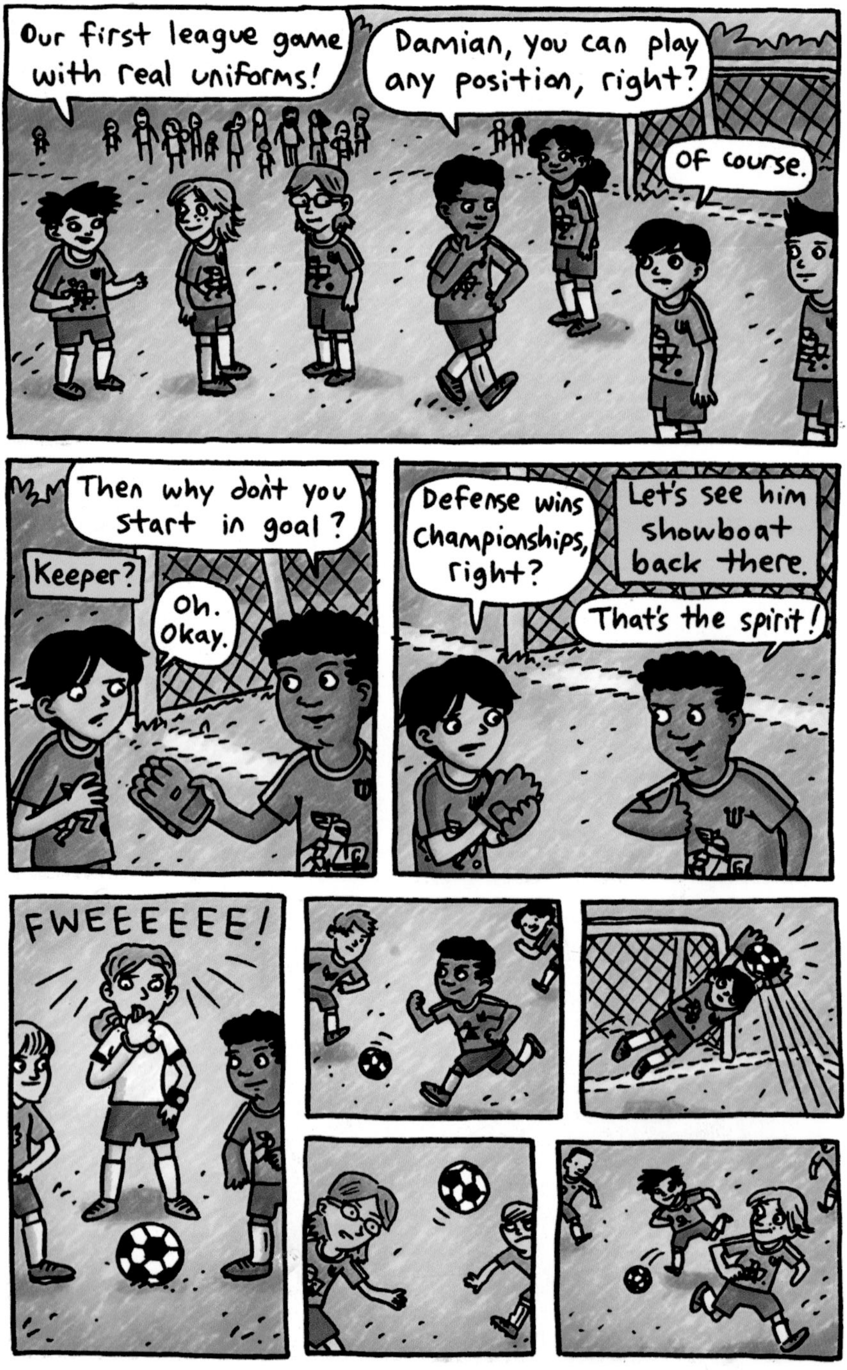
Our first league game with real uniforms!
Damian, you can play any position, right?
Of course.
Then why don't you start in goal?
Keeper?
Oh. Okay.
Defense wins Championships, right?
Let's see him showboat back there.
That's the spirit!
FWEEEEEEE!

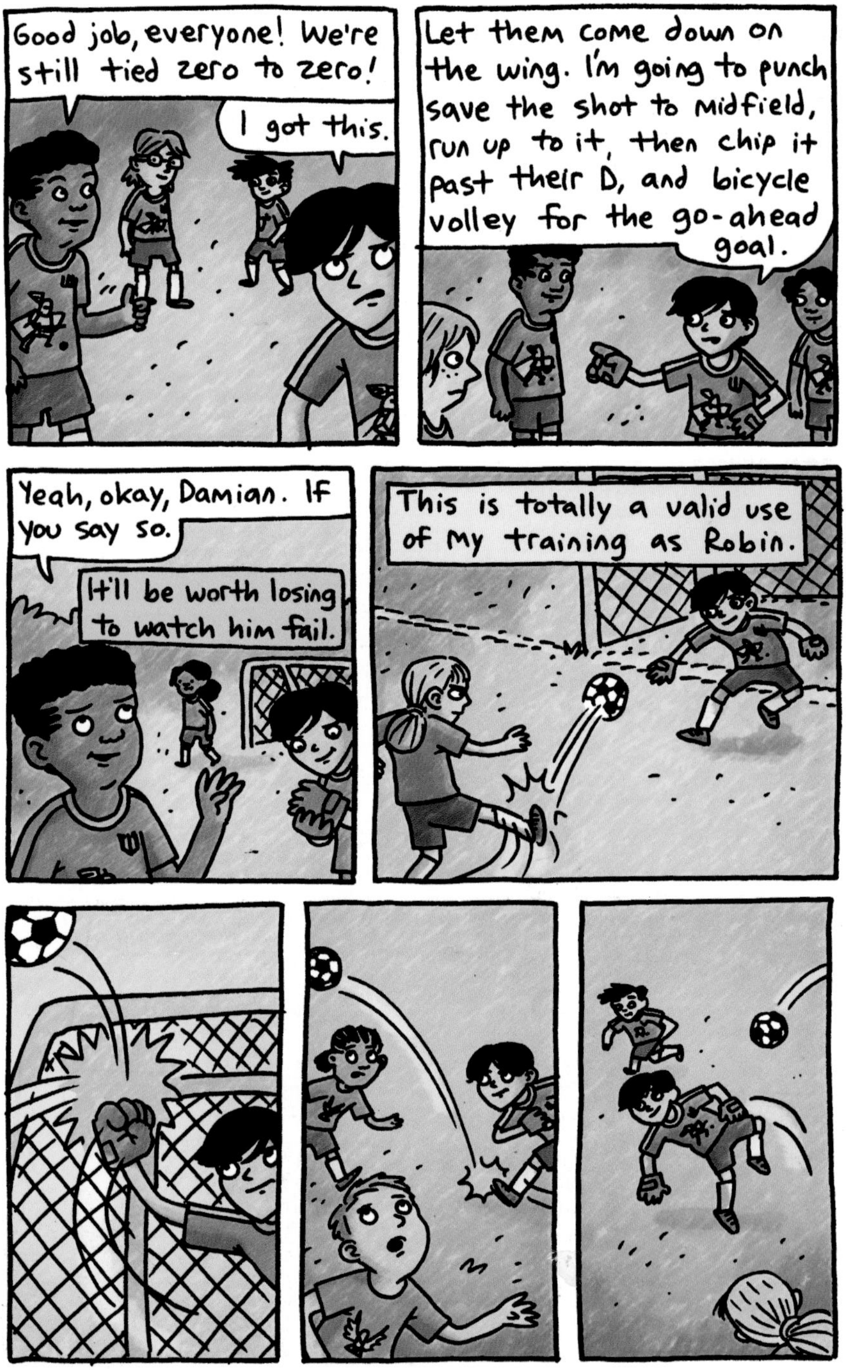
Good job, everyone! We're still tied zero to zero!
I got this.
Let them come down on the wing. I'm going to punch save the shot to midfield, run up to it, then chip it past their D, and bicycle volley for the go-ahead goal.
Yeah, okay, Damian. If you say so.
It'll be worth losing to watch him fail.
This is totally a valid use of my training as Robin.

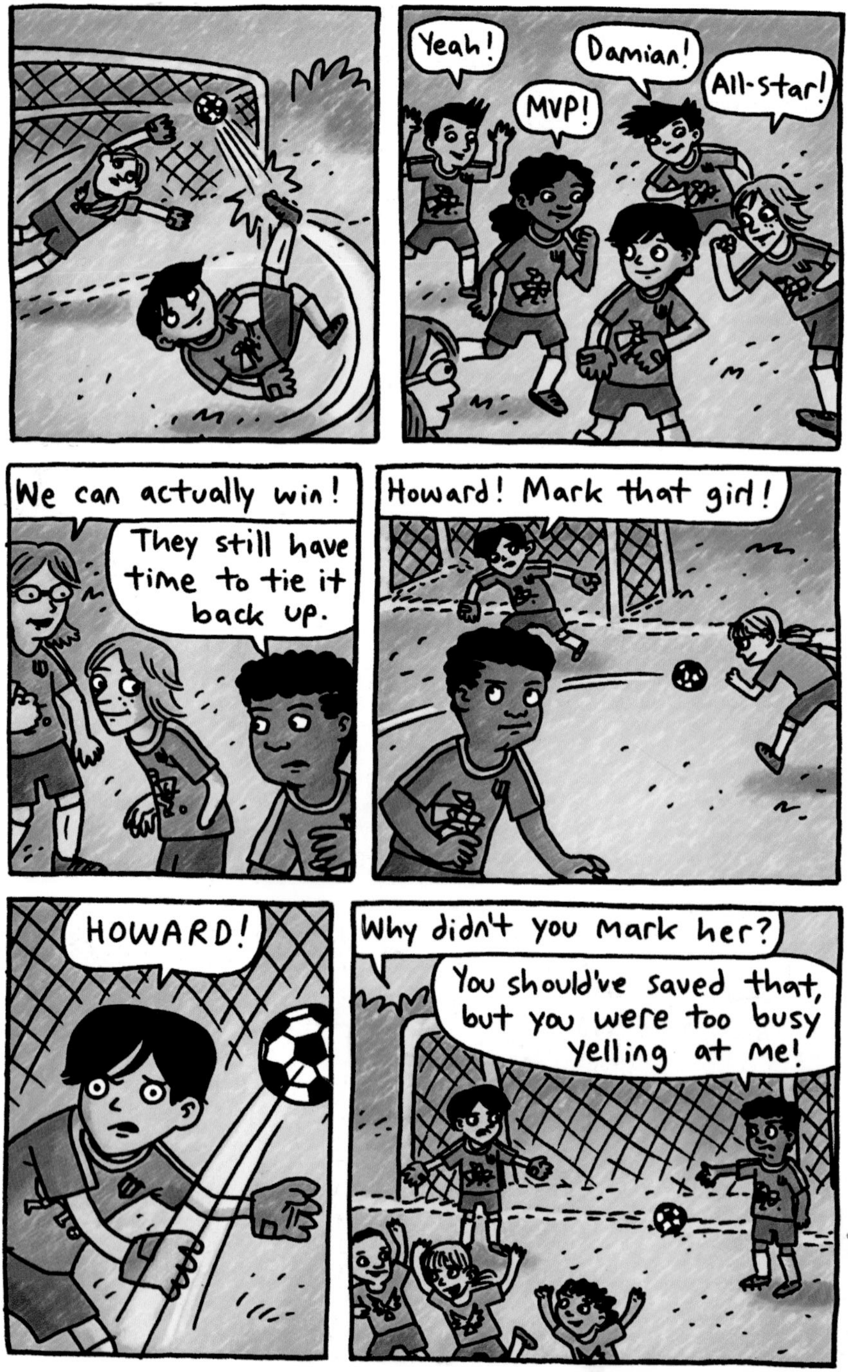
Yeah!
MVP!
Damian!
All-star!
We can actually win!
They still have time to tie it back up.
Howard! Mark that girl!
HOWARD!
Why didn't you mark her?
You should've saved that, but you were too busy yelling at me!

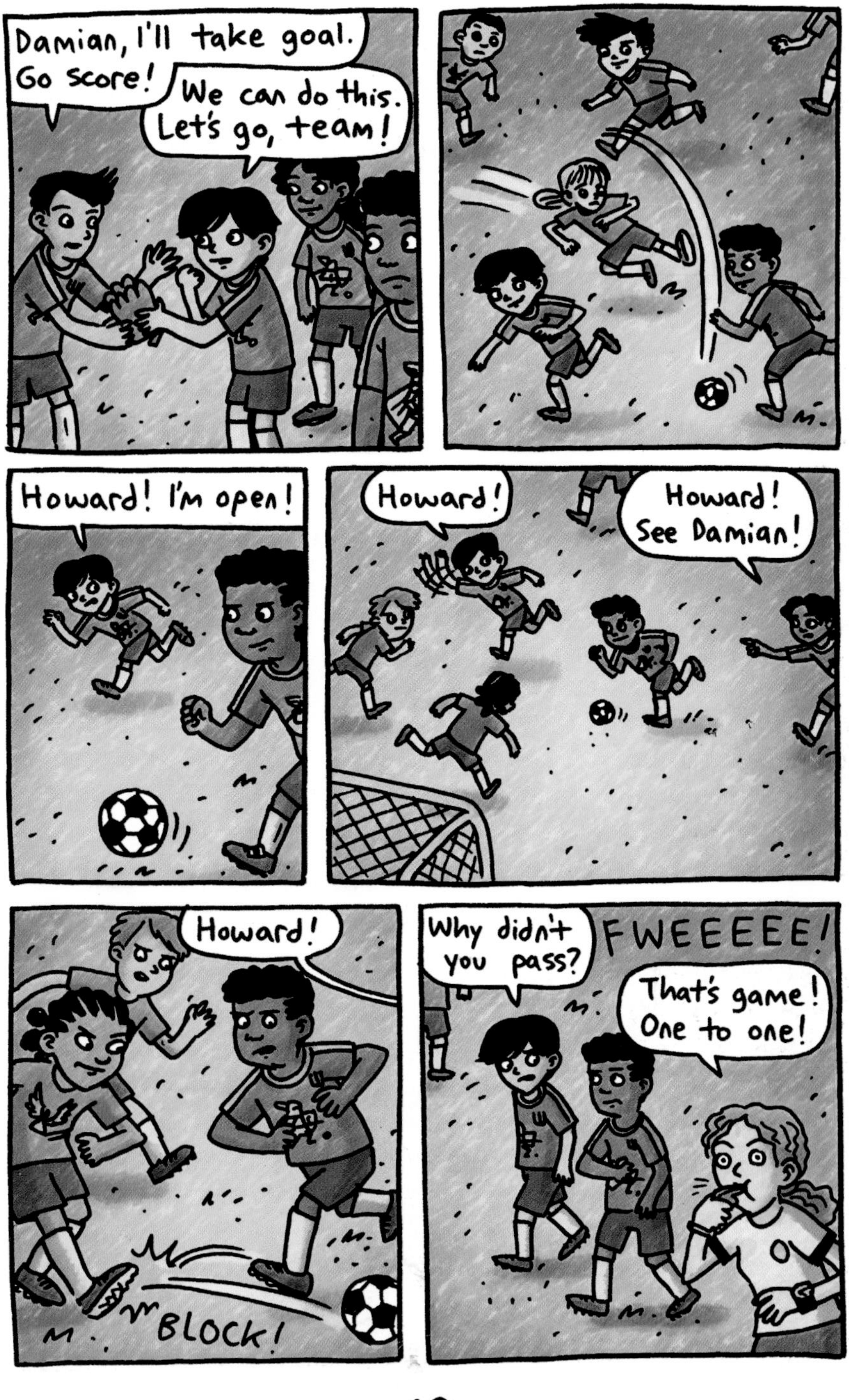

Damian, I'll take goal. Go score!
We can do this. Let's go, team!
Howard! I'm open!
Howard!
Howard! See Damian!
Howard!
BLOCK!
Why didn't you pass?
FWEEEEEE!
That's game! One to one!

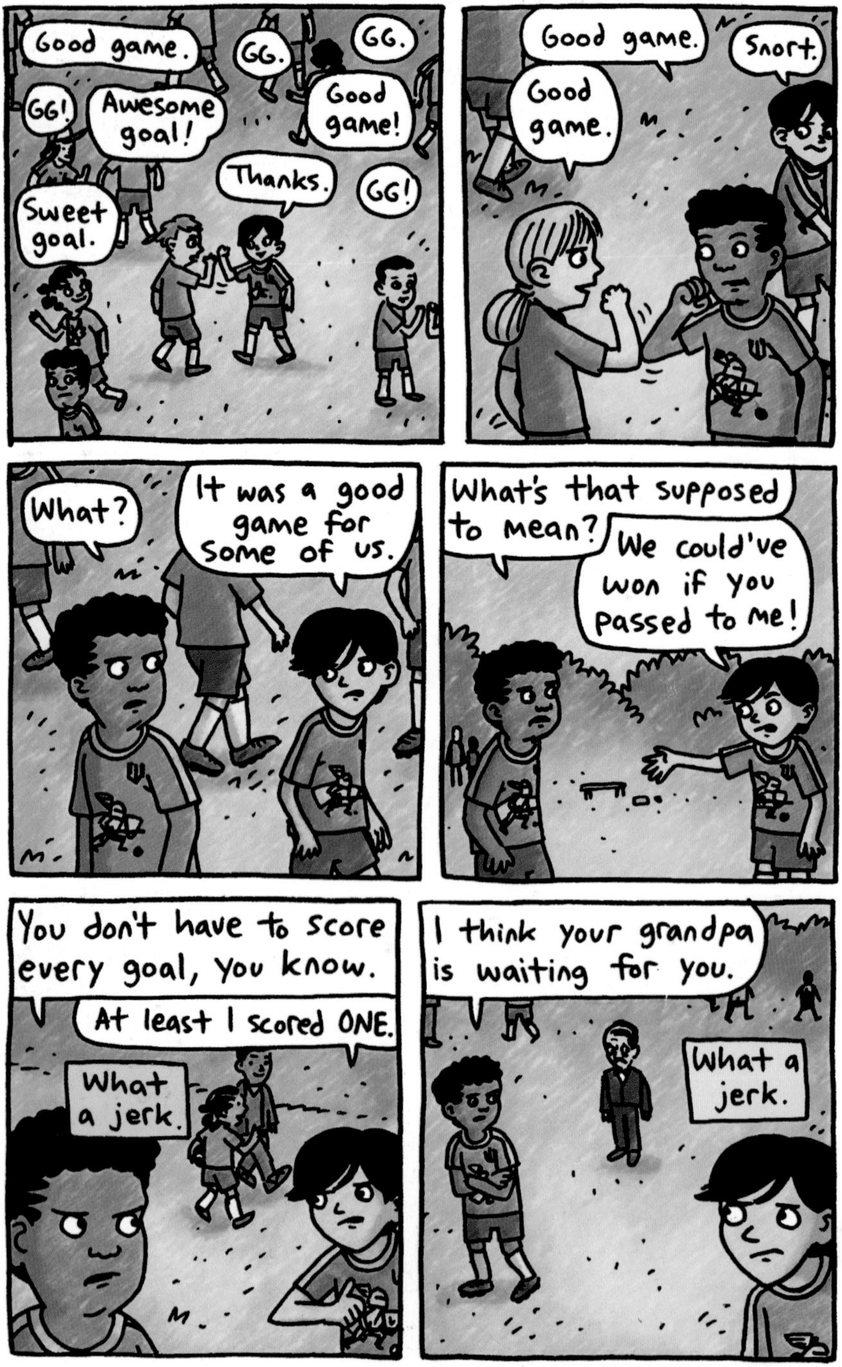
Good game.
GG.
GG.
GG!
Awesome goal!
Good game!
Thanks.
GG!
Sweet goal.
Good game.
Good game.
Snort.
What?
It was a good game for some of us.
What's that supposed to mean?
We could've won if you passed to me!
You don't have to score every goal, you know.
At least I scored ONE.
What a jerk.
I think your grandpa is waiting for you.
What a jerk.

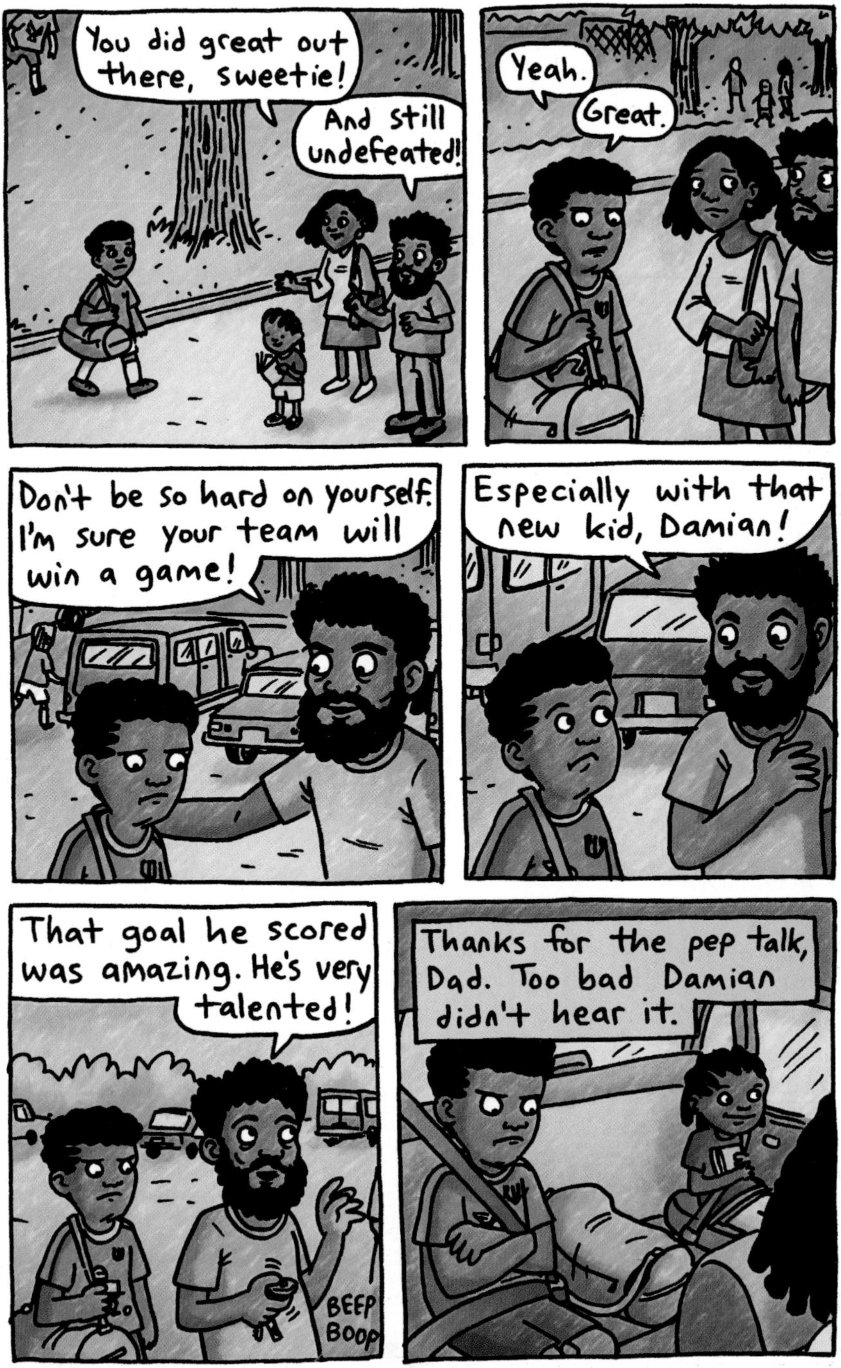
You did great out there, sweetie!
And still undefeated!
Yeah.
Great.
Don't be so hard on yourself. I'm sure your team will win a game!
Especially with that new kid, Damian!
That goal he scored was amazing. He's very talented!
BEEP BOOP
Thanks for the pep talk, Dad. Too bad Damian didn't hear it.

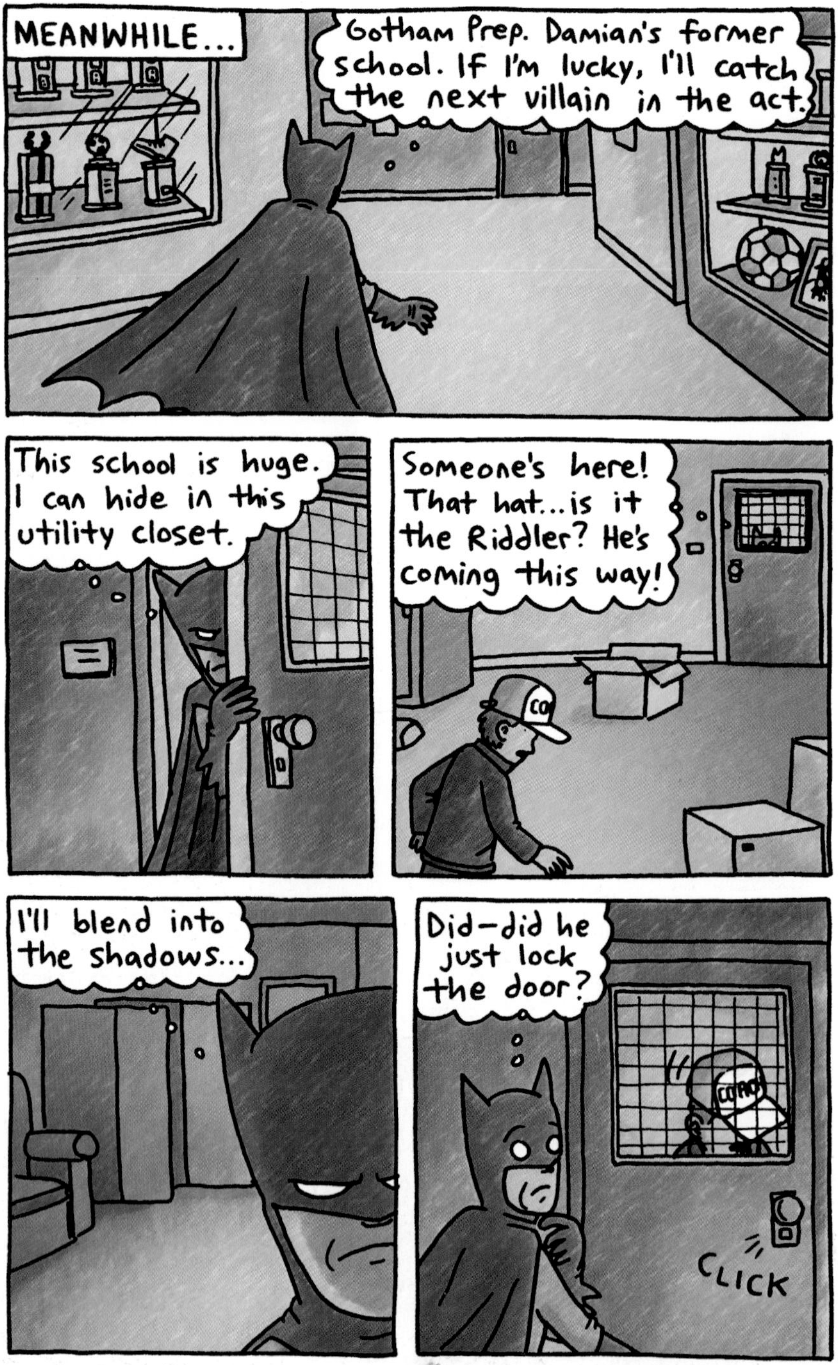
MEANWHILE...
Gotham Prep. Damian's former school. If I'm lucky, I'll catch the next villain in the act.
This school is huge. I can hide in this utility closet.
Someone's here! That hat...is it the Riddler? He's coming this way!
CO
I'll blend into the shadows...
Did—did he just lock the door?
COACH
CLICK

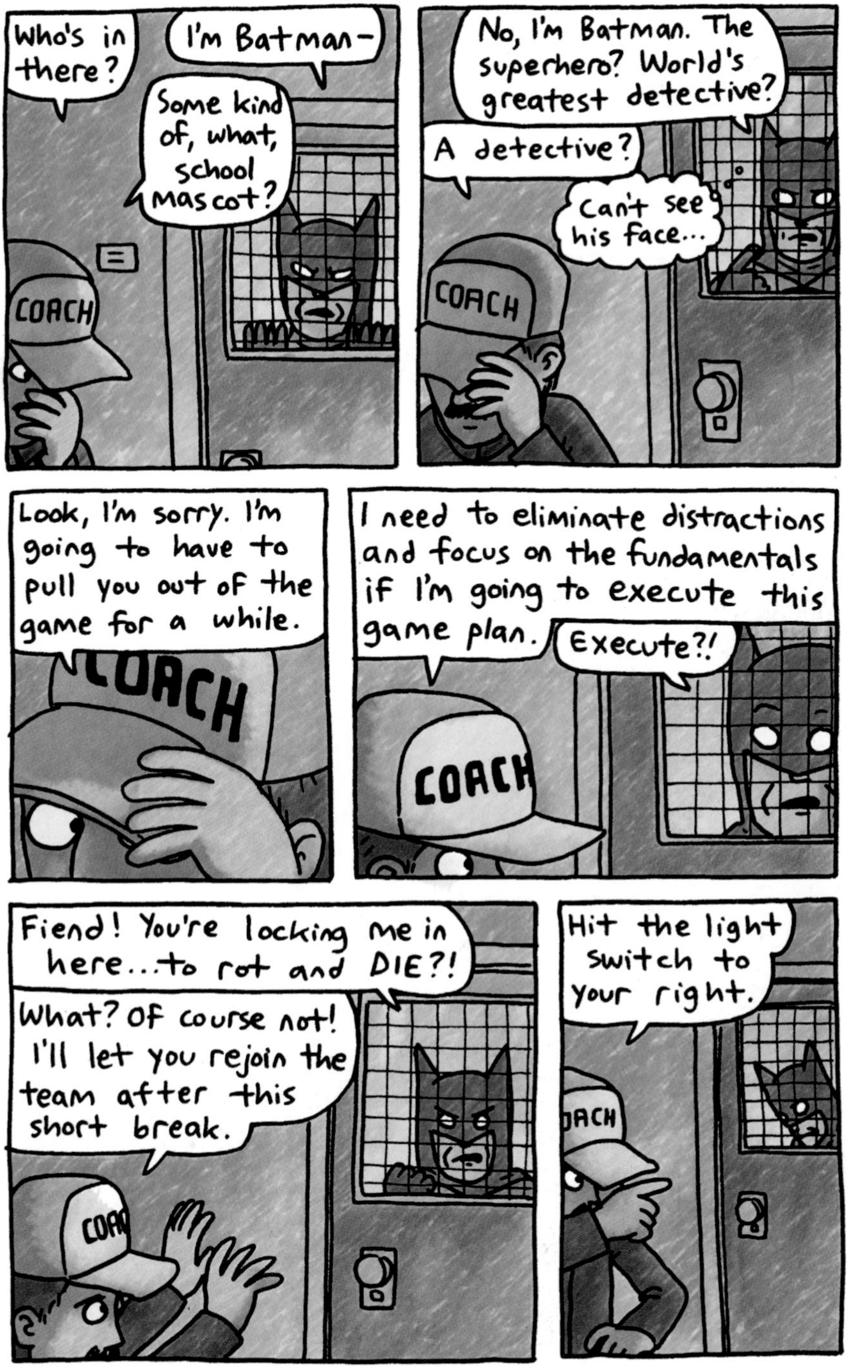
Who's in there?
I'm Batman—
Some kind of, what, school mascot?
COACH
No, I'm Batman. The superhero? World's greatest detective?
A detective?
Can't see his face...
COACH
Look, I'm sorry. I'm going to have to pull you out of the game for a while.
COACH
I need to eliminate distractions and focus on the fundamentals if I'm going to execute this game plan.
Execute?!
COACH
Fiend! You're locking me in here...to rot and DIE?!
What? Of course not! I'll let you rejoin the team after this short break.
Hit the light switch to your right.

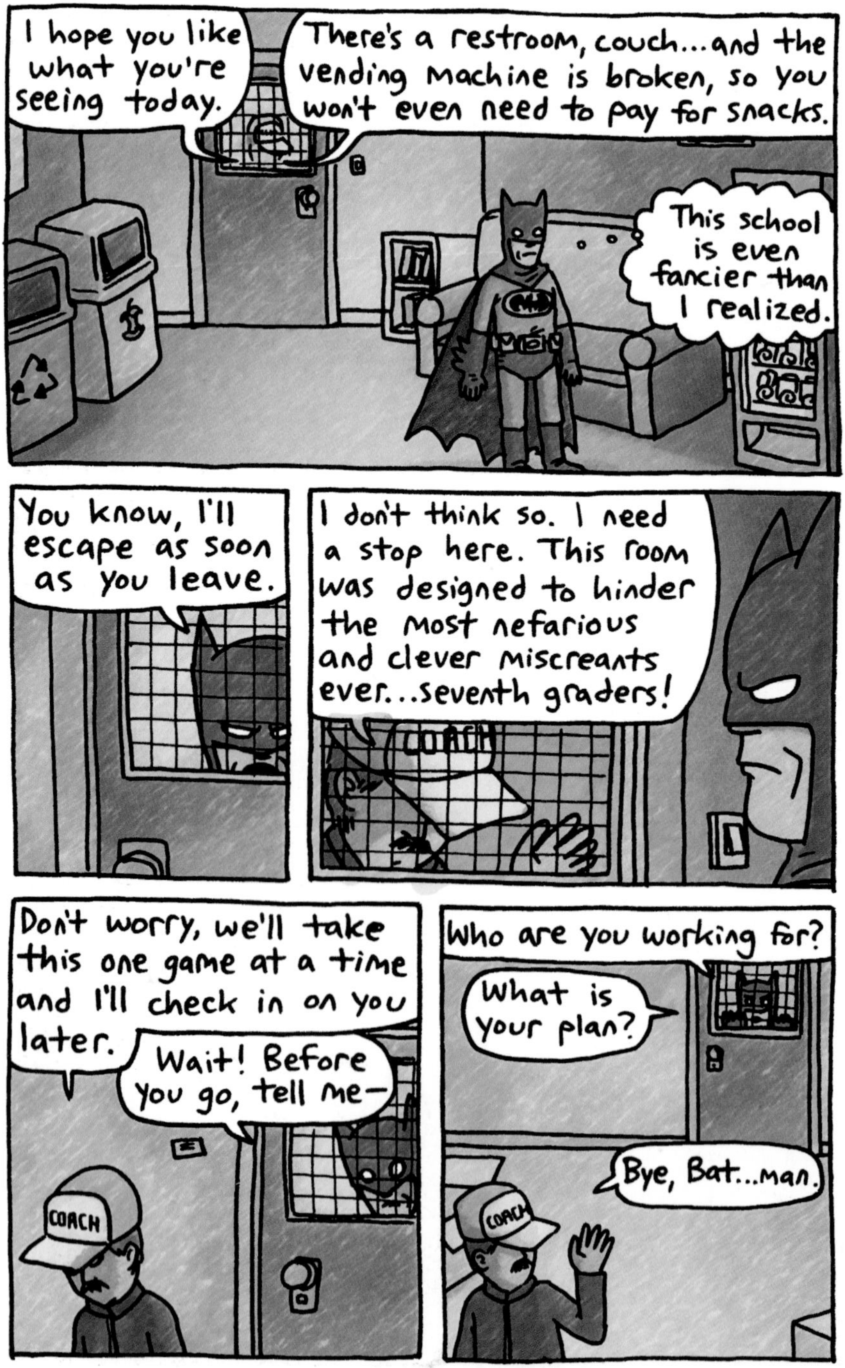
I hope you like what you're seeing today.
There's a restroom, couch...and the vending machine is broken, so you won't even need to pay for snacks.
This school is even fancier than I realized.
You know, I'll escape as soon as you leave.
I don't think so. I need a stop here. This room was designed to hinder the most nefarious and clever miscreants ever...seventh graders!
COACH
Don't worry, we'll take this one game at a time and I'll check in on you later.
Wait! Before you go, tell me—
COACH
Who are you working for?
What is your plan?
Bye, Bat...man.
COACH

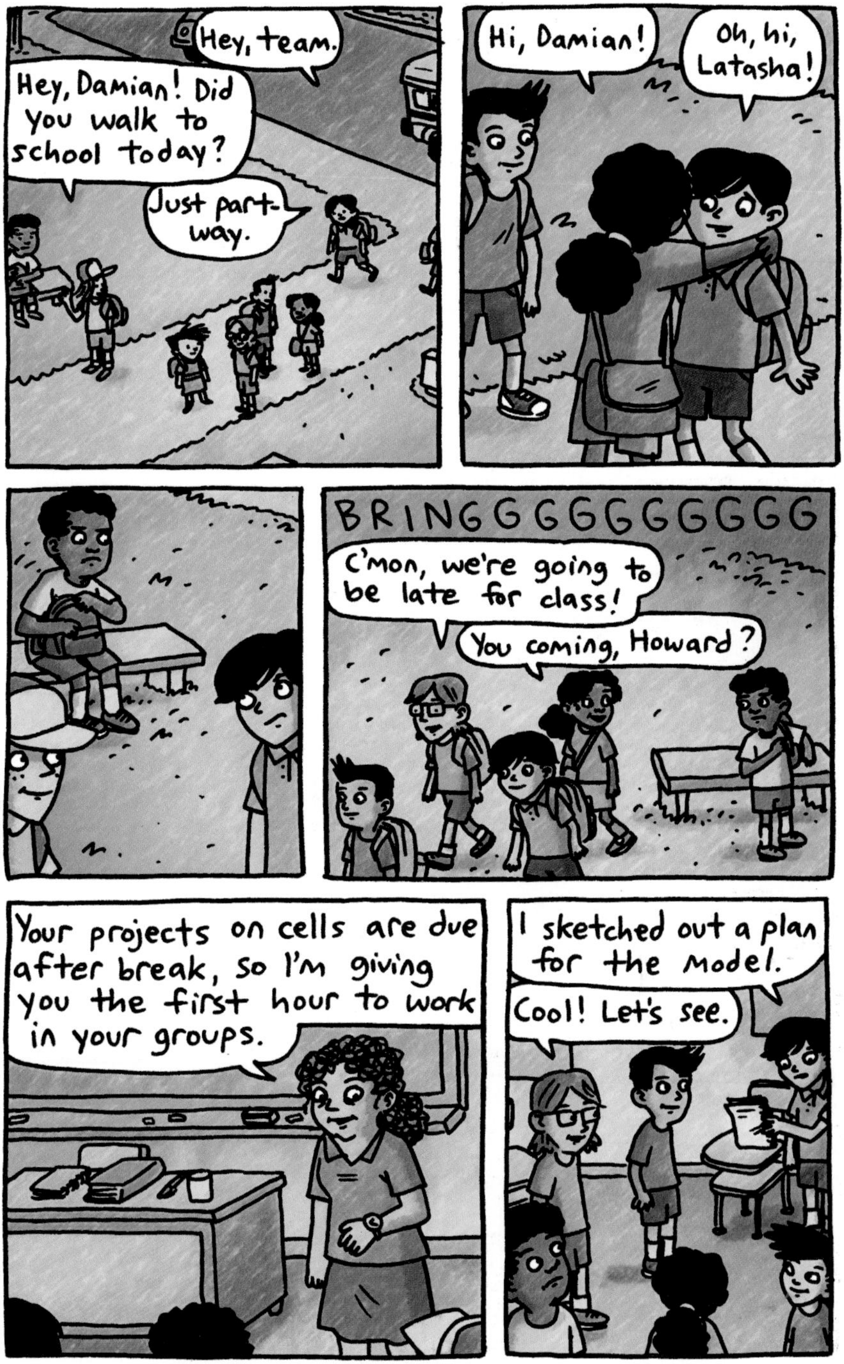
Hey, team.
Hey, Damian! Did you walk to school today?
Just part-way.
Hi, Damian!
Oh, hi, Latasha!
BRINGGGGGGGGG
C'mon, we're going to be late for class!
You coming, Howard?
Your projects on cells are due after break, so I'm giving you the first hour to work in your groups.
I sketched out a plan for the model.
Cool! Let's see.

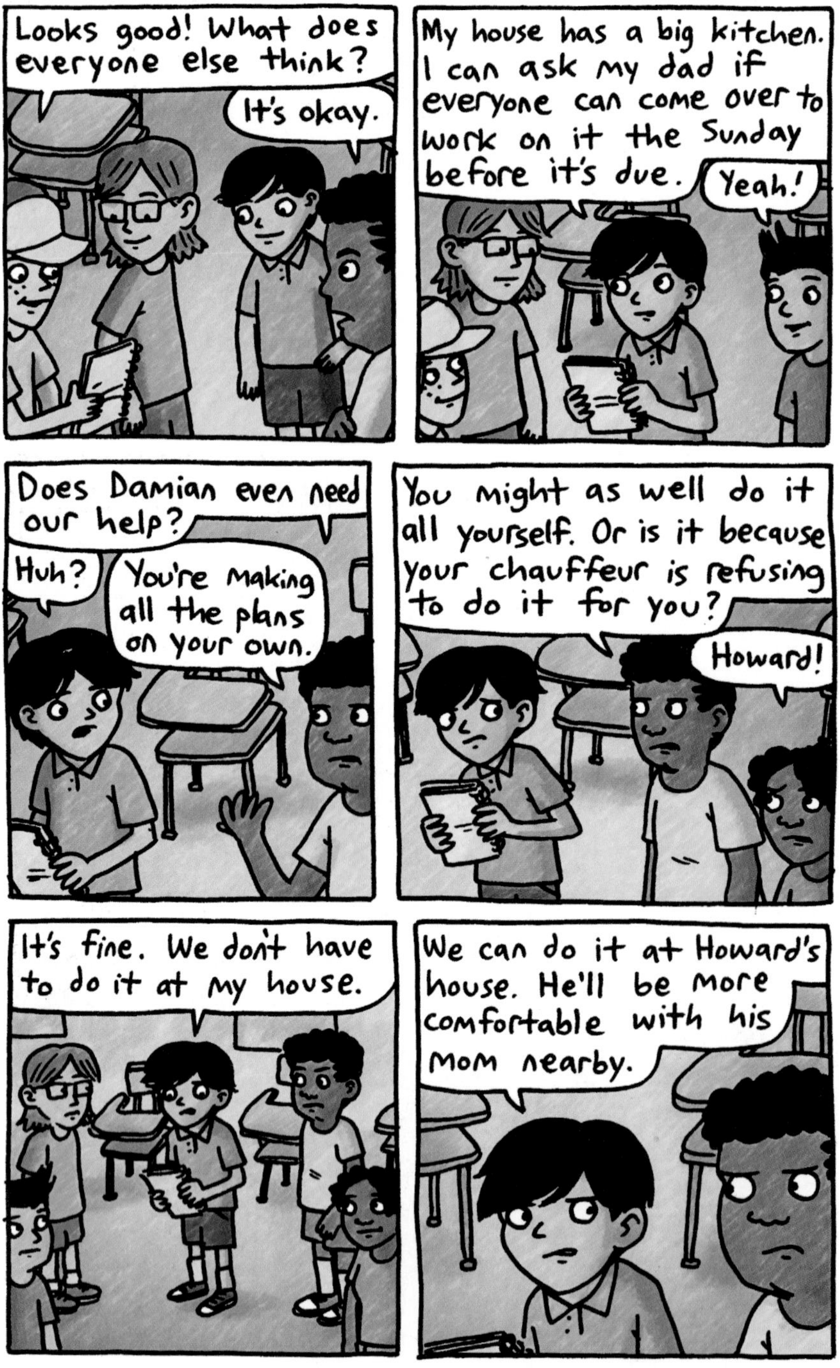
Looks good! What does everyone else think?
It's okay.
My house has a big kitchen. I can ask my dad if everyone can come over to work on it the Sunday before it's due.
Yeah!
Does Damian even need our help?
Huh?
You're making all the plans on your own.
You might as well do it all yourself. Or is it because your chauffeur is refusing to do it for you?
Howard!
It's fine. We don't have to do it at my house.
We can do it at Howard's house. He'll be more comfortable with his mom nearby.

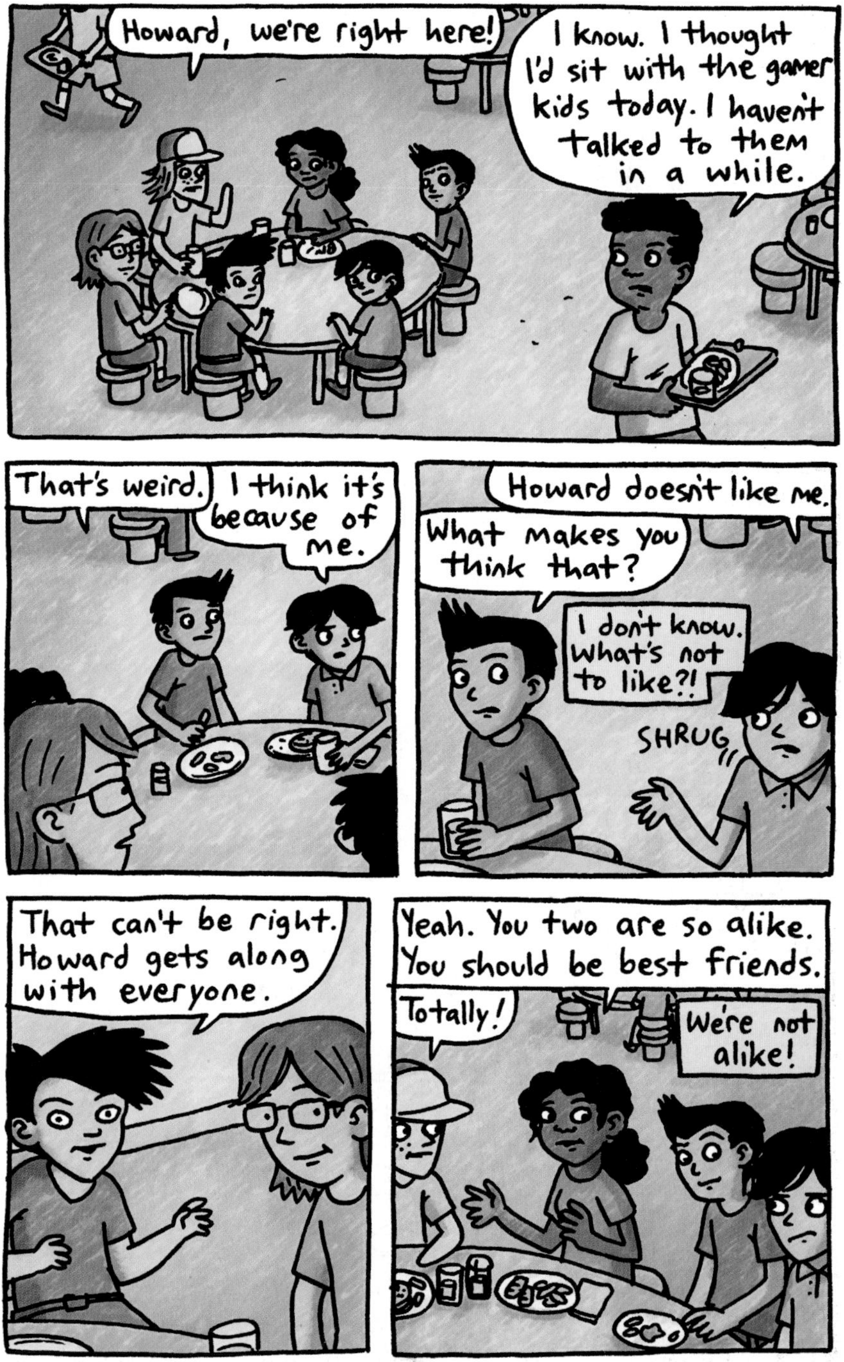
Howard, we're right here!
I know. I thought I'd sit with the gamer kids today. I haven't talked to them in a while.
That's weird.
I think it's because of me.
Howard doesn't like me.
What makes you think that?
I don't know. What's not to like?!
SHRUG
That can't be right. Howard gets along with everyone.
Yeah. You two are so alike. You should be best friends.
Totally!
We're not alike!

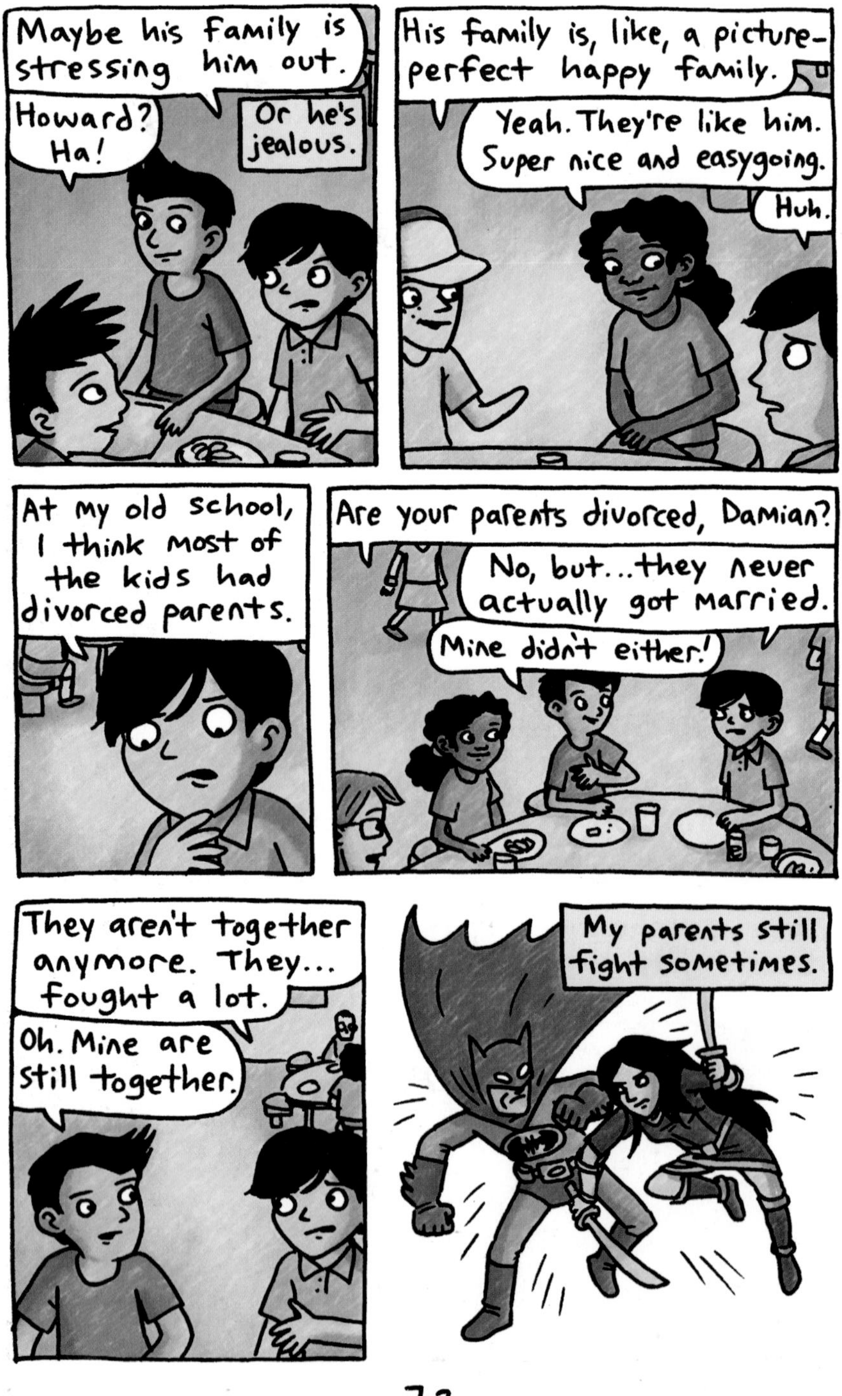
Maybe his family is stressing him out.
Howard? Ha!
Or he's jealous.
His family is, like, a picture-perfect happy family.
Yeah. They're like him. Super nice and easygoing.
Huh.
At my old school, I think most of the kids had divorced parents.
Are your parents divorced, Damian?
No, but... they never actually got married.
Mine didn't either!
They aren't together anymore. They... fought a lot.
Oh. Mine are still together.
My parents still fight sometimes.

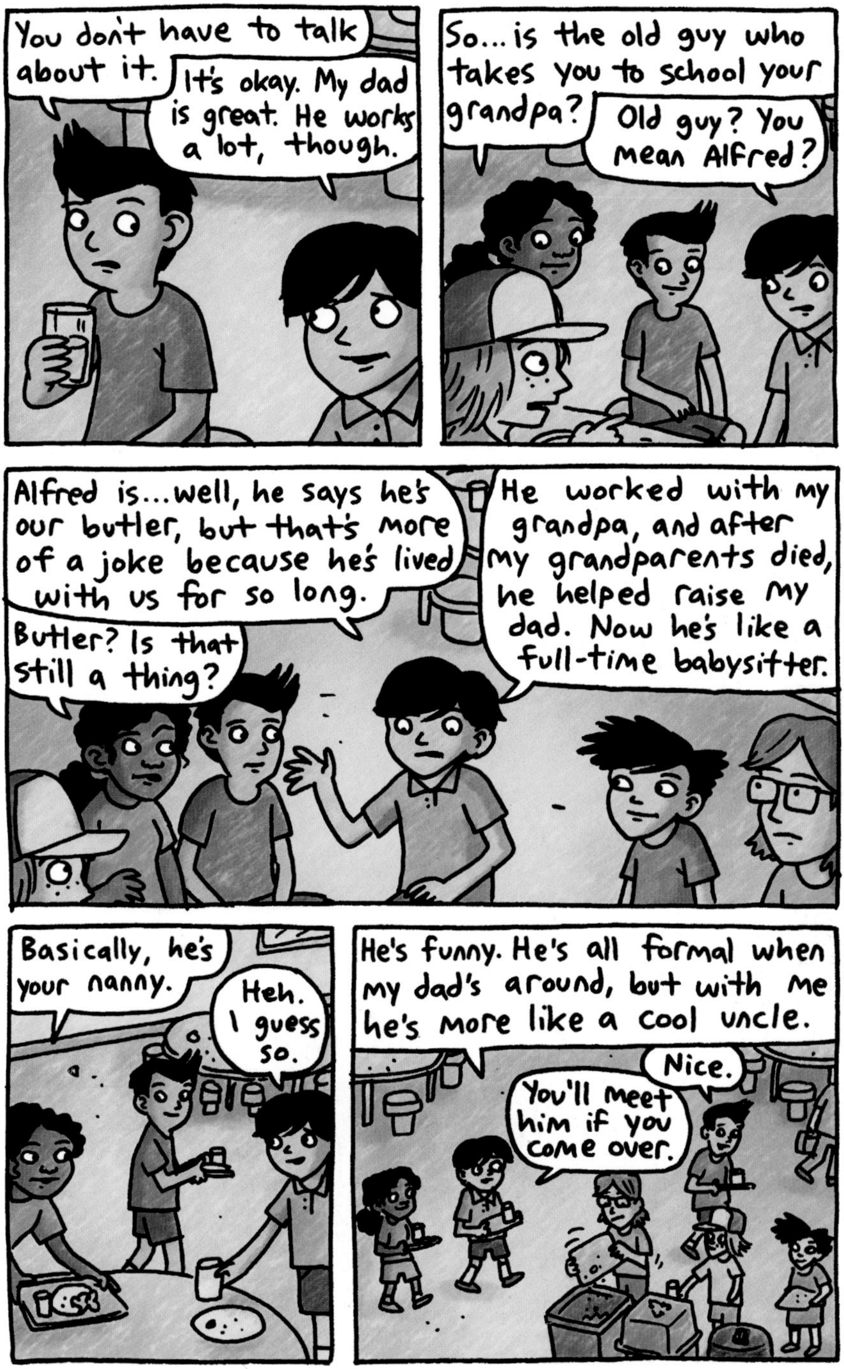
You don't have to talk about it.
It's okay. My dad is great. He works a lot, though.
So... is the old guy who takes you to school your grandpa?
Old guy? You mean Alfred?
Alfred is... well, he says he's our butler, but that's more of a joke because he's lived with us for so long.
Butler? Is that still a thing?
He worked with my grandpa, and after my grandparents died, he helped raise my dad. Now he's like a full-time babysitter.
Basically, he's your nanny.
Heh. I guess so.
He's funny. He's all formal when my dad's around, but with me he's more like a cool uncle.
Nice.
You'll meet him if you come over.

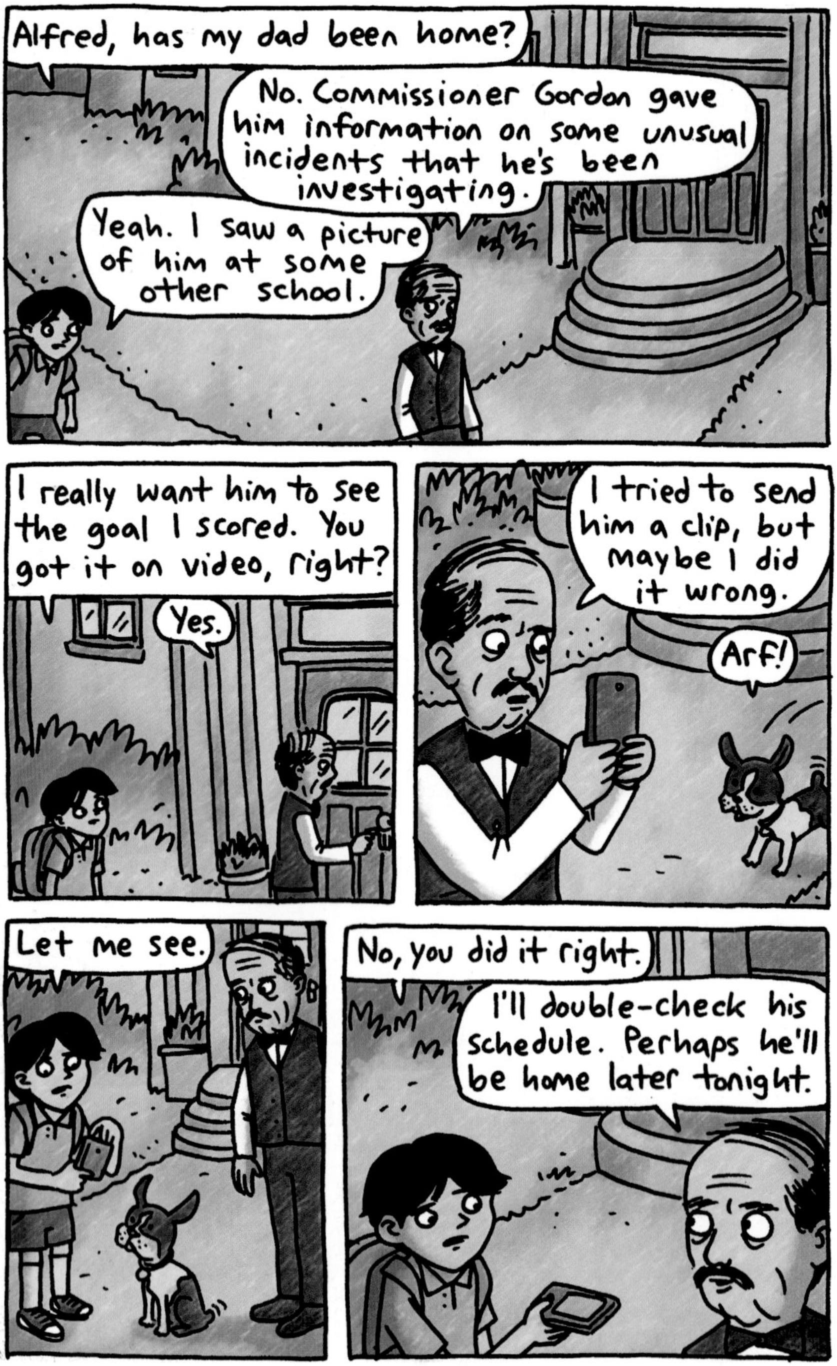
Alfred, has my dad been home?
No. Commissioner Gordon gave him information on some unusual incidents that he's been investigating.
Yeah. I saw a picture of him at some other school.
I really want him to see the goal I scored. You got it on video, right?
Yes.
I tried to send him a clip, but maybe I did it wrong.
Arf!
Let me see.
No, you did it right.
I'll double-check his schedule. Perhaps he'll be home later tonight.

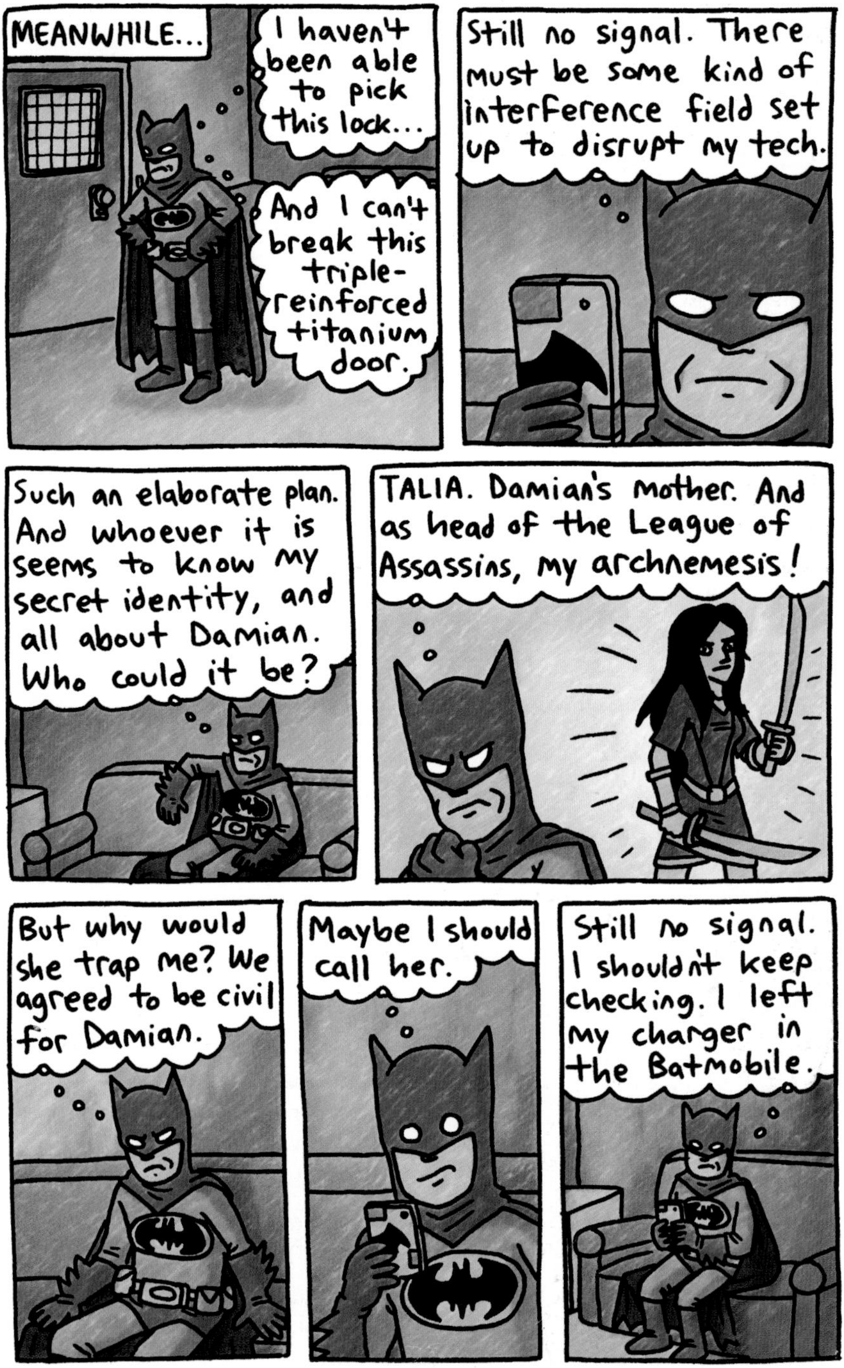
MEANWHILE...
I haven't been able to pick this lock...
And I can't break this triple-reinforced titanium door.
Still no signal. There must be some kind of interference field set up to disrupt my tech.
Such an elaborate plan. And whoever it is seems to know my secret identity, and all about Damian. Who could it be?
TALIA. Damian's mother. And as head of the League of Assassins, my archnemesis!
But why would she trap me? We agreed to be civil for Damian.
Maybe I should call her.
Still no signal. I shouldn't keep checking. I left my charger in the Batmobile.

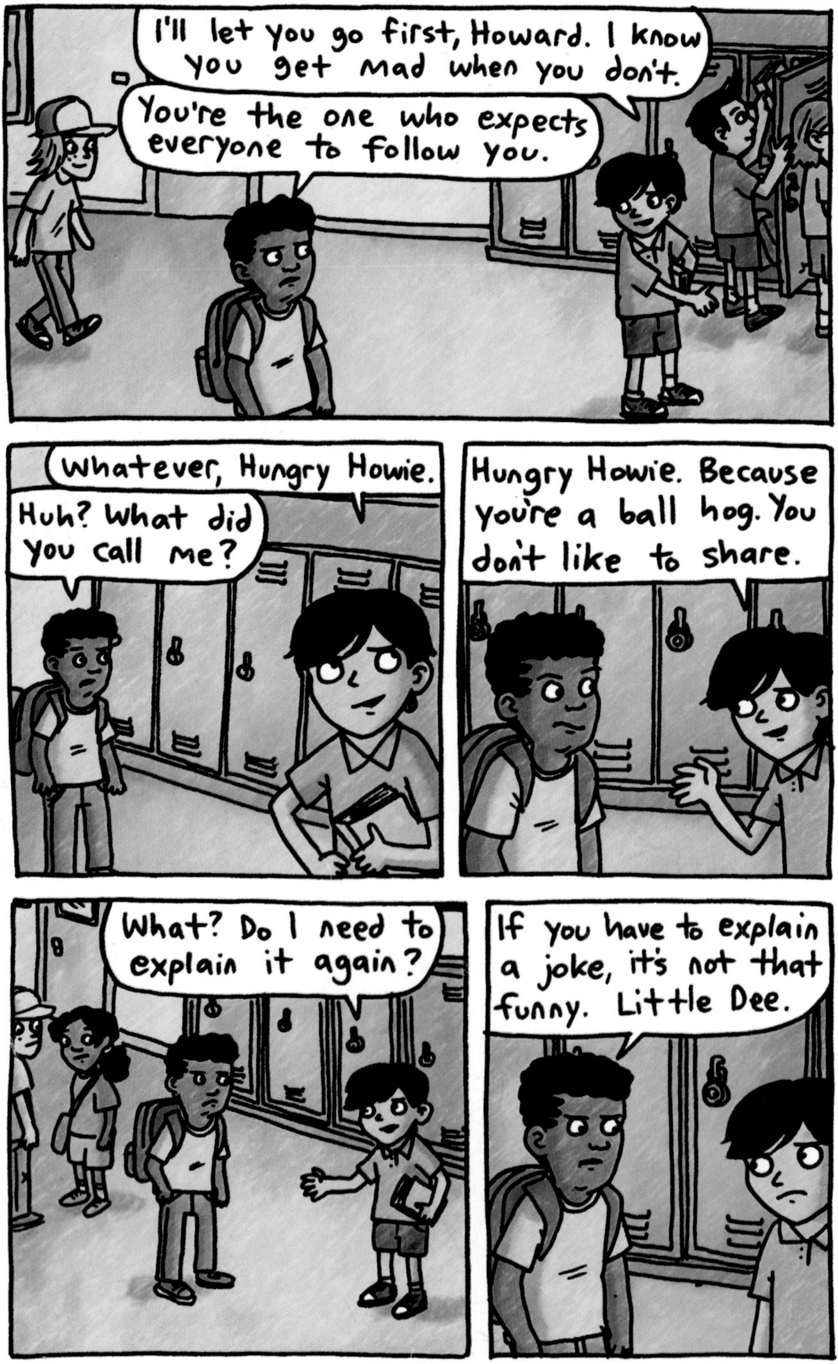
I'll let you go first, Howard. I know you get mad when you don't.
You're the one who expects everyone to follow you.
Whatever, Hungry Howie.
Huh? What did you call me?
Hungry Howie. Because you're a ball hog. You don't like to share.
What? Do I need to explain it again?
If you have to explain a joke, it's not that funny. Little Dee.

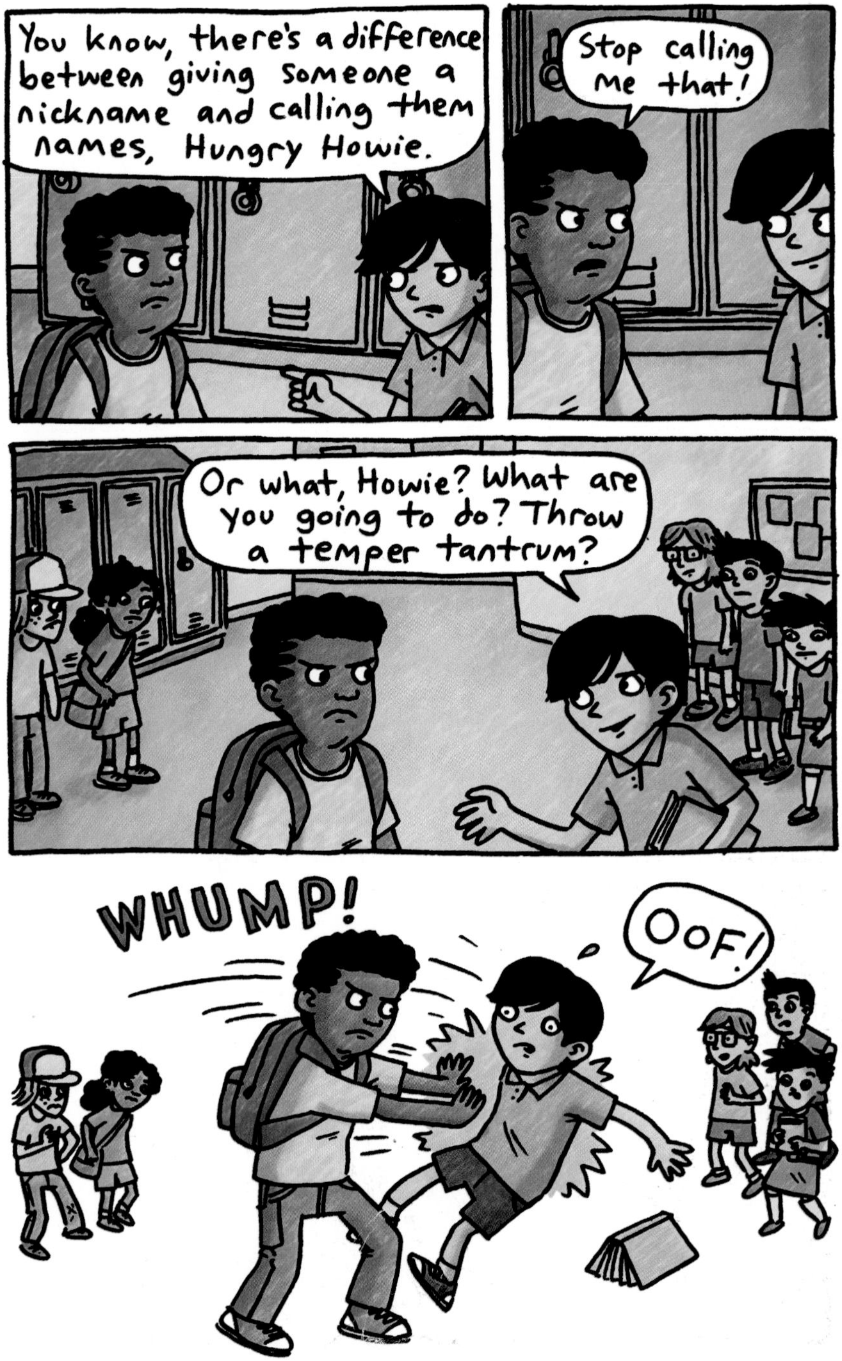
You know, there's a difference between giving someone a nickname and calling them names, Hungry Howie.
Stop calling me that!
Or what, Howie? What are you going to do? Throw a temper tantrum?
WHUMP!
OOF!

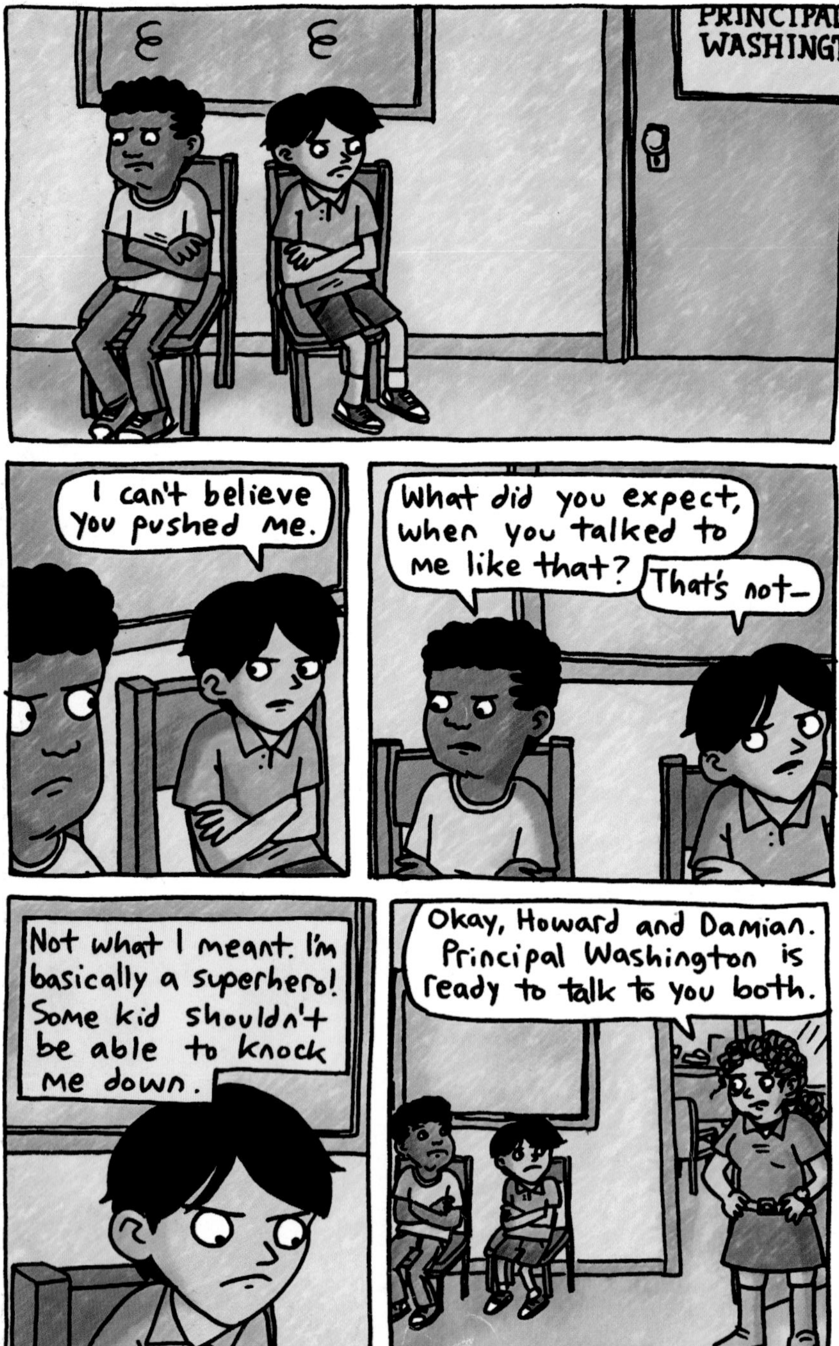
PRINCIPAL
WASHINGT
I can't believe you pushed me.
What did you expect, when you talked to me like that?
That's not—
Not what I meant. I'm basically a superhero! Some kid shouldn't be able to knock me down.
Okay, Howard and Damian. Principal Washington is ready to talk to you both.

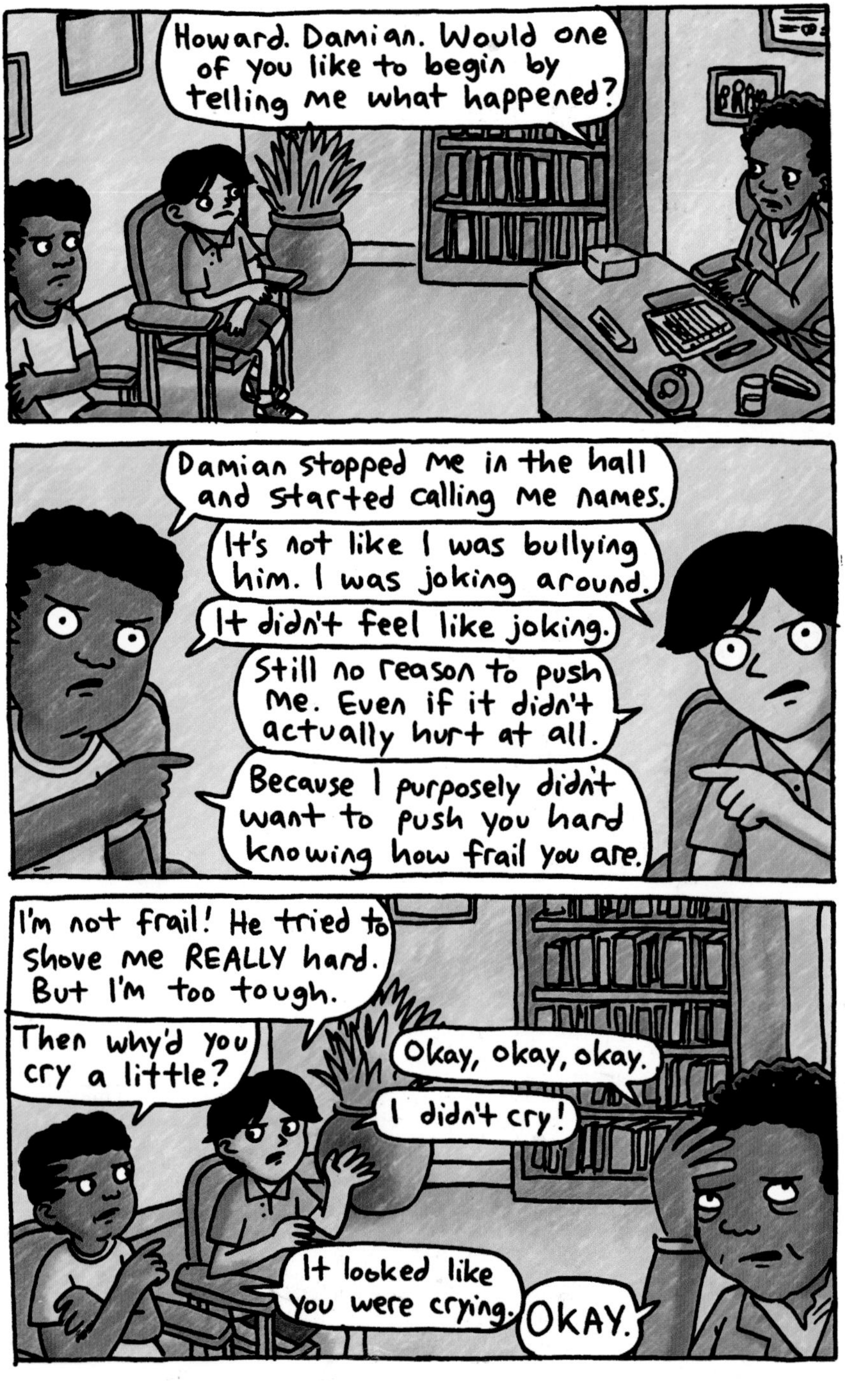
Howard. Damian. Would one of you like to begin by telling me what happened?
Damian stopped me in the hall and started calling me names.
It's not like I was bullying him. I was joking around.
It didn't feel like joking.
Still no reason to push me. Even if it didn't actually hurt at all.
Because I purposely didn't want to push you hard knowing how frail you are.
I'm not frail! He tried to shove me REALLY hard. But I'm too tough.
Then why'd you cry a little?
Okay, okay, okay.
I didn't cry!
It looked like you were crying.
OKAY.

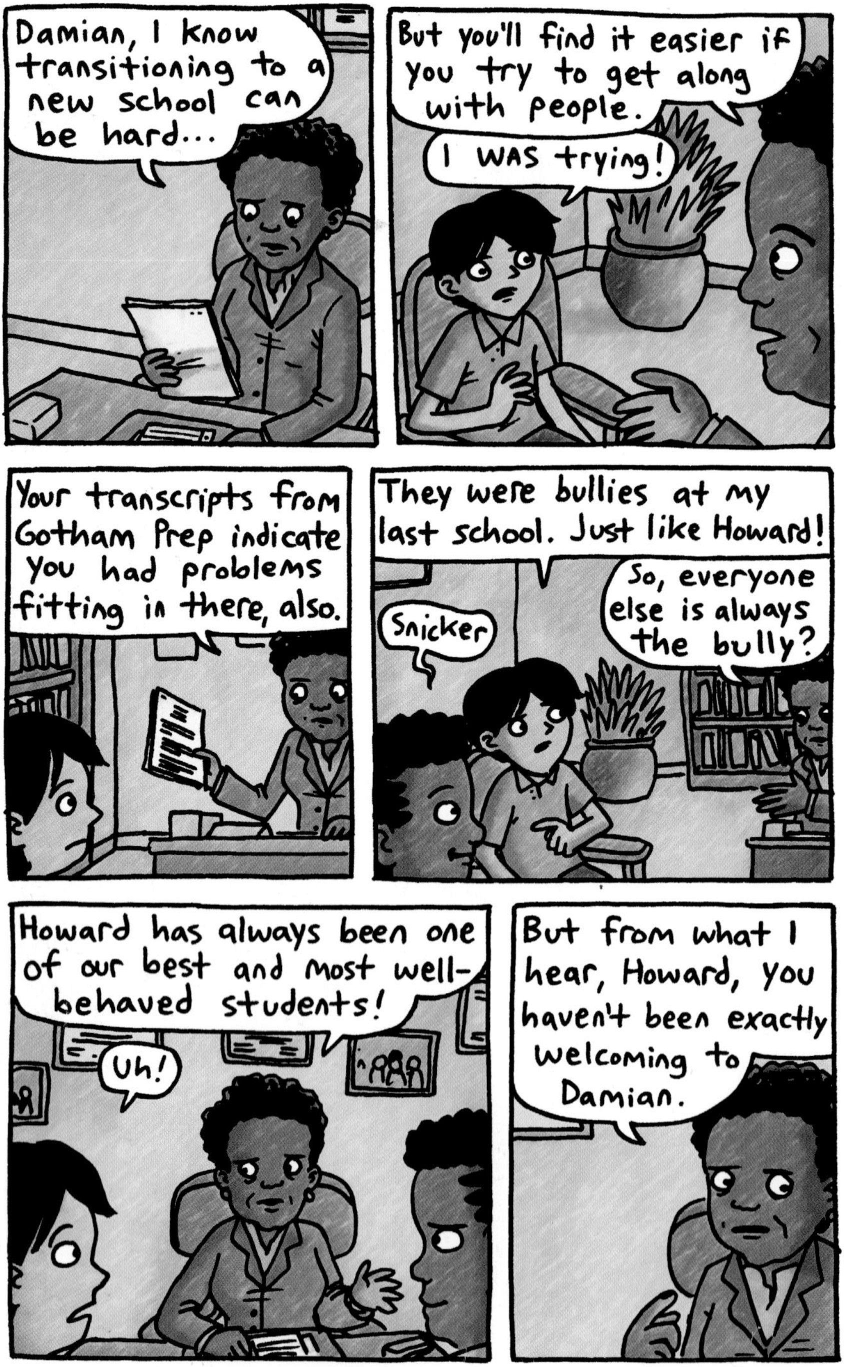
Damian, I know transitioning to a new school can be hard...
But you'll find it easier if you try to get along with people.
I WAS trying!
Your transcripts from Gotham Prep indicate you had problems fitting in there, also.
They were bullies at my last school. Just like Howard!
Snicker
So, everyone else is always the bully?
Howard has always been one of our best and most well-behaved students!
Uh!
But from what I hear, Howard, you haven't been exactly welcoming to Damian.

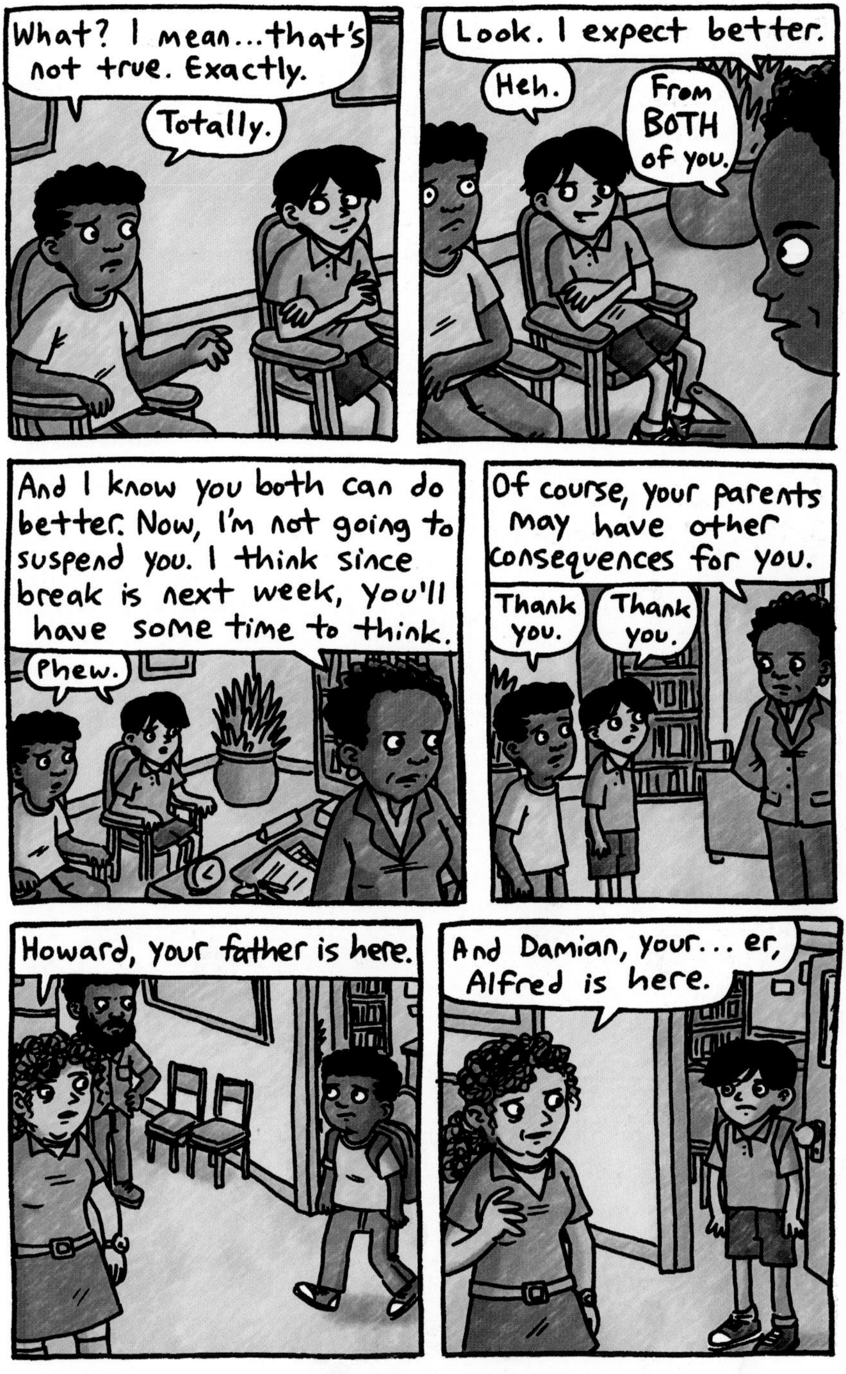
What? I mean...that's not true. Exactly.
Totally.
Look. I expect better.
Heh.
From BOTH of you.
And I know you both can do better. Now, I'm not going to suspend you. I think since break is next week, you'll have some time to think.
Phew.
Of course, your parents may have other consequences for you.
Thank you.
Thank you.
Howard, your father is here.
And Damian, your... er, Alfred is here.

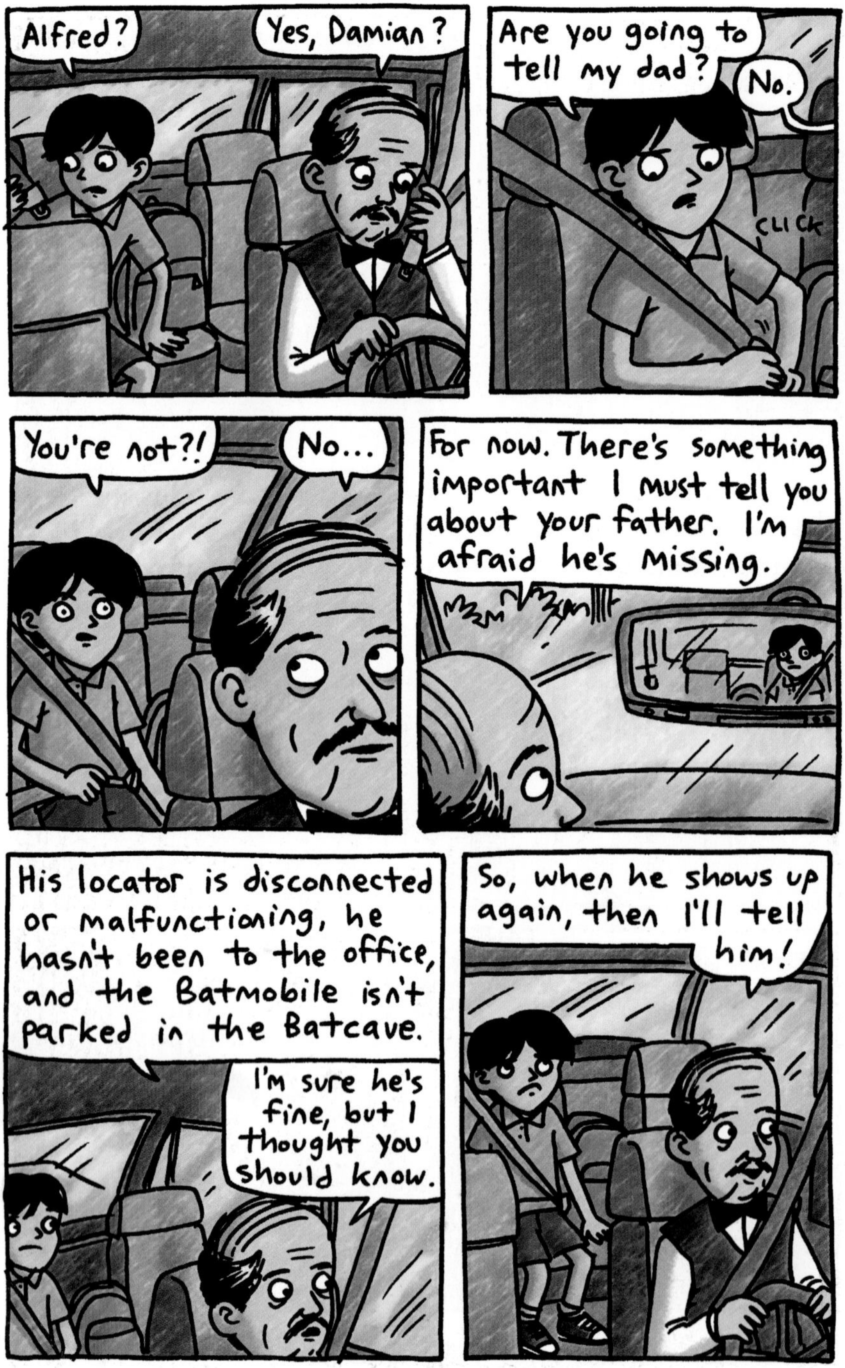
Alfred?
Yes, Damian?
Are you going to tell my dad?
No.
CLICK
You're not?!
No...
For now. There's something important I must tell you about your father. I'm afraid he's missing.
His locator is disconnected or malfunctioning, he hasn't been to the office, and the Batmobile isn't parked in the Batcave.
I'm sure he's fine, but I thought you should know.
So, when he shows up again, then I'll tell him!

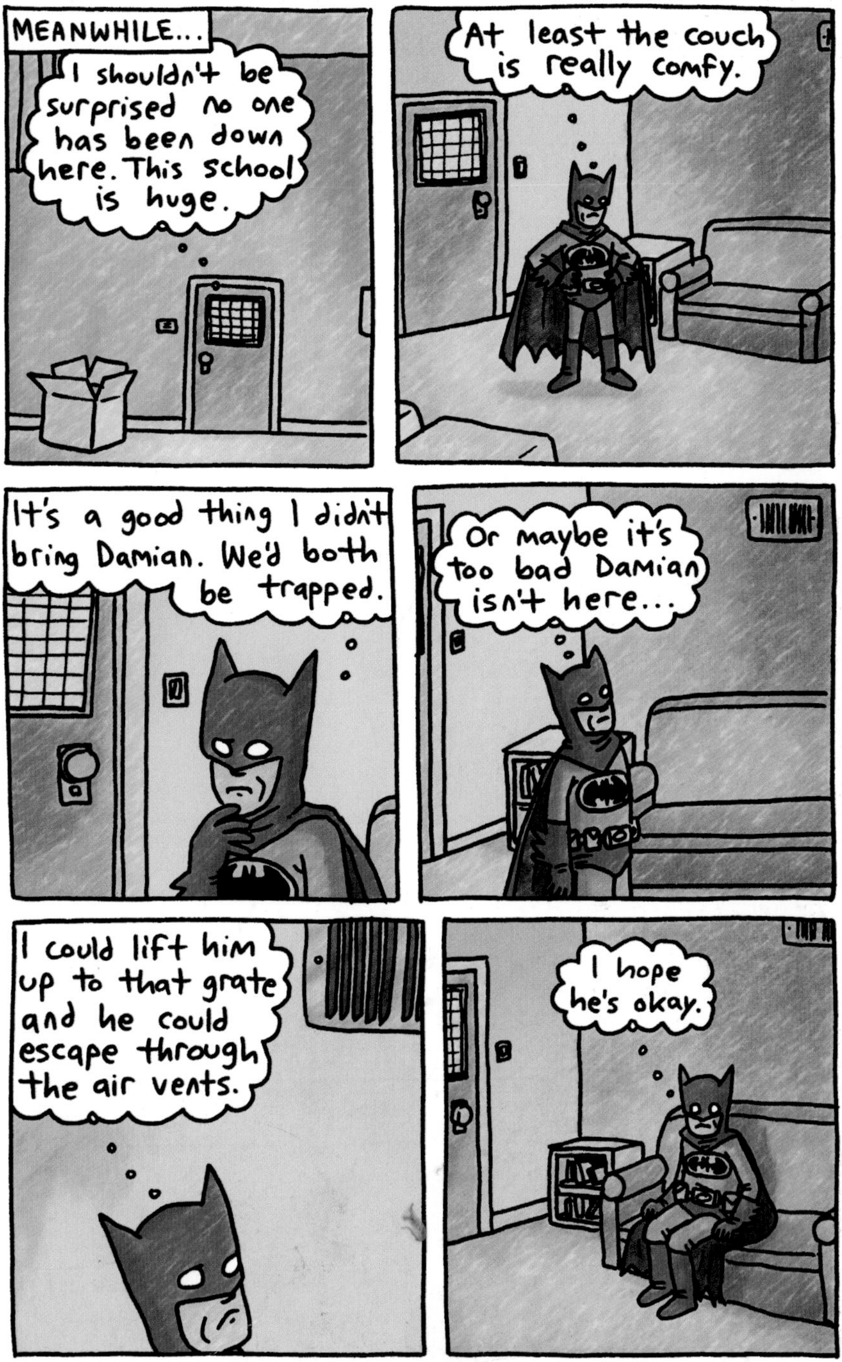
MEANWHILE...
I shouldn't be surprised no one has been down here. This school is huge.
At least the couch is really comfy.
It's a good thing I didn't bring Damian. We'd both be trapped.
Or maybe it's too bad Damian isn't here...
I could lift him up to that grate and he could escape through the air vents.
I hope he's okay.

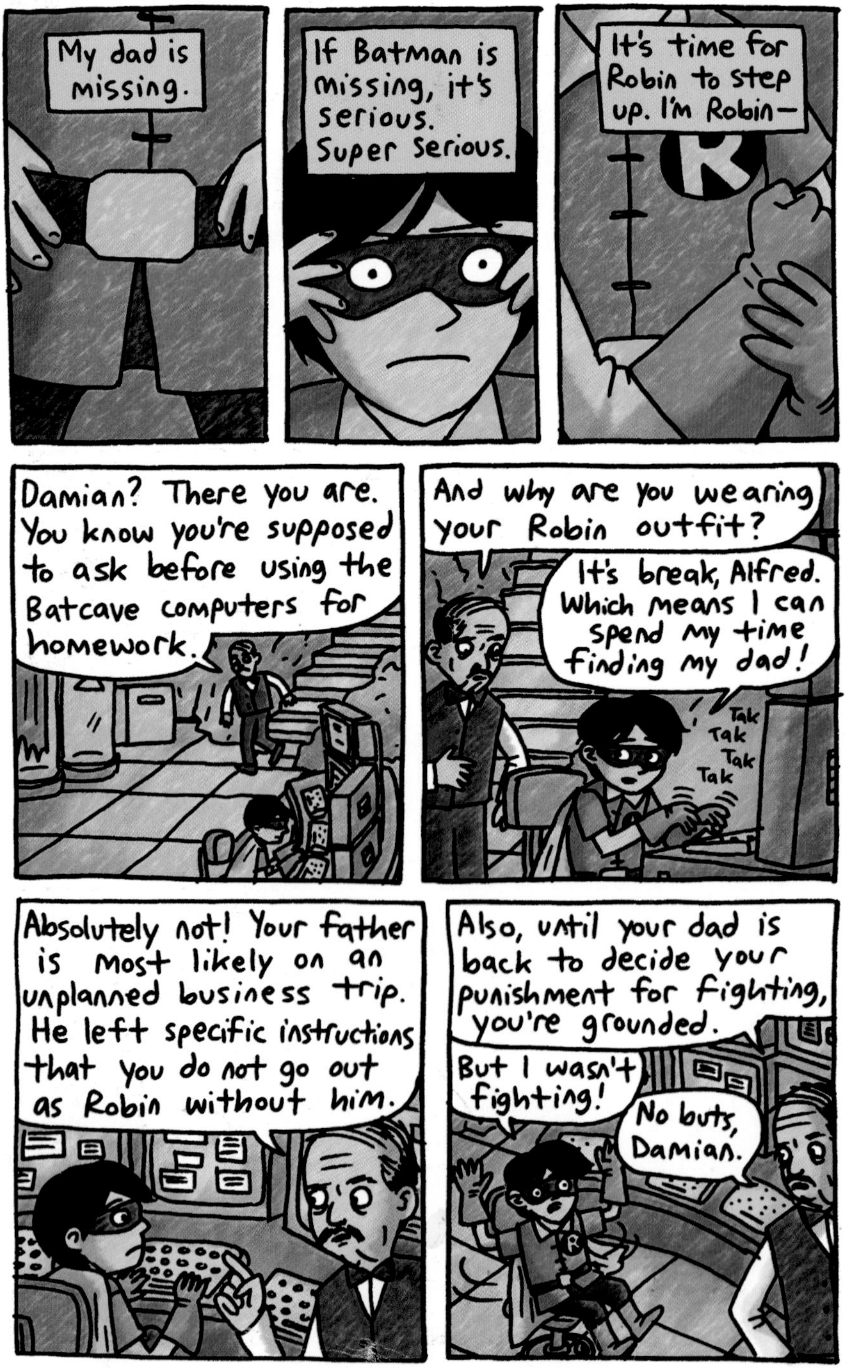
My dad is missing.
If Batman is missing, it's serious. Super serious.
It's time for Robin to step up. I'm Robin—
Damian? There you are. You know you're supposed to ask before using the Batcave computers for homework.
And why are you wearing your Robin outfit?
It's break, Alfred. Which means I can spend my time finding my dad!
Tak Tak Tak Tak
Absolutely not! Your father is most likely on an unplanned business trip. He left specific instructions that you do not go out as Robin without him.
Also, until your dad is back to decide your punishment for fighting, you're grounded.
But I wasn't fighting!
No buts, Damian.

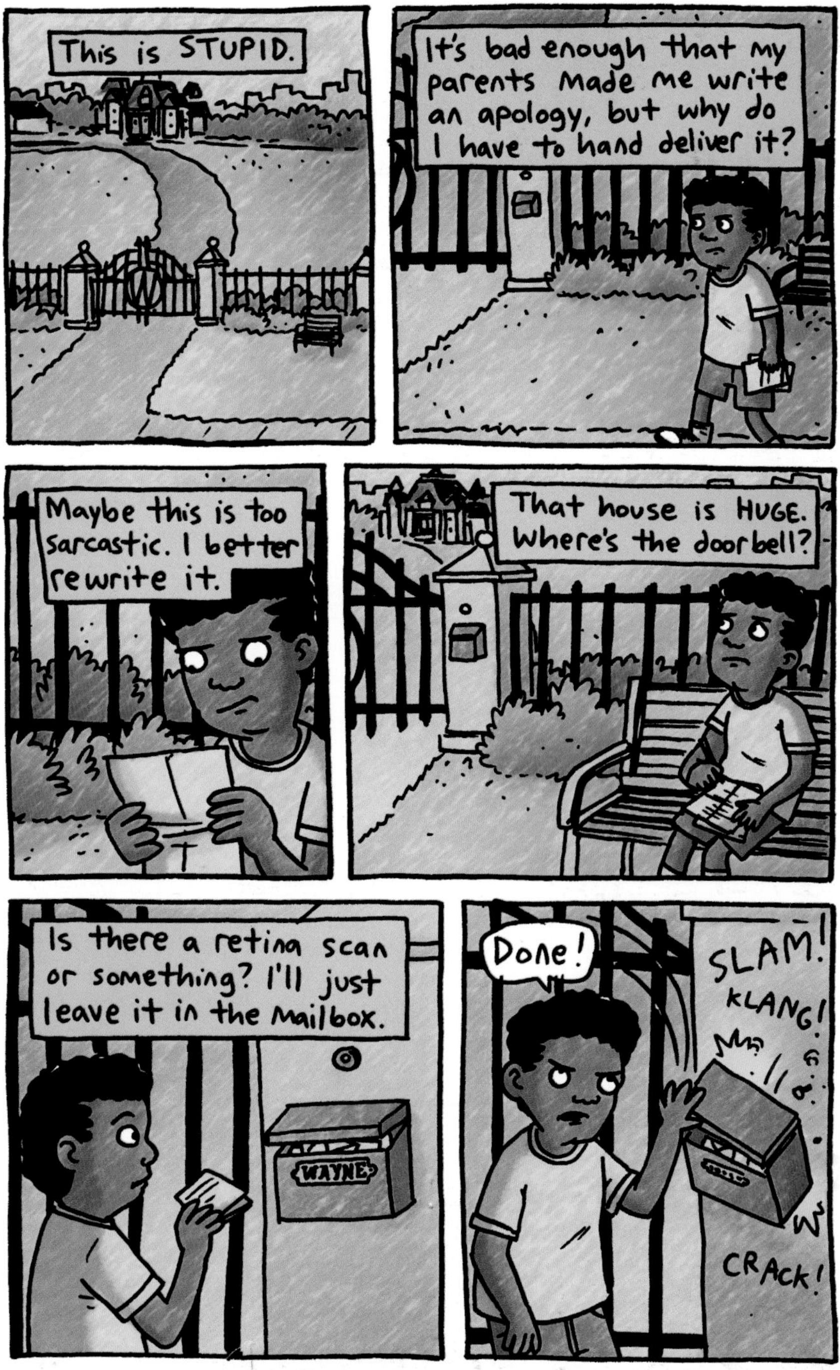

This is STUPID.
It's bad enough that my parents made me write an apology, but why do I have to hand deliver it?
Maybe this is too sarcastic. I better rewrite it.
That house is HUGE. Where's the doorbell?
Is there a retina scan or something? I'll just leave it in the mailbox.
WAYNE
Done!
SLAM!
KLANG!
CRACK!

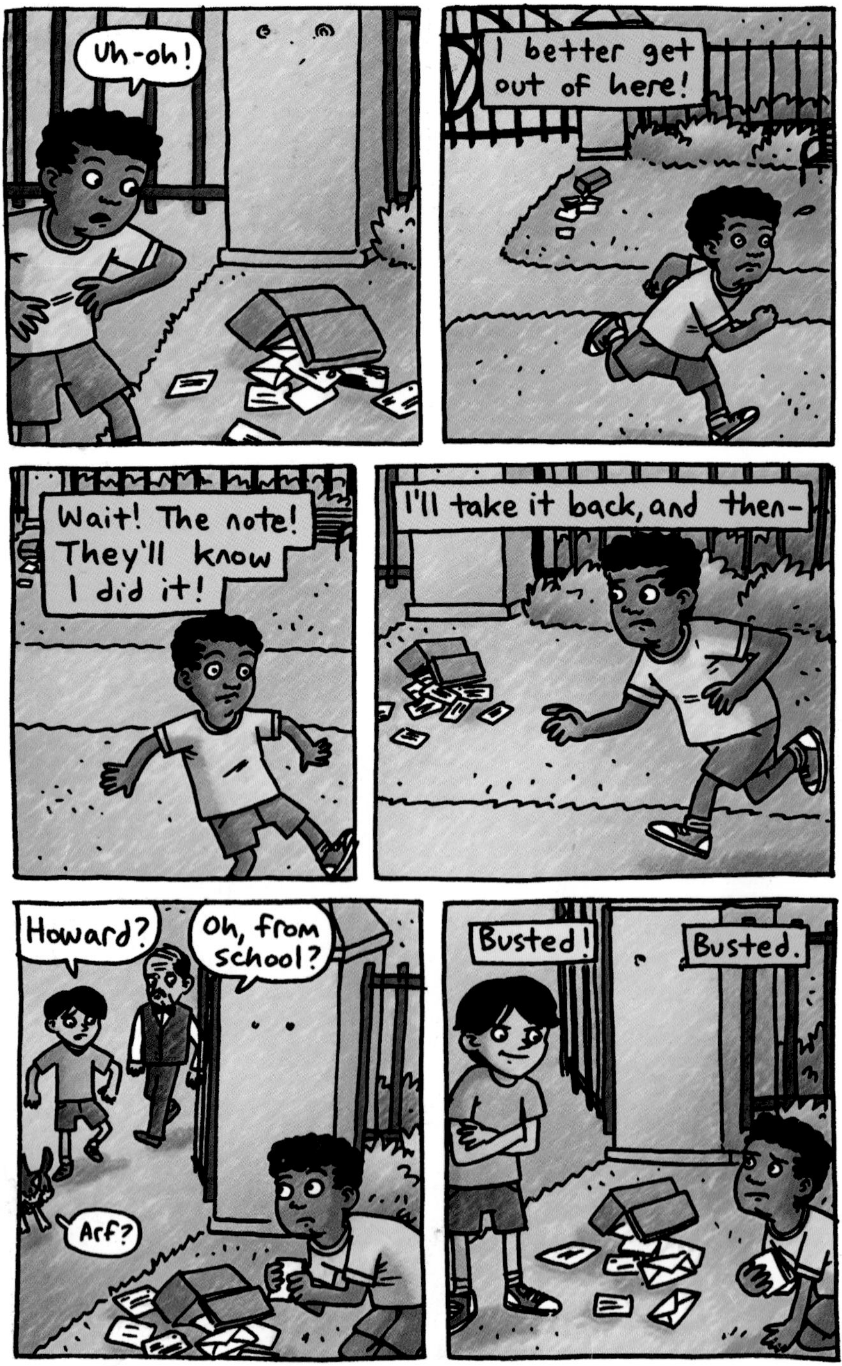
Uh-oh!
I better get out of here!
Wait! The note! They'll know I did it!
I'll take it back, and then-
Howard?
Oh, from school?
Arf?
Busted!
Busted.

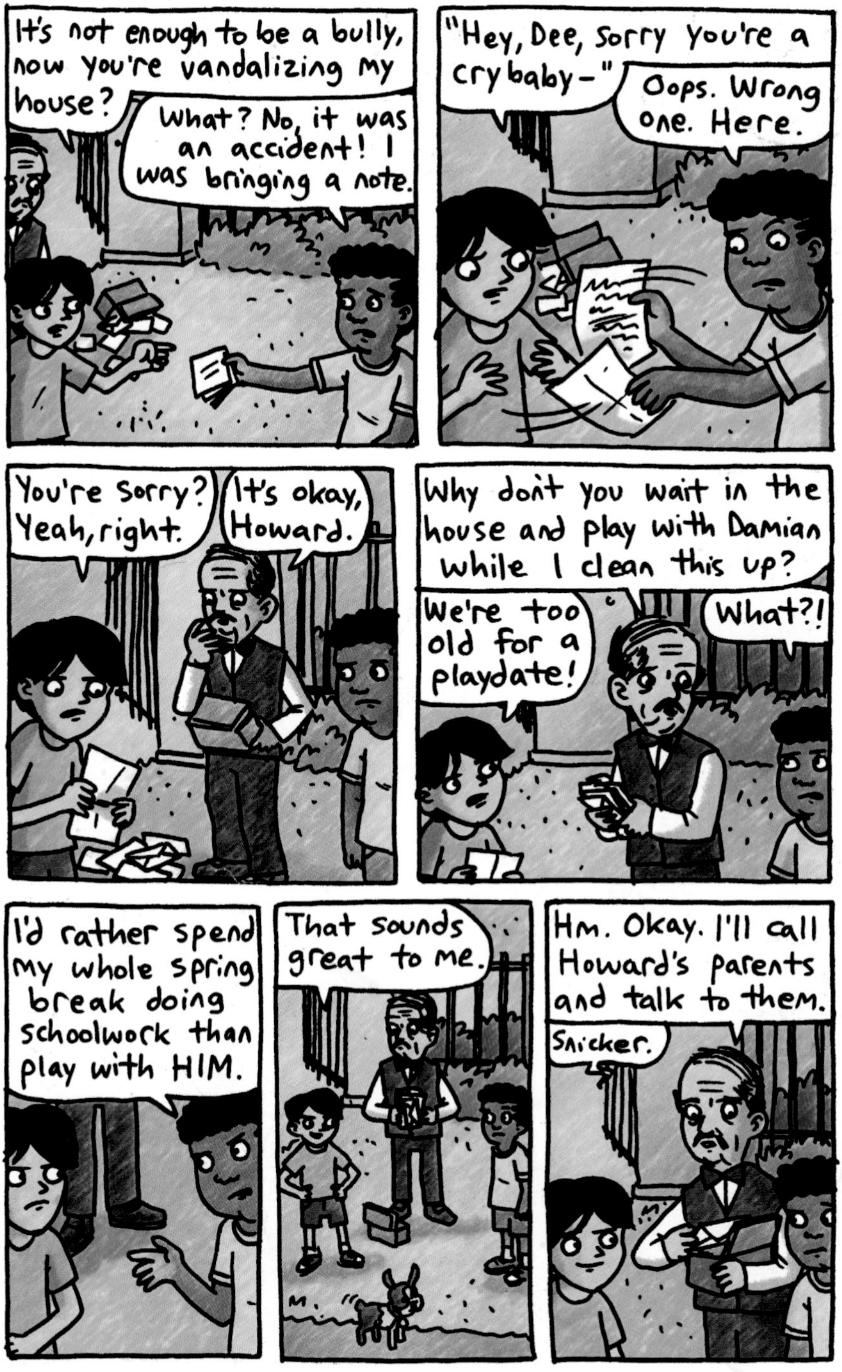
It's not enough to be a bully, now you're vandalizing my house?
What? No, it was an accident! I was bringing a note.
"Hey, Dee, sorry you're a crybaby-"
Oops. Wrong one. Here.
You're sorry? Yeah, right.
It's okay, Howard.
Why don't you wait in the house and play with Damian while I clean this up?
We're too old for a playdate!
What?!
I'd rather spend my whole spring break doing schoolwork than play with HIM.
That sounds great to me.
Hm. Okay. I'll call Howard's parents and talk to them.
Snicker.

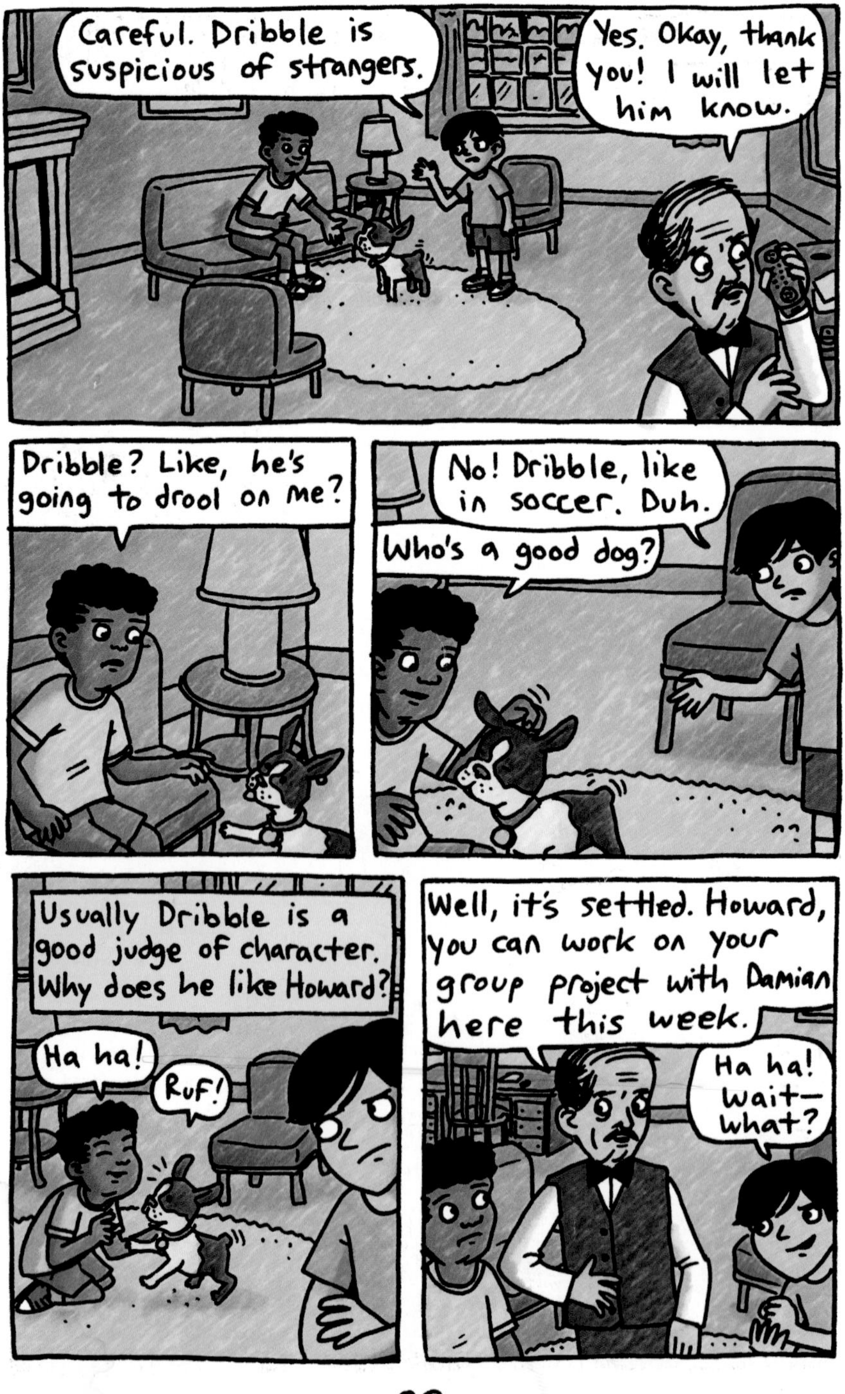
Careful. Dribble is suspicious of strangers.
Yes. Okay, thank you! I will let him know.
Dribble? Like, he's going to drool on me?
No! Dribble, like in soccer. Duh.
Who's a good dog?
Usually Dribble is a good judge of character. Why does he like Howard?
Ha ha!
Ruf!
Well, it's settled. Howard, you can work on your group project with Damian here this week.
Ha ha! Wait—what?

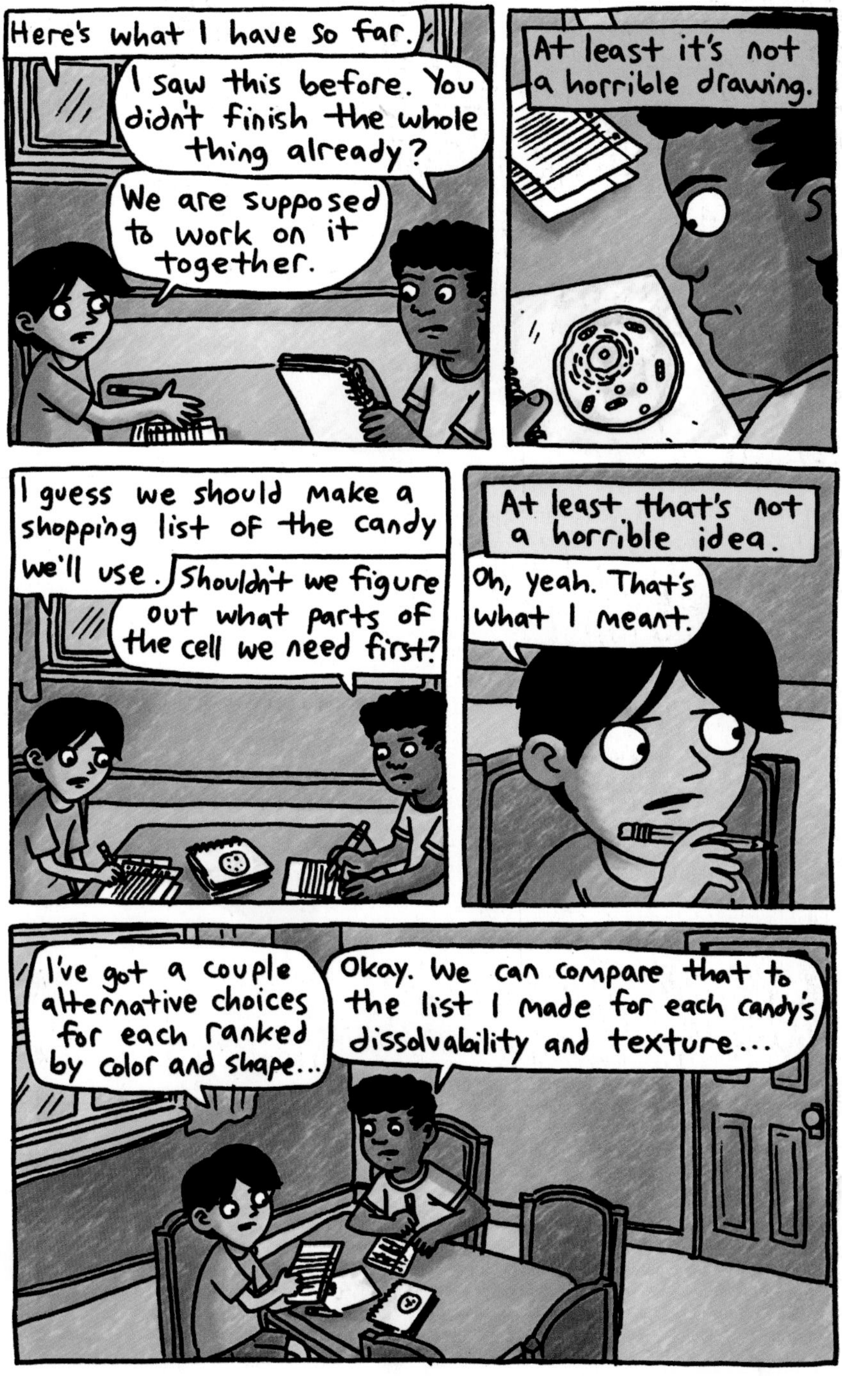
Here's what I have so far.
I saw this before. You didn't finish the whole thing already?
We are supposed to work on it together.
At least it's not a horrible drawing.
I guess we should make a shopping list of the candy we'll use.
Shouldn't we figure out what parts of the cell we need first?
At least that's not a horrible idea.
Oh, yeah. That's what I meant.
I've got a couple alternative choices for each ranked by color and shape...
Okay. We can compare that to the list I made for each candy's dissolvability and texture...

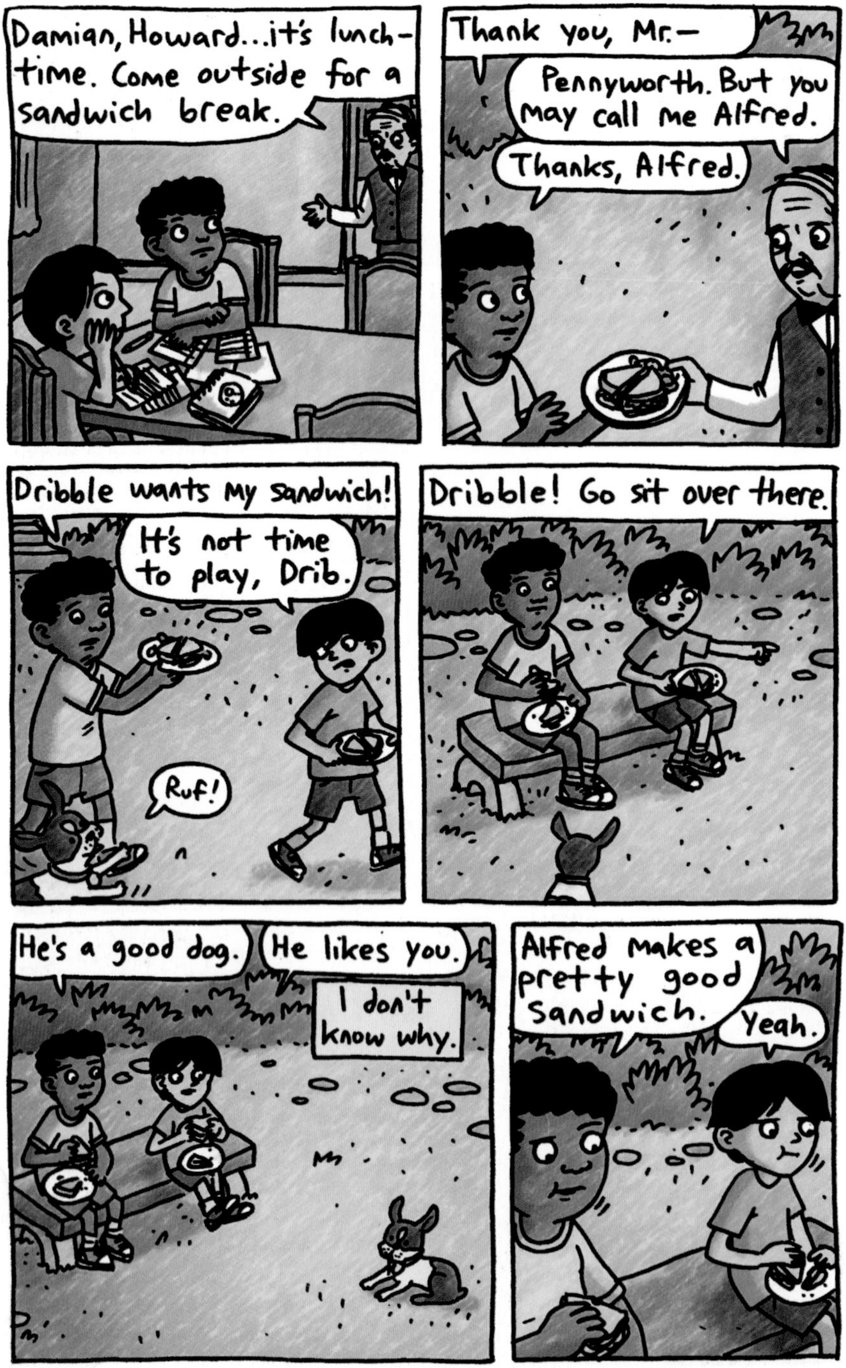
Damian, Howard...it's lunch-time. Come outside for a sandwich break.
Thank you, Mr.—
Pennyworth. But you may call me Alfred.
Thanks, Alfred.
Dribble wants my sandwich!
It's not time to play, Drib.
Ruf!
Dribble! Go sit over there.
He's a good dog.
He likes you.
I don't know why.
Alfred makes a pretty good sandwich.
Yeah.

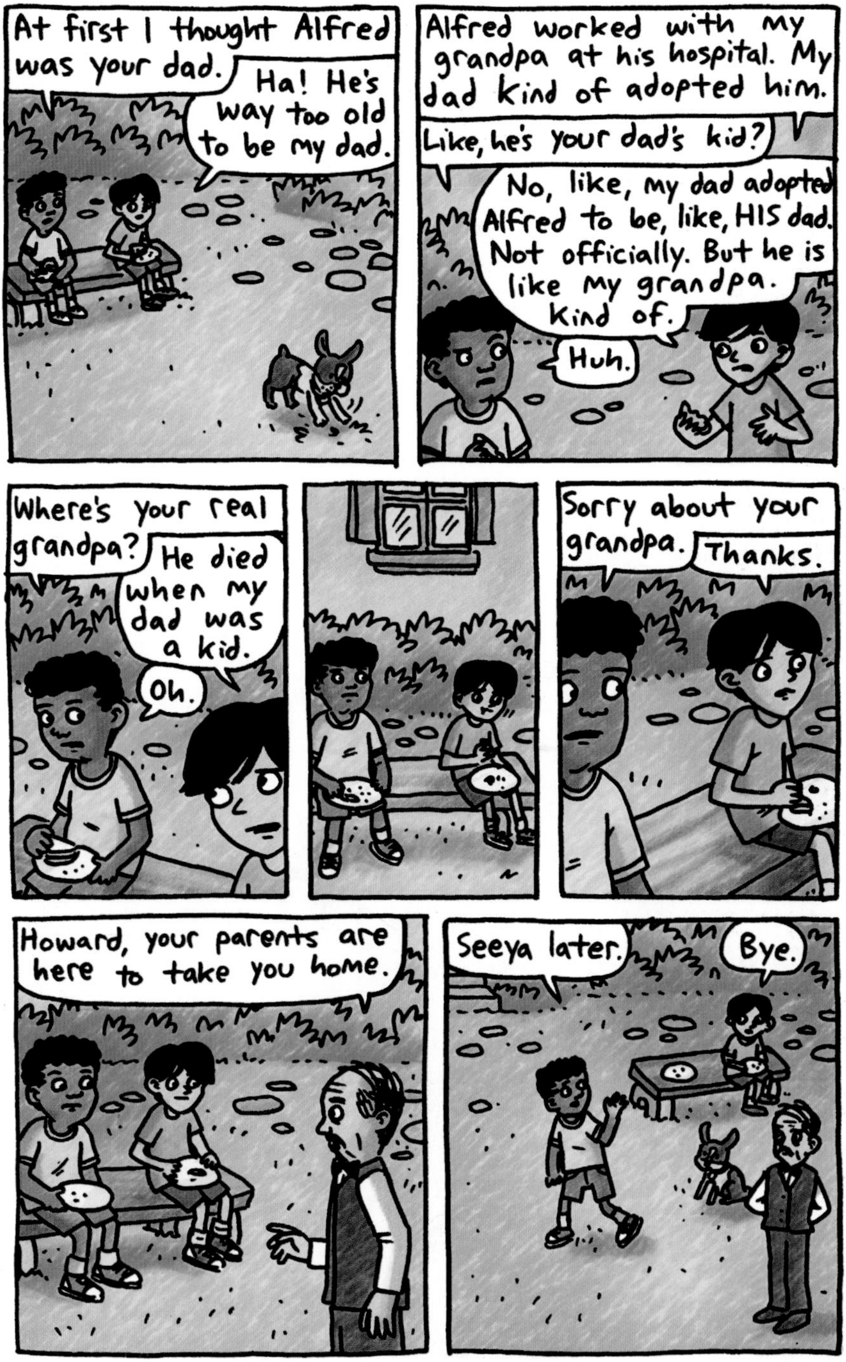
At first I thought Alfred was your dad.
Ha! He's way too old to be my dad.
Alfred worked with my grandpa at his hospital. My dad kind of adopted him.
Like, he's your dad's kid?
No, like, my dad adopted Alfred to be, like, HIS dad. Not officially. But he is like my grandpa. Kind of.
Huh.
Where's your real grandpa?
He died when my dad was a kid.
Oh.
Sorry about your grandpa.
Thanks.
Howard, your parents are here to take you home.
Seeya later.
Bye.

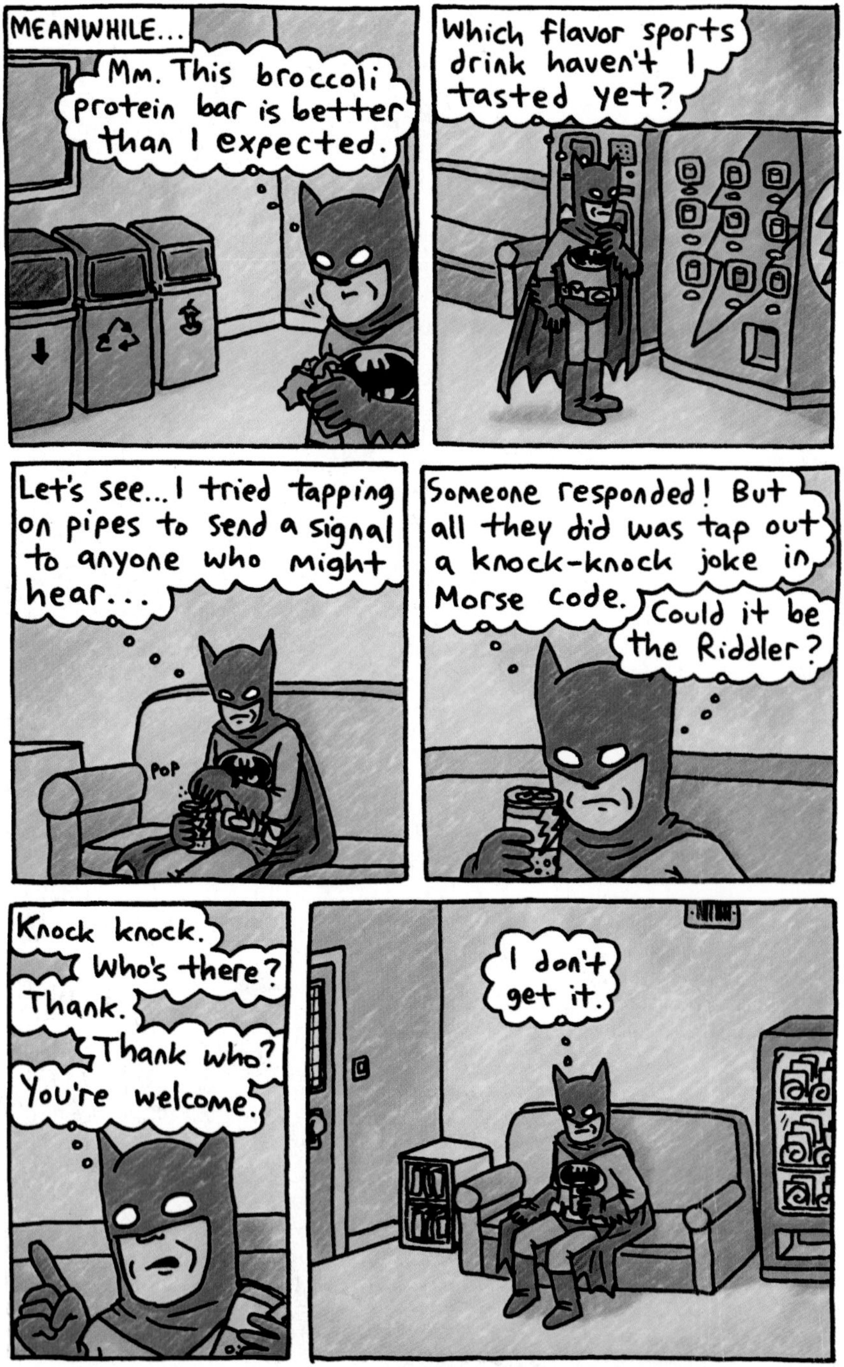
MEANWHILE...
Mm. This broccoli protein bar is better than I expected.
Which flavor sports drink haven't I tasted yet?
Let's see... I tried tapping on pipes to send a signal to anyone who might hear...
POP
Someone responded! But all they did was tap out a knock-knock joke in Morse code.
Could it be the Riddler?
Knock knock.
Who's there?
Thank.
Thank who?
You're welcome.
I don't get it.

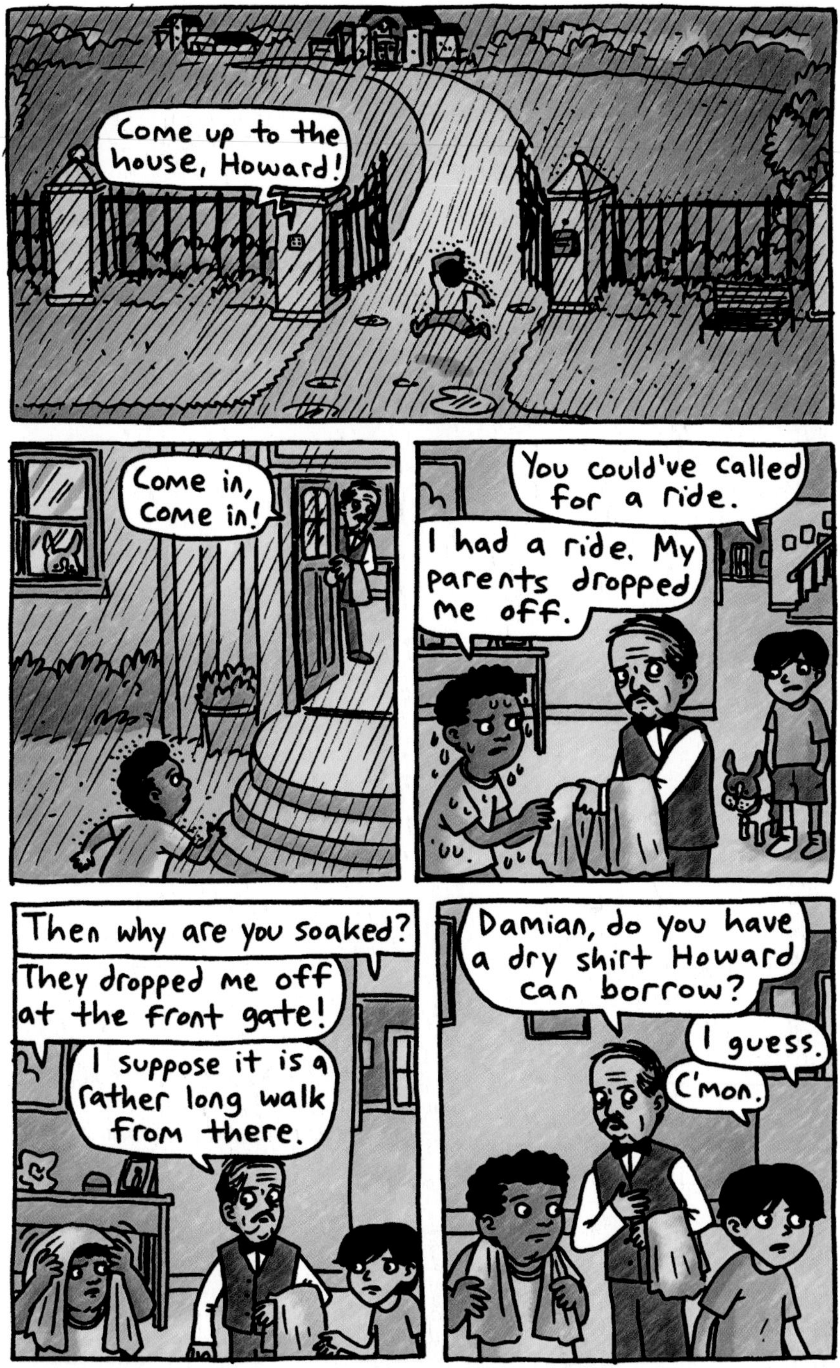
Come up to the house, Howard!
Come in, come in!
You could've called for a ride.
I had a ride. My parents dropped me off.
Then why are you soaked?
They dropped me off at the front gate!
I suppose it is a rather long walk from there.
Damian, do you have a dry shirt Howard can borrow?
I guess.
C'mon.

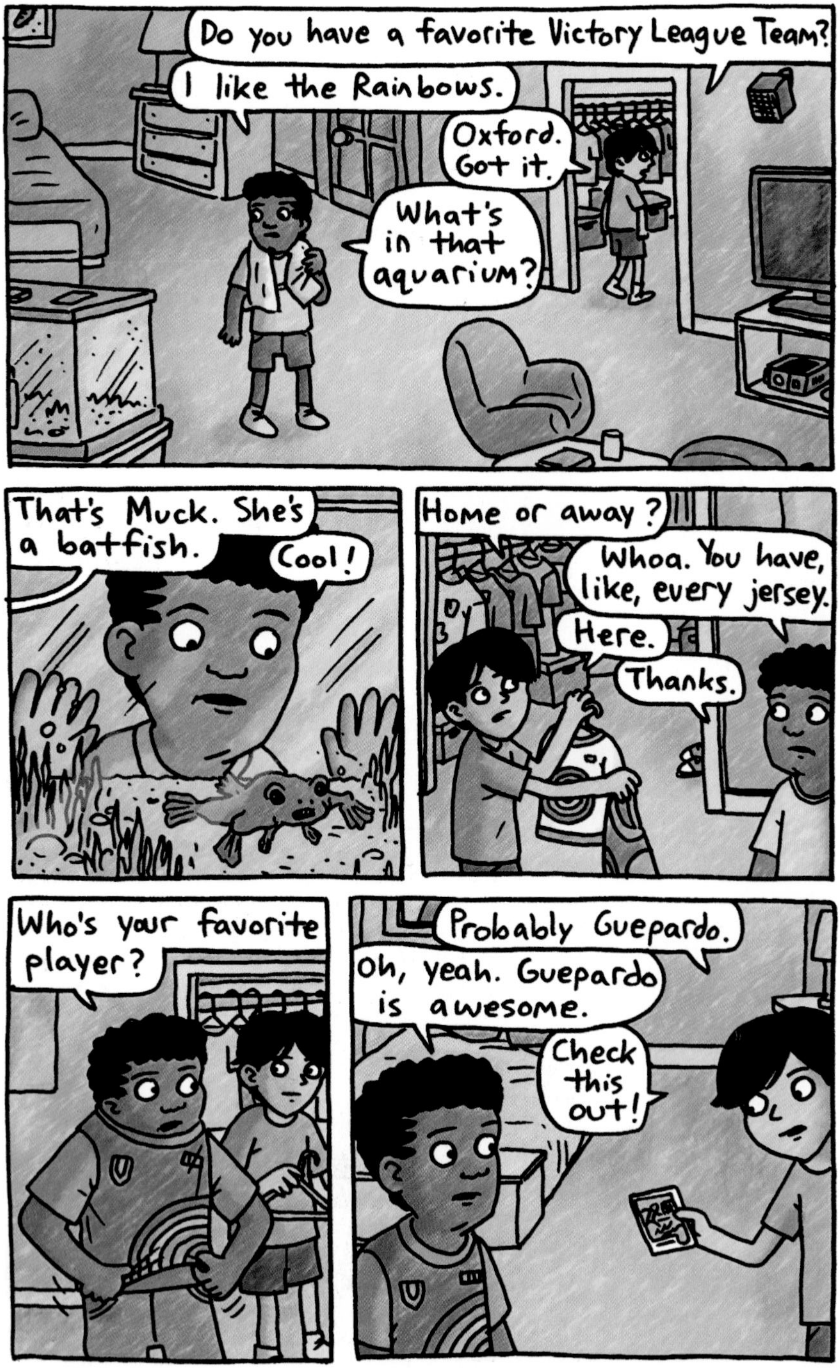
Do you have a favorite Victory League Team?
I like the Rainbows.
Oxford. Got it.
What's in that aquarium?
That's Muck. She's a batfish.
Cool!
Home or away?
Whoa. You have, like, every jersey.
Here.
Thanks.
Who's your favorite player?
Probably Guepardo.
Oh, yeah. Guepardo is awesome.
Check this out!

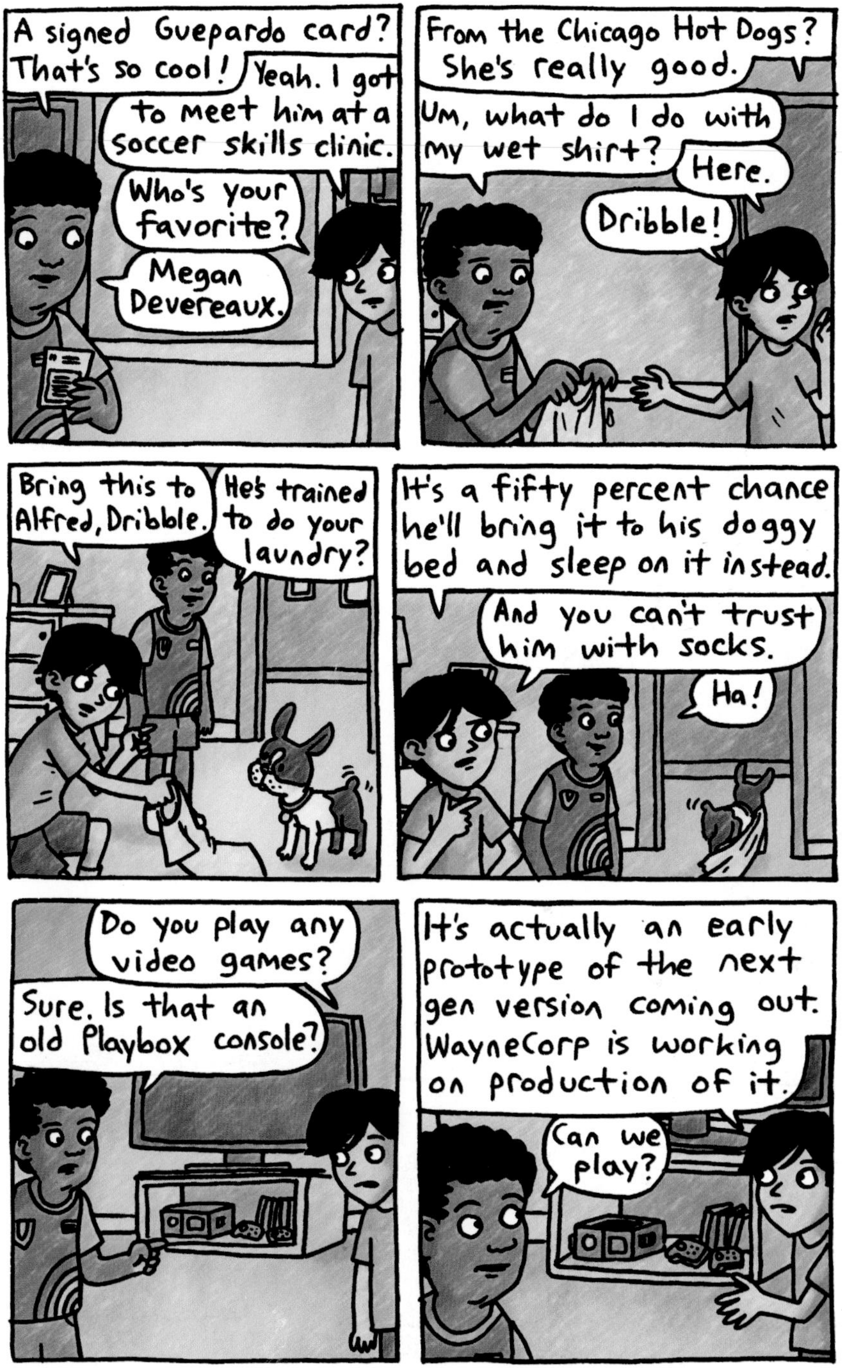
A signed Guepardo card? That's so cool!
Yeah. I got to meet him at a soccer skills clinic.
Who's your favorite?
Megan Devereaux.
From the Chicago Hot Dogs? She's really good.
Um, what do I do with my wet shirt?
Here.
Dribble!
Bring this to Alfred, Dribble.
He's trained to do your laundry?
It's a fifty percent chance he'll bring it to his doggy bed and sleep on it instead.
And you can't trust him with socks.
Ha!
Do you play any video games?
Sure. Is that an old Playbox console?
It's actually an early prototype of the next gen version coming out. WayneCorp is working on production of it.
Can we play?

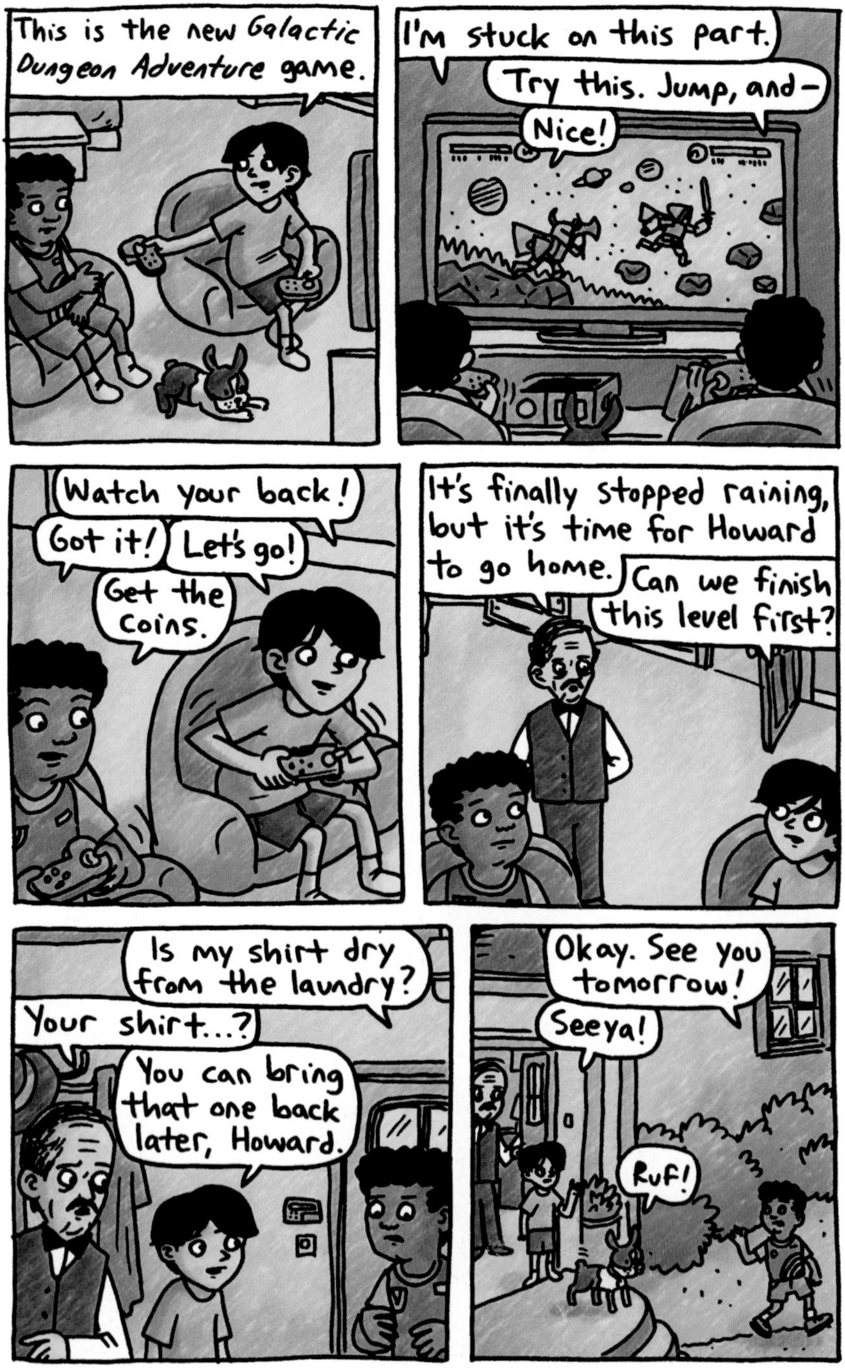
This is the new Galactic Dungeon Adventure game.
I'm stuck on this part.
Try this. Jump, and—
Nice!
Watch your back!
Got it!
Let's go!
Get the coins.
It's finally stopped raining, but it's time for Howard to go home.
Can we finish this level first?
Is my shirt dry from the laundry?
Your shirt...?
You can bring that one back later, Howard.
Okay. See you tomorrow!
Seeya!
Ruf!

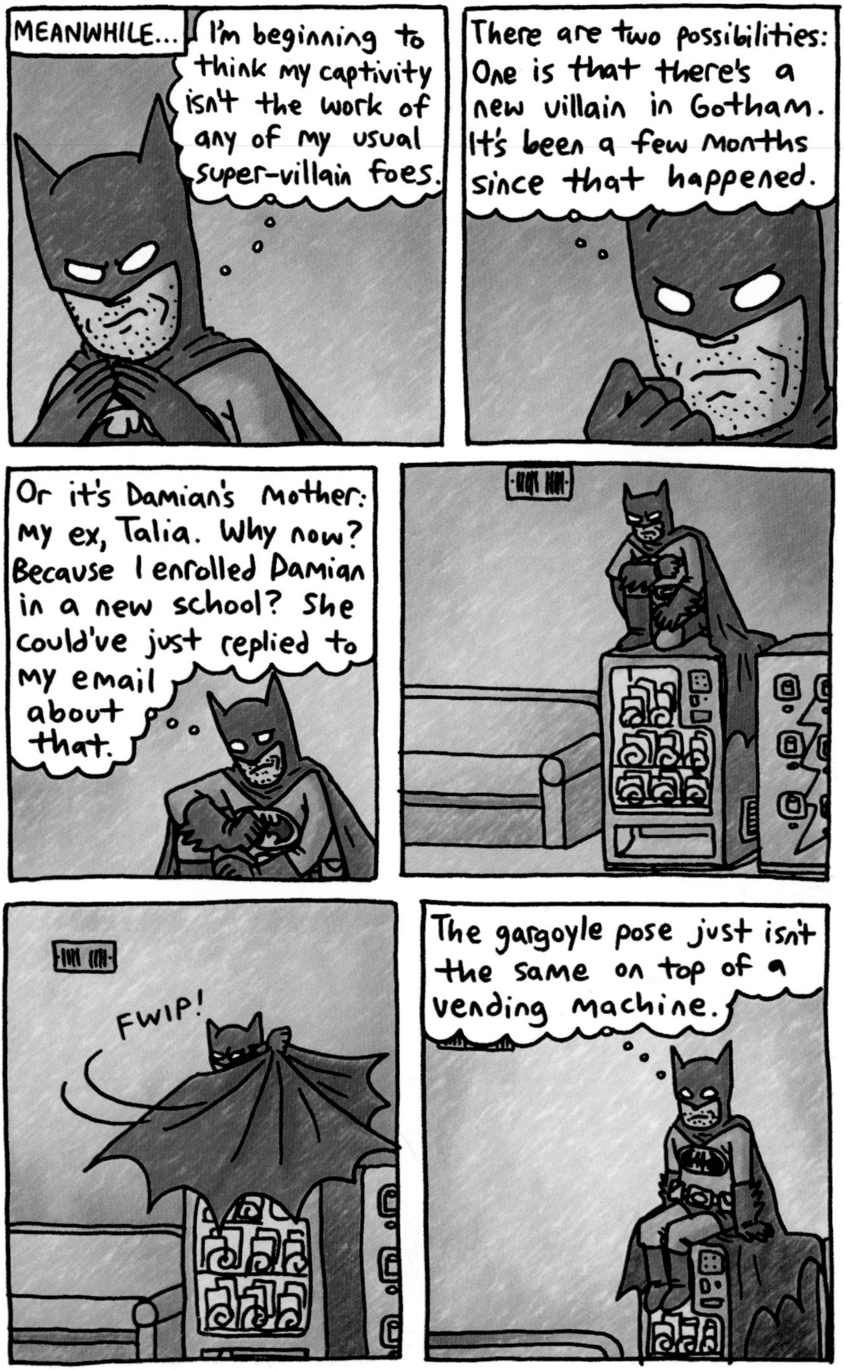
MEANWHILE...
I'm beginning to think my captivity isn't the work of any of my usual super-villain foes.
There are two possibilities: One is that there's a new villain in Gotham. It's been a few months since that happened.
Or it's Damian's mother: my ex, Talia. Why now? Because I enrolled Damian in a new school? She could've just replied to my email about that.
FWIP!
The gargoyle pose just isn't the same on top of a vending machine.

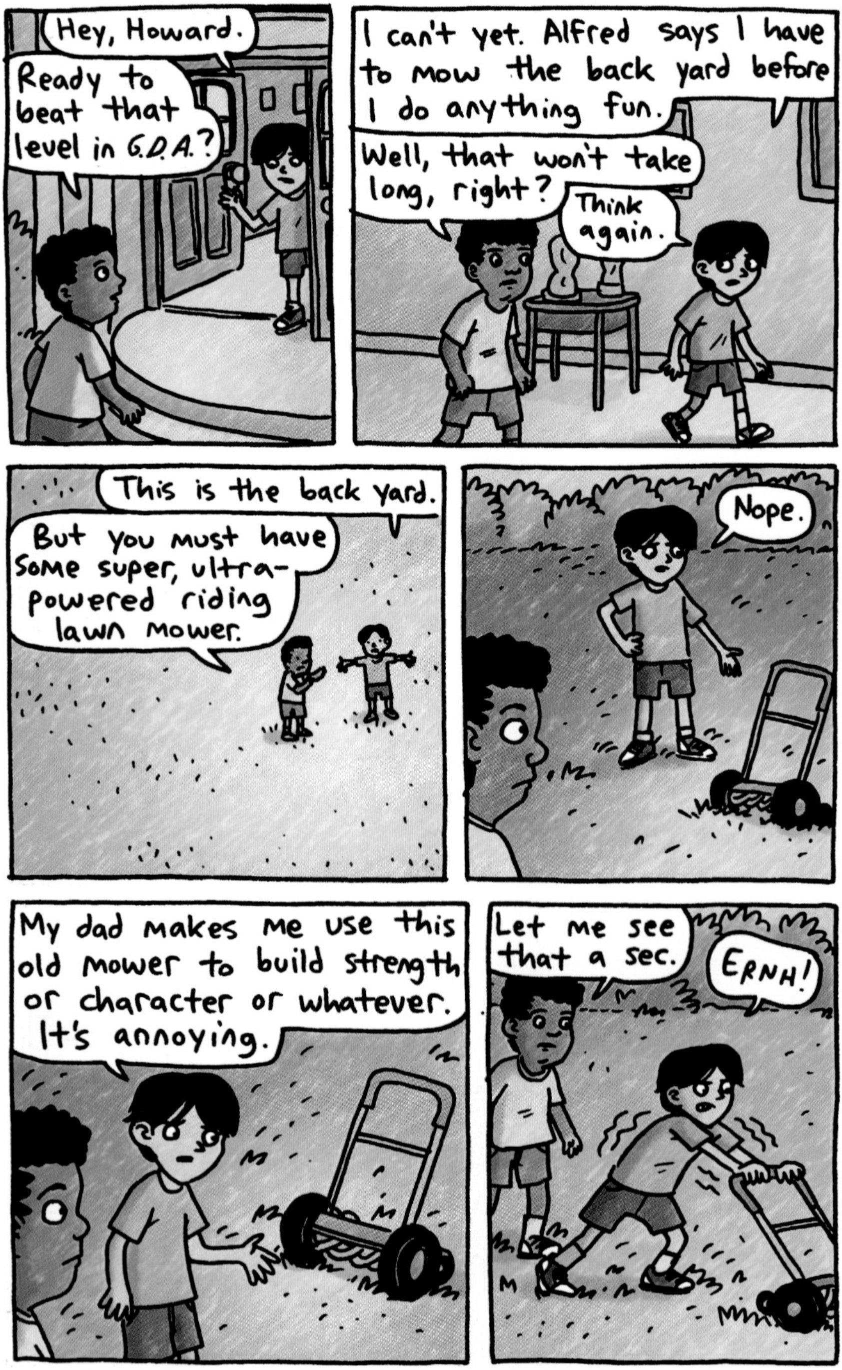
Hey, Howard.
Ready to beat that level in G.D.A.?
I can't yet. Alfred says I have to mow the back yard before I do anything fun.
Well, that won't take long, right?
Think again.
This is the back yard.
But you must have some super, ultra-powered riding lawn mower.
Nope.
My dad makes me use this old mower to build strength or character or whatever. It's annoying.
Let me see that a sec.
ERNH!

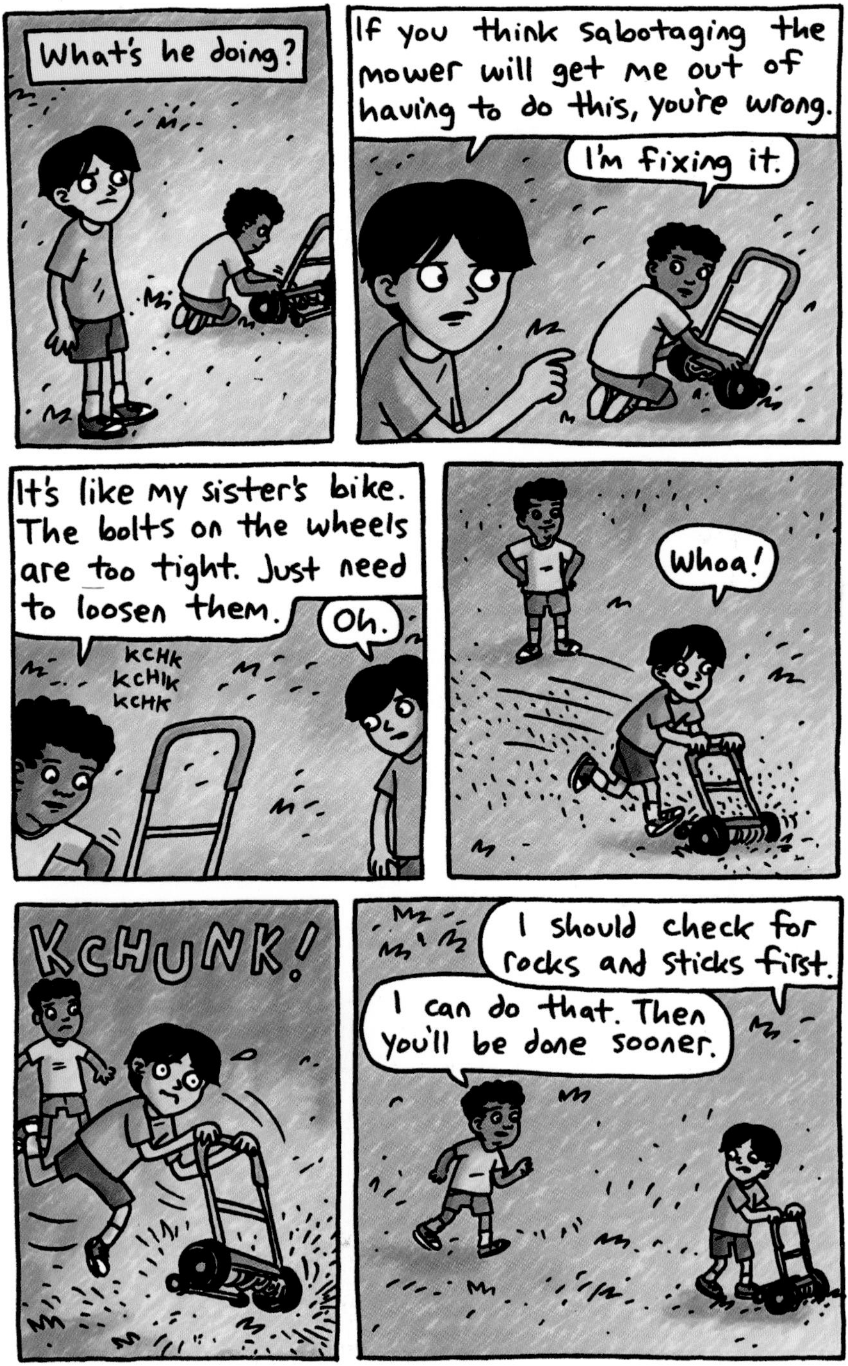
What's he doing?
If you think sabotaging the mower will get me out of having to do this, you're wrong.
I'm fixing it.
It's like my sister's bike. The bolts on the wheels are too tight. Just need to loosen them.
KCHK KCHK KCHK
Oh.
Whoa!
KCHUNK!
I should check for rocks and sticks first.
I can do that. Then you'll be done sooner.

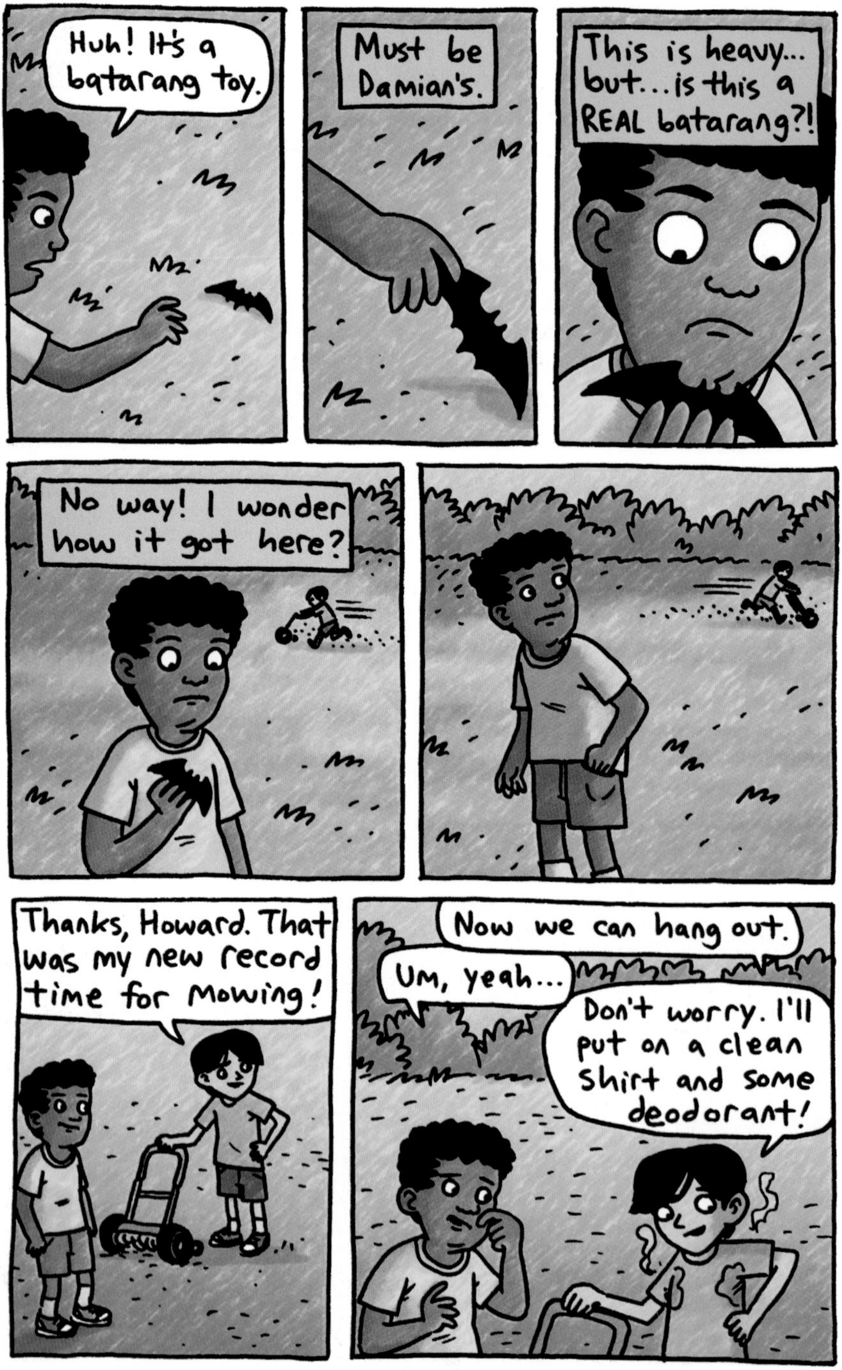
Huh! It's a batarang toy.
Must be Damian's.
This is heavy... but... is this a REAL batarang?!
No way! I wonder how it got here?
Thanks, Howard. That was my new record time for mowing!
Now we can hang out.
Um, yeah...
Don't worry. I'll put on a clean shirt and some deodorant!

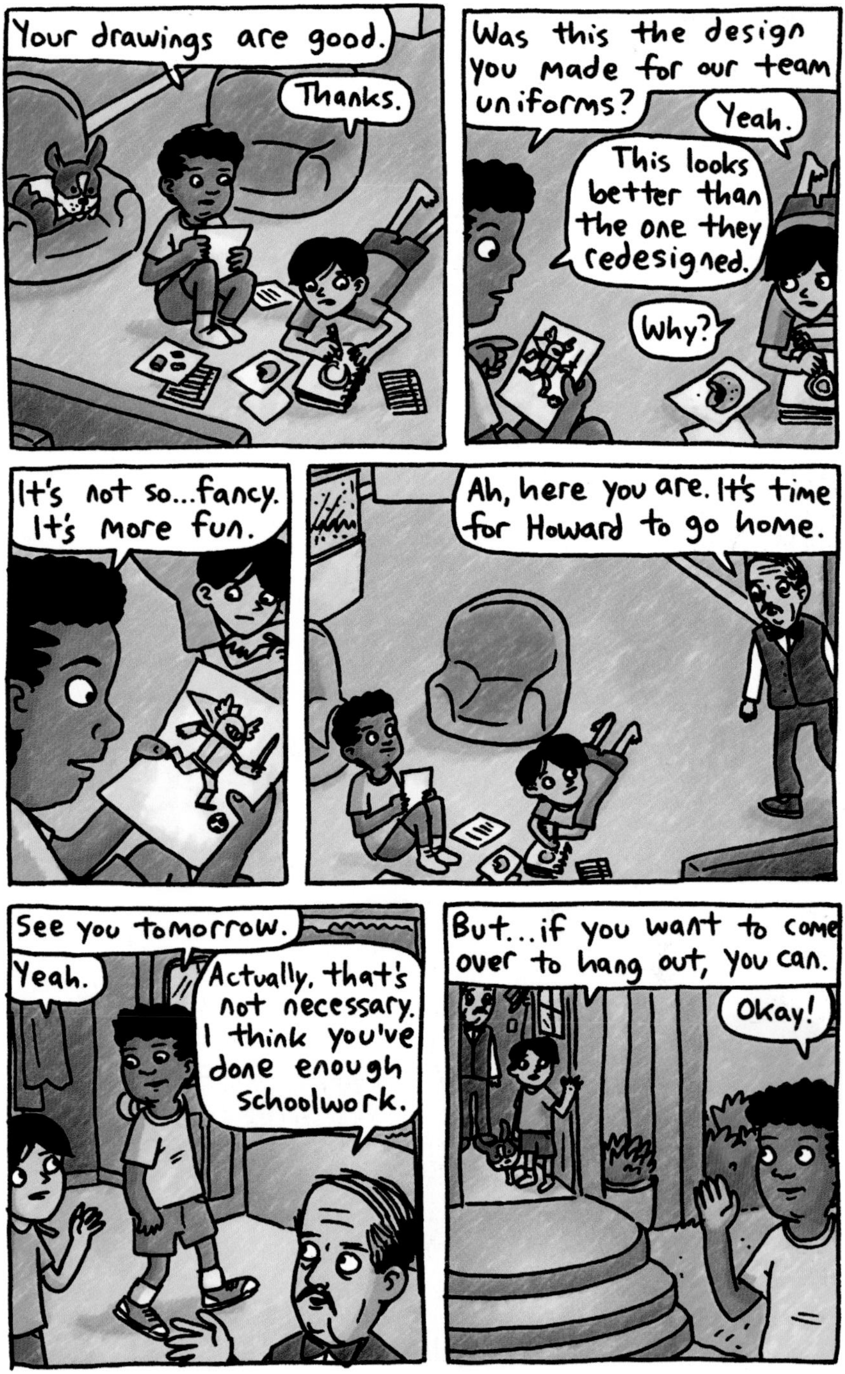
Your drawings are good.
Thanks.
Was this the design you made for our team uniforms?
Yeah.
This looks better than the one they redesigned.
Why?
It's not so...fancy. It's more fun.
Ah, here you are. It's time for Howard to go home.
See you tomorrow.
Yeah.
Actually, that's not necessary. I think you've done enough schoolwork.
But...if you want to come over to hang out, you can.
Okay!

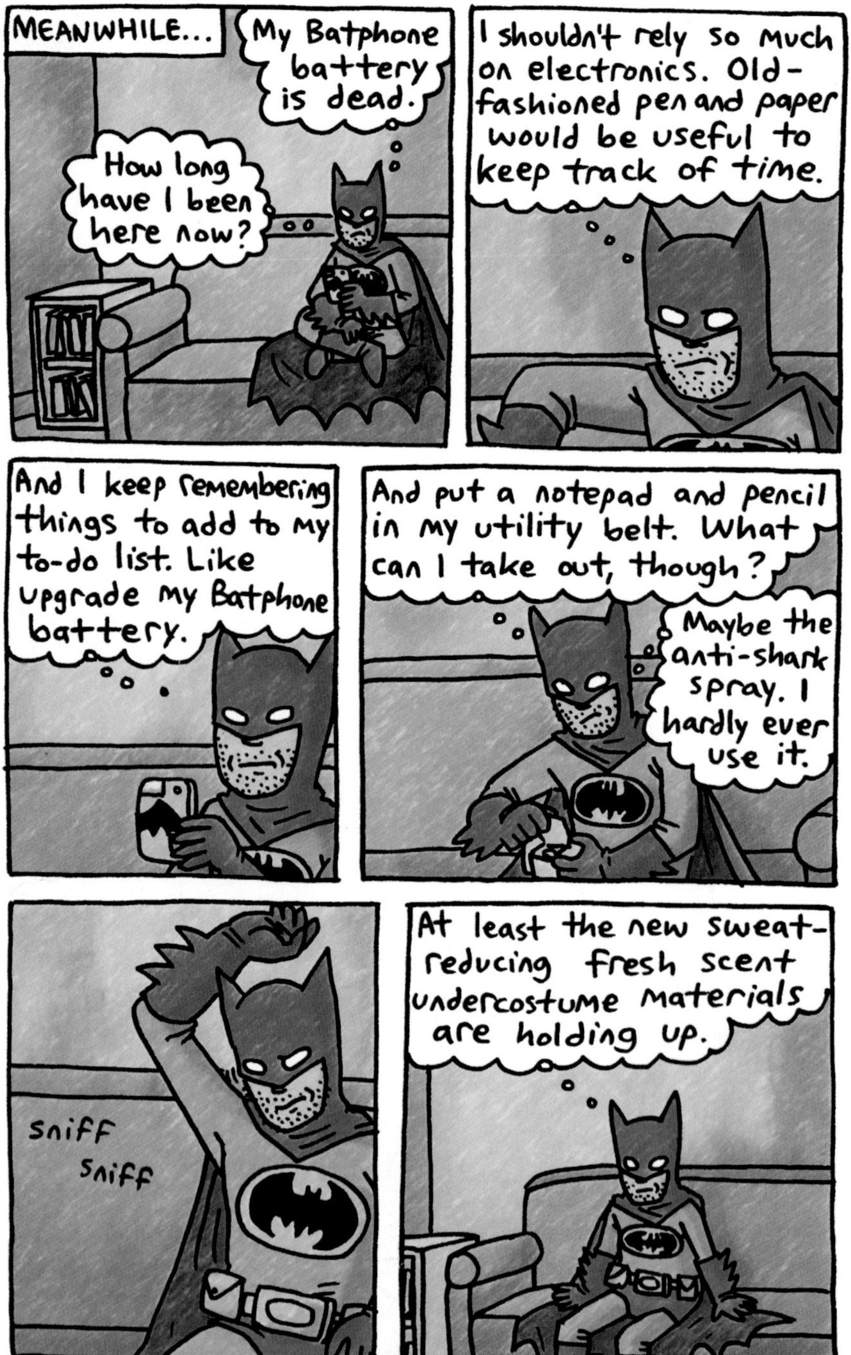
MEANWHILE...
My Batphone battery is dead.
How long have I been here now?
I shouldn't rely so much on electronics. Old-fashioned pen and paper would be useful to keep track of time.
And I keep remembering things to add to my to-do list. Like upgrade my Batphone battery.
And put a notepad and pencil in my utility belt. What can I take out, though?
Maybe the anti-shark spray. I hardly ever use it.
sniff
sniff
At least the new sweat-reducing fresh scent undercostume materials are holding up.

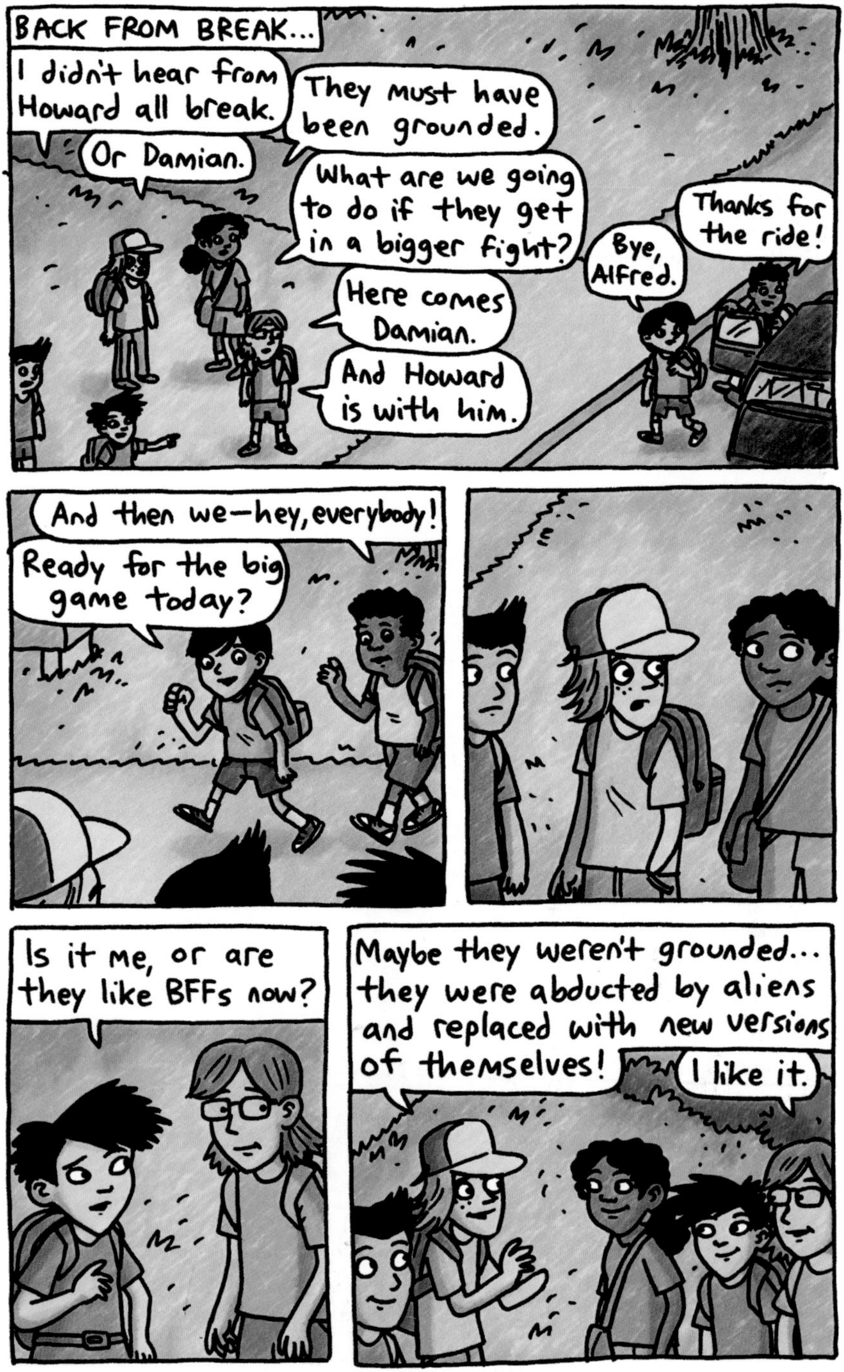
BACK FROM BREAK...
I didn't hear from Howard all break.
Or Damian.
They must have been grounded.
What are we going to do if they get in a bigger fight?
Here comes Damian.
And Howard is with him.
Bye, Alfred.
Thanks for the ride!
And then we—hey, everybody!
Ready for the big game today?
Is it me, or are they like BFFs now?
Maybe they weren't grounded... they were abducted by aliens and replaced with new versions of themselves!
I like it.

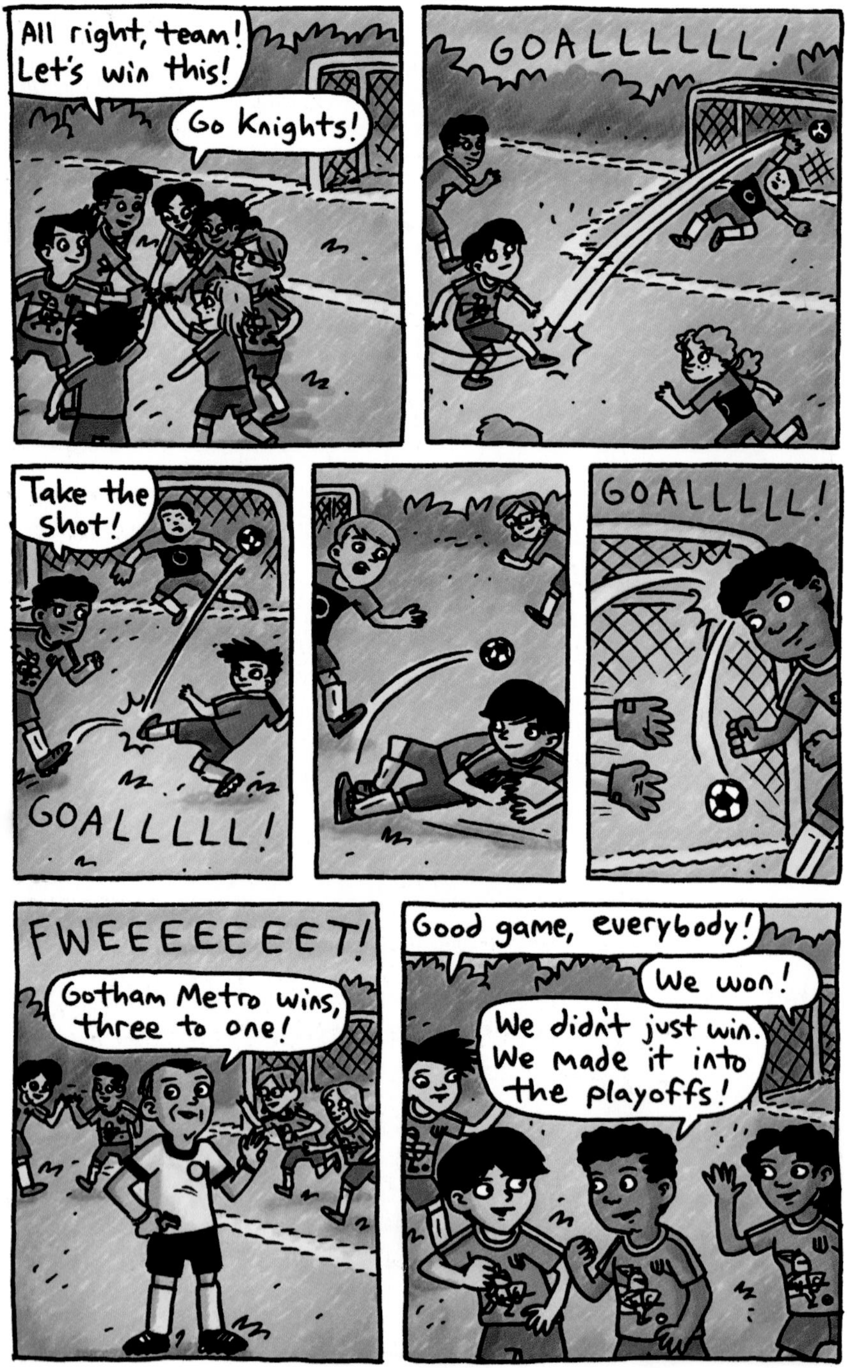
All right, team! Let's win this!
Go Knights!
GOALLLLLL!
Take the shot!
GOALLLLL!
GOALLLLL!
FWEEEEEEET!
Gotham Metro wins, three to one!
Good game, everybody!
We won!
We didn't just win. We made it into the playoffs!

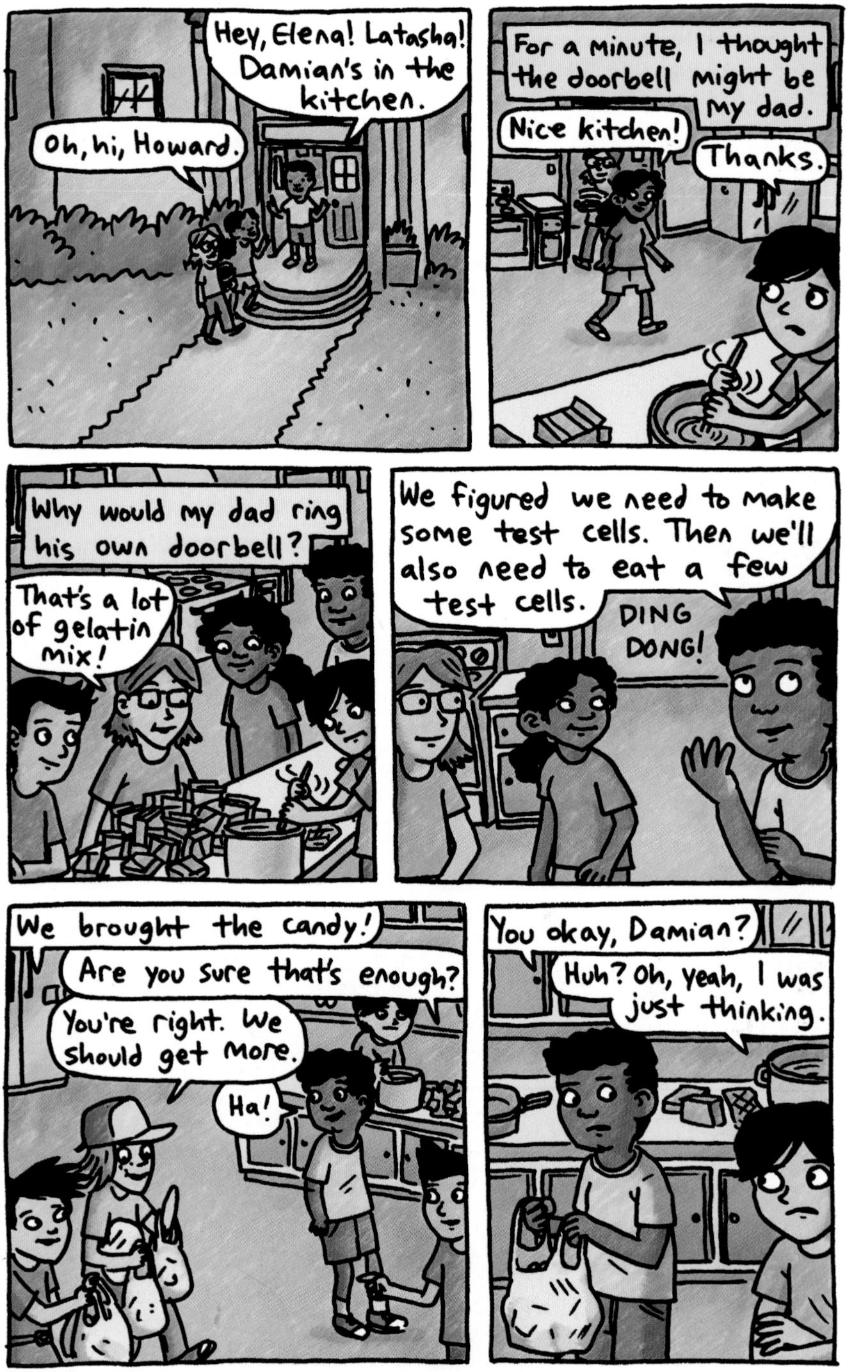
Hey, Elena! Latasha! Damian's in the kitchen.
Oh, hi, Howard.
For a minute, I thought the doorbell might be my dad.
Nice kitchen!
Thanks.
Why would my dad ring his own doorbell?
That's a lot of gelatin mix!
We figured we need to make some test cells. Then we'll also need to eat a few test cells.
DING DONG!
We brought the candy!
Are you sure that's enough?
You're right. We should get more.
Ha!
You okay, Damian?
Huh? Oh, yeah, I was just thinking.

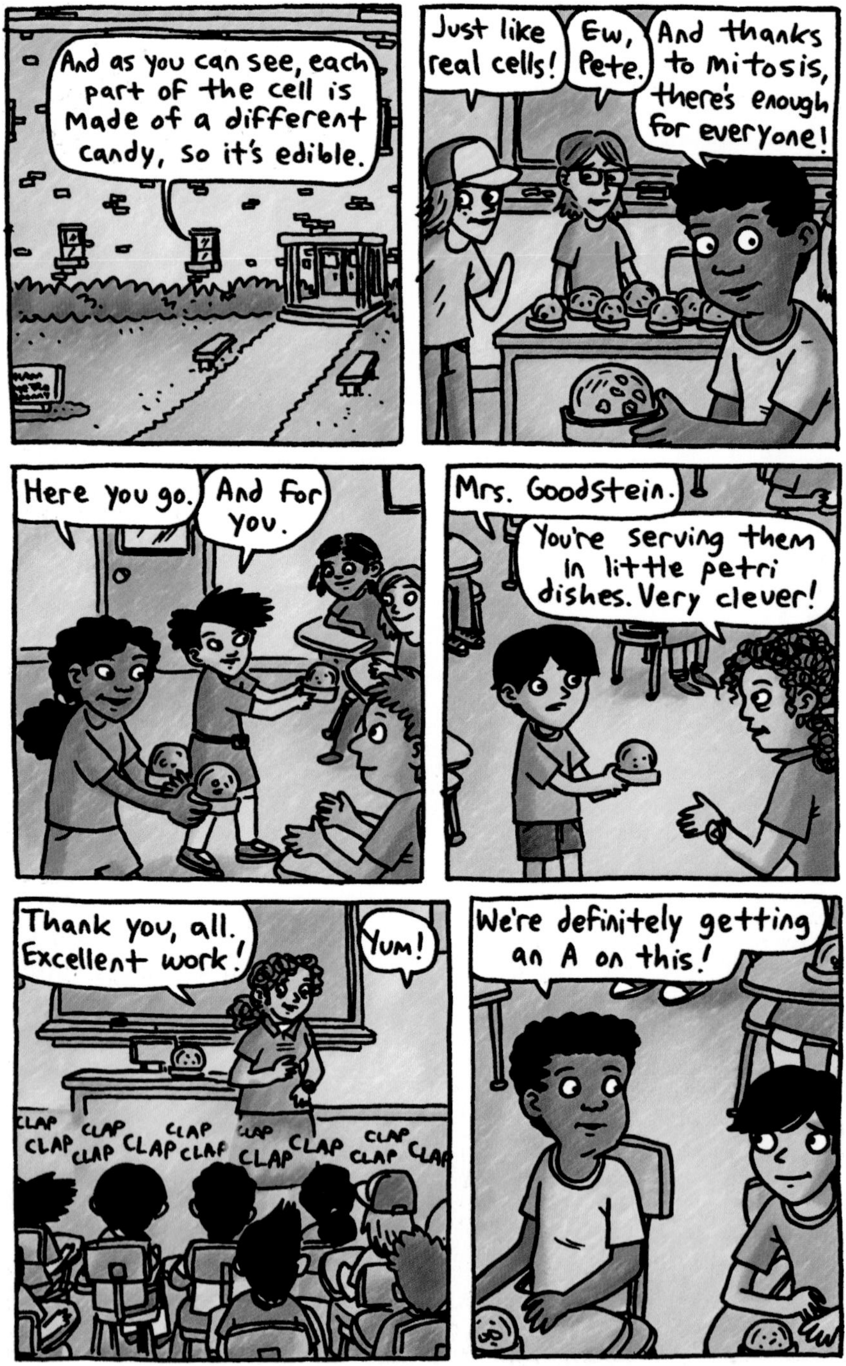
And as you can see, each part of the cell is made of a different candy, so it's edible.
Just like real cells!
Ew, Pete.
And thanks to mitosis, there's enough for everyone!
Here you go.
And for you.
Mrs. Goodstein.
You're serving them in little petri dishes. Very clever!
Thank you, all. Excellent work!
Yum!
CLAP CLAP CLAP CLAP CLAP CLAP CLAP CLAP CLAP CLAP CLAP CLAP CLAP
We're definitely getting an A on this!

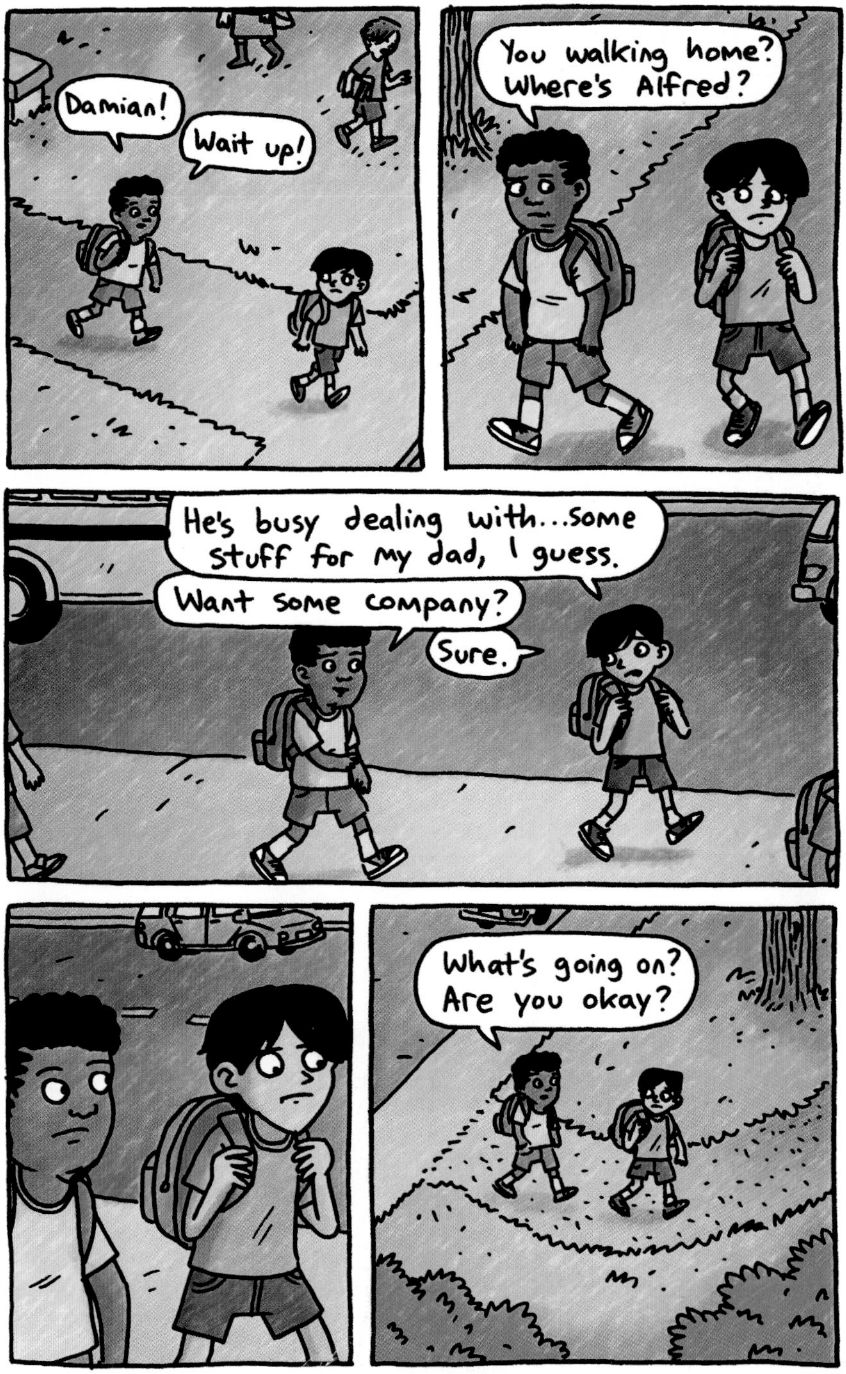
Damian!
Wait up!
You walking home? Where's Alfred?
He's busy dealing with...some stuff for my dad, I guess.
Want some company?
Sure.
What's going on? Are you okay?

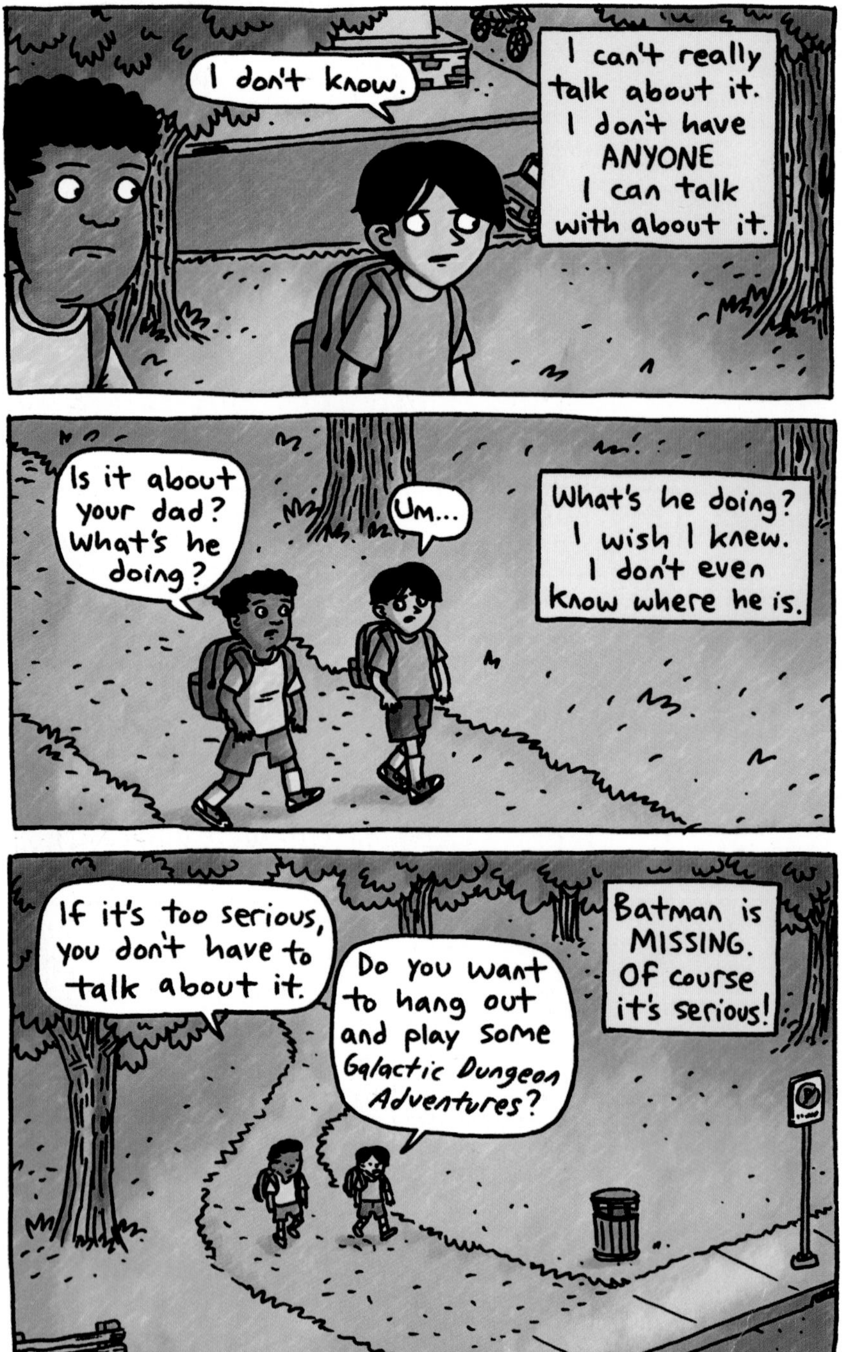
I don't know.
I can't really talk about it. I don't have ANYONE I can talk with about it.
Is it about your dad? What's he doing?
Um...
What's he doing? I wish I knew. I don't even know where he is.
If it's too serious, you don't have to talk about it.
Do you want to hang out and play some *Galactic Dungeon Adventures*?
Batman is MISSING. Of course it's serious!

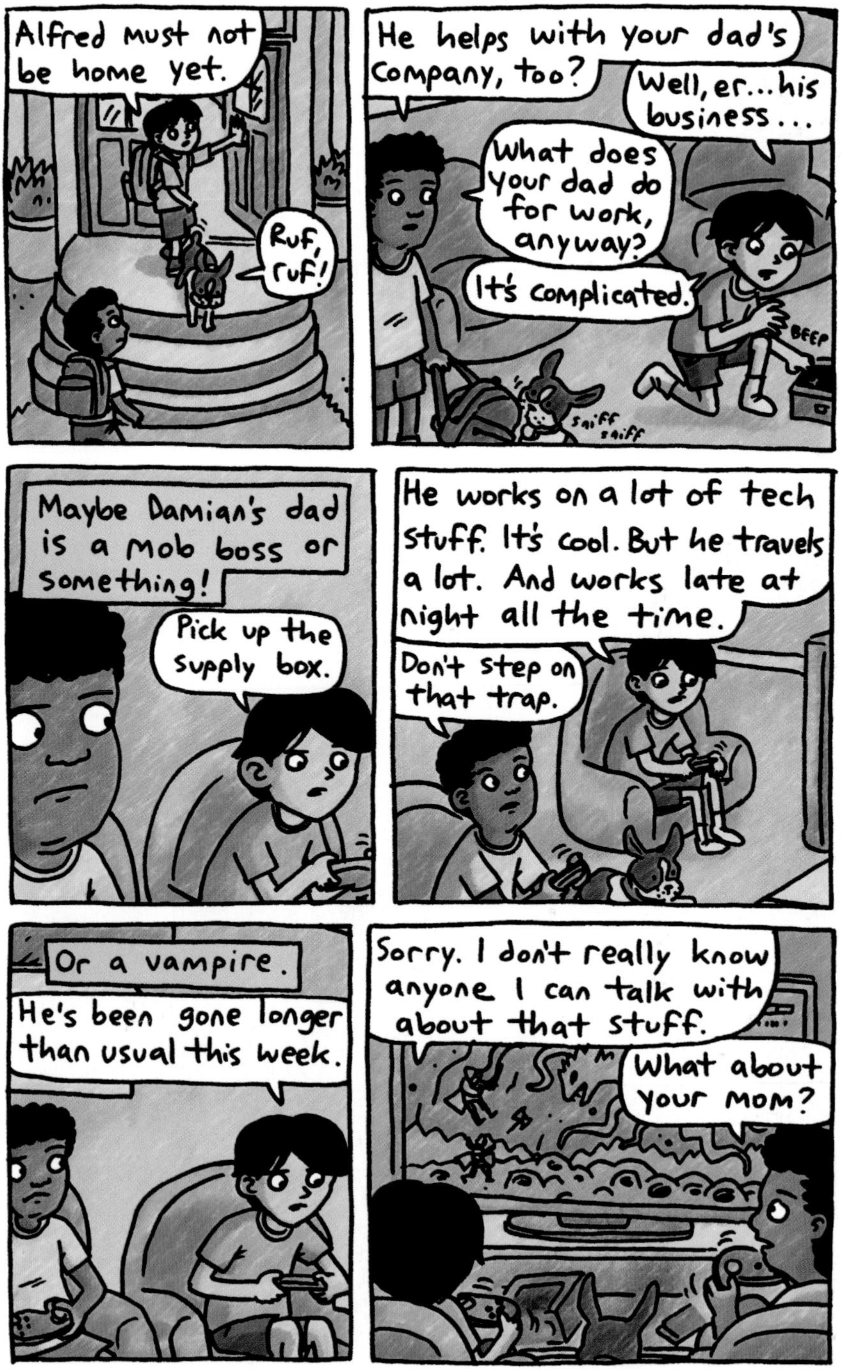
Alfred must not be home yet.
Ruf, ruf!
He helps with your dad's company, too?
Well, er... his business...
What does your dad do for work, anyway?
It's complicated.
BEEP
SNIFF SNIFF
Maybe Damian's dad is a mob boss or something!
Pick up the supply box.
He works on a lot of tech stuff. It's cool. But he travels a lot. And works late at night all the time.
Don't step on that trap.
Or a vampire.
He's been gone longer than usual this week.
Sorry. I don't really know anyone I can talk with about that stuff.
What about your mom?

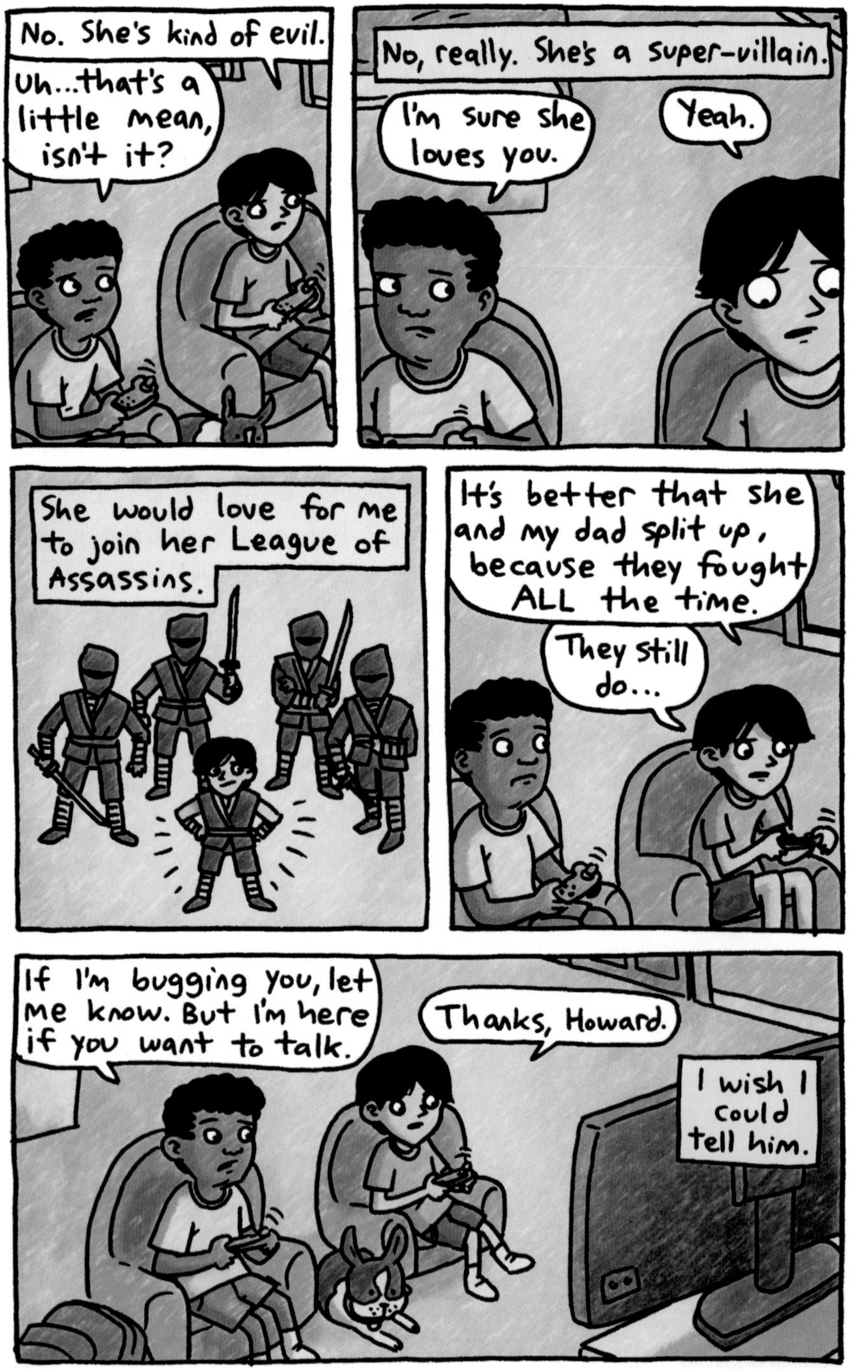
No. She's kind of evil.
Uh...that's a little mean, isn't it?
No, really. She's a super-villain.
I'm sure she loves you.
Yeah.
She would love for me to join her League of Assassins.
It's better that she and my dad split up, because they fought ALL the time.
They still do...
If I'm bugging you, let me know. But I'm here if you want to talk.
Thanks, Howard.
I wish I could tell him.

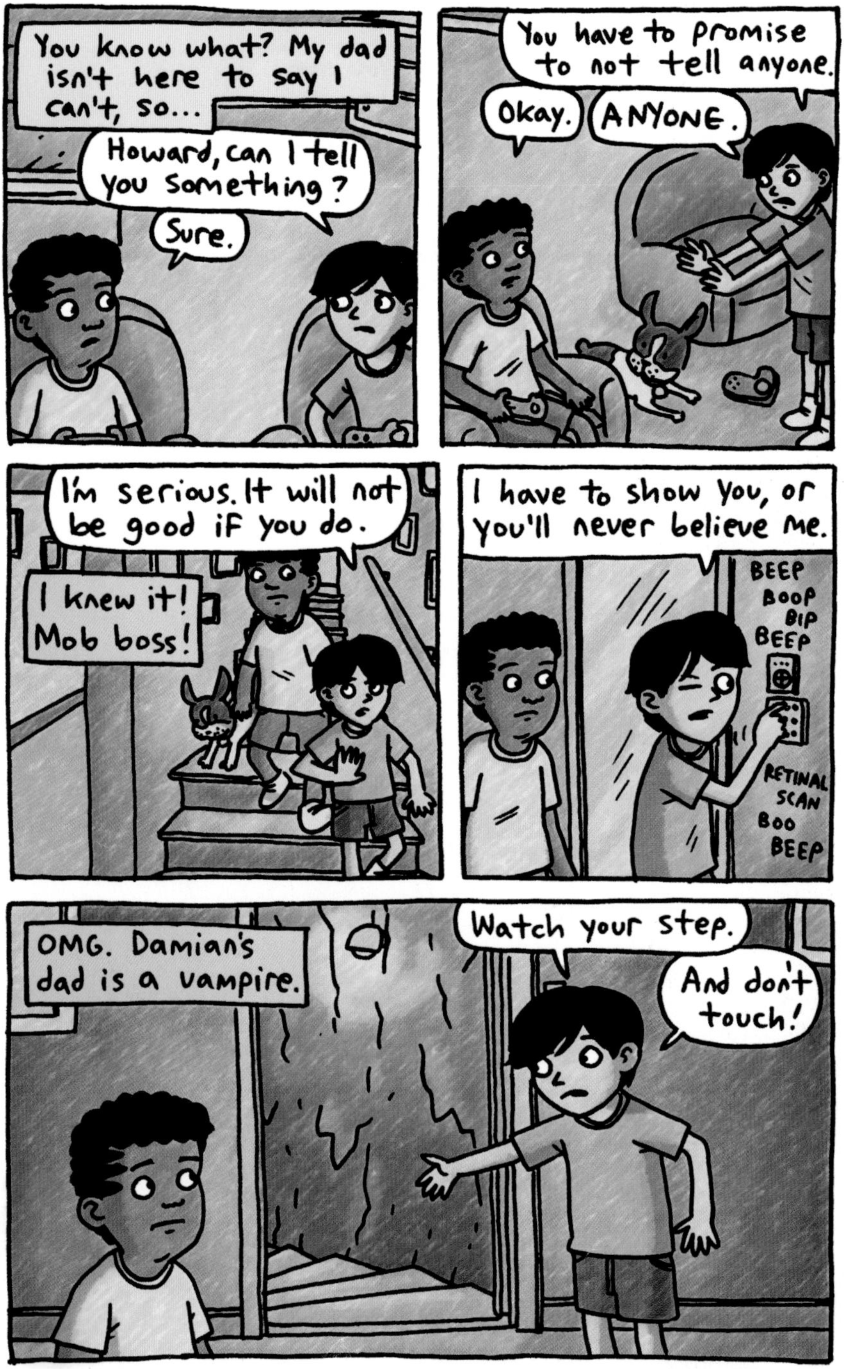

You know what? My dad isn't here to say I can't, so...
Howard, can I tell you something?
Sure.
You have to promise to not tell anyone.
Okay.
ANYONE.
I'm serious. It will not be good if you do.
I knew it! Mob boss!
I have to show you, or you'll never believe me.
BEEP
BOOP
BIP
BEEP
RETINAL SCAN
BOO
BEEP
OMG. Damian's dad is a vampire.
Watch your step.
And don't touch!

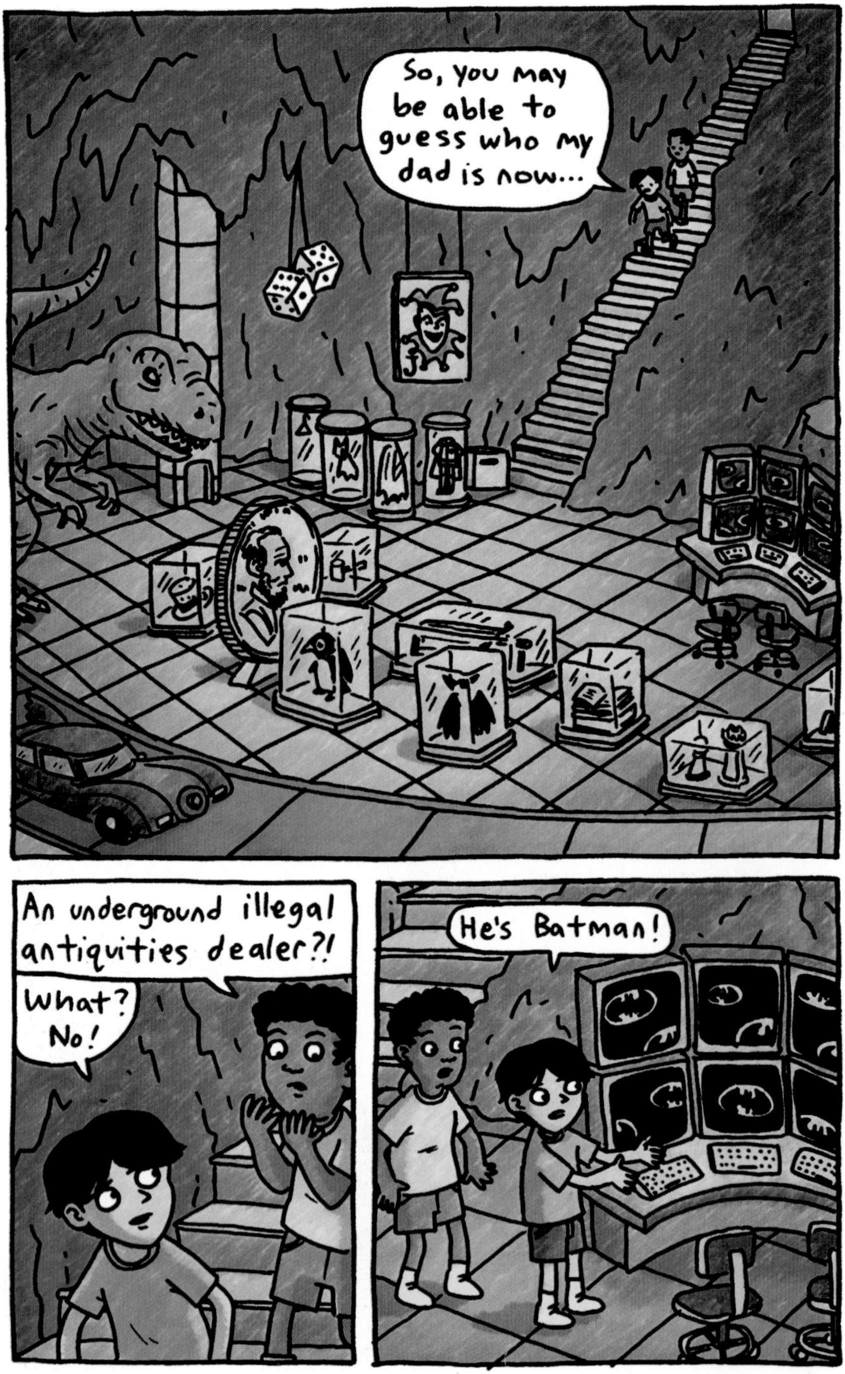
So, you may be able to guess who my dad is now...
An underground illegal antiquities dealer?!
What? No!
He's Batman!

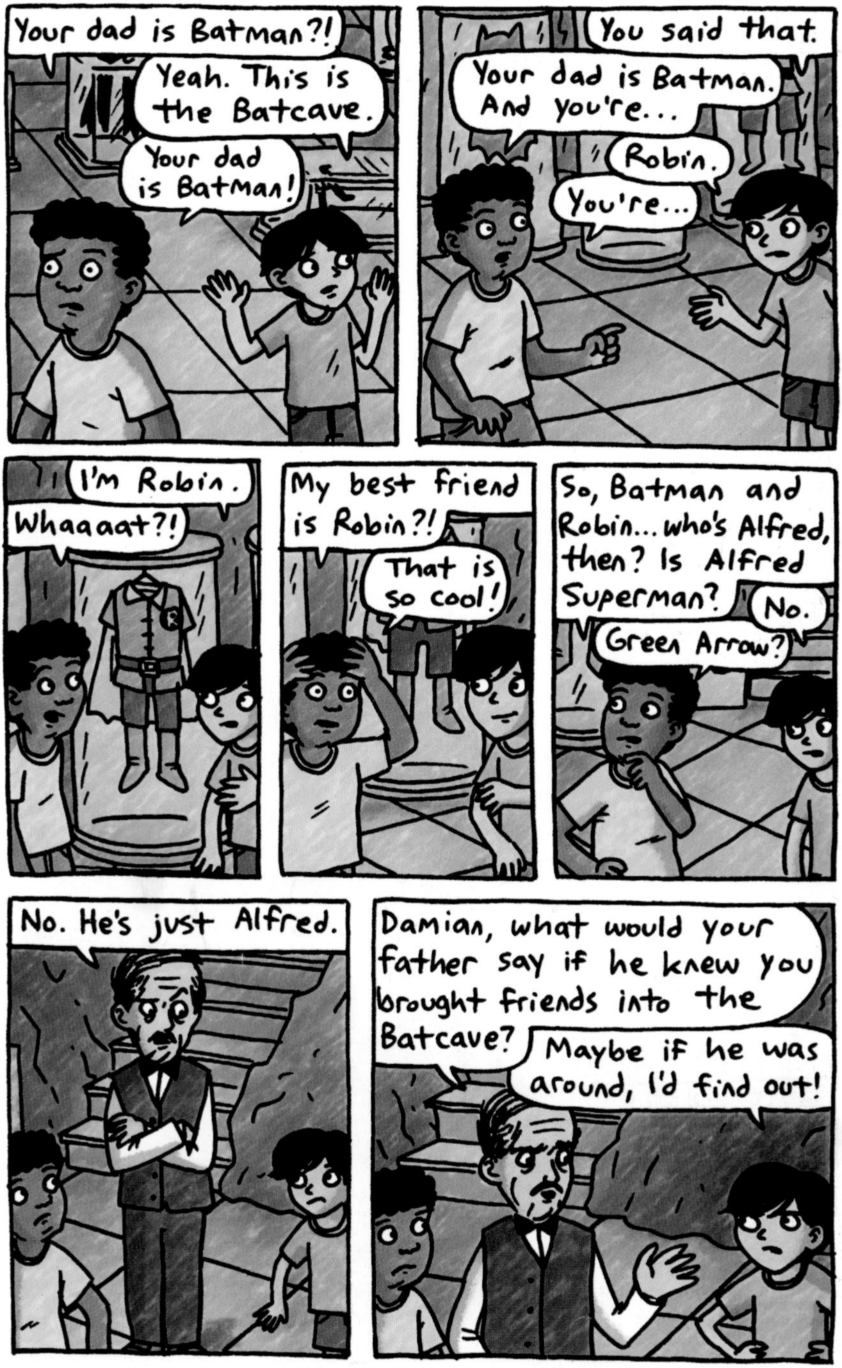
Your dad is Batman?!
Yeah. This is the Batcave.
Your dad is Batman!
You said that.
Your dad is Batman. And you're...
Robin.
You're...
I'm Robin.
Whaaaat?!
My best friend is Robin?!
That is so cool!
So, Batman and Robin... who's Alfred, then? Is Alfred Superman?
No.
Green Arrow?
No. He's just Alfred.
Damian, what would your father say if he knew you brought friends into the Batcave?
Maybe if he was around, I'd find out!

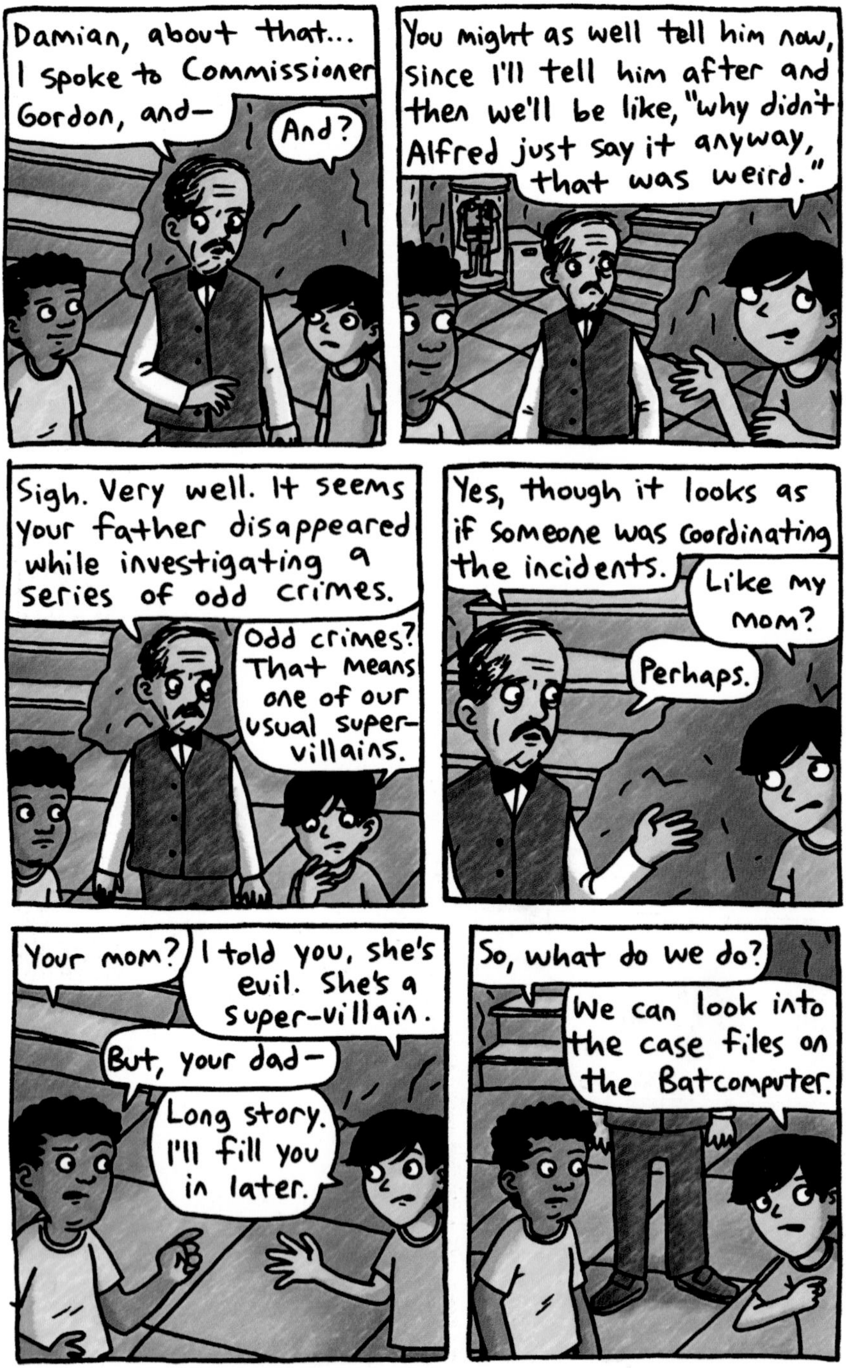
Damian, about that... I spoke to Commissioner Gordon, and—
And?
You might as well tell him now, since I'll tell him after and then we'll be like, "why didn't Alfred just say it anyway, that was weird."
Sigh. Very well. It seems your father disappeared while investigating a series of odd crimes.
Odd crimes? That means one of our usual super-villains.
Yes, though it looks as if someone was coordinating the incidents.
Like my mom?
Perhaps.
Your mom?
I told you, she's evil. She's a super-villain.
But, your dad—
Long story. I'll fill you in later.
So, what do we do?
We can look into the case files on the Batcomputer.

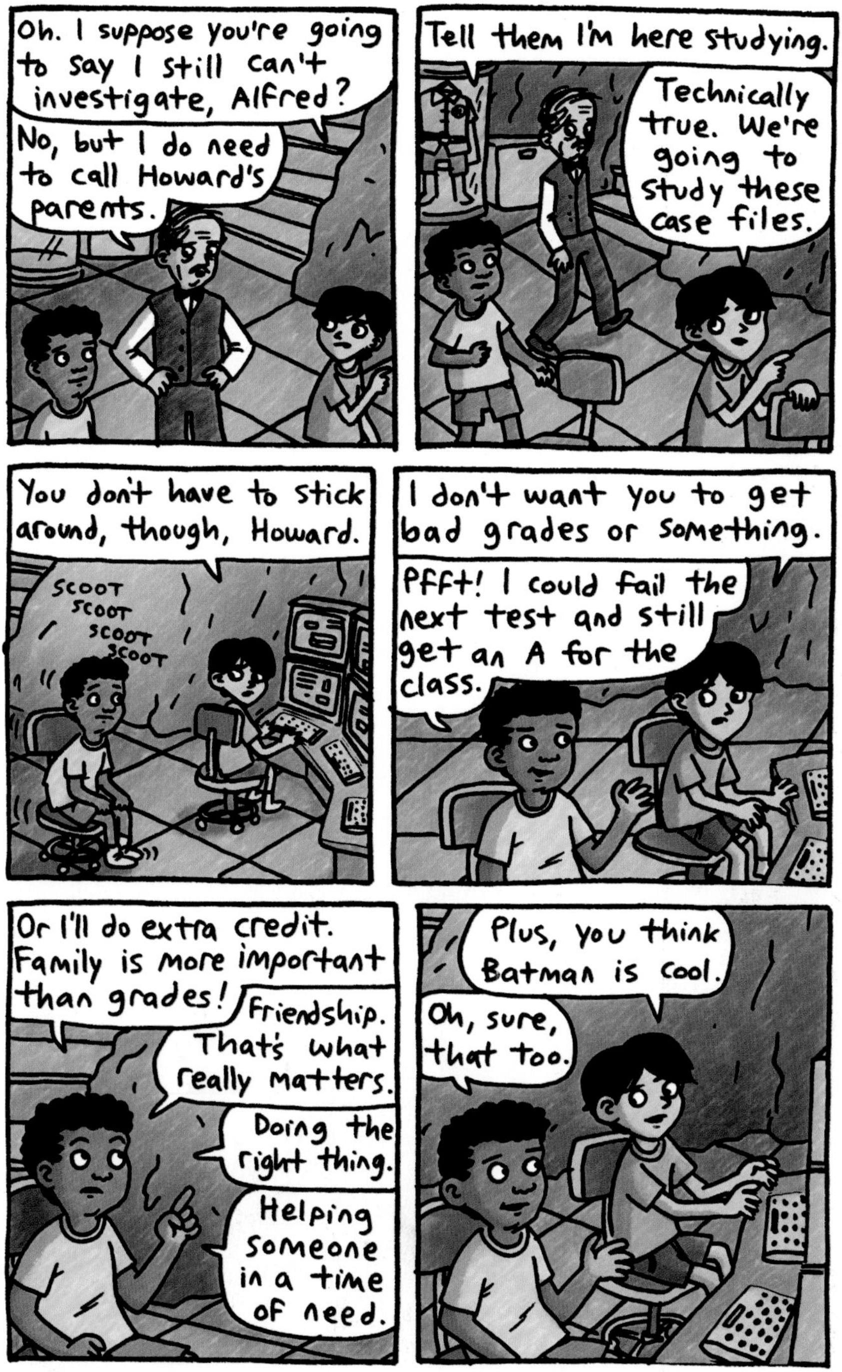
Oh. I suppose you're going to say I still can't investigate, Alfred?
No, but I do need to call Howard's parents.
Tell them I'm here studying.
Technically true. We're going to study these case files.
You don't have to stick around, though, Howard.
SCOOT SCOOT SCOOT SCOOT
I don't want you to get bad grades or something.
Pfft! I could fail the next test and still get an A for the class.
Or I'll do extra credit. Family is more important than grades!
Friendship. That's what really matters.
Doing the right thing.
Helping someone in a time of need.
Plus, you think Batman is cool.
Oh, sure, that too.

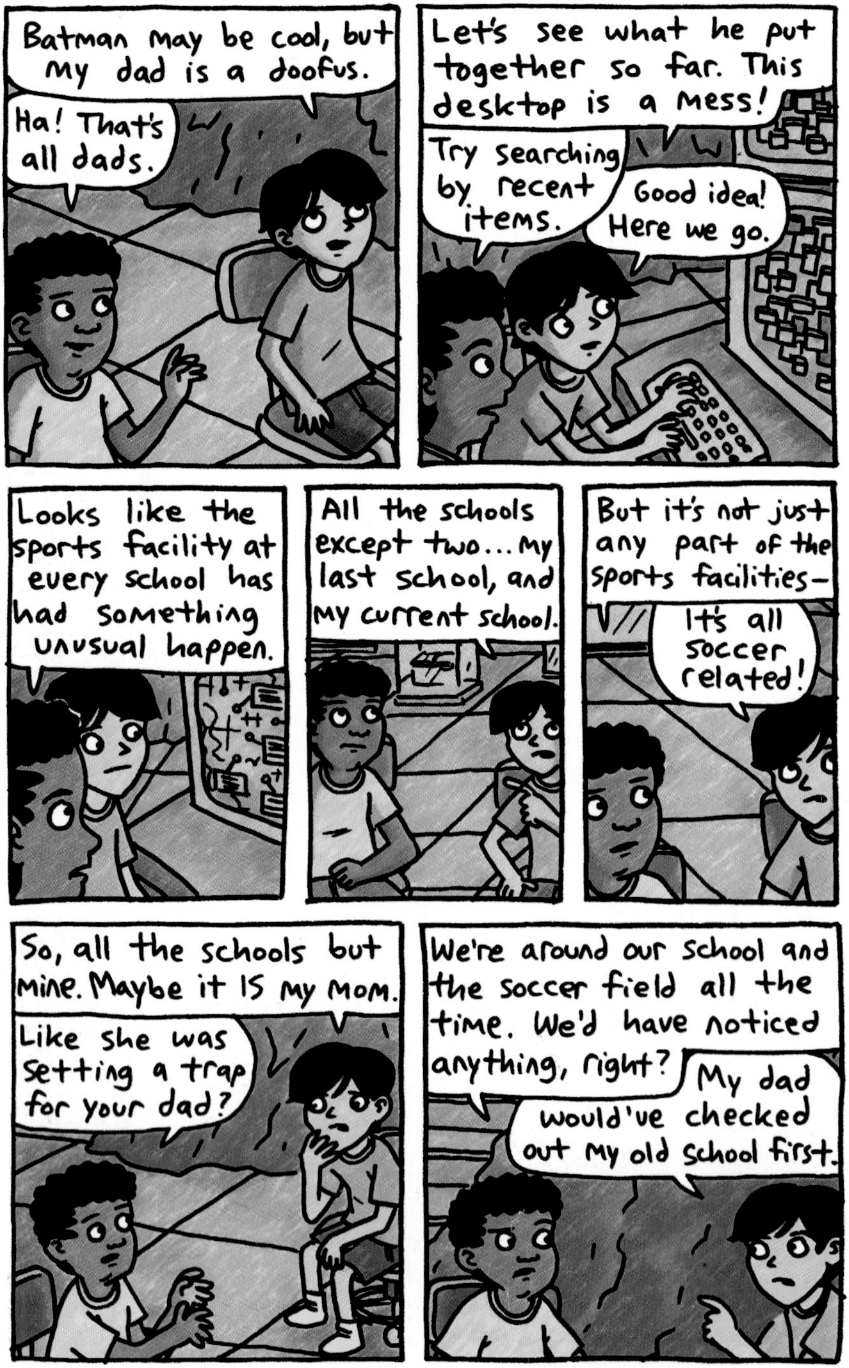
Batman may be cool, but my dad is a doofus.
Ha! That's all dads.
Let's see what he put together so far. This desktop is a mess!
Try searching by recent items.
Good idea! Here we go.
Looks like the sports facility at every school has had something unusual happen.
All the schools except two... my last school, and my current school.
But it's not just any part of the sports facilities—
It's all soccer related!
So, all the schools but mine. Maybe it IS my mom.
Like she was setting a trap for your dad?
We're around our school and the soccer field all the time. We'd have noticed anything, right?
My dad would've checked out my old school first.

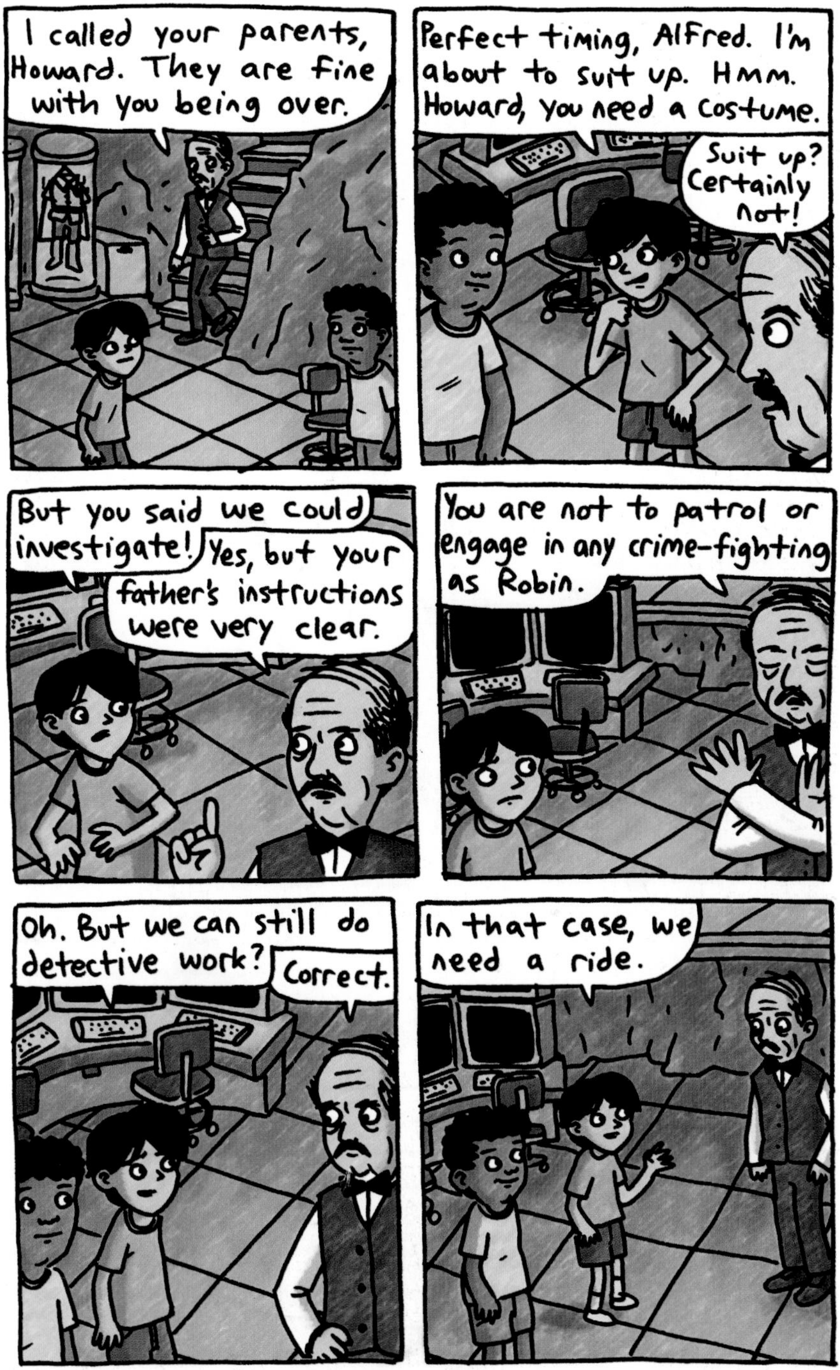
I called your parents, Howard. They are fine with you being over.
Perfect timing, Alfred. I'm about to suit up. HMM. Howard, you need a costume.
Suit up? Certainly not!
But you said we could investigate!
Yes, but your father's instructions were very clear.
You are not to patrol or engage in any crime-fighting as Robin.
Oh. But we can still do detective work?
Correct.
In that case, we need a ride.

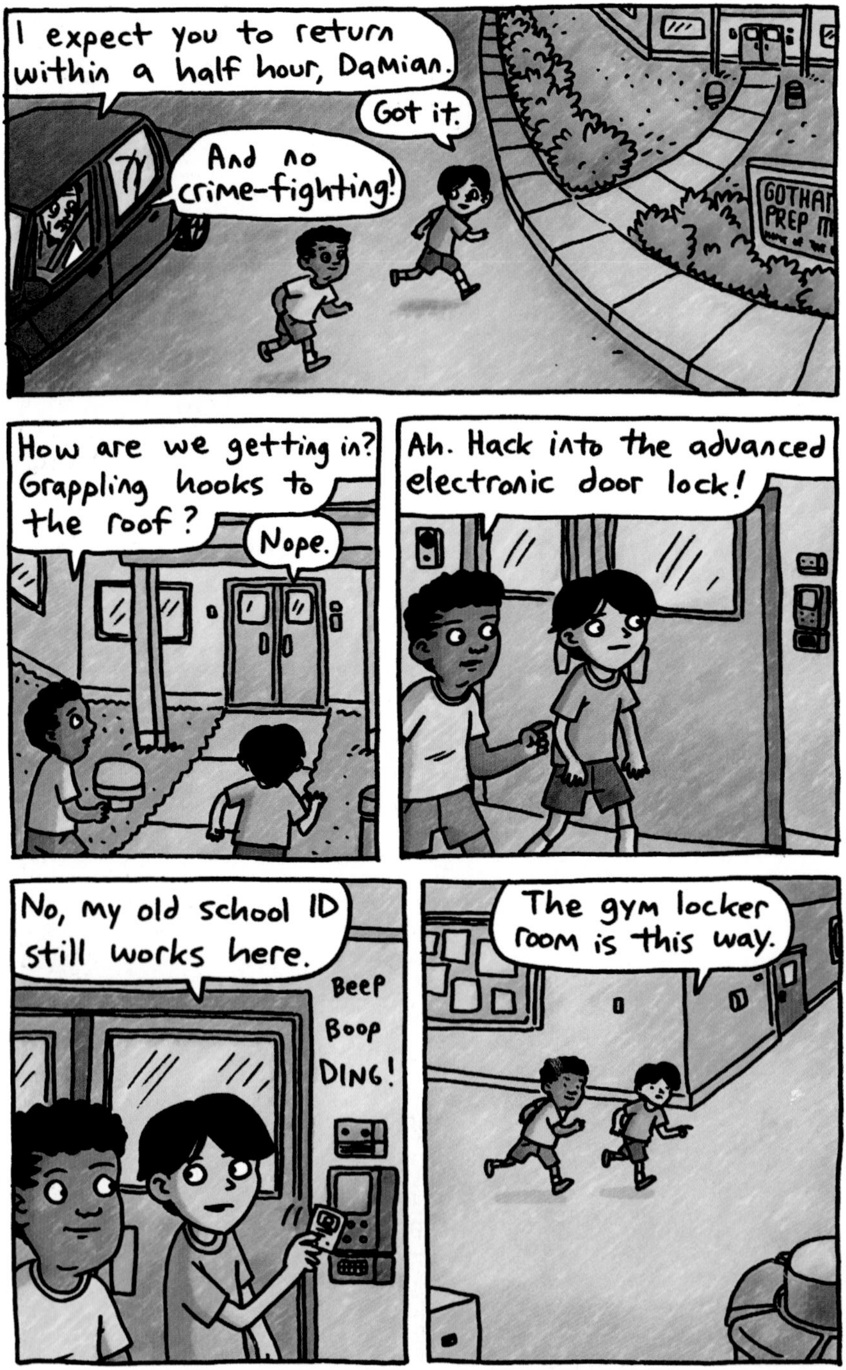
I expect you to return within a half hour, Damian.
Got it.
And no crime-fighting!
GOTHAM PREP
How are we getting in? Grappling hooks to the roof?
Nope.
Ah. Hack into the advanced electronic door lock!
No, my old school ID still works here.
Beep
Boop
DING!
The gym locker room is this way.

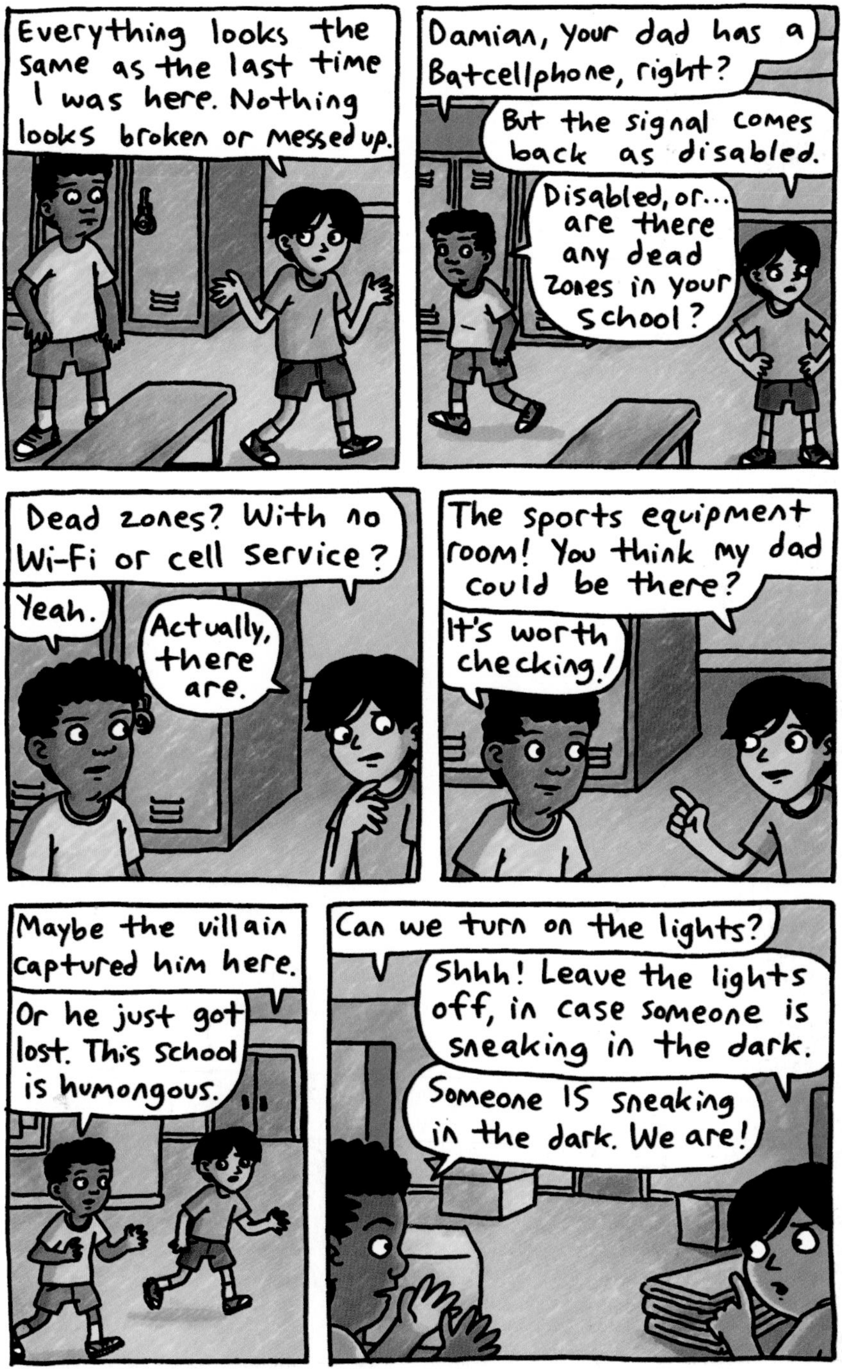
Everything looks the same as the last time I was here. Nothing looks broken or messed up.
Damian, your dad has a Batcellphone, right?
But the signal comes back as disabled.
Disabled, or... are there any dead zones in your school?
Dead zones? With no Wi-Fi or cell service?
Yeah.
Actually, there are.
The sports equipment room! You think my dad could be there?
It's worth checking!
Maybe the villain captured him here.
Or he just got lost. This school is humongous.
Can we turn on the lights?
Shhh! Leave the lights off, in case someone is sneaking in the dark.
Someone IS sneaking in the dark. We are!

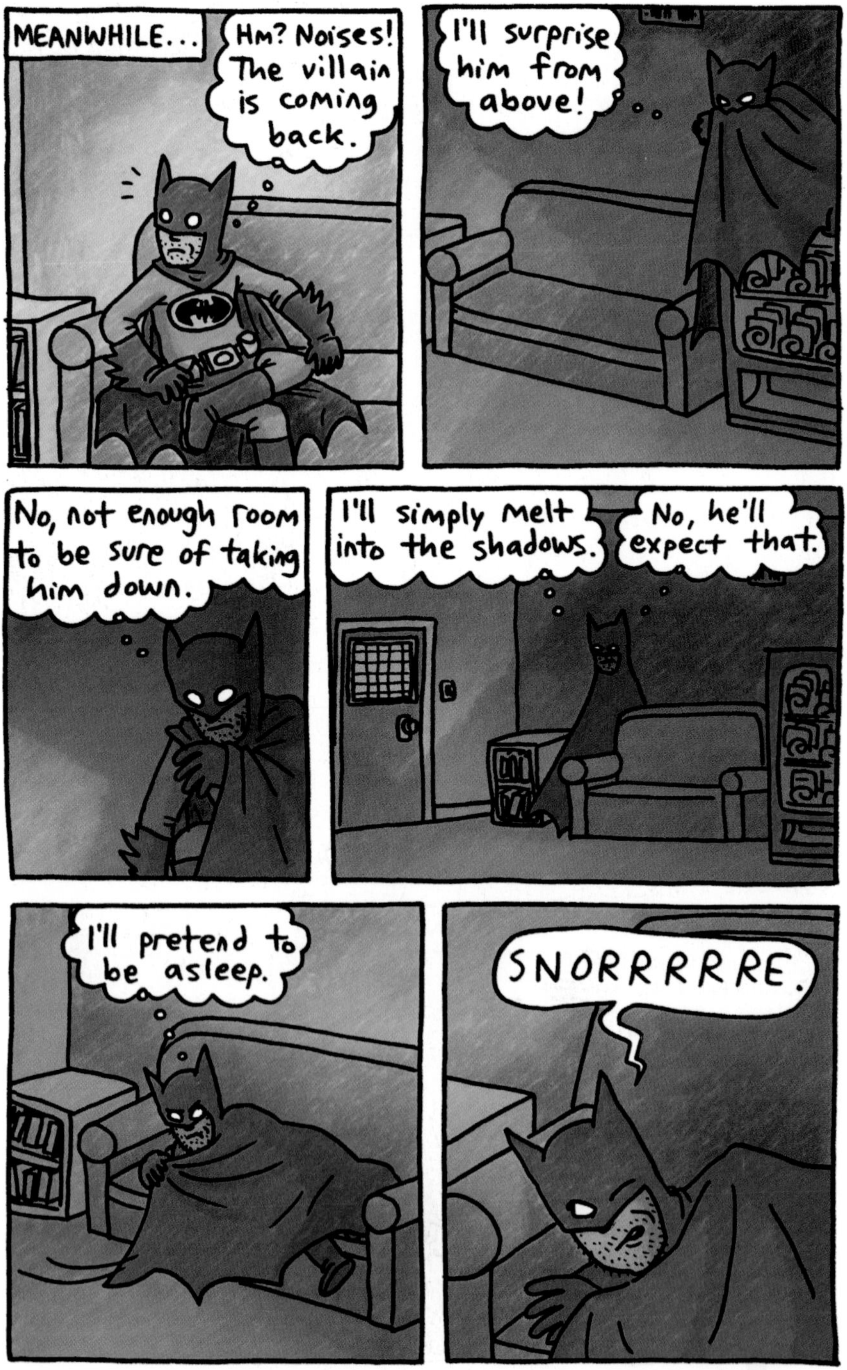
MEANWHILE...
Hm? Noises! The villain is coming back.
I'll surprise him from above!
No, not enough room to be sure of taking him down.
I'll simply melt into the shadows.
No, he'll expect that.
I'll pretend to be asleep.
SNORRRRRE.

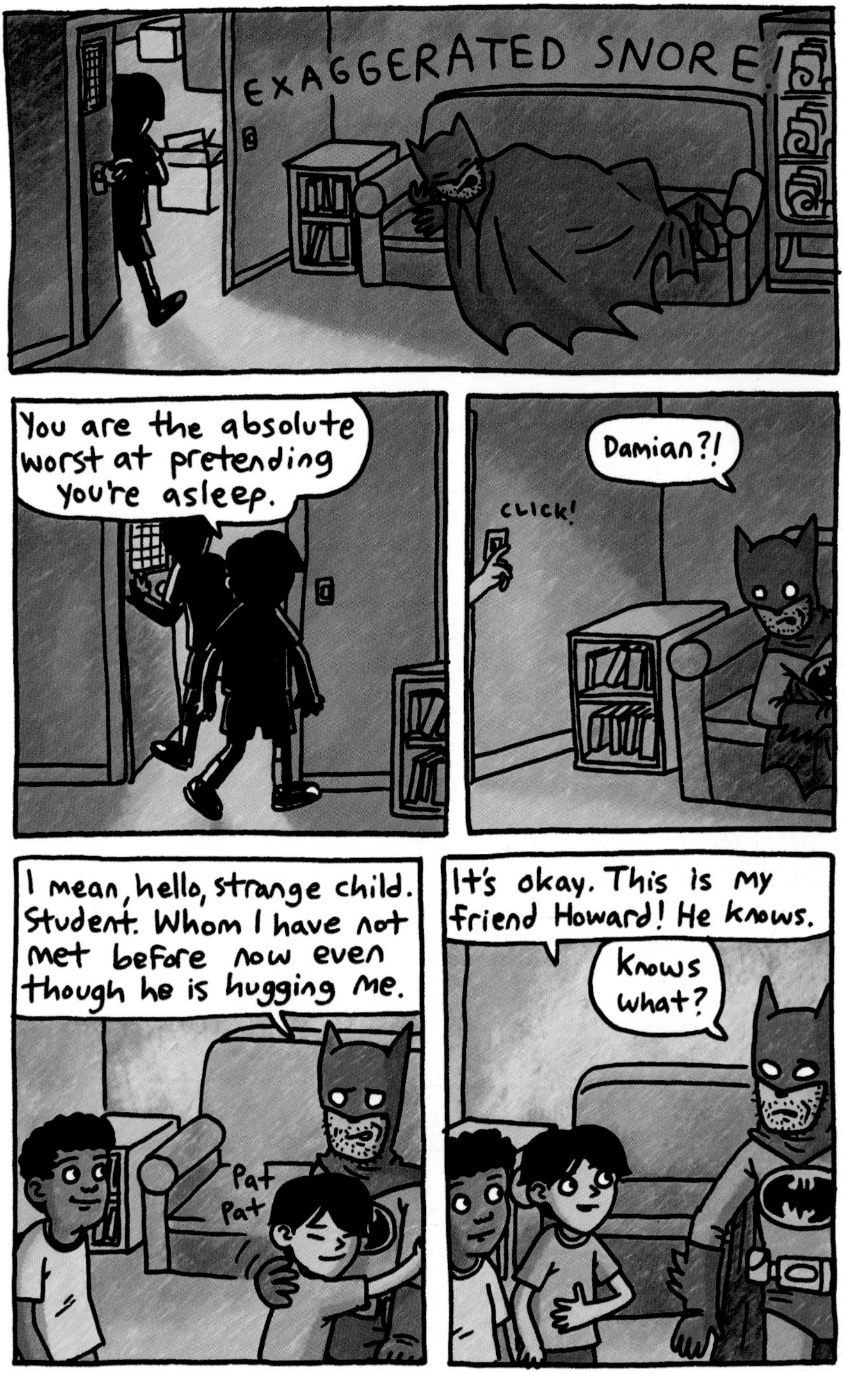
EXAGGERATED SNORE!
You are the absolute worst at pretending you're asleep.
CLICK!
Damian?!
I mean, hello, strange child. Student. Whom I have not met before now even though he is hugging me.
Pat Pat
It's okay. This is my friend Howard! He knows.
Knows what?

Everything.

Everything?!

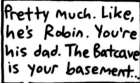

Pretty much. Like, he's Robin. You're his dad. The Batcave is your basement...

Damian, you know they're called SECRET identities?

Yeah.

But sometimes you have to trust someone you don't know well to help someone you love.

Damian! You're—right.

That was from our reading assignment!

Yeah. I totally swiped it.

So, did you lock yourself in here by accident?

No. Someone else locked me in.

Who?

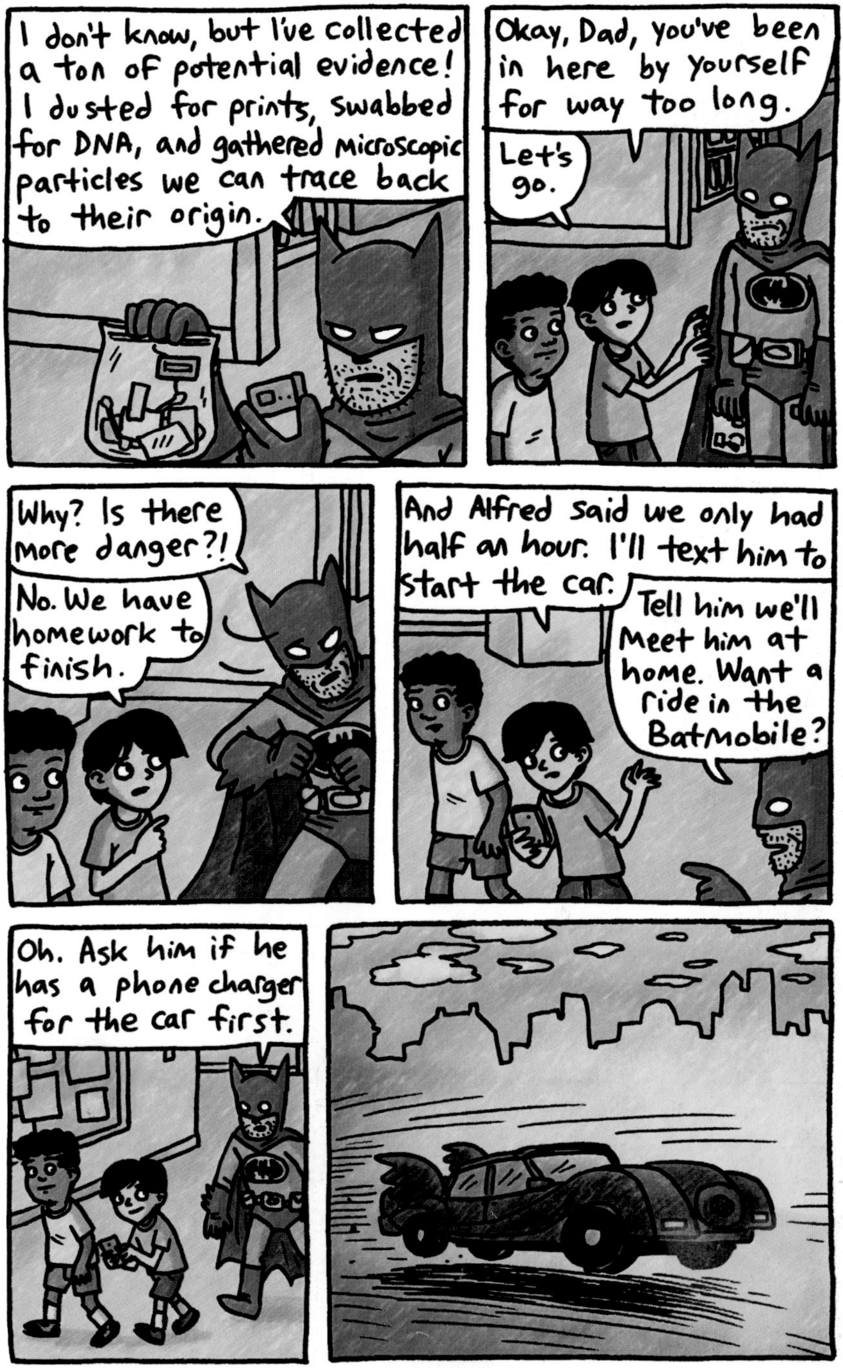
I don't know, but I've collected a ton of potential evidence! I dusted for prints, swabbed for DNA, and gathered microscopic particles we can trace back to their origin.
Okay, Dad, you've been in here by yourself for way too long.
Let's go.
Why? Is there more danger?!
No. We have homework to finish.
And Alfred said we only had half an hour. I'll text him to start the car.
Tell him we'll meet him at home. Want a ride in the Batmobile?
Oh. Ask him if he has a phone charger for the car first.

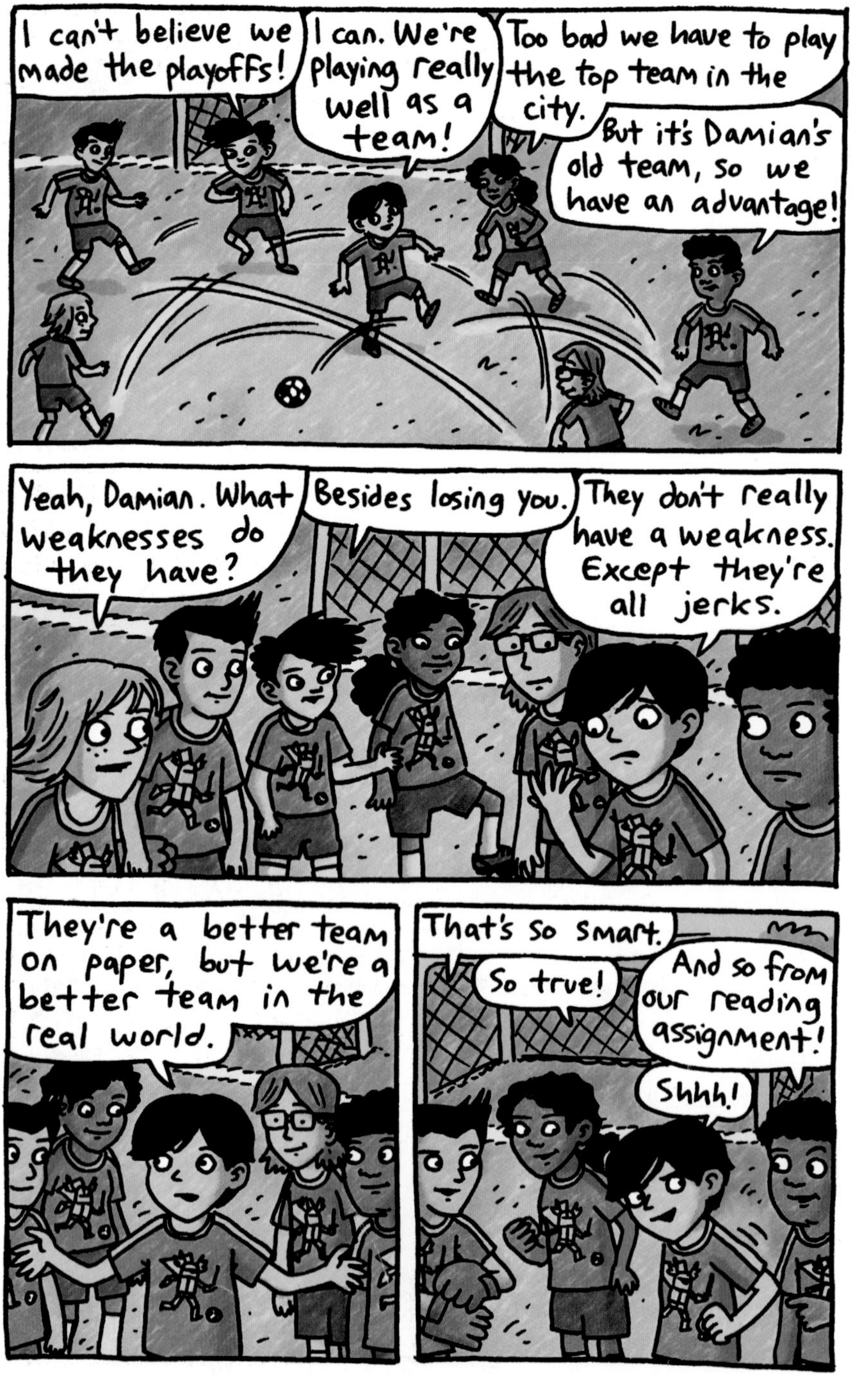
I can't believe we made the playoffs!
I can. We're playing really well as a team!
Too bad we have to play the top team in the city.
But it's Damian's old team, so we have an advantage!
Yeah, Damian. What weaknesses do they have?
Besides losing you.
They don't really have a weakness. Except they're all jerks.
They're a better team on paper, but we're a better team in the real world.
That's so smart.
So true!
And so from our reading assignment!
Shhh!

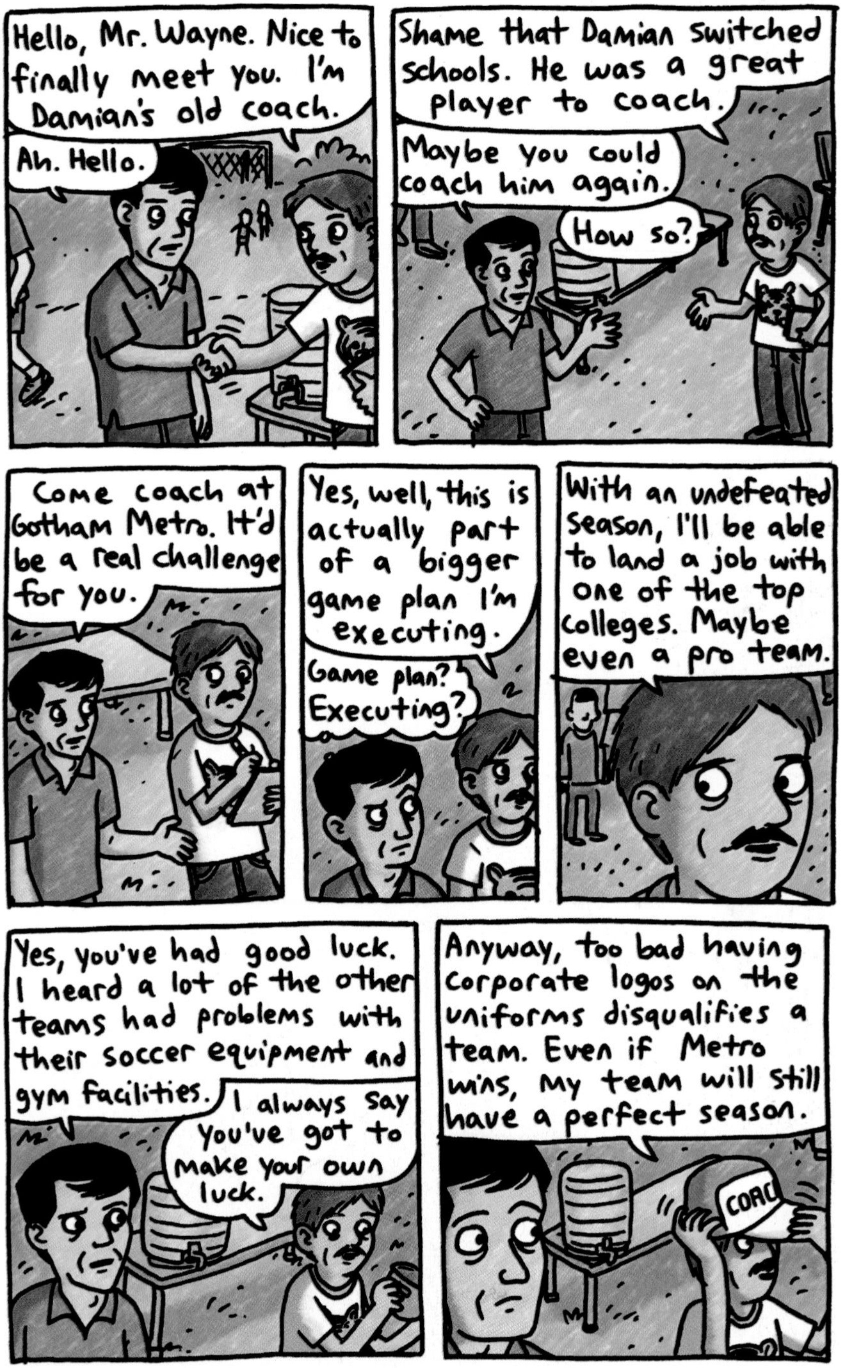
Hello, Mr. Wayne. Nice to finally meet you. I'm Damian's old coach.
Ah. Hello.
Shame that Damian switched schools. He was a great player to coach.
Maybe you could coach him again.
How so?
Come coach at Gotham Metro. It'd be a real challenge for you.
Yes, well, this is actually part of a bigger game plan I'm executing.
Game plan? Executing?
With an undefeated season, I'll be able to land a job with one of the top colleges. Maybe even a pro team.
Yes, you've had good luck. I heard a lot of the other teams had problems with their soccer equipment and gym facilities.
I always say you've got to make your own luck.
Anyway, too bad having corporate logos on the uniforms disqualifies a team. Even if Metro wins, my team will still have a perfect season.
COAC

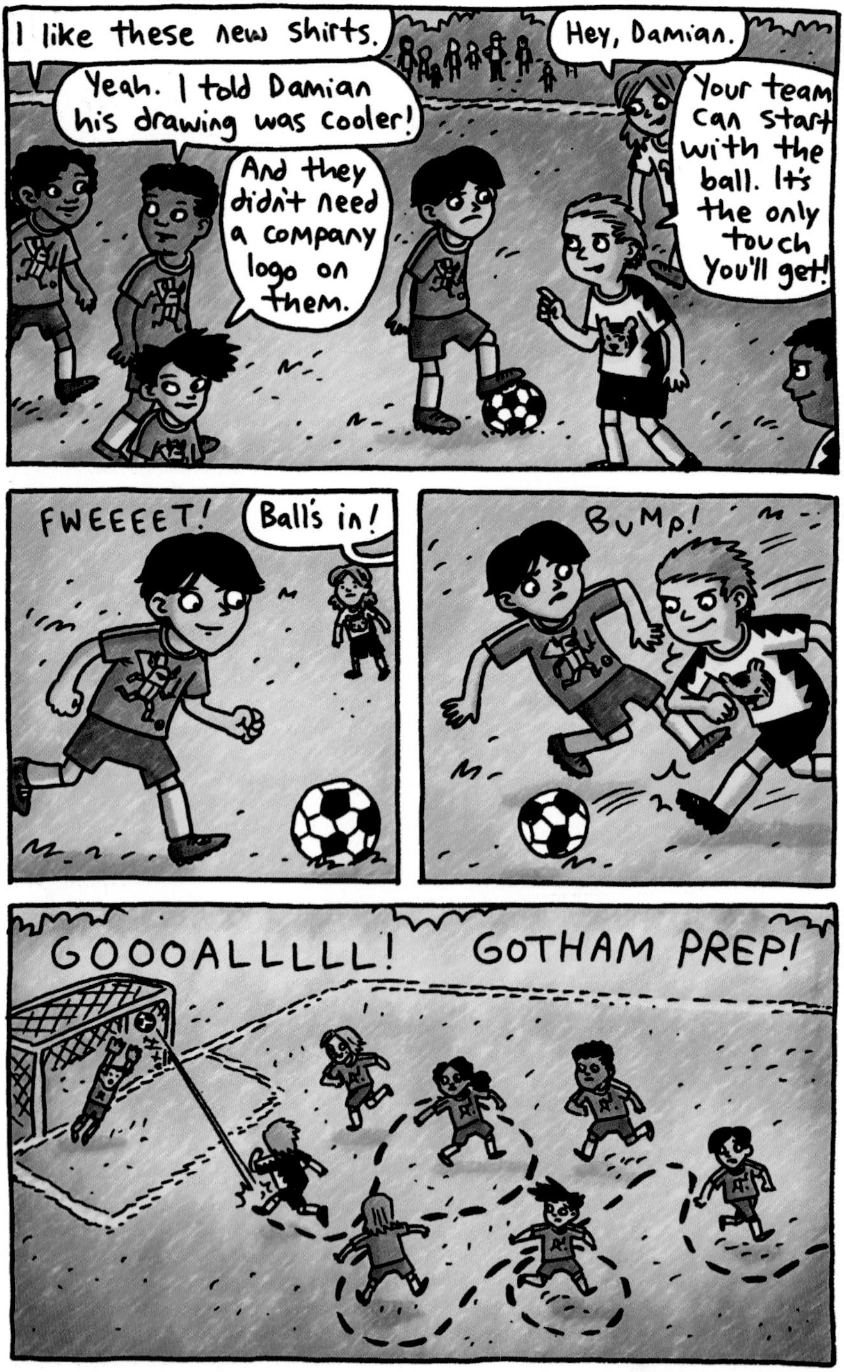
I like these new shirts.
Yeah. I told Damian his drawing was cooler!
And they didn't need a company logo on them.
Hey, Damian.
Your team can start with the ball. It's the only touch you'll get!
FWEEEET!
Ball's in!
BUMP!
GOOOALLLLL! GOTHAM PREP!

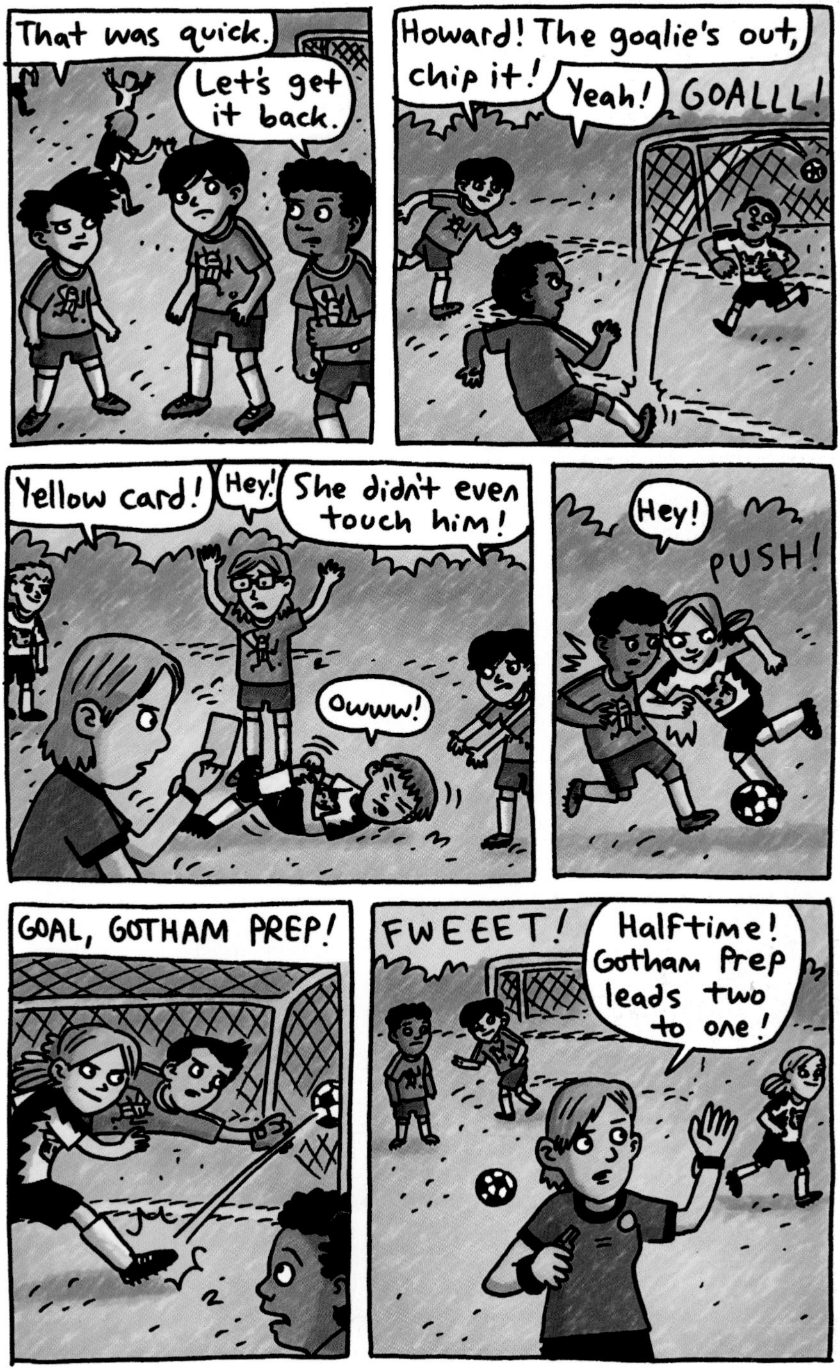

That was quick.
Let's get it back.
Howard! The goalie's out, chip it!
Yeah!
GOALLL!
Yellow card!
Hey!
She didn't even touch him!
Owww!
Hey!
PUSH!
GOAL, GOTHAM PREP!
FWEEET!
Halftime! Gotham Prep leads two to one!

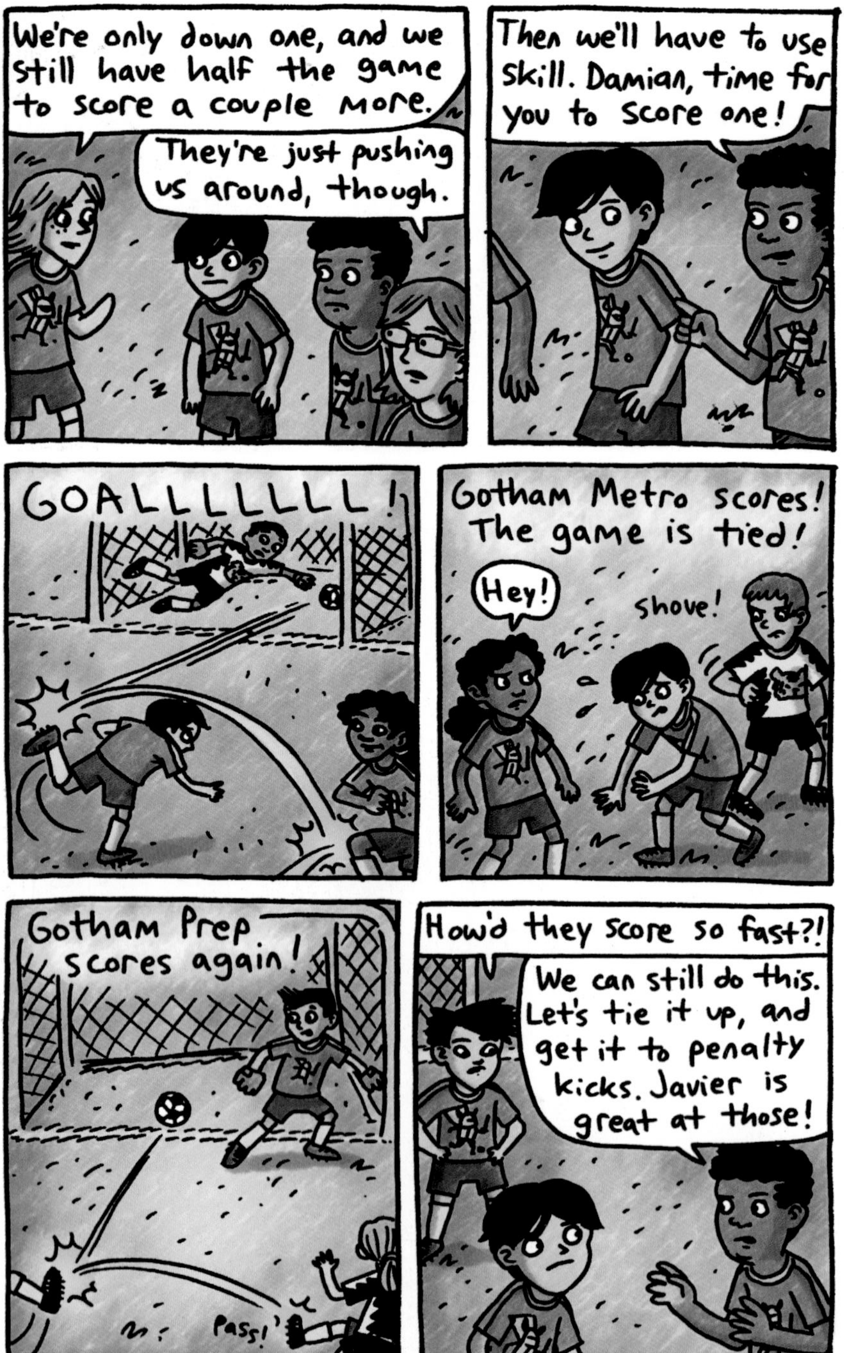

We're only down one, and we still have half the game to score a couple more.
They're just pushing us around, though.
Then we'll have to use skill. Damian, time for you to score one!
GOALLLLLLLL!
Gotham Metro scores! The game is tied!
Hey!
Shove!
Gotham Prep scores again!
Pass!
How'd they score so fast?!
We can still do this. Let's tie it up, and get it to penalty kicks. Javier is great at those!

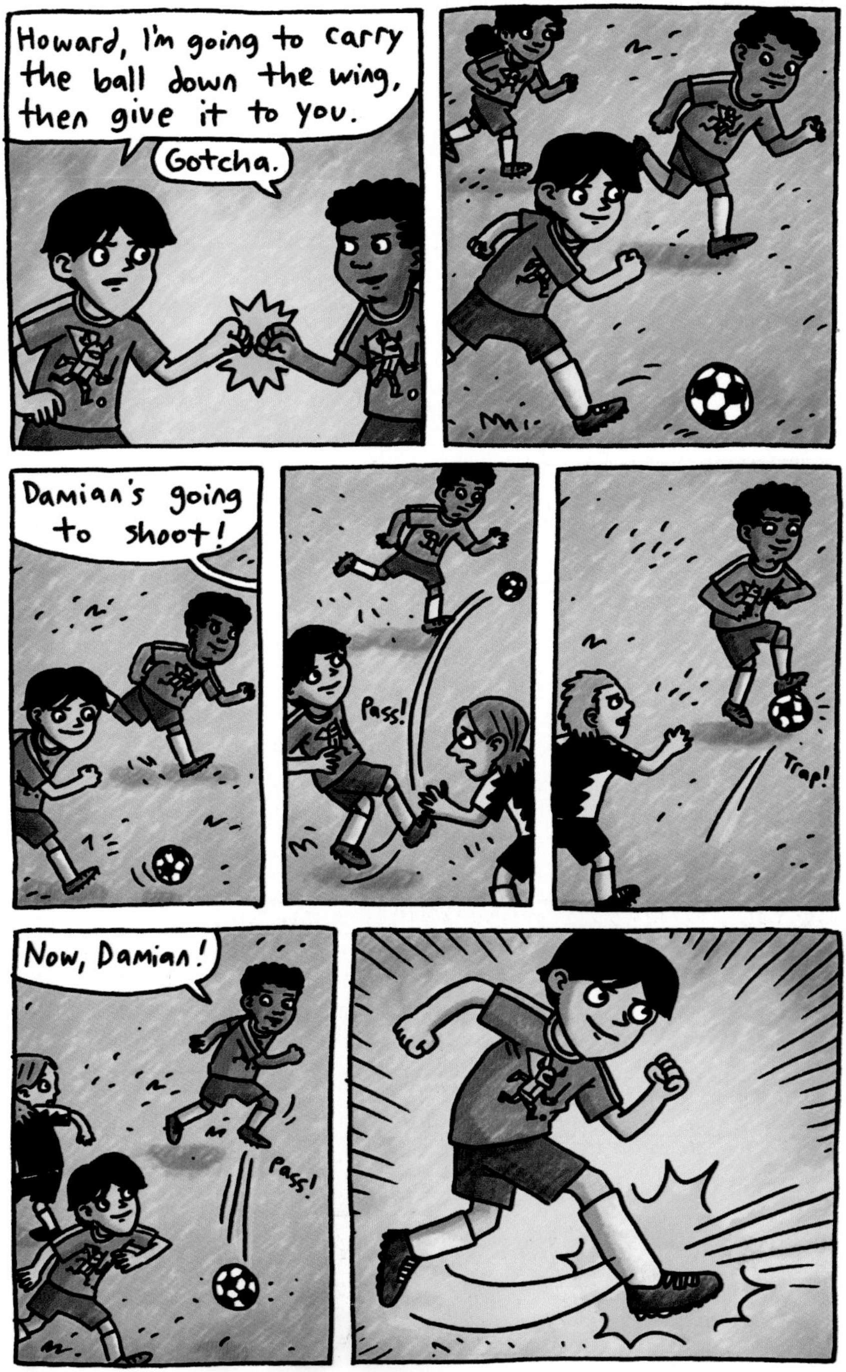
Howard, I'm going to carry the ball down the wing, then give it to you.
Gotcha.
Damian's going to shoot!
Pass!
Trap!
Now, Damian!
Pass!

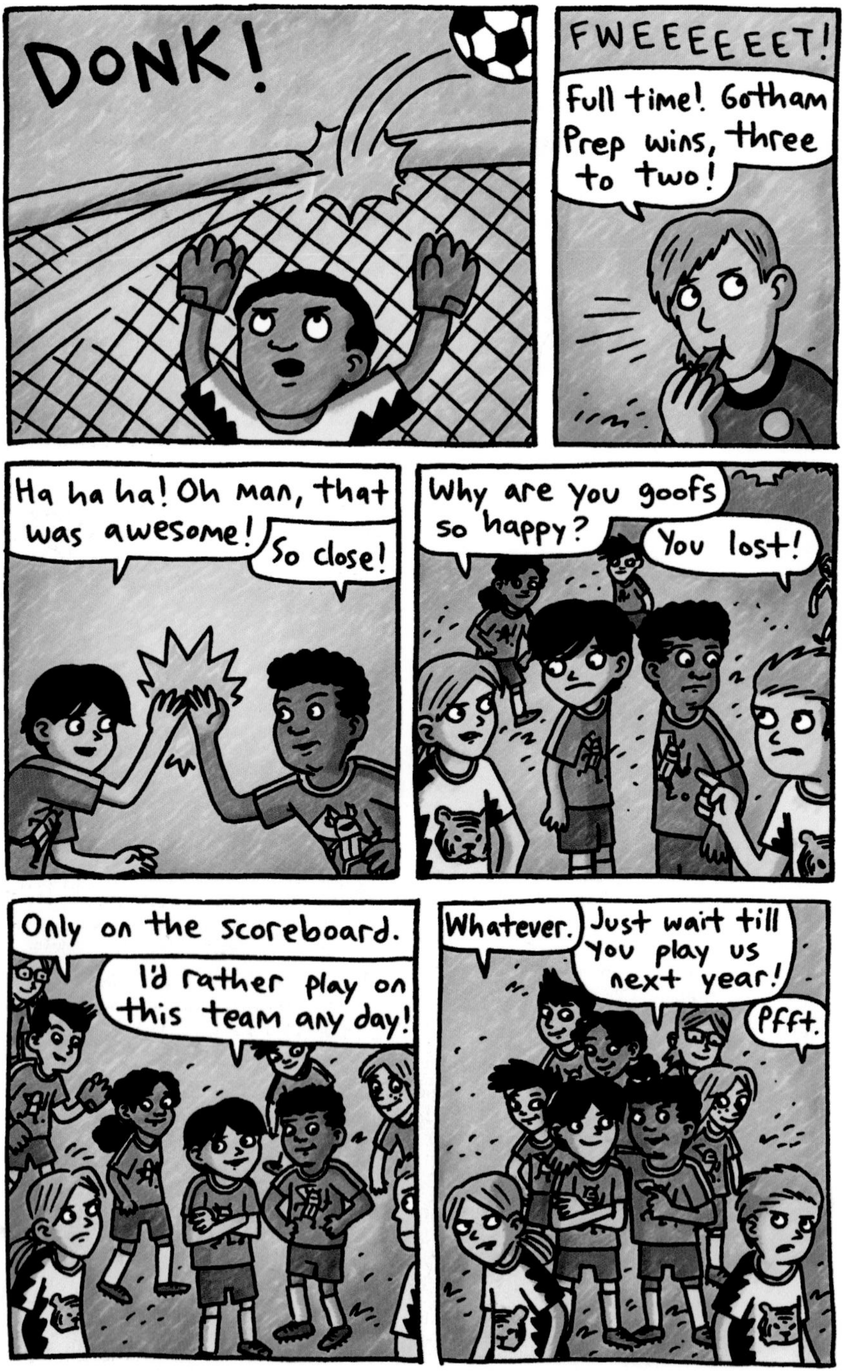
DONK!
FWEEEEEEET!
Full time! Gotham Prep wins, three to two!
Ha ha ha! Oh man, that was awesome!
So close!
Why are you goofs so happy?
You lost!
Only on the scoreboard.
I'd rather play on this team any day!
Whatever.
Just wait till you play us next year!
Pfft.

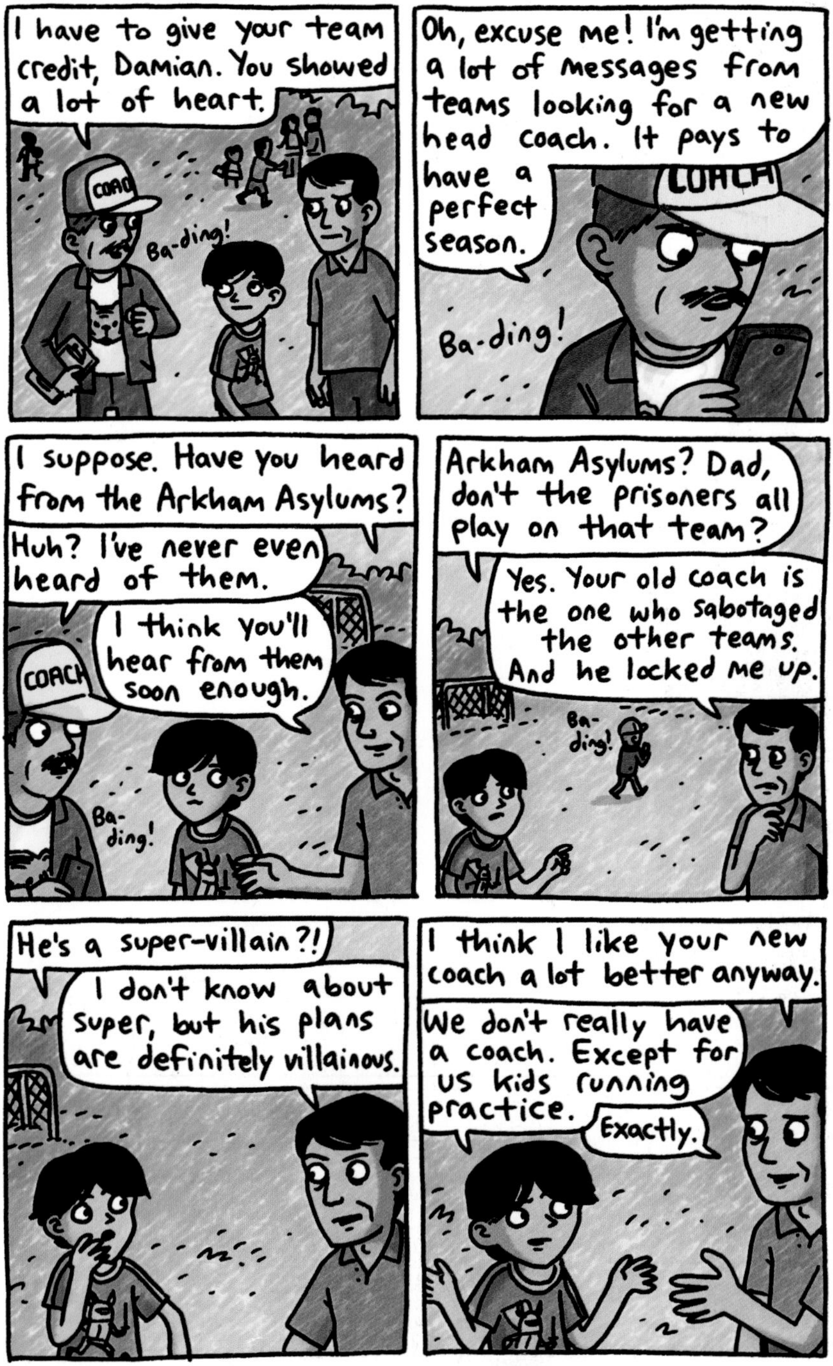
I have to give your team credit, Damian. You showed a lot of heart.
Ba-ding!
Oh, excuse me! I'm getting a lot of messages from teams looking for a new head coach. It pays to have a perfect season.
COACH
Ba-ding!
I suppose. Have you heard from the Arkham Asylums?
Huh? I've never even heard of them.
I think you'll hear from them soon enough.
COACH
Ba-ding!
Arkham Asylums? Dad, don't the prisoners all play on that team?
Yes. Your old coach is the one who sabotaged the other teams. And he locked me up.
Ba-ding!
He's a super-villain?!
I don't know about super, but his plans are definitely villainous.
I think I like your new coach a lot better anyway.
We don't really have a coach. Except for us kids running practice.
Exactly.

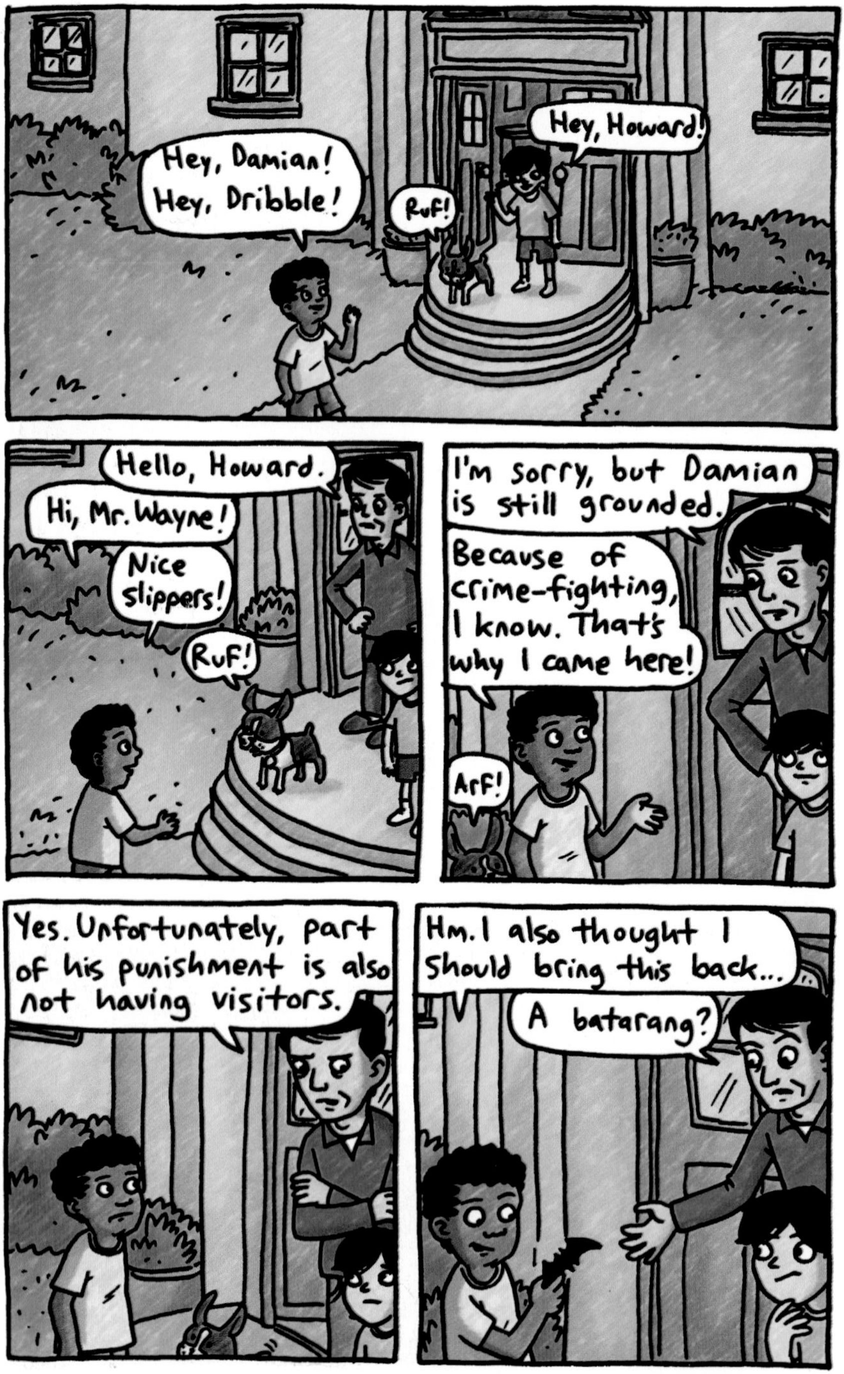
Hey, Damian!
Hey, Dribble!
Ruf!
Hey, Howard!
Hello, Howard.
Hi, Mr. Wayne!
Nice slippers!
Ruf!
I'm sorry, but Damian is still grounded.
Because of crime-fighting, I know. That's why I came here!
Arf!
Yes. Unfortunately, part of his punishment is also not having visitors.
Hm. I also thought I should bring this back...
A batarang?

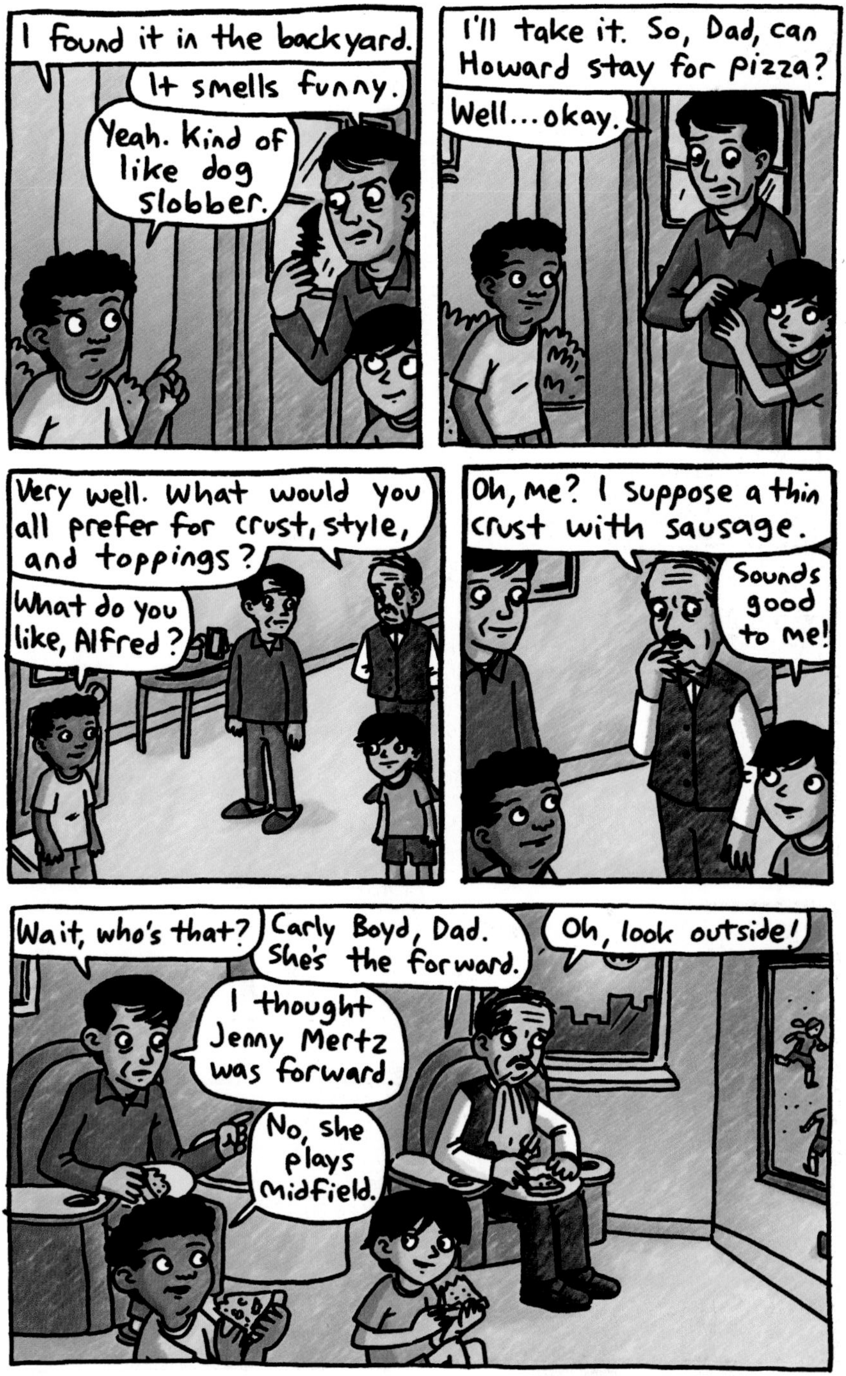
I found it in the backyard.
It smells funny.
Yeah. Kind of like dog slobber.
I'll take it. So, Dad, can Howard stay for pizza?
Well...okay.
Very well. What would you all prefer for crust, style, and toppings?
What do you like, Alfred?
Oh, me? I suppose a thin crust with sausage.
Sounds good to me!
Wait, who's that?
Carly Boyd, Dad. She's the forward.
I thought Jenny Mertz was forward.
No, she plays midfield.
Oh, look outside!

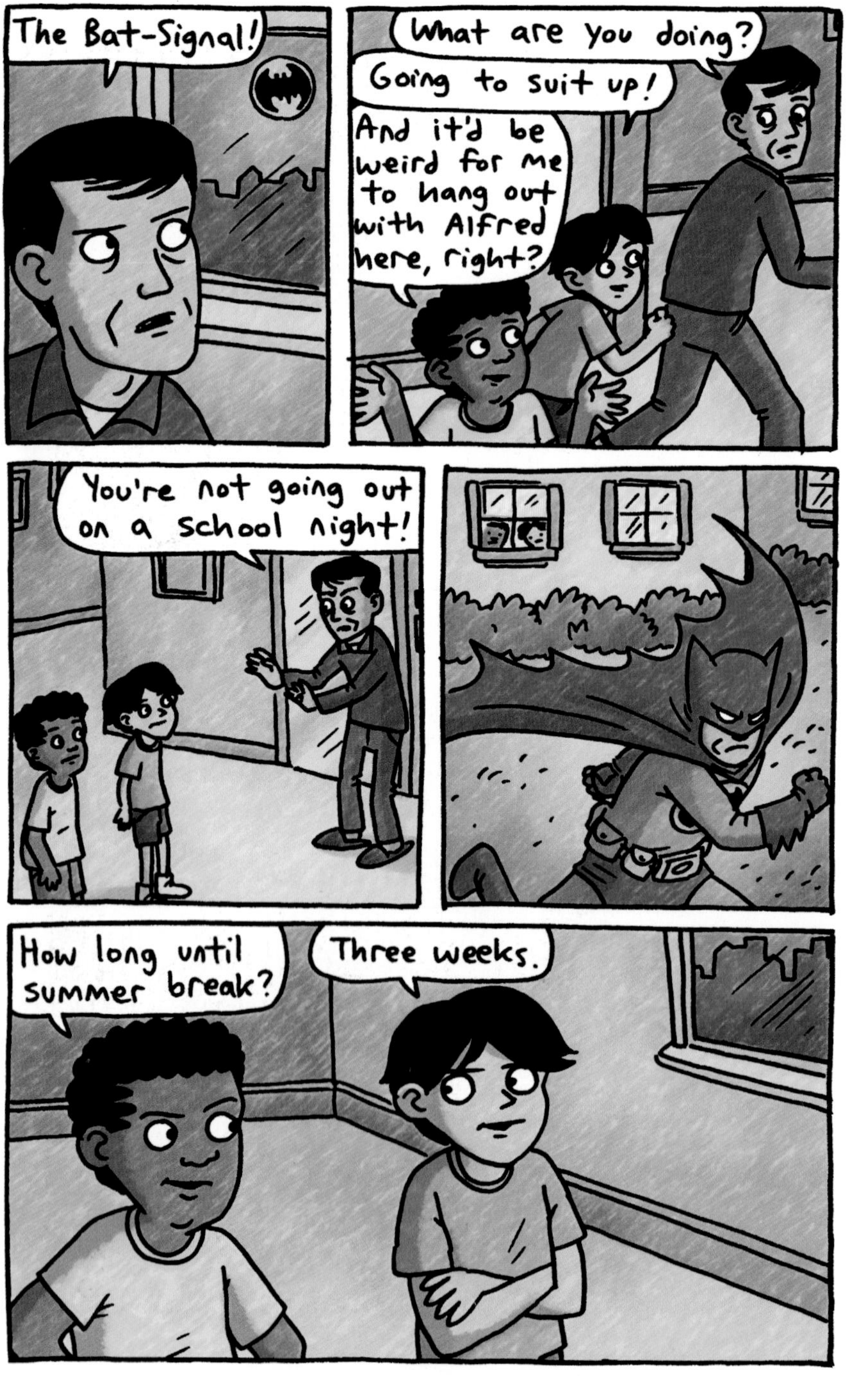
The Bat-Signal!
What are you doing?
Going to suit up!
And it'd be weird for me to hang out with Alfred here, right?
You're not going out on a school night!
How long until summer break?
Three weeks.

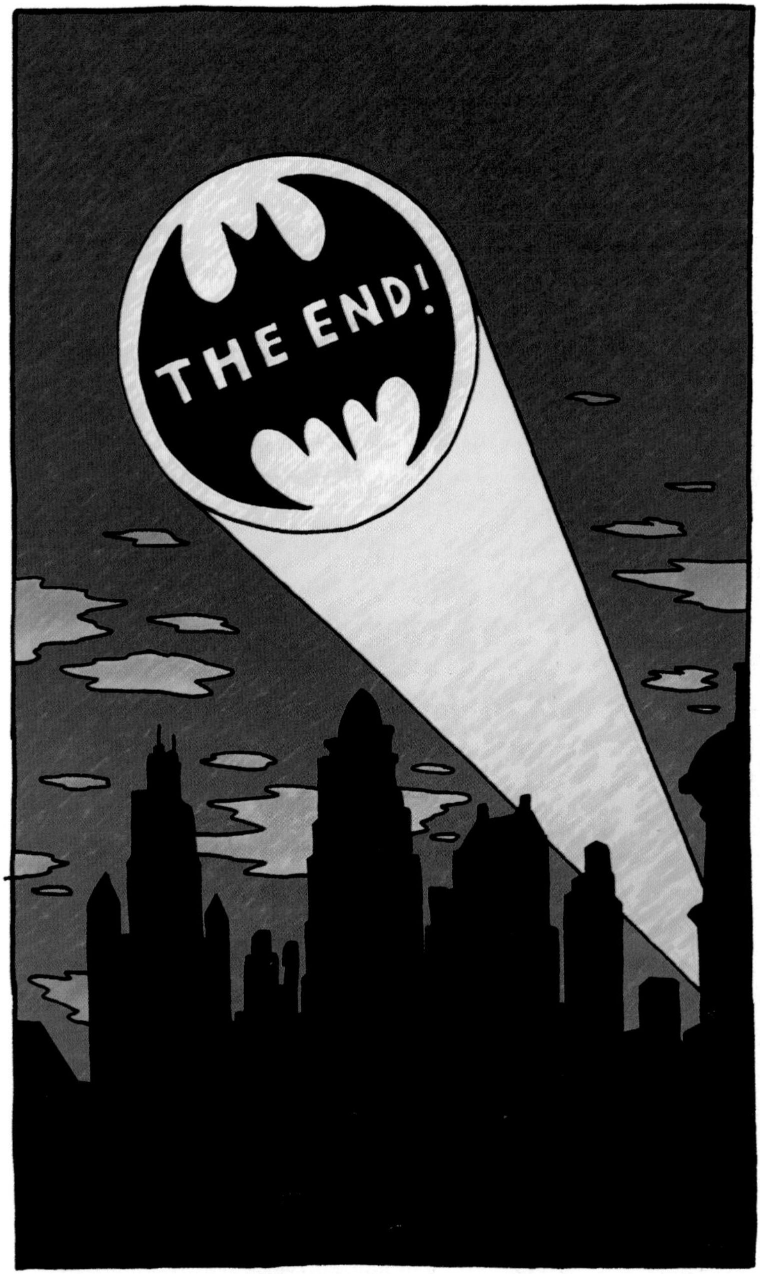
THE END!

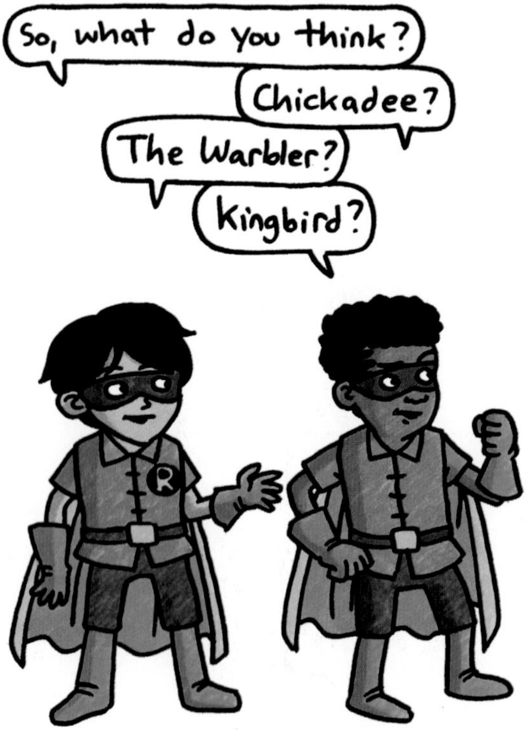
So, what do you think?
Chickadee?
The Warbler?
Kingbird?

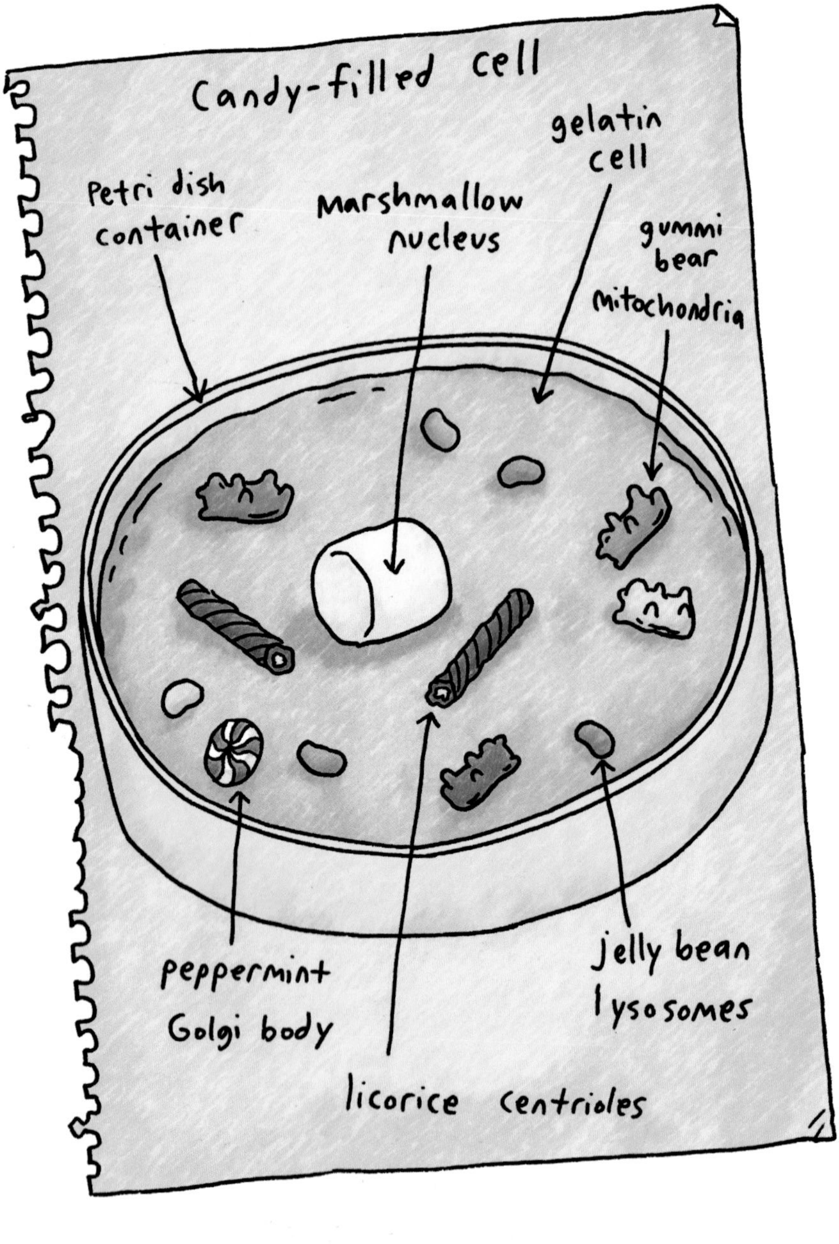
Candy-filled cell
gelatin cell
Petri dish container
Marshmallow nucleus
gummi bear mitochondria
peppermint Golgi body
jelly bean lysosomes
licorice centrioles

JEFFREY BROWN is the bestselling
author of the Darth Vader and Son
and Jedi Academy series, as well as
Lucy & Andy Neanderthal and Space-Time!
He lives in Chicago with his wife,
two sons, and cat. When he's not
busy drawing superhero sidekicks
playing soccer, Jeffrey likes to
go out and play soccer himself.

(He cannot
actually
play while
wearing
a Batsuit.)

www.jeffreybrowncomics.com
P.O. Box 120
Deerfield, IL 60015-0120
USA

I just thought of what my sidekick name could be. NIGHTWING!
That is an AWESOME name.

DIG IN AND BLAST OFF WITH MORE GRAPHIC NOVEL FUN FROM JEFFREY BROWN!

Learn more at RHKidsGraphic.com

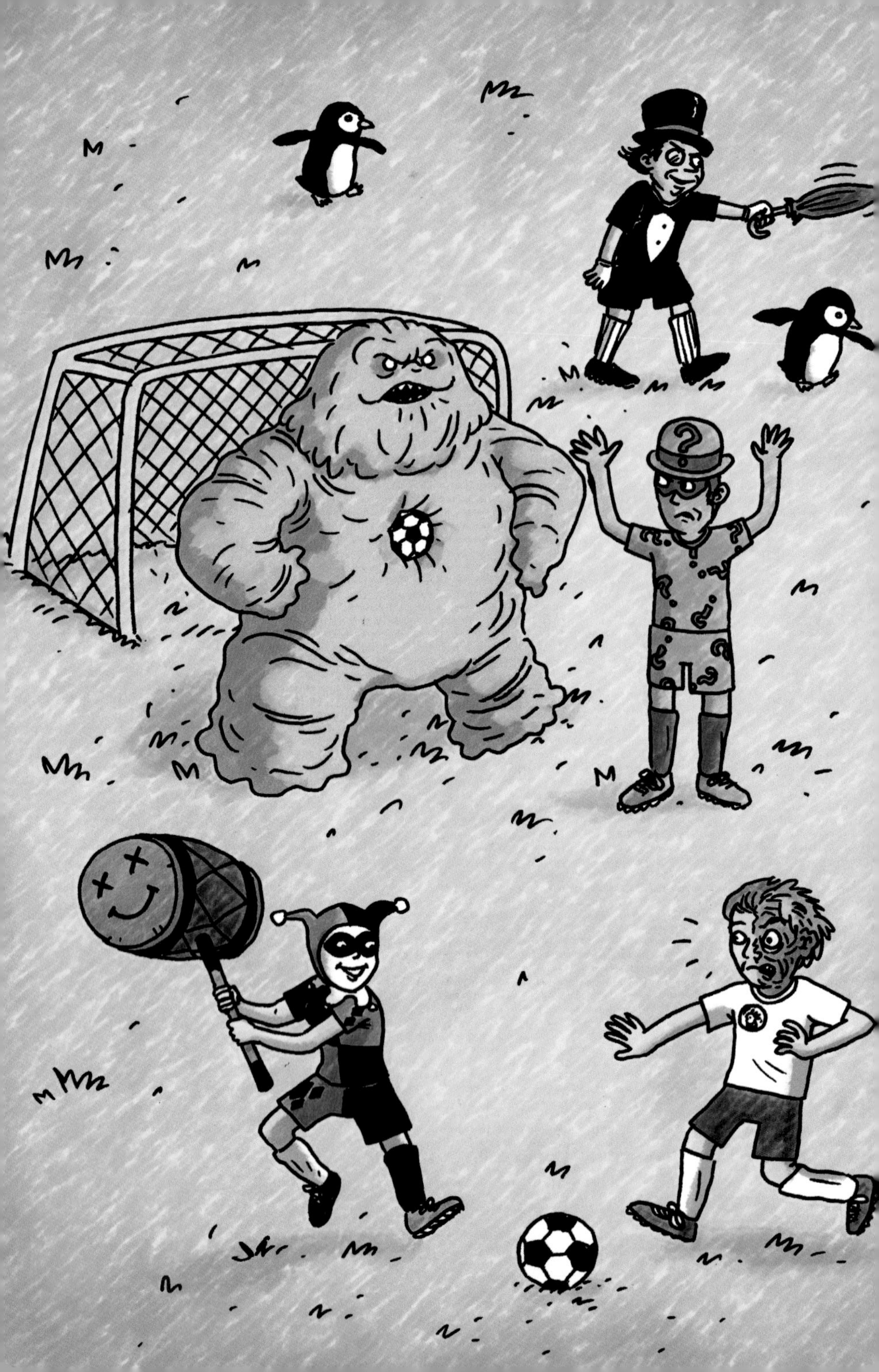

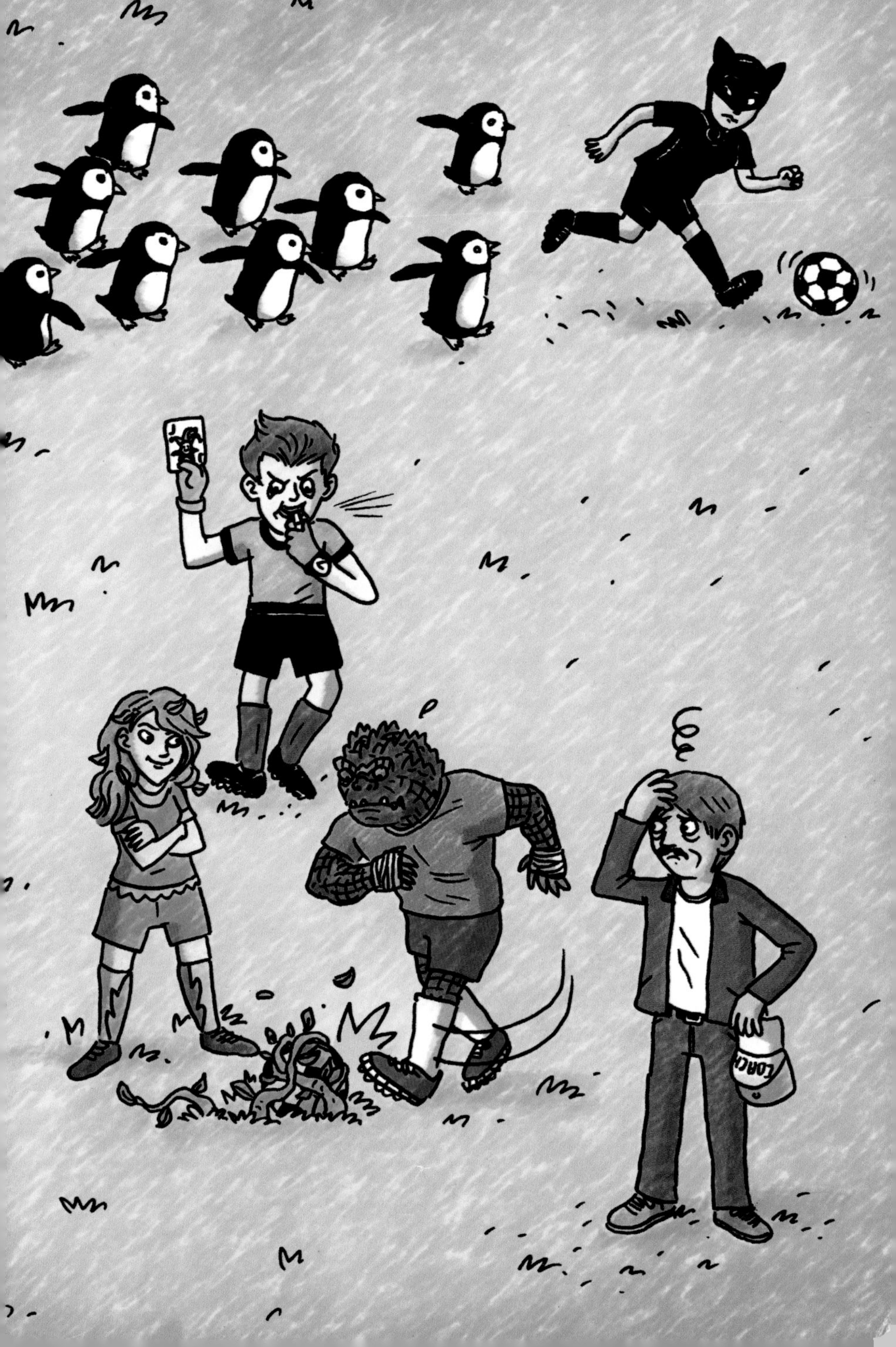
COACH

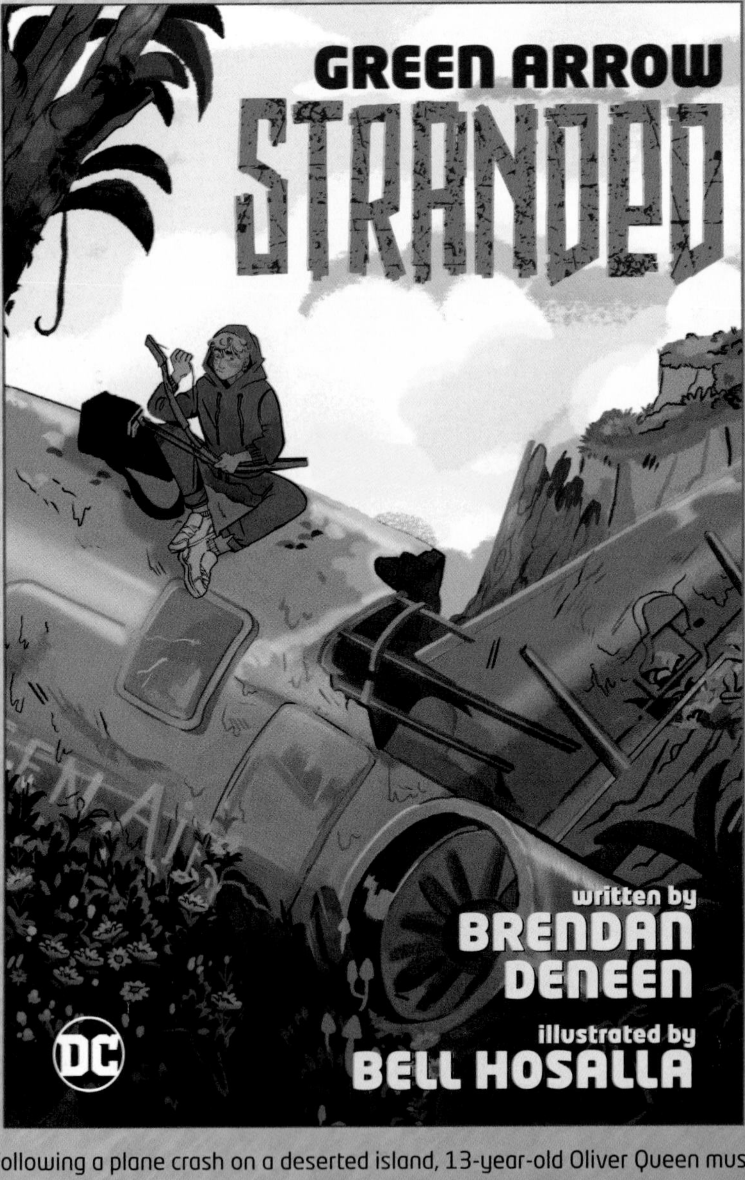
GREEN ARROW
STRANDED
written by
BRENDAN DENEEN
illustrated by
BELL HOSALLA
DC

Following a plane crash on a deserted island, 13-year-old Oliver Queen must learn the skills he needs to survive and to protect his injured father.

Find out how Ollie first learned how to become a master archer and how he started on the path that would make him the hero known as Green Arrow. This fast-paced and suspenseful tale from award-winning author **Brendan Deneen** and artist **Bell Hosalla** is sure to keep you on the edge of your seat!

Read on for a sneak preview of the graphic novel, on sale in March 2022.

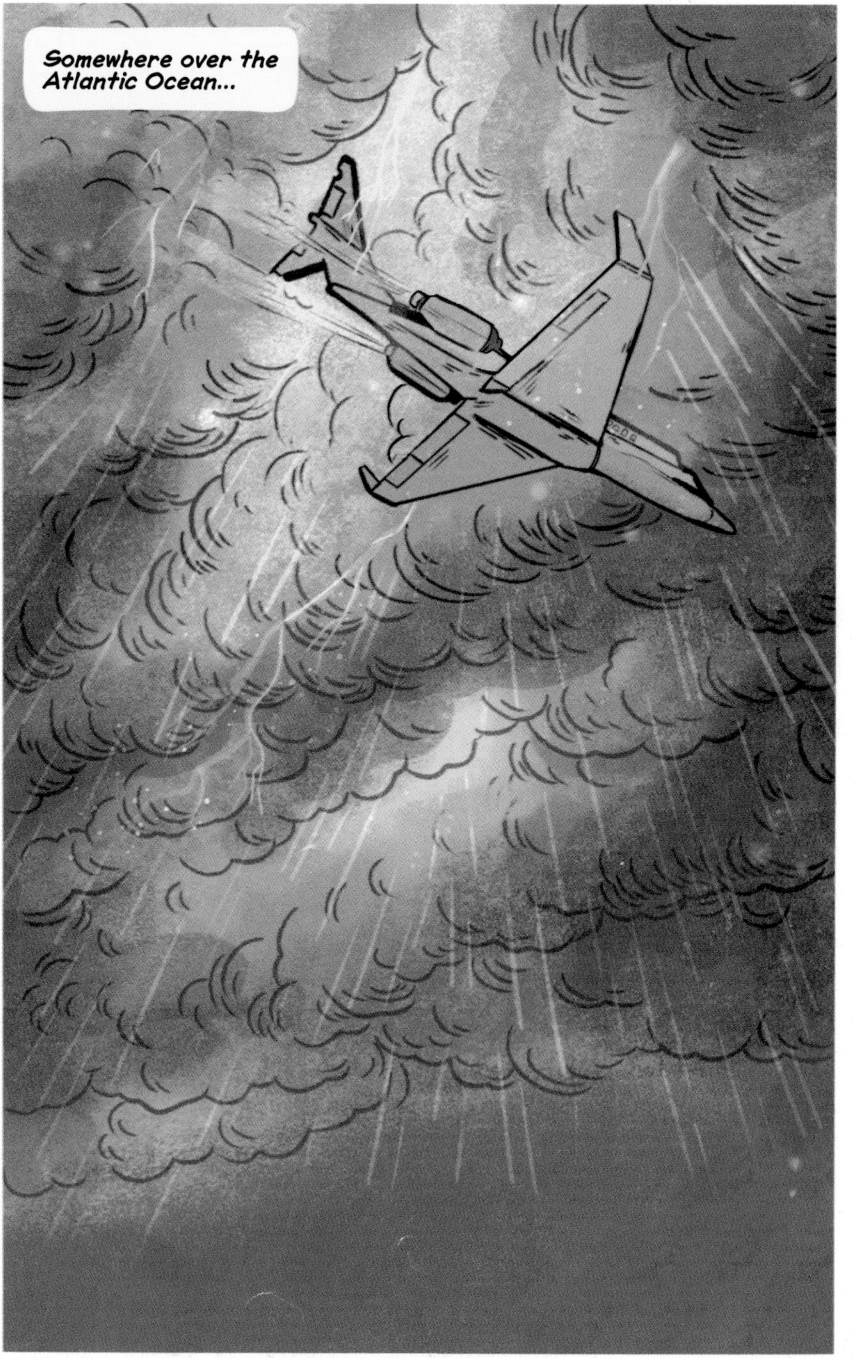
Somewhere over the Atlantic Ocean...

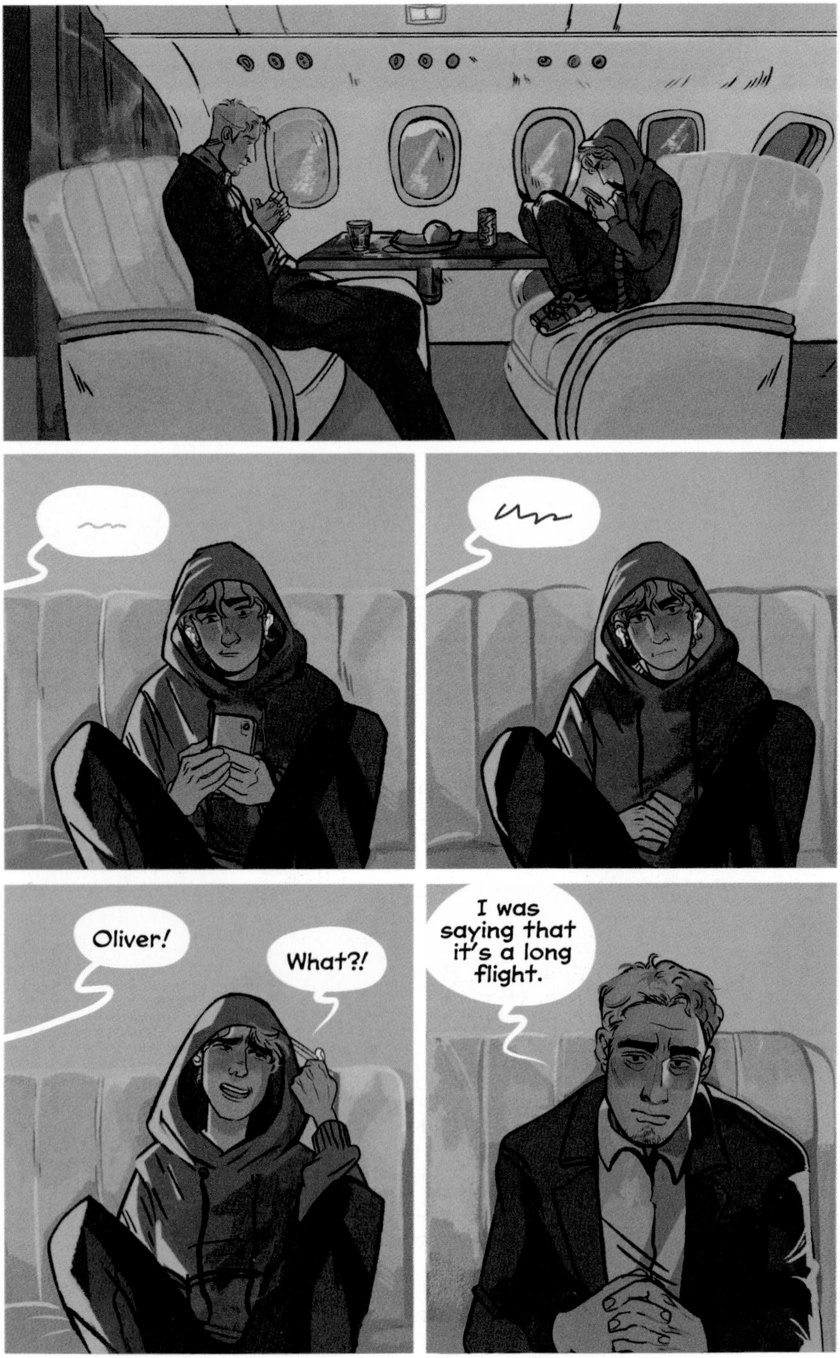

Oliver!
What?!
I was saying that it's a long flight.

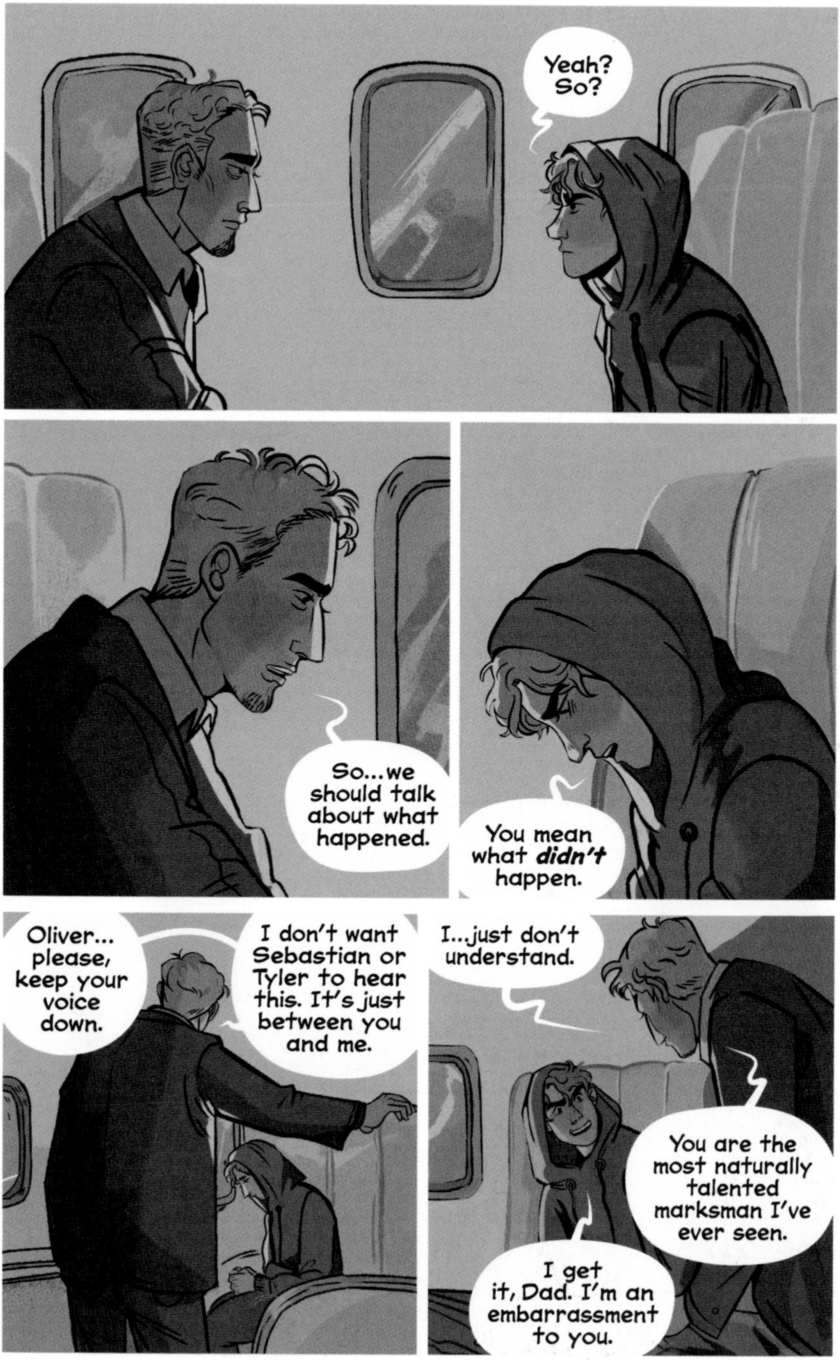
Yeah? So?
So...we should talk about what happened.
You mean what ***didn't*** happen.
Oliver... please, keep your voice down.
I don't want Sebastian or Tyler to hear this. It's just between you and me.
I...just don't understand.
You are the most naturally talented marksman I've ever seen.
I get it, Dad. I'm an embarrassment to you.

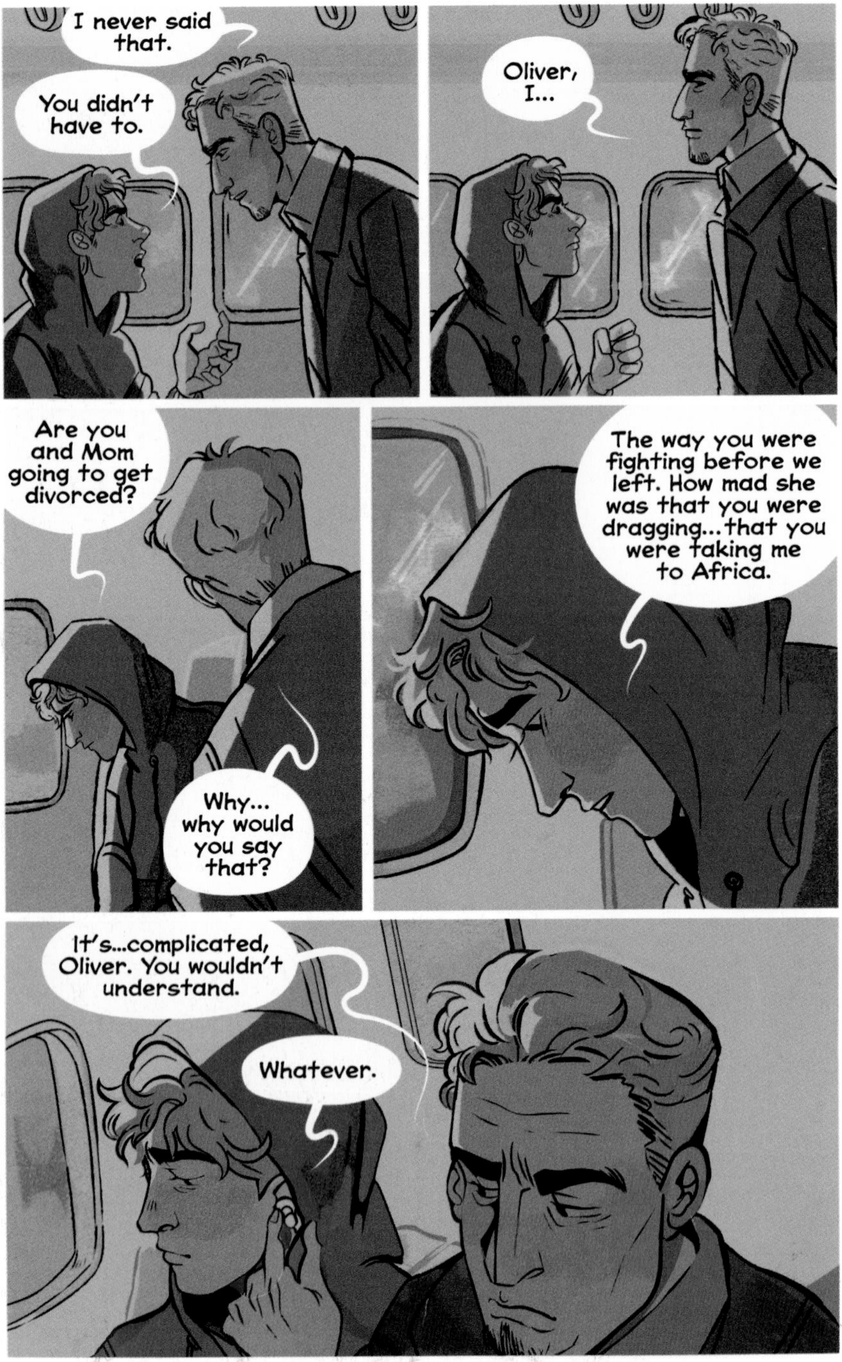
I never said that.
You didn't have to.
Oliver, I...
Are you and Mom going to get divorced?
Why... why would you say that?
The way you were fighting before we left. How mad she was that you were dragging...that you were taking me to Africa.
It's...complicated, Oliver. You wouldn't understand.
Whatever.

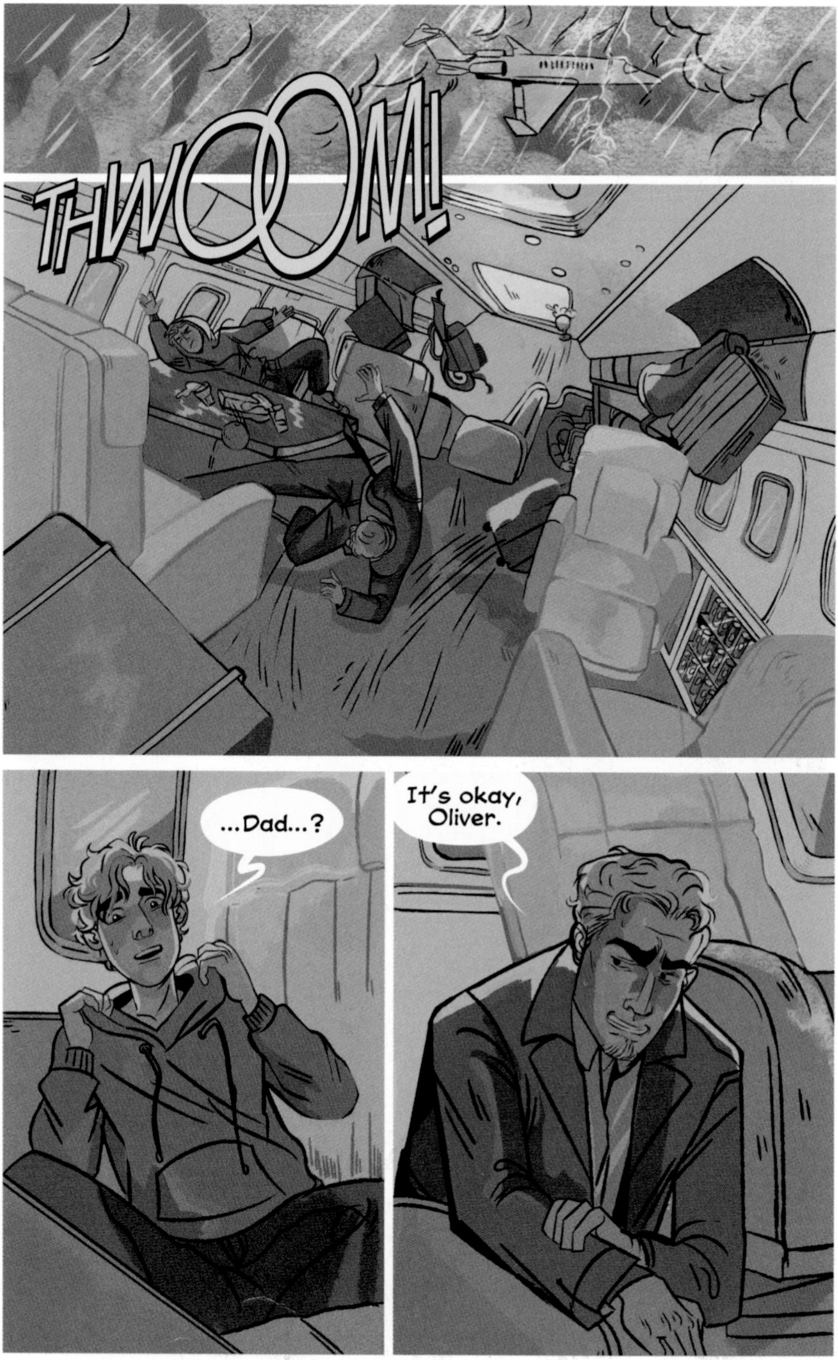
THWOOOM!
...Dad...?
It's okay, Oliver.

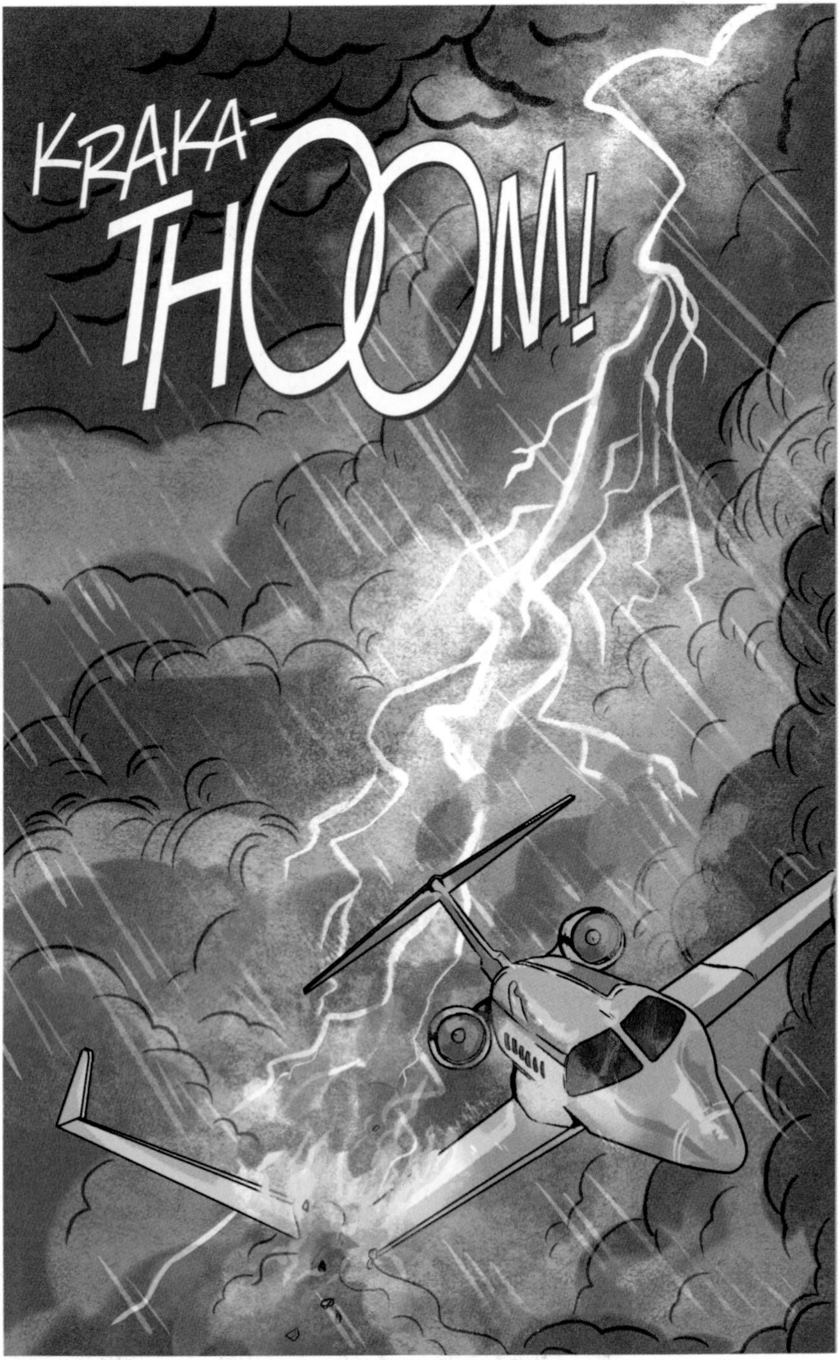
KRAKA-
THOOM!

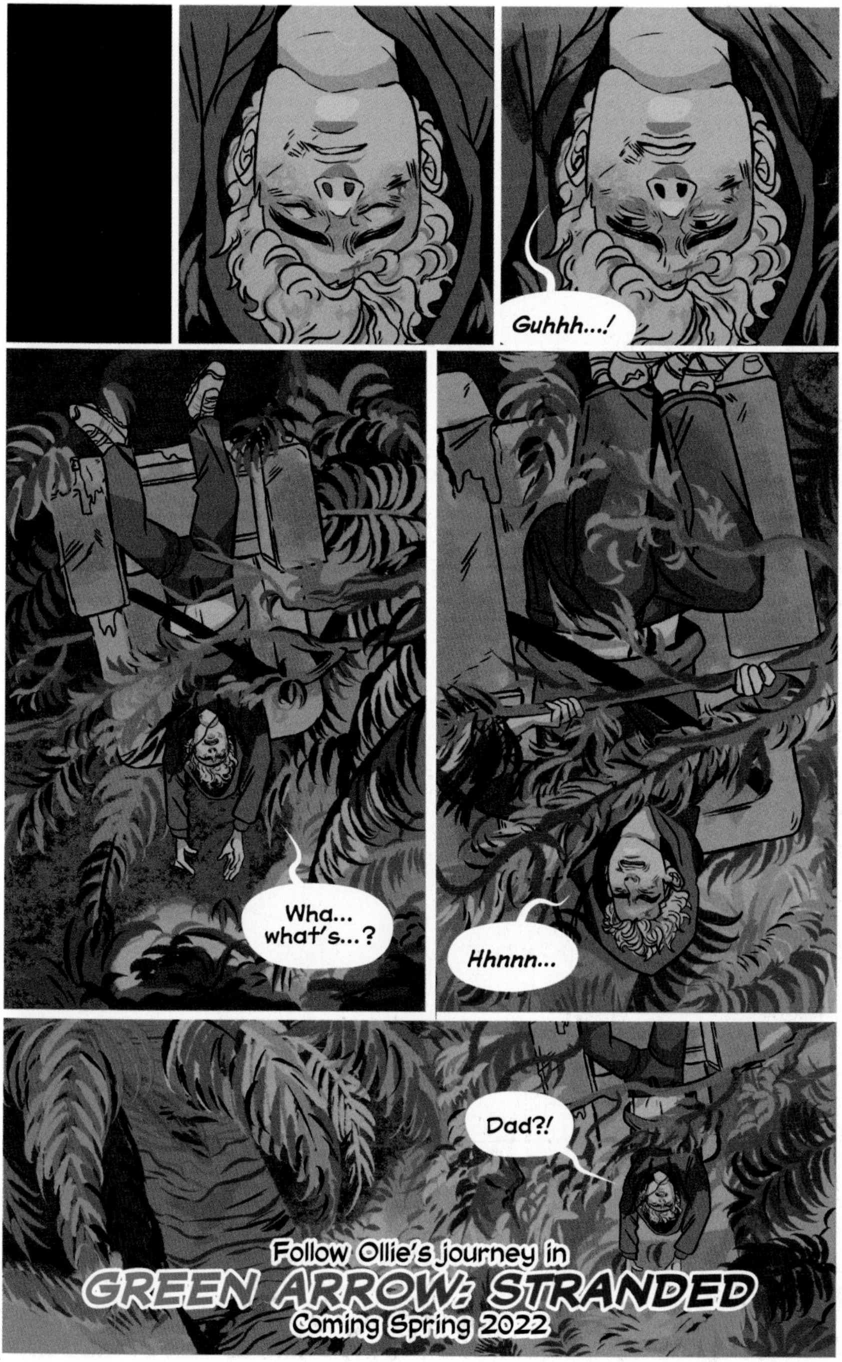

Guhhh...!
Wha... what's...?
Hhnnn...
Dad?!
Follow Ollie's journey in
GREEN ARROW: STRANDED
Coming Spring 2022